DEVIL'S ACRE

☆

JONATHAN BASTABLE

THEREFORE PUBLISHING

This is a Therefore book
This edition is published in 2013

Devil's Acre
© Jonathan Bastable

ISBN: 978-0-9576835-1-8

Design by Ian Denning

Set in Sabon and Coliseum

To Mark and to David,
who read it first.

The weak son of a sickly generation,
I'll not go searching for the alpine bloom.
No murmuring waves, no thundery morning's boom
Will furnish me with joyful exultation.

But there are some things precious to me still:
The diamond mountains with their weeping heights;
The dancing patterns of a fire at night;
Bouquets of roses wilting on a sill.

And when my head is swathed in sleep at last,
I read the antic fable of my dreams:
Books burned and unremembered words. It seems
Trembling I kiss them, in a sleeper's mist.

– Innokenty Annensky (1855–1909)

When we build, let us think that we build forever.

– John Ruskin (*The Seven Lamps of Architecture*)

February 21, 2012

"Cover your heads."

"What?"

"Put your scarves on your heads – that's the custom here. We're not at Bloomingdale's."

The two young women exchanged a glance, then did as their mother said. They followed her as she strode up the steps onto the broad pavement outside the cathedral. This threesome made an eye-catching sight, or would have done if there had been anyone there to see them: the older woman, elegant and self-assured, a vivid red pashmina wrapped loosely round her greying head; her two dark daughters, shadowing her like bodyguards as they tugged their own scarves up over their long hair.

"Was this one of your places?" asked the younger one as they approached the high doorway of the cathedral.

"Yes – well, no. It wasn't here in my time."

"This old church wasn't here?"

"It's not old. It's about the same age as you."

They passed through the south portal, beneath the massive bronze figures on the high lintel. "Those statues are not quite right," she said out loud.

Inside it was dark and warm – a pleasing relief from the bitter cold wind outdoors. The women turned left and found themselves facing a little stall selling long thin candles that looked like waxen straws.

"Is it OK to buy one?"

"Sure, Kira."

"Alix, have you got any roubles?"

Alix fished in her coat pocket for some coins, gave some to Kira, and they bought a candle each.

"You take it to any icon that you like the look of," whispered their mother. "Light it from a candle that's already there, and stand it in one of the little holders."

"Do we have to say a prayer?"

She looked to see if they were joking, but her girls had already wandered off into the huge cave-like body of the church. She didn't mind. She was glad to be alone for a moment or two, to drink in the incense-tinged air and think her own thoughts. The church was almost empty, which pleased her, and there was no service in progress. The girls, she could see, were exploring one of the side-chapels. She walked to the central point on the floor of the cathedral, directly below the great dome, and stopped to contemplate the iconostasis. It looked like a house – or rather, a huge teepee studded with saints. Strange and rather unorthodox. She smiled to herself. It was lovely to be back in Moscow.

She had turned away and was about to find the girls when there was a sudden commotion behind her. She swung back to see four women skipping onto the steps in front of the iconostasis. They were in brightly coloured shift dresses and – bizarrely – they were all disguised in masks, like balaclavas, with only an inverted triangle of holes for eyes and mouth. From somewhere a tinny heavy-metal soundtrack began to play, and the women started to kick like showgirls, then jump and bob to the tuneless music while making punching movements towards the ground. They began to chant in unison.

All at once Alix and Kira were beside her. "This is so *cool*," hissed Alix, her face a pantomime of thrilled amazement. "What are they saying?"

"I can't make it out," replied her mother, hoarsely. "It's too echoey." For reasons she could not have explained to her daughters, she felt tears pricking at her eyes, and a kind of dizzy nausea rising from her stomach. "They're singing something like 'God is crap',," she said – to herself now, as the sisters were gone again. Both had moved closer to the iconostasis, one to the left, the other to the right. They had taken out their phones and were filming, ignoring the outraged lay nuns who tried to shoo them away. Their mother saw them being edged back, holding their phones high as they went. She noted, with a blip of maternal admiration, their blithe lack of concern, the fact that they were not scared – merely amused and excited to have encountered something worth telling their friends back home.

She, meanwhile, did not move from the spot: she *was* scared – not for herself, but for the protesters (if that is what they were). She was frightened, and also unaccountably angry with them. She stared at the appalling and peculiar scene on the steps before her. One of the masked women was holding an electric guitar; she was not even pretending to play it – but how in the world had she got that into the church? Burly uniformed security men were in the act of pulling the instrument out of her hands. More guards were grabbing two of the other women. Somewhere off to the right an accomplice was filming the performance: out of the corner of her eye she could see the bright sharp light of a professional video camera, and she could hear someone barking at the cameraman to stop. Still the blasphemous chanting went on, growing fainter and more ragged as the women were bundled off the dais: *sran gospodnya, sran gospodnya...* In another moment of detachment, it occurred to her that 'holy shit' might be a neat translation of that unlikely and unnatural Russian phrase.

Now only the rightmost young woman was left in sight (it was clear, despite the terrorist-style masks, that they were all very young, probably no older than her own girls). This last protester dropped to her knees, slowly made the sign of the cross in the Russian Orthodox manner, then fell forward, arms outstretched and face to the floor in a parody of a Muslim at prayer. As a guard came for her she stood up of her own volition, and pranced away to join her friends...

The whole episode had lasted less than a minute. The American stood her ground for a few moments as lay nuns and security men scurried and flapped around her. The fact that she was outwardly still and calm seemed to have rendered her invisible to them. Then she turned and made for the exit, where she found her daughters waiting. The three of them went out together onto the broad snowswept square, which was as empty as when they had entered the church.

"That was amazing." said Alix. "Where are they? I want to talk to them."

"They're not here," said her mother, relieved. "They got away."

Baptism

This is my beloved son...

– Matthew 3:17

March 1982

The season for walking on water was almost over. Winter was at an end, and the river was beginning to move. Great flat sheets of ice slowly drifted and collided like continents on the snowy surface, jostling for position as the current and their own huge weight forced them downstream and out into the wide neck of the Finnish Gulf. Sometimes two slabs would grind into each other, and the pressure of their contact locked them together like antlers. One or other would always have to give way in the end, throwing up sheer peaks of green frozen water, or suddenly crumbling away in a slushy pulp.

On the Palace Embankment stood the lone figure of a young man, about seventeen years old. With his hands tucked for warmth into his armpits and his shoulders hunched against the biting wind, he watched the slow procession of ice floes. His feet performed a cold man's jig on the frosty pavement, and by his side was a small cardboard suitcase. He loved this tectonic sideshow. For a good half-hour he had been observing the little icy mountain ranges rise and fall. Most of all he enjoyed the sounds that the normally silent Neva produced as it thawed, and he closed his eyes to listen. The river creaked and groaned; it crackled and fizzed like a bonfire.

He opened his eyes and looked at the Peter and Paul Fortress on the far bank of the Neva. In that moment the golden spire caught a ray of early-morning sun, and its tip shone like a welding torch. With a shiver he recalled one of his elder brother's favourite rumours: that a month or two ago, in the dead of night, someone had painted the words YOU CANNOT KEEP THE SOULS OF THE PEOPLE IN CHAINS FOREVER in metre-high letters on the wall of the fortress. Mark said that they had removed all trace of the aphorism before the morning rush-hour.

He shivered again. The cold had thoroughly penetrated his inadequate overcoat, and it was time to go. He reached into an inside pocket and withdrew a stump of pencil and a small exercise book. On the cover was written the boy's name: Vadim Prichalov. He opened the tatty notebook to a fresh page and wrote with numb fingers: *5th March, Leningrad. Arrived from Moscow at six in the morning. Went to listen to the river."* He paused for a moment, then added: *Can't keep souls in chains – it seems most unlikely to me."*

Then he slipped the book back into his coat, picked up the suitcase and set off at a trot for the trolleybus stop at the top of Nevsky Prospekt.

December 1812

General Peter Kikin undid the stiff collar of his uniform, laid down the quill, and got up from the desk in his study. He rang a small brass bell on the mantelpiece by the log fire, and within a few seconds a house-serf appeared in the doorway.

"Zakhar, bring me a glass of tea, will you," he said. With a silent nod the serf disappeared. Kikin stared into the fire, and his mind drifted over the events of the war, which now, thank God, was coming to an end: the French invasion, the retreat, the occupation of Moscow and the terrible fire that followed.

In September he had entered the capital at the head of a column of cavalry. Moscow, beautiful Moscow, was then a smoking field of ash. The streets, insofar as streets could be discerned at all, were filled with black-faced urchins who spent their days rooting in the warm cinders for coins and candlesticks – for anything of value that might have survived the inferno. Kikin had not even been able to locate his own boyhood home in the ruins.

It was then, as he rode through the blackened rubble, that he had conceived the idea that he was now trying to put into words. Since that day, as the French retreated, the scheme had taken shape in his head, but he had hardly had a moment to get it down on paper. He was hoping it would be easier to get the proposal written and delivered during this short leave in Petersburg, but it had not proved so. For three days he had been pacing the floor of his study, and tomorrow he was to leave the capital and go back to his regiment in Vilna to continue the struggle. The French had now been pushed almost to the border. Another week or two and the last of the invaders would be driven from Russian soil.

Zakhar re-entered the room carrying a glass of tea and a silver plate of sweets, which he placed on the desk next to his master's writing instruments. With a sigh Kikin tore himself away from the fireside and went back to his desk. He took a sip of the hot tea, and popped a bonbon into his mouth. Then he dipped his quill and continued the letter:

... It is a good While since we have spoken, or written one to the other, and this Lapse does Credit to neither of us. Tho' be it said, Circumstances have been such that the Sword, not the Pen, has been our Chief Instrument of late. Moreover, each of us has suffer'd in his Soul, and every Heart has been constrained, in Expectation of Salvation from on high. Wherefore, then, describe our Feelings one to the other, when all feel a-like and grieve a-like?

And now that our Delivrance is nigh, who among us does not offer warm Prayers to the Almighty? Is there a Heart not filled with Gratitude to the Lord God, our sole Saviour? Who feels not in his innermost Soul the Desire to mark our Indebtedness for His Mercy to us? Why, Each and All of us, I am certain. This much is beyond Dispute; but each is Master of his own Mind, and every Man sees by his own Lights. Therefore I subject my Opinion to your enlightened Intelligence, trusting to its Justice. This is the Ground and the Goal of my Writing to you.

For all now cry out, saying that a Monument must be raised, but None can be made to agree as to what manner of Monument it shall be. Some call for an Obelisk, others a Pyramid, still others a Column, all to be dressed in eloquent Inscriptions according to the Phantasy of the various Auctors of these Designs.

I consider that the Monument should in all things be a Reflexion of its own Intention and a Mirror of its Epoch. This recent War, unleashed upon us by one whose Aim was to settle the Fate of Russia, to rock the Foundations of her Civil and Political Hierarchys, and to throw down Her very Religion, was a most uncommon Event; Its Monument must therefore be a most uncommon Object.

The Lord in His Mercy looked upon our Faith and upon the Zeal of our Nation, and He rescued us; to Him the Glory! God forbid that we, like unthinking Monkeys, should slavishly reproduce the heathen Forms of the Ancients, and think it well done. Are we Idolaters, then? Obelisks, Pyramids and suchlike merely flatter Men's Pride and encourage a Haughty Attitude, and in no Wise satisfy the noble Heart of a Christian when it is filled to overflowing with Thanks.

So I say to you: My Heart and my Intellect are at one in the Desire to see a Temple raised in Moscow. Let it be dedicated to the Saviour and be called the Cathedral of the Salvation, for this alone can in every Respect satisfy the Expectations of all our Countrymen. Let it be erected in an empty Square (there is now no Lack of them). I say: Let it be built in Moscow, for there, in the Heart of Russia, the Proud Foe determined to deal a Fatal Blow to the Russian People; there it was that he dared to mock our Holy Shrines; and there it was that Providence at last put a Stop to his wicked Plans for the Race of Men; there, in the Old Capital, began the Destruction of the unnumbered Legions of the Enemy.

Thus rendering unto God what is God's, we shall bind ourselves more closely to the True Faith. A Cathedral of the Saviour, standing on a new Square and rising from the Ashes of the Conflagration, will always be before our Eyes, and before the Eyes of our Descendants, a Symbol of our Indebtedness to the Lord God for His Salvation. Let it not be a strutting Peacock of a Monument, ascribing the Deed to our own Virtue. For it is written in the Scriptures: "Not ours, O Lord, not ours but Thine be the Glory!"

This is my earnest and heartfelt Opinion, for the little it is worth. Please make use of this Letter as you will. And God save the Tsar.

Your humble and devoted Servant,

Peter Kikin

Duty General of the Imperial High Command

St. Petersburg, 17th December, 1812

Kikin took another sip of tea. He folded the letter, sealed it with wax, and wrote the name of the addressee on the reverse. He carried it over to the mantelpiece and rang the brass bell again.

"Are my bags ready for the morning?" he asked Zakhar as he appeared in the doorway.

"All packed and waiting, your Excellency," replied the servant.

"Good. See that this note is delivered first thing."

The servant took the letter and left the room, bowing as he closed the door behind him. Kikin stayed by the fireplace for a long time, staring into the flames.

March 1982

When Vadim Prichalov opened the door of the flat on Marat Street he was surprised to see a light on in the kitchen. He was even more surprised to find that it was Mark, not his father, who was up and about at this early hour. Mark stood by the sink in his underpants, peering sleepily at the kitchen shelves through a tangle of long hair. "Hello, little brother," said Mark, "We seem to be out of clean cups."

"You could always wash one up," said Vadim, nodding at the pile of crockery in the sink.

Mark made a brief pantomime of considering the proposition. "I don't think so," he said. "Ira's coming today. If we can just last out a couple of hours..." He reached into the back of a cupboard and triumphantly extracted a 14-kopeck glass tumbler. Vadim sat down at the kitchen table and watched as Mark scanned the tiny kitchen for the teapot. When he located it, he poured a short finger of yesterday's strong brew into the glass and filled it from the boiling kettle on the stove. Then he sat down at the table opposite Vadim, and holding the rim of the hot glass gingerly between thumb and middle finger, took a noisy sip.

"Aren't you going to have one?" asked Mark. Vadim did not feel much like washing-up either – it wasn't his mess, after all. But he got up and rinsed a cup under the hot tap. He was still at the sink when his father shuffled into the room, the flippy-floppy rubber *vietnamki* slapping against the soles of his feet as he went. "Ah, welcome back," he said, tousling Vadim's hair. "The prodigal returns."

Vadim had never clapped eyes on a Bible in his life, but he had seen enough Dutch and Spanish art in the Hermitage to understand the allusion. "So have you slaughtered the fatted calf for me then, Dad?" he said.

"Afraid not," said Yuri Prichalov, pleased by his son's knowing joke. "But there's a butt-end of salami in the fridge. Dig it out and you can tell us about your trip over breakfast."

The kitchen was too small to accommodate three grown men at once – it was already crowded with essential furniture. In the far corner there was the outsize fridge that hummed in a deeply resonant monotone, like a Tibetan monk, each chant beginning and ending with a mighty shudder that shook the kitchen floor. Next to this was a low gas-stove sown with spent matches; then a set of drawers containing cutlery and a garlic-press; then, at the near corner, a square enamel sink, its whiteness stained an indelible brown in places like a smoker's nail. By the opposite wall stood a kitchen table. It was too large for the room and it forced the men to squeeze by each other, but the inconvenient kitchen table was tolerated as the family's one unchanging trysting-place, the point in space where their three lives crossed.

Four chipboard stools nestled under the table's legs, and a print of Valentin Serov's *Rape of Europa*, Yuri's favourite painting, adorned the wall above it. A postcard depicting the Dome of the Rock in Jerusalem was tucked into one corner of the frame.

Over the sink hung an aluminium plate rack, and nondescript cupboards occupied the remaining wall space. One cupboard contained a complete set of china, which at the insistence of Yuri's sister was brought out only on birthdays and other special occasions. This taboo was strictly observed, and it would never have occurred to Vadim or Mark to solve the crockery shortage by offending against it. Another cupboard contained stocks of dry food: a sixty-day supply of rice, buckwheat, home-made jam, macaroni, and flour. A third, decorated with a sticker bearing the legend *Olympiada 1980 Aeroport Sheremetyevo,* was home to everyday crockery: sole survivors of otherwise extinct tea-sets, three glazed mugs emblazoned with photo-transfers of the Admiralty, an eclectic collection of dinner plates and broad, shallow soup-bowls. These items rarely saw the inside of the cupboard, but wandered like the tribes of Israel back and forth across the triangular wilderness between the sink, the drainer and the table.

The men worked round each other with practised efficiency. Vadim finished the washing-up and sliced the sausage. Yuri fried some eggs, cracking them ostentatiously into the pan with one hand. Mark laid the plates and even deigned to make a fresh pot of tea.

"So how did it go?" asked Yuri, as they sat hunched over the feast. "Are they going to take you?"

"I don't want to tempt fate, Dad," said Vadim. "But yes, I think they are. As of this autumn."

"What were the tests like?"

"No problem. I passed. And the dean seemed happy with my performance when he interviewed me."

"And the university?"

"I liked it. I had a good look round the journalism faculty and the main building. They said that if I am accepted they will give me a place in the hostel."

"Hm. that's good." Yuri forked a piece of sausage. "Did you go to the theatre last night?"

"No tickets. I went swimming instead."

"At the Moskva? The open-air pool?" asked Mark.

"Yes."

Mark picked up his eggy fork and solemnly made the sign of the cross over Vadim's head. "I baptise you, my son, in the name of the Father, the Son and the Holy Ghost," he intoned.

Vadim looked at his brother in bewilderment, then to Yuri for an explanation.

"Take no notice," said Yuri.

"It's a private architects' joke," smirked Mark. "That was holy water you were splashing about in. Highly chlorinated, but holy all the same."

Vadim again looked from one to the other: his father, the qualified architect, and his brother, the student.

"You've heard of the Cathedral of Christ the Saviour?" said Mark.

"Yes, I've heard of it."

"Well, that's where it was before it was torn down."

"Oh?"

"Yes, on Stalin's orders."

"Why would Stalin want a swimming pool next to the Kremlin?"

"It wasn't intended to be a pool. He wanted the site for a Palace of Soviets, a skyscraper bigger than the Empire State Building with a huge Lenin on top."

Vadim knew Mark was just showing off his knowledge, and he resented it slightly. He had thought hard about bowing to the family tradition and applying to MArkhi, the Moscow Architectural Institute, but he was determined not to follow slavishly in his brother's footsteps. It was bad enough that he would be trekking after him to college in Moscow. What's more, Mark was a fine draughtsman, whereas Vadim could not draw a straight line if his life depended on it. No, Mark could have MArkhi. He would make a niche for himself at the university and concentrate on books and writing. He would never make a builder.

"So why the pool?"

"They found they couldn't get a building to stand on the shifting ground near the river," said Mark. "Still less the tallest building in the world. They couldn't even figure out how the tsarist engineers managed to put a building up there in the first place. So in the end they cut their losses, stuck a hosepipe in the hole they'd dug, and called it a swimming pool."

Vadim shrugged. There were still plenty of churches. So what if they were being used as museums, or even warehouses, the architecture was still there for those who were interested. He said as much to Mark.

"Christ the Saviour was no ordinary church," said Mark. "It was a giant cathedral, the biggest church in the world, built entirely with voluntary donations from peasants. Hundreds of thousands of ordinary people donated their kopecks. And then the people's party knocked it down. Can you imagine Leningrad without St. Isaac's? Can you see the English bulldozing St. Paul's, or the French Notre Dame, just to try and out-spit America?"

"I think that's putting it a bit strong," said Yuri, wanting to temper his son's anti-Soviet tone. "The Cathedral only stood for fifty years or so, and no-one liked it much, so you can hardly compare it with St. Paul's. And Konstantin Thon was no Wren – you know that. Perhaps they shouldn't have knocked it down, but it was no big loss. Of course, I'm glad they never built the Palace of Soviets – that would have been a monstrosity."

"No more monstrous than the Moscow University building, where Vadim's going to live," said Mark, getting up from the table. "Anyway, I'm off. I've got people to see."

"Put a hat on," said Yuri. "It's five below out there."

"Naturally. Catch you later, Vadim. Come over later if you like. I'll be at Artyom's – he'll be glad to see you."

December 1812

The seed planted by General Kikin did not fall on stony ground. He knew exactly what Shishkov would do with the letter when he received it, and he could not have picked a better champion. If anyone could win the tsar's sanction, it was his distinguished acquaintance Alexander Semenovich Shishkov.

State Secretary Shishkov read the letter in his chambers, and was

delighted by the idea. He had any number of lawyers and scribes at
his disposal, but he decided to pen this decree himself. He was sure
that the tsar would give his blessing.

He composed the first draft that evening. Unlike Kikin, he was
a skilled writer and the words flowed smoothly. As was his custom,
he put the paper on one side once he had a finished text. Though he
was not given to frivolity, Shishkov was fond of telling himself that
imperial decrees, like shot pheasant, are always the better for being
hung a few days. When he returned to it on Christmas Eve he made a
few stylistic changes and then gave the manuscript to his best scribe
to make a fair copy. He had an audience with His Imperial Majesty
the next day.

It was barely dawn when Shishkov's carriage arrived at chambers
the next morning. An elderly servant was cleaning the grate in his
office and preparing to light a new fire. "*S rozhdestvom khristovym*,
Your Honour – bless you on Christ's birthday!" said the servant as
Shishkov strode to his desk.

"God's blessing on you too," said Shishkov automatically, and sat
down. The decree was on the top of the pile of documents. He took
the parchment to the window and read it by the light of the winter
sunrise:

*On the Building of a Cathedral in Moscow, to be dedicated to the
Name of Christ the Saviour.*

*The Salvation of Russia from Her Adversaries, whose Cohorts
have been so various and strong, whose Designs and whose Actions
have been so wicked and unmerciful, but whose Destruction,
accomplished within this Half-Year, has been so complete that even
in fullest Flight only the smallest Fraction of their Number has been
able to quit our Territories, all this is a True Sign of the Grace of
God which anoints us; it is a very memorable Circumstance: one*

which shall not be effaced from the Annals and the Chronicles of our Nation, though Ages pass. In order that the unexampled Zeal, the Steadfastness and the Love of the Russian People for their Faith and for their Homeland be not forgotten, and in Commemoration of our Thankfulness for Divine Providence, which saved Russia from the Threat of Catastrophe, We have decreed that a Cathedral be raised in Moscow, where We are enthroned.

God bless Us in this our Undertaking, and grant that it be fruitful. May this Temple stand the Centuries long, and may the Thurible which burns within before the Seat of God bear Witness to our Gratitude before the last Generations, and so kindle in them Love for the Achievements of their Forebears, and also the Will to emulate them.

Shishkov grunted with approval. He put the unsigned decree in his despatch box with the other papers, and called for his carriage.

Yuri, Vadim's father, had been an architect for twenty years, and a widower for fourteen.

As a youth he had found it hard to decide on a career. But Efim Oskarovich, his father, believed in settling these matters early, and as soon as Yuri was thirteen he enlisted all his friends and relatives to have the boy come and spend some time at work with them. He thought that these days out at factories, in hospitals, on building sites, would help Yuri make up his mind about what to do with his life.

One such outing took Yuri to the school where his uncle Leonid taught *fizkultura*, physical education. Though his main interest at this time was painting, Yuri was not a bad athlete, and the life of a gym teacher seemed appealing enough. He found his uncle in the gym, presiding over a session of indoor football with two teams of sixteen-year-old girls.

Can I play? Yuri asked, and Leonid saw no reason why not. Yuri was naturally the best player on the pitch, and he had a lot of the ball. The girls giggled and yelped and chased him round the gym. But he was perhaps a mite young to appreciate his good fortune: he thought the best way to make an impression was to dazzle the girls with his sporting prowess. Two minutes before the end of the game the ball landed at Yuri's feet on the half-way line, and he saw the chance to make a spectacular dribble the length of the gym and score an individual goal. Head down, eye on the ball, he set off for the penalty area.

At this moment one of the less gifted girls decided to make up for her lack of talent with a display of courage. Her name was Natasha, she had green eyes, straight, dark hair, and she was a real Russian beauty. She stepped into Yuri's path, closed her eyes and extended one leg. Yuri did not see her. He was concentrating on his own feet, certain that the girl-defenders would make way as he sprinted for goal.

The top of Yuri's head made contact with the bridge of Natasha's nose at fifteen kilometres per hour. She went down like a sack of bricks, blood gushing bright and bubbly from both nostrils. She was out cold for a full minute, during which time utter pandemonium reigned in the gym. The girls screamed and bawled, and half a dozen fainted in sympathy. Yuri beat a hasty, somewhat cowardly retreat, ushered off the premises by Leonid, who was suddenly afraid for his job. By the time Natasha came round her eyes were two weeping purple slits, and her nose was swelling like a live thing.

Yuri was eaten up with guilt. The next morning he went to the hospital where Natasha was under observation for concussion. He brought expiatory gifts, but Natasha refused to see him. She did not want to see anyone while her face looked like a bowl of plums.

Driven by shame, Yuri persisted, and in the end Natasha accepted his offerings of flowers and books. Natasha came home and put herself under house arrest until the bruising was gone. Yuri visited her every day, at first as a form of penance, and then because he found that he enjoyed Natasha's company.

A strange friendship developed between them. Yuri discovered that he could make her laugh with little tales of his adventures at school, and he ransacked his life for nuggets of incident with which to amuse her. He also drew her portrait in charcoal, and blushed with pride when she hung the sketch in her room. Natasha forgave Yuri his reckless sportsmanship – he was just a boy, after all. And the small bump on her nose did not spoil her good looks; in fact, it gave a striking patrician air to her previously pretty, but unremarkable face.

After this Platonic beginning, it came as a shock to Yuri when he realised he was utterly in love with her. He never said a word, and the infatuation did not pass. For nearly five years he lived in a state of bittersweet misery, tending the rose of his unrequited love in the private garden of his own soul. These, at least, were the terms in which he saw himself: Byronic melancholy was the defining mood of his adolescence. Natasha guessed how her young friend felt, and she was flattered, but she saw boys of her own age and made plans for her future after leaving school. She wanted to be a nurse.

It took the might of the Red Army to stir Yuri to action. In the autumn draft of 1955 he was conscripted into the ranks of the Soviet armed forces. The day before reporting for call-up he was on his way to get his hair cut when on impulse he called in at Natasha's flat. She put the kettle on, and over tea and pumpkin jam he blurted out (with slight exaggeration) that he had loved her since the day he'd fractured her nose. He asked her to wait for him while he did his national service, and to his astonishment she said she would. She had become so used to his unspoken devotion over the years that she had failed to notice when she began to love him back. As they wept sweet tears at the thought of their impending separation, Yuri leaned across the kitchen table and kissed the little bony bump that was his personal contribution to her features.

After three months' basic training Yuri was granted a precious two-day pass to Leningrad. He turned up on Natasha's doorstep in uniform, stronger, stouter and, it seemed to her, a good five centimetres taller than when he went away. A kind friend lent them his one-room flat, and the lovers spent a sublime weekend eating thickly buttered caviar sandwiches, drinking Bulgarian wine, and sleeping in each other's arms. Yuri asked Natasha to marry him, and she said yes. Yuri was ecstatic, but even in this blissful moment he could not resist a facetious joke: "With a nose like that," he said, "I suppose it was inevitable that you would marry a Jew."

National service turned out to be more of an ordeal than Yuri could have suspected. At the end of his first year of service he found himself in Budapest, crouched in the driver's seat of a tank. Yuri killed no-one, but from inside the tank, which he steered through the narrow streets of Old Buda, he saw lives taken and lives given in the name of – in the name of what? When the crowds on the streets threw cobblestones at his rolling metal dungeon and yelled 'fascist', he had to agree: he was no better than a Nazi. The experience made a deep impression on Yuri, but he clung to his habit of silence. In the summer of 1957 he went home with the rank of sergeant, but locked away inside him, like a splinter of iron, there was a contempt for the Soviet regime that was as unspoken as his love for Natasha had been.

Back in Leningrad he made the decision that his father had been trying to wring out of him for eight years. He decided to train as an architect. Before applying to the Architectural Faculty of the Leningrad Institute of Building Engineering he took the sensible precaution of changing his Jewish surname, Shabad, to something more Russian-sounding. Thus he became Yuri Efimovich Prichalov, from the Russian *prichal*, mooring-post. He picked the name while out walking with Natasha near the port on Vasilievsky Island.

Yuri blew his first month's stipend on a wedding feast. Natasha moved in with her husband, sister-in-law and father-in-law. Efim Oskarovich and Ira vacated the two-room flat for a fortnight after the wedding to allow the couple a honeymoon. And when eighteen months later Natasha became pregnant, the family made an application to the local council for a separate flat. They were lucky. Their names came to the top of the list before Mark was out of nappies, and the Shabads, father and daughter, moved to a separate two-room flat in a brand-new five-storey *khrushchevka*.

The Prichalovs lived in a cheerful poverty that appealed to Yuri's romantic cast of mind. He studied ferro-concrete construction and the history of the Communist Party, and he made drawings of hypothetical bread factories and imaginary train stations. He leaned towards architectural theory and developed an interest in the immediate pre-revolutionary period. His student years coincided happily with the heady days of the Thaw. Yuri subscribed to *Novy Mir* and read *One Day in the Life of Ivan Denisovich* on the day it came out. He and Natasha sat by their reel-to-reel tape machine and listened solemnly to bootleg recordings of *Hound Dog* and *Love Me Do*. One day, to Natasha's horror, he came home from the institute with a samizdat translation of *Animal Farm* in his briefcase. He had been lent it just for the night: they bolted the door, put a pencil in the dial of the telephone, and through the small hours Yuri read the stylographed book to her in a whisper.

Vadim was born on 26th May, 1964. The Thaw was over, and the dull but dependable Brezhnev was easing himself into the general secretary's chair. Yuri was now teaching Architectural Theory, and working on the first draft of a dissertation on the history of *moderne*, Russian art nouveau. Natasha stayed at home with the babies, and

Ira helped with the housekeeping.

Natasha was sorry to leave nursing – she had qualified while Yuri was in the army – but she put her children first. She continued to be as accident prone as the day she and Yuri met, and he teased her constantly on this score. Yuri used to say that if she slipped over on the ice before Revolution Day, it was a sign that they were in for a hard winter. She decimated tea-sets and burned holes in frying-pans. Doorknobs would come away comically in her hands.

One sunny afternoon in August 1968 Natasha went for a walk in town. Yuri was in an archive somewhere, and she left the boys in Ira's safe hands. It was not often she got an hour or two of peace and quiet. She strolled down Nevsky in the direction of the Alexander Nevsky monastery. She bought an Eskimo ice cream, and picked off the delicious chocolate coating with her fingers before eating the white confectionery within. At the monastery she took a turn round the necropolis, stopping for a moment at Dostoyevsky's grave, where the bottom half of her ice-cream came away from the stick and plopped mortifyingly at the great writer's feet. On the way back up Nevsky she joined an excited queue for stockings and bought two pairs, one for her and one for Ira.

The afternoon flew by. She had told Ira she would pick up the boys at four o'clock, but at a quarter to five she was still twenty minutes' walk from home. At the kink in Nevsky, where the obelisk stands, she joined a knot of pedestrians waiting for the traffic lights to change. She pushed her way to the kerb, so as not to be slowed by the herd. As soon as the lights went red she set off across the road. She did not see the car that was attempting to skip across the busy intersection before the gap in the traffic closed. Even if she had spotted him, she had no way of knowing that the impatient driver had 150 grammes of vodka coursing through his veins, having just celebrated his brigade's victory in the previous month's socialist competition between guilds. When the car's bonnet shattered her

hip-bone and sent her somersaulting down the carriageway, the
incident marked not the beginning of a romance, as had her last
osteological trauma, but the end of Natasha's life.

Yuri came home at half-past six to an unexpected theatrical
tableau. His sister, red-eyed and drawn, was rocking Mark on her
knees. Mark, eight years old now, was stone-faced and tearless.
Efim Oskarovich was staring out of the window, the early-evening
sun streaming through his wispy white hair. And Vadim sat on the
parquet floor, playing nervously with a painted wooden model of
the Kremlin's Spassky Tower. He knew something was wrong, but
could not fathom it. No-one had found the words to tell him. He
dropped the toy when he saw his father and grinned a welcome.

The radio was on in the kitchen, as usual. An authoritative voice
was saying that a joint action of Warsaw Treaty forces was being
undertaken at the request of Czechoslovak Communist Party, and
was a necessary step to prevent the supporters of counter-revolution
from hi-jacking the fraternal socialist republic of Czechoslovakia.
Yuri was not a superstitious man, and he was not interested in
religion. But without ever formulating the thought he came to
believe that his wife's death was connected to his own part in the
invasion of Hungary, as if by some hidden karma his wife had been
taken in payment for the Czechs who were crushed under Soviet
tanks that day. He did not believe in God, but in his grief, and in
spite of his unbelief, he grew to hate the Almighty for His vengeful
sense of justice.

Perversely, he began to read the Bible – he borrowed one from
the same shady black market source that had lent him *Animal Farm*.
Stranger still, he put out feelers at work to see if he could become a
member of the KPSS, the Communist Party of the Soviet Union. It
was a career move: he wanted access to Western journals for his work
on *moderne*, and he needed a party card if he was to climb higher

up the teaching hierarchy within the Institute. He was well aware of the ironies, and in later years he derived a good deal of mirthless amusement from the idea that he was ostensibly in the vanguard of progressive Soviet society. He did not see that the contempt he cultivated for the world was slowly desiccating his soul.

December 1812

The streets were nearly empty when Shishkov left the Winter Palace and emerged onto the Embankment where his equipage was waiting. Most people were at home preparing for the celebration that marked the end of the Advent fast. Apart from his motionless carriage driver, the only living soul in view was a rather ragged boy scurrying across the ice towards the fortress.

Shishkov sucked in the fresh air, which was as cold and invigorating as champagne. Though he loved his Emperor, and was honoured to be received into his presence, he was always relieved when the meetings were over. Today's encounter had been friendly: what with holy day, and the fact that the French were now being harried across the frozen mud of Poland, the Emperor had been in a positively happy mood. Now Shishkov could go home to his own Christmas feast, the day's work done.

In the carriage he opened the leather blotter and read the day's business again. The decree that he had composed was now on the bottom of the pile. He went through it one last time, savouring his own language and the superb penmanship. With his finger he traced the curlicues of the large, elegant signature on the bottom, the spikes and troughs of which combined to form the single letter 'A', this being the autograph of Tsar Alexander the First.

Mandala

Thirty spokes
Share one hub.

– Lao Tzu, *Tao Te Ching*

December 1812

The boy whom Shishkov had spotted from his carriage trotted home through the quiet streets behind the fortress. His overcoat billowed behind him as he ran; his long, dark hair and the tails of his scarf streamed out at right angles to his lanky frame; he took long, loping strides, keeping an eye out for icy patches on the uneven, cobbled pavements, or skidding across them like a skater. His lungs ached from the cold air, and beads of sweat ran down his broad forehead and froze uncomfortably in his eyelashes. He had given his father a solemn promise to come straight back from the Academy and not to be late for the Christmas feast. But the morning had been so quiet and clear that he had not been able to resist taking a stroll on the English Embankment. Now he was paying for that half-hour's peace and solitude.

He turned the last corner at a run. He saw at once that a light was burning in his father's workshop, which was good. If father was still at his bench, then he was not late after all. He walked the last few yards to catch his breath. The sign over the shop was swinging creakily in the breeze. Not for the first time, it drew the boy's attention: though I say it myself, that is a good piece of work, he thought. His father had been pleased with it too, and had even given him a few coins for the job. "Well done, Konstantin," he said. "A paid commission – the first of many, I hope."

As the boy passed below the hanging sign he jumped and struck it with the tips of his fingers. It turned a circle on its hinges, which was a disappointment: his best effort was three full revolutions. The door had slammed behind him before the painted board came to rest. If there had been anyone else on the street, they could now have read its message. In fine gilt lettering on a black background the sign said: "Andrei Thon: goldsmith, jeweller."

March 1982

Ira had never had any children of her own, and she loved her two nephews with a love made strong by her sense of unfulfilment. Over the years she had slowly usurped the maternal functions of her dead sister-in-law, and the boys paid her back by loving her like a mother.

The boys' favourite food was mushroom soup, so at least once a week in summer and autumn Ira would get up at the first glint of dawn and take a bus to the forest on the edge of the city. Here she gathered the dew-covered mushrooms from among the roots of the trees. She was an expert picker and knew every kind of mushroom by name: the bitter *syroyezhka* with its purple cap; the brown, dimpled *serushka;* the *lisichka* with the yellow pie-crust lid that keeps its colour when pickled; and the pale *poganka,* or 'stinker', which looks like an ordinary white mushroom, but is deadly to eat.

Auntie Ira knew them all, but where the boys were concerned she took no chances. Back in her kitchen she would cut each mushroom in half and put the halves on two separate plates. Then she would make a batch of soup from one set of halved mushrooms and eat a bowl alone at her kitchen table. Only when she was sure she had not poisoned herself would she make another batch of soup from the rest of the mushrooms for Mark and Vadim. She carried it hot to the Prichalovs' flat in an aluminium milk-churn wrapped in a blanket. And in her cloth shopping-bag there was always a jar of fresh *smetana* and a half-moon of rye-bread.

The flat where Ira lived with her father was not far from Marat Street. Efim Oskarovich was her responsibility too, so in effect she had four men to look after: father, brother, nephew, nephew. In her bag today (the mushroom season still some months away) were curd-cheese *bliny* warm from the pan.

Vadim, meanwhile, was on his own in the flat in Marat Street. Yuri had left for work soon after Mark. He went to the bedroom that he shared with his brother and sat down at the large scroll-top secretaire, a solid, coffin-like piece of furniture bequeathed to the flat by grandfather before Vadim was born.

He was planning to do some work, but something was interfering with his concentration. He was strangely disturbed by the conversation over breakfast. It was not just that his curiosity had been roused; that was part of it, but there was also something sinister in his disquiet. Vadim tried to analyse the sensation. If he worked at it with the proper concentration, he knew he could usually find the buried source of any unexplained emotion.

He quickly deduced that it was Mark, not his father, who had upset him. He put Yuri out of his mind and focused on his brother. First, there was Mark's habit of putting an anti-Soviet spin on everything he said. He did not mind the opinions themselves, though he thought it was a waste of energy to despise the system to the extent that his brother and father did. But Mark did not have father's sense of caution, and Vadim was afraid for him. His tendency to say exactly what he thought had got him into trouble before, and was liable to become a real danger unless he learned to think twice before he opened his mouth. There was no way Vadim could say this to Mark, who would interpret any comment as proof that his bravado was having a properly shocking effect.

Was it something to do with the story of Christ the Cathedral? Yes, this seemed more likely. The sheer vandalism of it? Vadim thought not. He knew well enough that many churches had become victims of the official ideology. So had many people, and living souls are more important than buildings. He knew about the purges in the Thirties. Not from school or books, naturally, but Grandad had been through them and his maternal grandparents had both died in them. He knew the broad facts of 1937, the ones that were not in the text books, and he lost no sleep over them. And as for the cathedral, father said that it was not a great work and that the architect was a third-rater.

Konstantin Thon. He had come across that name in his reading somewhere recently. Again, he knew that if he concentrated, he would be able to pluck the reference from the card index of his mind.

The scrape of a key in the front door made Vadim jump. His train of thought was broken for the moment. He went to meet aunt Ira in the corridor.

"Hello there, *rybka*, my little fish. Welcome home." Ira took Vadim's head in both hands, inclined it toward her, and kissed his curly fringe. "You look thin. There's no food in Moscow?"

"Of course there's food, Ira. More than there is in Piter, anyway. And I can't be thinner. I was only gone three days."

"Three days is a long time with nothing to eat. Sit down, I have your breakfast here."

It was useless to protest that he had eaten less than an hour before. Vadim did as he was told and ate a second meal. He told her about his success in the university, and she listened with sombre attention. "So now I lose you both to Moscow," she said. "Dad will be miserable too."

"My dad or your dad?"

"Both, as it happens. You might go round and see Grandad today. He'll want to hear your news, and you know what day it is today."

Vadim said not.

"You know. March the fifth. It always puts him in such a temper, and the only thing that sets him right is if he can talk to someone about the war."

Vadim twigged. "I'm not sure I want to go and commiserate with Grandad on Stalin's death," he said. "I think it's a pity Stalin didn't die earlier, it would have saved everybody a good deal of trouble."

"Now, don't you start," said Ira sharply, lowering her voice at the same time. "You sound like your brother."

"What if I do?" said Vadim, reddening. "I think Mark is right about a lot of things."

"Well, right or wrong, just mind you don't go expressing any political opinions. Not just when you are setting out on a university career."

"I know better than that, Ira," said Vadim, blushing again. "I am not stupid."

Ira saw now that she had offended him. "I know you're not, *lapochka*, little paw." She stroked his head. "I'm sorry. But do go and see Grandad. It's nothing to make a fuss about – just pop round and cheer him up."

Vadim said that he would. "But first I must do some work."

"Of course. What do you want for tea tonight? I think we should have a small celebration."

"Let's not be hasty. I keep telling you, I might not be in yet. You ought not count chicks in spring."

"Well it's spring now, and I saw them unloading frozen Hungarian chickens at the *gastronom* on Herzen Street just yesterday. I call that a happy omen. I'll go and buy one, and a bottle of *shampanskoye*. Tonight we are having a little party."

Vadim laughed, and a thought or a memory bubbled to the surface of his mind.

At the end of the summer term of 1814, in his eleventh and penultimate year at the Academy, Konstantin Thon was awarded the silver medal. His father and brothers all turned out for the prize-giving ceremony.

The main topic of discussion at the occasion was the sensational news about Karl Vitberg. He was barely out of the Academy, but had defeated all his old teachers in the competition to win the commission for the Cathedral of Christ the Saviour in Moscow. Konstantin's brother had studied composition with Vitberg. "He was a good painter," was the verdict of the older Thon. "But he couldn't build a dog kennel." It seemed everybody at the Academy, from the president to the nightwatchman, had an opinion on the subject of Vitberg's triumph, and they were all disapproving. "The mother of the arts entrusted to a babe," quipped one professor. "The child now cradles the madonna in its arms." It became the most-repeated remark of the day.

Konstantin vaguely remembered Vitberg, who had spent only two years at the Academy and was several years his senior. He had never spoken to his brother's classmate, but had often seen him in the corridors. Vitberg had struck him as a melancholy, dreamy figure – not at all unsympathetic. Thon wondered what professor Voronikhin would make of the news. He decided to pay his favourite teacher a visit once the prize-giving was over.

The professor was in his apartments at the Academy – he did not often leave them these days. "Ah, master Thon," said Voronikhin on opening the door. He was wearing a long dressing gown and a velvet cap with a tassel. His thin face was pale, but his skin and eyes glowed almost luminously. He was in the final stages of consumption. "Come to show me your medal, have you? Bravo, my congratulations to you."

"And my commiserations to you, professor."

"Commiserations? Whatever for? I'm not dead yet."

"No, of course not, professor," said Thon, shocked. "I meant the competition."

"Oh that," said the teacher, kicking one of the piles of drawings and plans that lay strewn on the floor. "I am not too concerned about that."

"You should have won it."

"Ha! Thank you for your loyalty, Konstantin. But I never expected to receive the commission, and I never hoped for it. It is not my time. Vitberg is a worthy victor. He will build a fine church, I am sure."

"That's not what they are saying downstairs."

"Sour grapes, nothing more. You too must get used to that kind of talk."

The young man was abashed. "What will you do now?" he asked.

The teacher smiled. "Never mind me. What will you do?"

"What do you mean, professor?"

"I mean you must win the gold medal next year and go abroad."

Thon picked up one of the scattered drawings. "No-one goes abroad any more, professor. You know that."

"The war will not last much longer, Konstantin. We are in Paris, after all. Once peace returns to Europe, there will be no reason to deny gold medallists their scholarship. You must win it and go to Rome. It will be the making of you."

Thon looked at the drawing in his hands. It was one he had seen dozens of times before, but it never failed to move him. It depicted the main façade of Voronikhin's design for the Cathedral of Christ.

The church had a grand ovoid dome at the centre topped with a bulbous sixteenth-century cupola. Around the dome were four steep tent-roofs, like those over the gates of monasteries in old Muscovy, and these too were topped with slim little onion-hats. The decoration consisted of spade-shaped *zakomary* and round arches. All these elements were taken from an ancient Russian tradition, yet the effect was strikingly original. The church was both old and new. It owed nothing to the Greek models that (Thon had been taught) were the acme of architectural form and could never be improved upon.

"Nothing of Rome in this, professor. This makes it look rather as if you disapprove of the classics," said Konstantin at length.

"I most certainly do not disapprove of them. I merely disapprove of the use they are put to."

"How so?"

"Go to Europe, and you will learn how so."

Thon nodded. "I love this drawing," he said.

"Then keep it. It is yours."

"Professor, I didn't…"

"I know. Do not be embarrassed, I want you to have it. To me it is bread cast upon the waters."

"What do you mean?"

"Win the gold medal and go to Europe, Master Thon. That is the last piece of advice I shall give you."

The end of this remark was lost in a violent fit of coughing. Konstantin wanted to wait and talk some more. He wanted to hear about his future. But the professor waved his pupil out of the door. The gesture was so urgent that Thon dared not protest. He left with a bow, the drawing tucked under his arm. He never saw Voronikhin alive again.

March 1982

After Ira left for the shops, Vadim went back to his desk, having first gone to his father's room for a book. He leafed through the book, breathing in the sour, woody aroma that wafted off the coarse paper. Vadim could not help but congratulate himself: Ira had given the clue to him without knowing, but he had been sharp enough to catch the thought in flight. Here it was in Alexander Herzen's *Past and Thoughts*, the paragraph he was thinking of. He had read it less than a year before, which was itself pure chance. He set the book on the secretaire before him and copied the passage into his own notebook:

In a society remarkable only for the absence of faith, and of any defining circumstances whatsoever, it was difficult to endow a created thing with the breath of life. The strain of the attempt shewed in the new churches, which reeked of hypocrisy and anachronism: they were either pentacephalous cruet-sets with cupolas for corks, all decked out in the Indo-Byzantine garb favoured by Nikolai and Thon; or else they were the angular, Gothic concoctions, offensive to the artistic eye, like those with which the English are wont to embellish their little towns.

Certainly Herzen was in no doubt about Thon. But it sounded like he had an axe of his own to grind. There was a footnote: see Stasov, V.V. *25 Years of Russian Art*. Dad was bound to have that, it was his period. He went again to the other room, replaced the Herzen, and scanned the wall of shelves for Stasov. Yes, it was there. Vadim took volume two of the three and went back to his own room.

His heart was thudding – why? He was doing nothing wrong. He tried to define his feeling: it was an adrenalin rush, like being a hunter. He suspected that he was on the trail of something big, that this was a significant beginning. He checked the book: it was the right edition, probably the only Soviet edition of Stasov. What was it Chekhov had called him, 'the Inky Impaler'?

Vadim turned to the index of names and there he was, Thon K.A., page five hundred and five. The cross-reference turned out to be a typically venomous passage:

...He was an entirely mediocre engineer, he had no talent whatsoever. He was at best a capable stonemason, but completely lacking in education and in artistry. The ungifted and tasteless structures that he erected betrayed utter ignorance of Ancient Russia; they were cobbled together using elements plundered in haste from a handful of Muscovite sources, and even these were reproduced in a slapdash and corrupted form. He knew nothing of Russian architecture outside of Moscow (why indeed should he? To go travelling round Russia would have been an awful bore!), and what little he saw he interpreted in the most clumsy fashion imaginable. His works were the architectural equivalent of such twopenny reproductions of well-known paintings as idle office-boys are wont to turn out on their day off. This was clear as daylight to all but the authorities. Everybody else was opposed to Thon, and at a loss to find the smallest grain of true national feeling in his sorry brick-built doggerel...

Vadim copied out this passage too. Now he was interested, and suspicious too. If Thon was really as mediocre as all that, why resort to such strong language, even allowing for Stasov's caustic style? He could understand Soviet critics being opposed to the chief architect of Nikolai I, but why were his contemporaries so dead set against him? Vadim decided to see what else he could find out, but not now. He had to go and see Grandad.

☆

"Before a battle the sergeant would come round with a bucket of homebrew vodka," said Efim Oskarovich. "We could drink as much as we liked. I used to knock it back by the billycanful."

"Wasn't it hard fighting Germans when you were drunk."

"Drunk? We weren't drunk. We were just warm, and perhaps a little more courageous than we might otherwise have been. Also, it was for many the last tipple of their lives. We would toast Stalin, wish each other luck, and then it was over the top."

"You toasted Stalin?"

"Naturally. All of us went into battle with the words 'For Stalin and for Motherland' on our lips. For us Stalin and Motherland were the same thing. When he died I thought the world had come to an end. I did not know how I could go on living."

"But you did, didn't you. So Stalin and Motherland are not the same thing, are they?"

"They were for us. Oh, I know mistakes were made. God knows, there were plenty of mistakes. But we knew our cause was just. We made our choice in 1917, and don't you forget it. There was no turning back then, and there is none now, whatever you might hear from certain quarters. And it was the right choice. The Revolution gave us a proper army and the heavy industry to back it up. Without them, and without Stalin, we would never have defeated Hitler. Remember, you will have to serve in the army yourself sooner or later."

"Mark didn't."

"Never mind Mark. You would never get away with that, and I wouldn't want you to try."

This was an episode that Efim Oskarovich viewed with the utmost distaste. Yuri had taken advice from a doctor friend as to how his elder son should go about avoiding the army. The doctor said Mark should fake a faint on the underground six months before his draft board, and provided detailed clinical information on how he should go about it. Yuri gave the man a copy of *Master and Margarita* for his trouble. Mark was told what to do and he pulled the whole thing off with confidence and theatricality: rush hour, Revolution Square, out like a light. He did not so much as twitch an eyelid until he had been in hospital for an hour. The doctors were baffled, but it went on his medical notes and at his subsequent draft board he was pronounced unfit for military service.

"...two things really churn you up inside," Efim Oskarovich was saying. "The first time you kill an enemy, and when someone you know gets killed. It needn't even be a close friend necessarily. With me it was just someone I had noticed because he had bright red hair and a permanent grin, not Russian-looking at all. He was not in my platoon, and I didn't even know his name – I'd just seen this hair and this great toothy smile. We were on the march, and I hadn't spotted him for a while. Then one day I was thinking out loud at mealtime, and I said: 'Where's that carrot-top?' 'Copped it last week,' someone said. 'Got his legs blown off at the thigh and bled to death in a field hospital.' 'No,' I said. 'Yes,' he said. 'I was with him. Wasn't laughing at the finish, I can tell you.' Well, I had seen plenty of raw meat by that time, but that really got to me. I couldn't finish my food; in fact, I threw up. And I had to go for a walk so the others wouldn't see me cry. And I didn't even know him – don't know his name to this day."

Vadim's mind wandered. He did not object to his grandfather's stories about the war. But the ones that interested him most were the ones he heard from Yuri and Ira. Efim Oskarovich had been an engineer and a professional soldier before the war. He was arrested in 1938, during the mass purges of the Red Army officer corps. His wife Nadya was at that time pregnant with their second child. He was held in a labour camp until early 1942, and considered himself immensely fortunate not to have been shot within a few months of his arrest, as most were. But he suffered dreadful torments from not knowing what had become of his wife, and from the shame of being labelled an enemy of the people. He was a patriot and a communist, and he never stopped believing that his dishonour was a terrible mistake. His steadfastness was rewarded: he was released and sent to the front, where his particular engineering skills were needed. This reprieve was his second piece of luck. He never said a word to anybody about his time in the camps. He was just grateful for the chance to atone for whatever sin had got him jailed in the first place.

His war ended violently when he was felled by a shrapnel blast during the battle for the Kursk salient. He was hit for a second time as his bleeding body was being carried off the field. This blast killed the two stretcher-bearers, and left Efim Oskarovich 'shredded like a cabbage', as he himself put it.

All the time he was fighting he had no idea what had become of his wife and daughter. He thought they were in besieged Leningrad, but in fact they had been evacuated to Tashkent in the first days of the war. Yuri was born there, but always thought of himself as a Leningrader, even though he did not set foot in the city until he was six years old. Nadya, Efim's wife, died of typhoid far from home under warm Uzbek skies, and Yuri and Ira were looked after by a kind neighbour who was evacuated with them. They sat out the war, two little orphans in Asia, but came back to Leningrad as soon as circumstances permitted after the lifting of the blockade. They greeted Victory Day in their home town.

Efim Oskarovich also came back. He made it to Leningrad in the summer of 1945, an 'invalid of the first group'. It took him three hours to walk the half-mile from the Moskovsky Station to the flat on Marat Street, stopping to rest at every lamp-post, every windowsill and every kerbside along the way. He found his daughter, then ten years old, and the son he had never even set eyes on, camping in the bombed-out shell of the apartment block where Yuri still lived nearly forty years on. Ira recognised him at once, the gaunt, sweaty cripple who limped into their yard on crutches. She could never say how, but it was true: she instantly knew that Efim was her father.

The severity of his wounds meant that Efim Oskarovich spent long periods in hospital. This turned out to be a third and final blessing, albeit in disguise: it was while he was in an infirmary ward that the NKVD came to the flat on Marat Street to arrest him for a second time. They left when they did not find him at home, and for some reason never returned. Thus Efim Oskarovich avoided doing a second stretch in the gulag.

The doctors gave Efim Oskarovich five years to live. But his constitution proved stronger than their predictions, and he not only lived but slowly recovered his health. For years after the war he would fish lumps of shrapnel out of his body. He would start by complaining of a pain in his arm or leg. This would last for a day or two. His mood would darken and he would sink into silence, until finally he announced: tonight it's coming out. Come the evening he would sit in front of the electric heater in the kitchen kneading a discoloured patch of flesh on, say, his thigh. This process was time-consuming, sometimes two hours, sometimes three. When he felt he had worked it into the right position near the surface he would make a small incision with a penknife, freshly sterilised in a pan of boiling water. Yuri always insisted on being present for the last stage of the operation when, while Ira cried squeamish tears of sympathy in the corridor, Efim Oskarovich extracted thin slivers of German metal from his body with a pair of tweezers.

April 1819

In the spring of 1819 foreign scholarships were reinstated and Thon was informed that, as a gold medallist of the class of 1815, he

was to be sent to Italy. Alexei Olenin, President of the Academy of
Arts, had petitioned the tsar himself to allow young Konstantin to be
included in the group. His Imperial Majesty not only consented, but
even awarded a larger stipend to Thon than to the other scholars.

Thon felt he had earned it. The four years since graduation had
been full of drudgery. At his father's insistence he'd taken a job in
the Hydraulic Committee of the Petersburg Planning Department.
It had been crushingly dull, and he longed for Sundays and holidays,
when he continued to hone his architectural and engineering skills
through his one freelance commission. This after-hours job had
given the young man a first small taste of fame. For Count Zubov he
had designed a steam-heated orangerie that also supplied hot water
to the Count's laundry. It was efficient and highly ingenious; and for
a short while it was the sensation of Petersburg.

But now Thon's great adventure was to begin. Travelling in the
company of his friend Karl Bryullov, he set off across the western
reaches of the Russian Empire, through the Ukraine, Poland and on
to Prussia. They stopped and admired the crowded Gothic spires of
Dresden and the imperial pomp of Berlin, before turning south for
Vienna. They crossed the Alps and laced their way down the boot of
Italy – Venice, Bologna, Siena, Florence – and finally to Rome, where
their serious studies began.

The Russian community in Rome was inclined to stick together.
The embassy, headed by Prince Gagarin, was the centre of social life,
and the diplomats and their wives were glad of the lively company
of this band of artists and architects. For their part, the Petersburg
scholars were grateful for the little private commissions that they
received from the well-heeled government servants.

Thon was much in demand at the soirées given by the beautiful
Princess Volkonskaya, where he would sing while she accompanied
him on the piano. 'Long Thon with the short name' she called him,
and he was known as an accomplished ladies' man. "He would argue

and trade insults like a gypsy tinker," recalled Bryullov, "just to set the ladies' fans a-rustling. He boasted shamelessly about himself, and would put on a ludicrous face whenever a pretty girl passed by."

Bryullov painted a portrait of his friend around this time. It shows a skinny fellow (he did not run to fat until his middle years), swarthy, mop-headed, with dark, thoughtful eyes and full lips. He seems soulful, but capable of having fun, and he bears a more than passing resemblance to his contemporary Alexander Pushkin.

After a year or so in Rome, Thon decided the moment had come for a new voyage of discovery. He packed his bag and set off for Paris, this time with a new friend in tow, a promising musician by the name of Mikhail Glinka. Paris made an indelible impression on the two Russian travellers, as it does on all visitors from Russia even today. This was Napoleon's capital, the seat of the Great Enemy. Barely five summers since, the Russian imperial armies had marched through these streets in triumph. Thon could not understand how a force so destructive could have issued from a place so accomplished, so civilised, so confident. He walked the maze-like corridors of the Louvre in awe, and purposefully paced the length of the Ile de France like it was a ship's deck and he its captain. He filled notebooks with sketches. More than Rome or even Venice, Paris made Moscow look a muddy village, and Petersburg like an empty, painted stage-set.

Now Thon asked himself whether there might not be some middle way between the cold, derivative classicism of the northern capital and the colourful anarchy of Muscovite architecture. He enrolled at the École Polytechnique where he studied architecture and mechanics. He read widely, searching for the middle path. He began to think that the classicism of the Greeks was not an unchanging canon. *Ars longa*, but nothing in art is eternal. What made Greek civic architecture great was its individuality and its inventiveness, its appropriateness to the epoch and to the ideals of statehood it expressed. Could not the fountainhead of the Russian ethos be tapped in the same way? Did not the achievements of the Russian Empire merit it? And was this what old man Voronikhin had been trying to tell him?

He spent a year in Paris, then returned to the sunny conviviality of Rome in general, and of Princess Volkonskaya in particular. Thon was still a great success on the social circuit, but his career was progressing more slowly than he would have liked. He had important municipal commissions, such as the restoration of the Templum Fortunae in Rome, but none of these brought him the glory he longed for. The princess remarked affectionately that "Konstantin has rebuilt the Shrine of Good Luck, now he need only walk through its doors."

The years of work and study passed smoothly by, but Thon was restless. He cast about for a suitable Italian girl to marry. He was a mature man, after all, and it was high time he found a wife – or so everyone told him.

In the winter of 1825, news reached the emigré community of the death of Tsar Alexander and an armed uprising in St. Petersburg against the new tsar Nikolai. But the snow-swept Venice of the North seemed very distant, and the details of the incident were few and far between. No-one felt inclined to rush back home, and Thon was adept enough in the mores of polite society to avoid discussing it at dinner. Everyone had an opinion, however, on the scandalous news that Nikolai had *personally* interrogated the officers who plotted against him.

March 1982
Vadim climbed the stairs to the fourth floor and rang the bell. Artyom opened the door and his long face lit up. "Give peace a chance," he said to Vadim in English, his usual greeting. "Your

brother's drunk, and so am I."

"Hello, Tyoma," said Vadim, pleased to see him. Vadim handed over his gifts, two oblongs of processed cheese and a cylindrical half-kilo of sausage. "I expect you'd like something to eat then."

"Thanks. Do you know they have just passed a law in Novosibirsk reducing the amount of sawdust you can put in sausage?"

"I didn't know there was any sawdust at all in sausage."

"Exactly! Why do they tell us this stuff like it's good news? Do they think we want to know we are eating shit?"

Vadim liked Artyom and his wife Marina, and they liked him. They were hippies. Mark had met them some years before, on the day he became a member of the Komsomol. He had been putting it off for months, and was by far the oldest non-*komsomolets* in his school. This, coupled with Mark's reputation for shooting his mouth off, made Mark's chances of getting into further education look slim. (In the sixth year he had written a frank essay on the topic "My attitude to the Motherland", which now constituted the first page of his KGB file.) Yuri had been forced to beg his son to join the Komsomol, and finally Mark acquiesced. The only problem was that the plenary meeting of the committee, his last chance to sign up, was on the same day tickets went on sale for Elton John's Soviet tour. Mark joined the ticket queue at the crack of dawn. He asked the person behind him to keep his place while he went and joined the All-Union Leninist Communist League of Youth. That person was Artyom. He was so amused by the situation that he shared his last beer with Mark on his return. They went together to enjoy the greatest gig ever seen on Soviet soil, and became firm friends in the process.

Artyom was an electrical engineer by training, and had been making a decent career for himself in the technical division of the Ministry of External Trade. He would soon have been co-opted into the party and allowed to go on trips abroad, but at the end of 1980 he suffered a kind of nervous breakdown, and gave up his job. Now, to avoid the crime of parasitism, he worked for the local housing committee as a lift technician. His job consisted of checking that all the lifts in all the buildings on his patch were properly earthed. He had a little meter for this purpose, but it was a superfluous piece of equipment since all he really needed to do was peep into the lift shaft and assure himself that the two-metre earthing girder was still buried in the ground. If it was, the lift was earthed. No-one had ever heard of an earthing girder being stolen; nevertheless Artyom had to check each lift every day because that was his job. After two years he had got to the stage where he could cover the whole beat in an hour and a quarter. It was the ideal post, as it left the balance of the day free for his real interests.

Artyom's job paid ninety roubles a month. This would not have been enough for the couple to live on, but Marina still had her job at the ministry, where they had met. She was an economist, a specialist in Scandinavian commercial institutions and a fluent speaker of Swedish and English. She spent her mornings knitting jumpers for Artyom's friends, and in the afternoons she would sneak out of the office to go and hunt for groceries. In her spare time she dabbled in Buddhism.

Artyom and Marina lived on Middle Prospekt, the central core of the tear-shaped Vasilievsky Island, and their flat was the unofficial headquarters for a whole tribe of Leningrad longhairs. There was hardly a moment when they did not have uninvited guests in the flat, which, though smaller than average and on the fourth floor, was known across Leningrad as *Peshchera*, The Cavern. Some visitors would bring a small gift with them: a packet of tea, a tin of sardines, a bootleg tape to listen to, a bottle of scarlet Kindzmarauli, and on rare occasions an ounce or two of Uzbek grass. Most came empty-handed to bum off Artyom's hospitality or to share their troubles with Marina. She and Artyom were only in their early thirties, but this and the fact that they were married made them a veritable rock of ages in the eyes of their young circle of friends.

Artyom and Marina's flat also functioned as a concert venue. Once in a while they held little unofficial soirees where young musicians could present new work, so long as it was not so loud or tuneless as to upset the neighbours or attract the attention of the militia.

But Artyom's status among Leningrad's hippies was due only in small part to his activities as an impresario. His reputation rested mainly on the fact that he was undisputedly the city's leading authority on the oeuvre of The Beatles. His knowledge of the group was encyclopaedic, and all the more impressive for having been acquired without any access to published sources. Sometimes his friends gathered at The Cavern to try to catch him out: Where did Wings make their debut? What does Yoko mean in Japanese? He always answered with complete confidence, and if he ever bluffed, nobody had been able to prove it.

Artyom had a nickname: *Zhuchonok*, Baby Beetle. It had been with him for ten years, ever since he first developed his obsession with the band. But it caught on in a big way after the shooting of John Lennon. This was the event that provoked Artyom's mental crisis. When he heard the news on the BBC World Service that winter morning he nearly died of shock himself. He felt he no longer wanted to make a contribution to a world where such wicked things happen. He did not want to live in a world where there was no John Lennon.

He went to bed and did not get up for six weeks. He lost weight dramatically, and his hair grew longer. When he finally emerged it was as if he had undergone a metamorphosis. His gaunt features made his nose and chin more prominent; he had developed a slight stoop; he had become in short the spit and image of his dead idol. Once he had grown his hair longer still and put on a pair of little round glasses, the resemblance was truly uncanny. When he was out on his elevator rounds people clapped their hands to their mouths as if they had seen a ghost. And for those who knew Artyom well, the most amazing thing about his transformation was that it was altogether unintended. He never set out to be a Lennon lookalike. It just happened in some mystical way during his period of mourning. Artyom's hippy friends looked on his mutated appearance with a kind of reverent awe: Artyom bore the Beatle stigmata, and that commanded respect.

Vadim took off his coat and winter boots and slipped on the pair of sandals that Artyom proferred. "How was Moscow, little Vad?" asked Artyom.

"The girls made me sing and shout," said Vadim. Artyom nodded gravely, as if the statement summed up all that he had ever thought about the state of womanhood in the capital.

They passed through into the main room. This room was a work of art famed throughout Soviet hippydom. It was a vast mural on the theme of the Beatles, a Sistine Chapel dedicated to the Fab Four. The main wall was a lifesize copy of the sleeve of *Sergeant Pepper* executed in the minutest detail; every face, every button and tassel on their bandsmens' uniforms was meticulously reproduced. The adjoining wall was an epic fantasy on motifs from the *Yellow Submarine*: cohorts of Blue Meanies; the phallic glove; the whitebeard submarine captain – serene as a Pskov icon; and up at the ceiling the Nowhere Man weeping bitter tears of self-pity. The opposite wall was divided into black-and-white squares, each one containing a stylised portrait of one of the members of the band in the manner of the *Hard Day's Night* cover. The far wall was a clever piece of *trompe l'oeil*; it depicted the four Beatles trying to climb out the window of Artyom's flat: moptop Ringo, Paul – anachronistically – in a walrus suit, George in skis and a top hat, and a loutish teenage

John. The ceiling was devoted entirely to Lennon. Around a central
portrait were scenes from his life: the neon lights of Hamburg,
American *auto da fes* of Beatles LPs, John and Yoko defiantly abed
in Amsterdam, the white Imagine piano, and a phalanx of number
nines marching with the red banners of revolution.

There was very little furniture in the room, apart from two
battered orange armchairs, in one of which Mark slouched reading
a typewritten manuscript; there was also a coffee table, and a low
cupboard that contained Artyom's record collection. A turntable
and a tape deck stood on top, and were connected to an unwieldy
Soviet amplifier. A telephone lay unplugged in one corner, where
there was also a sizeable throng of empty beer bottles. The only
other item was an upright piano that stood in the centre of the room.

"Give that man a beer," said Mark, full of smiles. Artyom
obediently brought two beers from the fridge, then went back to the
kitchen to make sandwiches with the groceries Vadim had brought.

"Vadik," he called out. "What exactly is custard?"

"A kind of English egg sauce, I think," said Vadim.

"I knew it would be something unpleasant, but that sounds
really nasty."

"Doesn't it. Why are you asking?"

"I'll tell you in a minute."

Mark meanwhile had put down the typescript and was opening
the two bottles of beer by locking the caps in a special grip and
tugging them both off in one movement. It was a trick he had
learned at the Architectural Institute.

"How's Grandad," asked Mark.

"All right," said Vadim, sitting down opposite his brother and
taking a sip of beer.

Artyom came back in with a plate of rough-hewn sandwiches.
Mark pounced on them hungrily.

"Where is Marina?" asked Vadim.

"She is in the bedroom," said Artyom indicating the connecting door in the black-and-white wall. "But she can't come out right now." Vadim did not enquire further, but Artyom supplied a cryptic explanation. "She is half-way through a sand mandala," he said. "The whole thing will go to hell if anyone opens that door."

Vadim and Artyom took a sandwich each, and Mark tucked into his second. They munched in silence for a few moments, then Artyom made an announcement through a mouthful of bread:

"My life's work has begun," he said. "I know that I was born for this."

Vadim sat up. There was a note of real seriousness in Artyom's voice that he had never heard before. "For what?" he asked.

"For this," said Artyom raising his voice, and his greasy forefinger stabbed the typescript that now lay on the coffee table. It is why I am alive."

"What is it?"

"It is part one of a three-volume history of the *Bitly*," said Artyom, and passed the sheaf of papers on to Vadim. He flicked through them: they were translations into Russian of Beatles songs. On top was *I Am the Walrus*.

"The first volume will be the definitive Russian edition of the poetry of Lennon and McCartney," Artyom was saying. "I have made a start, but even with Marina's help my English is not up to it. I intend to gather a team of scholars and devotees to perform the task. Volume Two will be an annotated commentary and a concordance of all the songs. It will also answer questions like: Where is Penny Lane? What is significant about Blackburn, Lancashire? Why was there rice in the church where the wedding had been?"

"Yes, that is something I have wondered about," said Vadim. "Perhaps at English weddings they distribute food to the poor?"

"For this I will need the help of historians," continued Artyom. "Also literary specialists and musicologists."

"Musicologists?"

"Certainly."

"Where will you find them?"

"Here, there and everywhere," put in Mark.

Artyom leaped up and went to the piano. "A case in point," he said. He struck a chord and began to sing. "To lead a better life..." Channg! – a new chord – "...I need my love to be here..." Channg! Channg! "Hear that? It is a rising arpeggio in G major that moves to a minor-key harmony on the mediant in the second bar – that is to say on the upper dominant – followed by another arpeggio on the minor third melodically identical to the first, but harmonically in the new tonic. Bach would be proud of a progression like that. It is piece of pure genius."

"And the third volume?" asked Vadim.

"Ah, the third volume. That is the meat of it. It is an exhaustive encyclopaedia of the Beatles. I am going to write it myself: *Artyom Pankin's Bitlopaedia*. Everything I know in one book. Thousands of entries in alphabetical order on every aspect of their life and work from the Quarrymen to the present day. It will be a seminal piece of *bitlologiya*. There is nothing even remotely like it, even in the West."

"Sounds ambitious," said Vadim. "I think we should drink to it."

They raised their bottles and clinked them. "To success," they said, and they all swigged deeply.

At this moment Marina came out of the bedroom and carefully closed the door behind her. She guessed the nature of the toast. "So you have heard about the planned magnum opus," she said to Vadim. She came over and kissed him on both cheeks where he sat.

"Hi, Marina."

"Hello. Nice to see you back." She went to the kitchen to put the kettle on; Vadim followed.

"Are you all right?" he asked. "When Tyoma said you couldn't come out I thought you might be ill."

"I'm fine, thanks," she said. "True, I've taken a few days' sick leave, but that is because I wanted some time to meditate, restore my inner energy, you know." She ran her fingers like a comb through her long hair, and readjusted the bead headband that she wore when she was not at work. The headband was the only outward sign that she considered herself a hippy; the rest of her attire was the usual poor-quality Soviet hotchpotch.

"Are you going to translate all the Beatles' songs for Tyoma?"

She made a half-laugh. "I'm not going to do the work for him. I'll help if he's serious about it, but he has got to overcome his idleness first. I think it would be good for him to produce something."

"What is that you are making in the other room – it sounds very fragile."

"Oh, that's different. It's a mandala."

"What's a mandala?"

She lit the gas and blew out the match. "It's an aid to meditation, a ritual, a dwelling-place for the gods."

"A picture?"

"It is a symbolic pattern, but not necessarily a picture. The main thing is it has a centre and an edge, that's what the Buddha teaches. The world seen from space is a mandala – you might say it is the original mandala. So is Stonehenge in England; so are the ripples of a stone falling in water."

"So is the hammer-and-sickle," said Artyom, who had come into the kitchen for some more beer.

Marina pouted and aimed a kick at her husband. "No it isn't, because it has no centre and it is all lop-sided."

"A fried egg is a mandala," said Artyom. "A bumprint on the beach is a mandala." He beat a retreat with his beers.

"He's such a fool," said Marina to Vadim, smiling. "But what can you expect from a grown man who worships a pop group?"

"Artyom said your mandala was made of sand," said Vadim.

"Yes, it's a Tibetan ritual. It is meant as a kind of culmination to my week of meditation. Come on, I'll show you."

Marina led the way back through the painted room, where Mark was doing the two-bottle trick again, but this time succeeded only in spilling half a pint of frothing beer into his lap. Marina opened the bedroom door, as if there was a sleeping baby in there. She ushered Vadim through, and closed it gently behind her. The bedroom was dark. The only light came from two candles on the floor and a third on the windowsill. The furnishing was as spartan as in the other room: an unmade bed, a wardrobe and a small bookcase. A small jade Buddha stood on the bookcase, the only decoration. The air was filled with the sweet smell of burning sandalwood – a joss stick protruded from the base of one of the candlesticks. There was no Lennoniana in the room at all.

"I've never been in here," whispered Vadim, not noticing that he had lowered his voice.

"This is where I come when I am fed up with sharing the flat with a lunatic and a dead rock star," said Marina. "It is the only place I can meditate in peace."

Vadim surveyed the room. As his eyes grew accustomed to the half-light he could see that there was a wooden board on the floor next to the bed where the candles burned, along with a jumble of artists' instruments, a small bell, and some other objects he could not identify.

"Tread as softly as you can." ordered Marina.

She walked round to the far side of the board and gracefully sat down crosslegged on the floor. The candles threw a warm uplight on her face and made her blond hair glow. With a gesture of her hand she indicated that it would be best if Vadim inspected her work from the vantage point of the bed. He did as she told him. Crouching on the edge of the mattress he looked down on the unfinished mandala.

It was an intricate geometric maze of different colours. To Vadim
it looked like a stylised rose. By this light he could not make out
the hues, just the light and dark, but he could see the fine grains of
sand glinting separately in the mobile glimmer of the candles. He
marvelled at the distinctness of the image. Every figure looked like
it had been drawn with a ruler. Not a grain of sand was out of place.

"How do you make such straight lines with sand?" he asked, still
whispering.

"With this," she said, also in a hush. She picked up a short stick
and a slim brass horn that had a row of shallow fins down one side.
Laying the point of the horn against an empty edge of the board she
drew the stick lightly to and fro across the fins. The vibration sent a
narrow stream of sand out of a tiny hole at the end of the horn, like
salt shaken from a salt-pot.

"Is that ordinary sand?"

"Yes. It ought really to be ground soapstone, but I don't know
where to find that here. I get this sand from a beach on the Gulf
near Repino. It is the only place I know where the grains are fine
enough. I mix it with watercolour paint and when it dries it retains
the colour. I make the pattern starting from the centre and working
out towards the edge. That is how the Tibetan monks do it."

Vadim noticed a row of receptacles, mostly old teacups, with the
coloured sand.

"Did you invent the design yourself?"

"Yes, that is part of the meditation."

"Does it have to be abstract?"

"It is only abstract to European eyes. In Tibet everything in a
sand mandala has significance: the width and length of the lines, the
colours, the angles, the patterns."

Vadim stared at the strange design. It seemed to draw him closer,
and for a moment he felt about to tumble off the edge of the bed. "I
think it is hypnotising me," he said.

"That's good," said Marina. "A mandala is a power object. It attracts strength and benevolent spirits. It's their home."

"Aren't you afraid Tyoma might step on it?" asked Vadim.

"More than his life is worth. And anyway he is sleeping on the armchair in the other room tonight. I am not letting him near this while he is drunk."

"How are you going to move it when it is finished?" Vadim asked.

"I have no intention of moving it. Tomorrow afternoon I will finish it, and in the evening I will sweep it up."

"You are going to destroy it?"

"Not destroy it. The mandala is indestructible. Just sweep it up."

"It seems a terrible waste of effort."

"Not at all. Everything comes from emptiness, and to emptiness it returns. But I will have changed in the meantime, that's the point. Tomorrow evening I will say a prayer and ask the divinities to quit my mandala and return to their heavenly dwelling place. Then I will sweep the sand to the centre from eight directions. After the ritual sweeping I will have a small pile of grey sand that I must throw into the Neva. The consecrated sand cleanses the water, which eventually evaporates and turns into a cloud. Then it rains back down on the earth as a blessing."

"That is a very beautiful idea."

"Thank you," she said. "I think so too."

She raised her eyes to the ceiling, and Vadim saw that there were tears in her eyes. They caught the flickering candlelight. She blinked and the first droplet fell on the outer edge of her design.

"What's wrong?" asked Vadim.

"Nothing." She wiped her eyes with the back of her hand and stood up. "Let's go and have a glass of tea."

They went back out to the Beatle shrine, where Artyom and Mark were now both snoring noisily. They left the two drunks to their dreams and went to sit in the kitchen. The kettle had boiled dry.

Sparrow Hills

"You have made stones speak."

– Tsar Alexander I to Karl Vitberg

September 1982

It was a warm day when Vadim arrived in Moscow to begin his studies. He was carrying his cardboard suitcase and a guitar in a plastic sleeve. He got off the overnight train from Leningrad and followed the early-morning crowd into the cavernous expanse of Komsomolskaya metro station. Once on the train, he arranged his suitcases and his guitar neatly by the door and settled down for the half-hour journey. There were a couple of things he wanted to check out along the way.

The clipped recorded voice of a woman came over the intercom: "Careful, the doors are closing. Next stop Lermontovskaya." For Vadim the metro announcements were the signal that he was assuredly in Moscow. Back in Leningrad they sensibly announced the next stop when you arrived at a station; in Moscow they told you where you were going when you were already on your way and it was too late to change your mind. He counted off the underground mileposts on the road to his new life: Lermontovskaya. Kirovskaya. Dzerzhinskaya. Prospekt Marksa. Biblioteka imeni Lenina – Vadim had plans for the Lenin Library this term.

Then Kropotkinskaya. This was the stop for the swimming pool. He looked at the platform with a sharper interest than the last time he passed through. He noted the pinkish glow of the marble columns and walls and the subdued lighting. It was a rich but understated station, not as spectacular as some of the others.

"Careful, the doors are closing. Next stop Park Kultury." The long train heaved itself into motion. Vadim felt it dip as it moved into the dark tunnel for the long descent to the riverside station at Gorky Park. After Park Kultury, Frunzenskaya, then Sportivnaya – for the Olympic Stadium.

"...Next stop Leninskiye Gory."

The train chugged uphill, climbing out of a steep, subterranean valley. Then it emerged dramatically into the blinking sun. Some passengers craned round in their seats at this point to look at the view. The carriages were now on a bridge, high above the broad ox-bow bend in the Moscow River. The train slowed down, for the glazed-in bridge was also Lenin Hills Metro Station, its platforms hanging like a Promethean equals-sign in mid-air. It was an impressive feat of engineering on its own, but that was not all there was to the Metro Bridge. The roof of the station doubled as the main road-bridge into central Moscow. Tonnes of traffic flowed north and south directly above the heads of the metro passengers, while the river flowed west to east beneath their feet. As they waited for their trains, the people on the platform could listen to the adjacent thunder of the former while watching the silent, liquid progress of the latter down below.

But it was not the wafer biscuit of the bridge that interested Vadim. He was looking out of the right-hand side of the train towards the far bank of the river. The forested slope rose sharply from the Sparrow Embankment, its ascent broken by a sudden plateau about as far above the bridge as the bridge was above the river. The man-made plane, at the very brow of the hill, overlooked the central point in the river's horseshoe.

At the left-hand corner of the plateau was the long loop of the university ski-jump, like a Spanish question mark resting on the edge of the bluff. Farther back, the xiphoid spike of MGU punctured the skyline. From here one could see its great height, but not its massive width. This, the largest university building in the world, was to be home to Vadim for the next five years.

"Careful, the doors are closing. Next stop Universitet."

The train plunged back into the darkness of the tunnel on the far side of the bridge. It clattered south-west through the hill, and six minutes later Vadim was on the surface. As he emerged from the nether-world of the metro he fished in his pocket among the loose change for his komsomol badge, a golden profile of Lenin on a background of a little red flag. He pinned the badge to his lapel, thinking it right to observe the formalities for these first few hours of his higher education.

He crossed over to the bus-stop on the corner of Universitetsky and Vernadsky Prospekts. There were three other freshmen at the bus-stop. They exchanged glances, but Vadim did not feel inclined to strike up a conversation with any of them. He observed that each of them looked a lot more nervous and uncomfortable than he did, and that made him feel good. A canary-yellow Ikarus bus, the 119, happened along almost immediately, and Vadim climbed in the back where there was plenty of space for his bags. Yes, it was going to be a good term, of that he was sure.

1828

After ten years abroad, Thon and the other 'Romans' returned to Russia. He had continued to be unlucky in love to the very end of his foreign sojourn – that Italian wife had never materialised – but now his professional career did at last take an upward turn.

Alexei Olenin was still president of the Academy, and Thon was still very much his favourite. His candidacy for membership of the

Academy was immediately proposed, and Olenin set about getting Thon some prestigious work. Thon first carried out a capital repair of the Academy building on the embankment where he had spent his boyhood. He made a fine job of it. The board was greatly impressed with his technical expertise, and even more so with the fact that he had finished the project well under budget.

At the same time as he was refitting the Academy building, Thon reconstructed the quay itself. It became one of his favourite spots. The two granite sphinxes brought from Thebes, which Thon installed here, seemed to him to dispense an aura of serenity. He often came to this spot in later years. He found it soothing when he was working on his masterpiece to be with these relics of a long-dead empire.

He lived in a modest flat with his sister, who kept house for him. It was, as he had expected, a duller existence than in Italy, dominated by work and teaching responsibilities. In 1830, after some delay, Thon and most of the other Romans were made Fellows of the Academy. It was an honour they deserved, but it was a political move too: Olenin deliberately packed the Academy with young turks, his own protegés, as a means of forcing through the reforms that he had in mind, and that were somehow symbolised by Thon's ruthless gutting of the old building.

Thon was now thirty-five years old, successful and comfortable. He was well respected in his field, and could already claim to have left his mark on the city of his birth. He could have retired at this point, and feel assured of a creditable mention in any history of Russian architecture. He could have devoted his time to the search for the domestic happiness that still eluded him. Instead he found himself embarking on a new project, the one that was to be his life's work. Konstantin Thon was about to be visited by Christ the Saviour.

☆

8th November, 1982

Barely a month into his university career, and Vadim was regretting bringing his guitar along. It was the only half-decent instrument in the hostel, and it had quickly become clear that he was going to be in constant demand for komsomol-sponsored cultural events. He had already been volunteered to play at a fraternal socialist tea-party with the university's Vietnamese contingent, and next week he was slated to go along to some dull speechfest with Angolan trade unionists.

But today, for October Revolution holiday, he had been co-opted for an altogether more interesting celebration. Lena, the komsomol organiser for the journalism faculty, had come by to see him early in the day. "As komsorg I have to tell you that you were not on the original list of invitees for this Friendship Evening," she had said. "We all have to earn the right to mix with westerners, and you have not been here long enough to prove yourself. But every nationality is going to do a song and introduce themselves, so we have to do one too."

"What song are we doing?"

"Moscow Nights."

Vadim grimaced. "Can't we do something more original?"

"It's been decided, Vadim. The student council does not need your advice. Your job is to come along, accompany the song, then leave. You can have a piece of cake, but then you have to go. Is that clear?"

"As day."

"Don't be late."

At 7.30 sharp he was there in the largest meeting hall in the central zone of the building. There was a table assigned to each national contingent. On every table stood two bottles of Borzhomi mineral water and a plate of biscuits. Vadim sat with the rest of the

Soviets, most of them second- or third- year students, plus one or two postgraduates. Lena sat opposite Vadim, nervously fingering her komsomol badge.

The foreigners had all arrived late. Each group came armed with a home-made paper version of its national flag, which they planted on their table. There were half a dozen Brits, some French girls, four West Germans, two Swedes. The Americans constituted the largest group: there was a dozen or more of them.

First there were speeches. The oldest of the Soviet postgraduates introduced himself as Sergei Tolchkov, chairman of the Central Committee of the Moscow University komsomol organisation. It was clear to all the Russians that he was here to keep a watchful eye on proceedings, but for now he gave a short and entirely apolitical address welcoming the foreign guests and dear international friends to Moscow University, which he described in high-flown terms as 'the leading temple of knowledge in the Union of Soviet Socialist Republics'.

Lena then got up and spoke about the global significance of the Great October Socialist Revolution. In her speech she mentioned that when Lenin was in London he would often walk from the West End to the East End of London, saying in English through gritted teeth, "Two nations". To Lena's consternation, this historical note had the British contingent roaring with laughter. Vadim suspected that the foreign guests were not about to take this 'Friendship' business as seriously as they might.

Now it was time for each country to do its piece. Vadim found it all absolutely fascinating. The Germans sang *Von Guten Mächten*, a rather beautiful hymn with words by Dietrich Bonhoeffer. They first explained – a mite too apologetically, Vadim thought – that Bonhoeffer was a Catholic martyr and a victim of fascism. Two young men from the English contingent got up and performed an interminable dialogue in barely comprehensible Russian –

something to do with a dead parrot. Everybody watched in utter bafflement apart from the Americans, who were completely helpless with hilarity. The two Swedes made a short speech saying how glad they were to be here, but unfortunately neither of them had any performing talent whatsoever and so had nothing to offer. This frank admission got the biggest round of applause of the evening. Then, in word-perfect Russian, the French girls sang *The Prayer of François Villon* by the semi-official bard Bulat Okoujava. It was a well-judged choice of song, thought Vadim: to sing in Russian was complimentary without being obsequious, and the theme was a tiny bit risqué but not actually subversive.

Last up were the Americans. Their spokesman explained that their item was a folk song for the Christmas holiday, that it was about a sleigh ride through the snow, and so seemed appropriate for the Moscow climate. The song, which sounded like a children's ditty to Vadim, got off to a shaky start, but was soon bowling along – "*jingle bells, jingle bells, jingle jingle...*" In the second chorus, one of the American girls produced a tambourine and shook it in time with the music. Vadim had barely noticed this girl until this moment, but now she caught his eye. Her dark hair fell across her face as she jigged somewhat arhythmically on the spot. She was enjoying herself, but was also clearly aware of the absurdity of it all. She laughed out loud when she altogether lost the beat and had to stop for a moment. The other Americans laughed with her. When the song ended, she alone gave a mock-theatrical bow, sweeping her hair off her face with her forearm as she stood up straight. Her cheeks were flushed, she was out of breath, and her brown eyes shone. Vadim followed her with his eyes as she walked back to the American table, chatting and laughing as she went.

The Soviets now got up to sing their song and bring the formal phase of the party to an end. After the Americans' relaxed performance it sounded an awful dirge. Vadim tried to liven it up, to inject a little pace, but his singers, picked on purely ideological grounds, were beyond salvation. As he played, he looked across to where the American girl was sitting. She had her back to him, and was talking to one of the Swedes at the next table.

Moscow Nights came to a merciful end. Vadim wondered if he dare go and introduce himself to the Americans – but the matter was taken out of his hands. Lena came over to speak to him. "Thanks Vadim," she said. "Sorry if I was a bit sharp this morning. Organising this has been a lot of stress."

"That's all right," said Vadim. "I am glad to be here. It's a chance to practise my English."

"Ah, I'm afraid you can't though. You have to go." She nodded in the direction of Tolchkov. "I think you have earned the right to stay, but Sergei says that only approved students should be representing the university on this occasion. He was very specific, and very insistent."

Vadim looked over at Tolchkov. He had one of the French girls locked in conversation.

"I understand. I'll go right away."

"He is just doing as he is told too, I suppose," said Lena. "Don't take it personally, Vadim."

Vadim went to pick up his guitar, then made for the exit. In the doorway of the hall, he turned round for a last glimpse of the lovely American girl, but he could not see her for the crowd.

Karl Magnus Vitberg, author of the first project for the Cathedral of Christ the Saviour, was born into a family of Russianised Swedes. His father, Laurens Vitberg, settled in the northern capital before Karl Magnus was born, so the boy grew up every inch a Russian, his cool Scandinavian Protestantism notwithstanding.

The imperial manifest of December 1812, announcing the competition to create the Cathedral of Christ the Saviour, inspired the young man. Despite his age (he was only twenty-five) and his utter lack of expertise (he specialised in painting battle scenes), he resolved to win the commission.

In the first years of the nineteenth century the job of professional architect did not exist in Russia. It is barely an exaggeration to say that the glorious new capital of Saint Petersburg, then a little more than a hundred years old, was built entirely by foreign professionals or gifted Russian amateurs. It was only in the middle years of the nineteenth century that the calling of architect came to command respect. So there was nothing to stop Karl Vitberg thinking himself as well qualified as anybody to build the Cathedral of Christ.

For the first six months of 1813 he gave himself over to the study of architecture. At the end of this period he felt sufficiently well versed to go to Moscow and devote himself to the design of the cathedral while at the same time continuing his studies: *"I had long desired to see Russia's Protokafedral Metropolis,"* recalled Vitberg in the days of his disgrace, *"One can with Ease surmise the Impression it made upon me in those Days, being wholly scotch'd, scorch'd and forsaken. Only the magnificent Kremlin, which had evaded Devastation in the past and alone was spared in the present Catastrophe, prevailed above the Ruins."*

This novice in architecture and newcomer to Moscow found himself in competition with the leading master-builders of his day: Giacomo Quarenghi, Alexei Voronikhin, Avraam Melnikov, Domenico Giliardi, Josephus Bove. With the single exception of Voronikhin, all submitted designs in the classical style then *de rigueur* for new buildings in post-conflagrational Moscow. None, however, caused the stir occasioned by Vitberg's design, which soon became the talk of the city. This circumstance worked very much in the young man's favour, and was abetted by Vitberg's wide circle of influential and like-minded friends. These same friends did what they could to win Vitberg a personal audience with Emperor Alexander so that he could present his designs to the best possible advantage. This goal was achieved, and in due course Vitberg was granted the commission.

But there was one small formality to be attended to before Vitberg could get down to work. The Emperor felt that the builder of a national monument of such far-reaching significance, one that commemorated the God-given triumph of the Russian people over Bonaparte the Anti-Christ, must be a child of the Russian Church. And so, to comply with the Tsar's pious stipulation, Karl Magnus adopted the Orthodox faith. He was by nature of an ecumenical disposition, believing that God was above any particular rite, so his conversion to the Eastern Church was not accompanied by long or painful soul-searching. Since the name Karl is unknown to the Orthodox canon, he was baptised Alexander in honour of his royal patron. Thus is he known to history: Alexander Lavrentiyevich Vitberg.

There was much discussion about where in Moscow the Cathedral of Christ would be located. Vitberg's first suggestion was that the new church should be built within the Kremlin walls. Again we have his own account of how the idea came to him, as dictated by him to his great friend and champion Alexander Herzen. (Herzen met the older man when they were both in exile in Vyatka. Vitberg dictated his entire life to the young writer, who later published Vitberg's wisdom in the course of his long and bitter polemic with the 'leaden hand' of the regime of Nikolai I.) Vitberg was with some friends on a stroll round Moscow when,

...my Eye was drawn to a low and empty Place between the Moskvoretsky Tower and the Magazin Gate. Leaving my Companions, I descended to the River-Bank, the better to look

upon the Kremlin – from below, as it were. From there I returned to my Fellows through the Gates. My Notion of the Temple, hitherto inchoate and dimly perceived, now acquired a solid Shape, and entranced by the Attraction of the Place, I express'd my Thoughts for the Temple, the Merit of its being raised within the Kremlin. And new Ideas for its Execution, born of the Location, crowded in on my Mind and complemented the religious Thought. There were two Blasted Parts in the Wall [i.e. two holes, damage inflicted by the French when they tried to blow up the fortress] *which, it seemed to me, might be fashion'd for an admirable Approach to the Temple. This Site was pleasing to me in other Ways also: The River and the sloping Topography did make a Place where the Church might be raised on the Gradient.*

But Vitberg's proposal was overruled by Alexander himself, who felt that it would be "unseemly to do violence to the ancient stronghold", and that the classical visage of Vitberg's plan would look odd amidst the onion domes of the older Kremlin churches. Others suggested that the cathedral be raised on the site of the gunpowder cellars next to the Simonov monastery on the industrial eastern extremity of Moscow (where, later, Konstantin Thon built a bell-tower). But this site was felt to be infelicitous both architecturally and geographically, though, of course, it was not the last time explosives would figure in the story of the Cathedral of Christ the Saviour. Eventually the choice of Vitberg and the Tsar fell on Sparrow Hills, the so-called 'Crown of Moscow'.

At that time the Hills were way beyond the limits of the city, separated from its outermost earthen fortifications, where the Garden Ring Road now runs, by the broad open expanse of Luzhniki and by the Moscow River. But the very fact of an intervening rural wilderness meant that the temple on the Hills would be visible from every corner of Moscow. Also Vitberg, a great lover of the

symbolism of buildings and places, was very conscious of the fact
that Sparrow Hills lay precisely on the central axis between the
route whereby the French entered Moscow, and that by which their
demoralised armies departed: that is between the Kaluga and the
Mozhaisk roads.

As to the form of the temple itself, this too was imbued with
symbolic significance. It was to be the tallest building in the world,
237 metres from the foot of the Hills to the top of the cross. The
church itself was to be 170 metres high, outdoing St. Peter's in
Rome by almost 30 metres. On the lower terrace were to stand two
triumphal columns, over 100 metres tall. One was to be made of
gun metal captured from the French on Russian soil, the other made
from the same metal, but captured during the long pursuit across
Europe to Paris.

How Vitberg loved his symbols! He wanted every outward
detail of the cathedral to be a reflection of the religious and patriotic
doctrine that inspired it. He saw a profound correlation between
the vision that inspired the project and its explicit concrete form.
Here is Vitberg's own exposition of the philosophical content of his
church:

*I thought it appropriate that each Stone in the Temple, and all
the many Stones taken together, should in some special Wise be
cogent Expressions of the Religion of Christ; That all the external
Forms should bear the Impress of the internal Idea; in short, that
this Temple be not a Heap of Stones craftily assembled, not a Temple
merely, but a Christian Phrase, a Devout Text. For is it not written:
"Ye are the Temple of God, and the Spirit of God dwelleth in you."*

*Therefore, the Arrangement of the Temple must be elicited from
the Spirituall Edifice which is Man-Kind.*

*But what is Man? Man is constituted of three Beginnings or
principia; to wit: Body, Soul, and Spirit. This Triplicity was bound*

to be express'd, in the purest possible Manner, through the Parts of
the Temple.

So I imagined the Creator as a Point in Space. To this Point I gave
the name Singularity, or God. Then I took up a Pair of Compasses,
and charted a Circle, whereof the centre was the first Point; the
Circumference I named Plurality. Thus, I had depicted Singularity
and Plurality, Creator and Creation. How now to join up the Point
and the Circumference? I studied my Sketch, and saw that the
opposing Legs of my Compasses did comprise a straight Line, that an
infinite repetition of such Lines, each being of the same Length and
issuing from the same Point, must constitute the Circle; That these
Lines, inter-secting at the middle Point, do form Crosses. Thus, an
Eternal Christian Truth was repeated in my idle Draughtsmanship:
The Creator was re-united with Creation by means of the Cross. In
this Manner, I descry'd a Connexion between three Figures: a Line, a
Cross, a Circle; together they composed a mysterious Shape in which
I found utter Peace and Consolation. In that moment I apprehended
the Mystery which had troubled me for so long. I at once resolved
to exploit my Discovery and apply it to the Construction of the
Temple.

A mathematical Line, when translated into corporeal Form,
produces a narrow Rectangle; and the Body of Man, when the Spirit
has departed, is laid down in a Grave of this same Shape. This is
the Form wherewith I endow'd the first Temple, called the Temple
Corporeal.

The Temple Corporeal was to be fix'd to the Earth and bury'd in
it, even as the Body of Man is fix'd to the Earth, and, finally, bury'd
in it. Three Sides were rooted in the Ground and only the eastern
Façade of the Temple showed above (for the Provision of the bare
Minimum of Light).

The lower Temple is joined to the middle Temple, the Temple
of the Soul, or the Temple Moral. It is set on the Cusp of the Hill

*and is open from all Sides. The Temple is cruciform, for as the first
Temple constituted a simple Line, so the second is an Intersection of
two Lines. As the Parallellogram befits the mortal Body, so the Cross
befits the Idea of the Soul, which is the Body when invested with the
Spirit of our present Life and Endeavor.*

*From the second Temple a Stair leads to the third and uppermost,
which is the Temple of the Spirit, or the Temple Divine. As the second
Temple consisted of a Cross derived from a Line, so the third consists
of a perfit Circle derived from a Cross. Inasmuch as it has neither
Beginning or End, it is the most apt Figure for the Expression of the
Idea of Eternity.*

*Even as the Cross was a Picture of the Soul, so here the Circle's
Circumference expresses the Spirit (insofar as any Material Form
can so do). The Temple is brightly illumined, to the full Extent that
Architecture will allow; as the lower Temple is all Gloom, so the
Temple of the Spirit is filled with Light, and the Brightness of the
upper Temple of the Spirit informs and illumines the middle Temple
of the Soul, which is part Light, part Darkness.*

*Such was the Conception of the Triplicate Temple as regards its
interior Parts; but its Exterior was to be a Seamless Whole, compleat
in itself and indivisible, like the Very Godhead.*

The geometry and theology of Vitberg's plan can be summed
up in one sentence: God is the Supreme Architect, and every moral
being is engaged in building a temple within.

11th November, 1982.

In the space of two hours, the red flags spread like an angry rash
across the face of the city. Hundreds of hammer-and-sickle banners
edged in black, slowly stiffened in the sharp frost. Vadim was in

the journalism faculty library on Prospekt Marksa all morning – a funereal place at the happiest of times – so when he stepped out of doors into this sea of red cloth it was the first he knew of it: Leonid Brezhnev was dead.

Vadim felt no sorrow for the old man, and no shame at feeling no sorrow. He registered only a twinge of sympathy for the men whose job it was to slot the flags into the little V-shaped iron brackets on the façades of every building in Moscow: they had only taken them down two days before, after the celebrations of the 65th anniversary of the Great October Socialist Revolution.

When he was a small boy, Vadim had believed that the flags appeared and disappeared by magic on every holiday. He was about five years old when, on a trip to the shops with Ira after Victory Day, he first saw two unshaven, hungover workers uprooting the flags like weeds and tossing them into the back of an open truck. Much to Ira's bewilderment, he had burst into tears.

Vadim tugged up his collar and headed for the metro. It was a straight toss-up which was nearer, Biblioteka or Prospekt Marksa. He plumped for Prospekt Marksa so as not to have to walk face into the wind. He wondered which of the old men would step into Leonid Ilyich's shoes. He was not much interested in the succession, but he knew it would be a topic of conversation when he got back to the hostel. Hussein, his room-mate of five weeks, would want to hear his views. Grishin? Possibly. Gromyko? Too old, even by politburo standards. Romanov, the Leningrad boss? No, it would surely be too ironical to have a Romanov in charge.

At the corner of Gorky Street, just before the entrance to the subway, he stopped to look across the road to Red Square. He liked the view of St. Basil's from this point, through the gap between the State Historical Museum and the Kremlin Wall. The redbrick façade of the museum was completely obscured by a thirty-metre full-length portrait of Lenin with his hands in his pockets and his

cap on. The clock in the Spassky Tower had just struck one, and if
he screwed his eyes up he could see the bayonet points of the honour
guard silhouetted against the pale sky as they bobbed away to the
far end of the square. General secretaries come and go, he thought
(though this was the first time one had gone in his lifetime), but
some things are eternal.

Vadim arrived at MGU to find the place abuzz with doleful
activity. The bookstalls were closed for the day; komsomol leaders
were rapidly organising committees; knots of silly girls were weeping
in corners; *stengazety* – wall-newspapers – were being hastily written
and glued together. Vadim found it all rather alarming, especially the
stengazety. He had already had to do a couple of these communal
scrapbooks, and he knew how immensely time-consuming they
could be. He was now regretting leaving the library, and wondered
where he might hide out for the rest of the day.

First he went back to his room. Hussein, his new Azerbaijani
friend, was home. He emerged from his side of the blok. He was
in his usual daywear – striped army *telnyashka*, blue jogging pants,
house slippers – but his dark countenance spoke of grief manfully
borne. "Vadim, have you heard the news?" he said, smoothing his
impressive black moustache.

"Of course. It's difficult to miss."

Hussein beckoned Vadim to him. Holding him by the coat lapel
he whispered in his ear, so close that the moustache tickled. "But
have you heard the real news?"

"What real news?" Vadim's voice was also a whisper.

"They are bringing in a colour television for the funeral. It is
going to be put in the recreation room on the fifth floor. The central
committee of the komsomol arranged it."

"Colour won't make the funeral that much more entertaining,
will it?"

Hussein gripped his friend's coat tighter. "You don't understand, you fool. There is a move to acquire the TV set on a six-month lease. If all goes well, we will have colour for the entire ice hockey season."

"Well, never a gale but a little sunshine peeps through," said Vadim. "But take my advice, wipe that grin of anticipation off your face before you step outside this room."

There was a sharp rap at the door that wiped the grins off both their faces. "Come in," they said in unison. It was Lena, the komsomol organiser. "Vadim," she said, "I need your help. We're doing a *stengazeta* for Leonid Ilyich" – his heart sank – "You wouldn't have any black paper, would you? The student committee says it has to have a black border."

Vadim inwardly sighed with relief. "I'm afraid not, Lena. Sorry." She tutted and left without another word. "That was close," said Vadim. "I thought she was going to ask me to write the damn thing."

"If you were a more progressive member of Soviet society you would have offered," said Hussein. "But I suppose it is too late now. Come into my blok, I have a bottle of Armenian cognac with which we can wish the old fellow godspeed on his final journey."

They locked their door and left the key turned in the hole. Hussein poured a finger into two glass tumblers while Vadim got out of his street clothes. Then Vadim went through to Hussein's room. He sat down and lifted his glass. Hussein put the plastic cork back in the neck of the cognac bottle, and was just about to embark on a toast when there was another knock on the door. The two young men froze in mid-chink. "Vadim, Vadim are you there?" It was Lena again, come to press-gang him after all, no doubt. She knocked again, but less resolutely. Then she kicked the door in frustration and they heard her stomp off down the corridor.

"*Za zdorovye*," mouthed Vadim, not yet daring to speak out loud.

"Peace be with Leonid Ilyich," breathed Hussein solemnly. "May the earth be soft as goosedown to him, and may Allah have mercy on his soul." They threw back the honey-coloured liquid in one.

1817

The search for a site, the architectural design of the cathedral, and the elaboration of a philosophical basis for the project occupied Vitberg for nearly three years. It was only in 1817 that the foundation stone was laid. The ceremony was all pomp and ritual, as the official record makes clear:

On the Morn of October Twelfth, [it begins] *on which Day, five Years previous, the Foe did quit Moscow, our many Regiments foregather'd on Maiden's Field. The Gentry and the Proletary of Moscow hurry'd from every Corner of the Citie to this same Field, and others made Haste to the Sparrow Hills. The Confluens of Citie-Folk on the Streets was so copious as to defy all Probability: they fill'd not just the High-Ways, but also the Houses, and the Windows and the Balconies in the Houses; Many took up positions on the Rooftops, or did make Turrets of Wood, the better wherefrom to observe the Ceremonial. At the tenth Hour His Majesty the Emperor with His most August Family came to Luzhniki, into the humble Church of the Mother of God of Tikhvino. Under the blessed Vaults of this remote and sequester'd Temple, the Autocrat of all Russia offer'd Prayers to the Almighty. In the meanwhile, the Regiments of the Tsar were drawn up beyond the New Nunnery of the Holy Virgin and in Luzhniki, in such wise that the Visage of all these many Warriors was directed toward the Sparrow Hills; Divines carry'd Gonfalons and Holy Ikons, and array'd their Selfs close by the Tikhvinsky Church in Expectation of the imminent Conclusion of the Liturgy within. Their Number was more than thirty Episcops, three hundred Sacerdotals, two hundred Deacons and Archdeacons, two Choirs of*

Singers (one synodical and one of the Court) all equipp'd in their best and costliest Cloathing. At the XII'th Hour a Procession with Cross and Banners passed over a Bridge of Wood, purposefully assembled for this Memorable Event. Beside the many Ecclesiastics who did climb the Sparrow Hills, the Procession included Courtiers of the Tsar and distinguish'd Officials of the Army and of the Secular State; they progress'd to the Chiming of Bells and to martiall Musick, under the Gaze of fifty Thousand Men-At-Arms and no less than four Hundert Thousand vulgar Folk. Soon thereafter His Majesty the Emperor with His most August Family, in the Company of many Noble Military and Civil Personages, emerged from his Private Communion. On the Middle Reaches of the Hills was a High Place, where stood the Altar of the Lower Temple. Through the Ranks of the Priests and Monks, the Laurel'd Progenitor of the Temple ascended to this Spot. A Consecration by Water was perform'd, and a deep Stillness did reign over the River and on the Heights of the Hill Of Sparrows; In all that Great Assembly, under the broad Canopie of the open Sky, no Sound was to be heard save the prayerfull Melody of Sacred Songs. The Consecration by Water being accomplish'd, the Sovereign Emperor did lay the First Stone at the Fundament of the Temple to Christ the Saviour.

Eighteen years later, an embittered Vitberg recalled that he caught a chill while waiting for the tsar to arrive.

It took until 1820 for the meticulous Vitberg to produce a budgeted estimate of the building costs for the tsar's perusal. Alexander gave his approval to the assessment, and before the year was out Vitberg arranged to borrow ten million roubles from the Council of the Muscovy Trusteeship. With this money he arranged to purchase 18,000 serfs in the provinces adjacent to Moscow. These serfs, it was proposed, would generate income through *metayage*, producing goods that could then be sold for profit and finance the building of the cathedral; they were also to be exploited as cheap labour on the building-site itself, or else they could pay a fee so that some other bonded peasant could be employed in their stead. By the spring of 1821, the Cathedral Commission had acquired 11,275 souls, and this was thought sufficient manpower to begin the work of levelling the vast potholed and craggy expanse, a kilometre square, where the lower level of the temple would be.

These early days of the practical work on the temple were the high point of Vitberg's good fortune. It is not hard to imagine him going about his business. He was a slight man with delicate, almost feminine features: hooded, long-lashed eyes and full, cupid lips, prominent cheekbones and a wisp of grey in the forelock of his dark hair. He used to stride about the fresh-broken earth on the windy hilltop with a hammer or a trowel in one hand and a sheaf of his own drawings and watercolours gripped in the other. Occasionally he would stop and look towards Moscow, as if seeking inspiration in its distant spires and its flashes of gold. At these moments, seeing him apparently idle, overseers and contractors would come to him with their queries and complaints, but with a wave of the hand he would send them away to talk to the clerk of works. He could not bother his head with trivia, because his job was to keep the grand vision before him. This was a task that required a huge effort of the creative imagination; it was a special kind of poetic mood, a fragile thing that could be shattered by the slightest dissonant note. It was his duty to preserve his equilibrium; this above all, for he was engaged in the erection of something worthy of the great Empire of which he was a citizen, and of the magnanimous Emperor of whom he was the humble subject.

But things very soon began to go wrong. The minister of finances, a rather sour and unpleasant character named Dmitry Guryev, began to make problems for Vitberg by raising objections to the release of state funds for the church. Vitberg also had enemies on the building commission itself, who, it seems, found various ways of siphoning off money: shady sub-contractors were hired for huge advances, and this without Vitberg's knowledge or approval. The first successful experiments in supplying stone by barge from quarries in the village of Grigorievo, far upstream from Moscow, proved deceptive. In the event it was impossible to raise the level of the Moscow River sufficiently for the transportation of large loads.

At the same time, Vitberg was caught in the crossfire of a court intrigue. His main ally at court, Prince Andrei Golitsyn, was the childhood friend of the Emperor. Golitsyn was involved in a struggle with Count Arakcheyev, the sinister and powerful *eminence grise* of the regime. Arakcheyev was deeply jealous of Golitsyn's position as the tsar's main informant on matters relating to the cathedral, and of the access that the position gave him. He was determined to find a way to undermine Golitsyn, and the failure of the alien Vitberg to cope with the twin Russian diseases of indolence and pilfering provided just the opportunity he was seeking.

Things came to a head in 1824. The number of serfs engaged in building work had more than doubled to 23,254. These slaves had shifted well over half a million cubic metres of earth, but still Vitberg could provide no definite information about the bedrock of Sparrow Hills, nor commit himself to a date for the start of building. Seven years after the ceremony of dedication, still only the lower terrace had been levelled. Tonnes of building materials had been amassed, but it was not clear how they were to be used. Some people began to doubt that the church would ever be built, and perhaps to pre-empt any accusations that they were responsible for the fiasco, they made their fears known to the Emperor. Alexander reluctantly sacked Golitsyn. This left Vitberg without a friend at court, and fuelled his conviction that he was the object of a campaign of slander and persecution. When, despite his protests, Vitberg's enemies on the building commission forced through a dubious payment of 300,000 roubles to a contractor, it was the last straw.

Vitberg left the chaotic building site in Moscow and rushed to Petersburg. The Emperor granted him an audience, but to the architect's dismay he cancelled at the last moment – he was due to leave the next morning on a long trip to the provincial city of Taganrog, and had matters of state to attend to. Alexander bade Vitberg explain himself instead to Count Arakcheyev, his worst enemy. This was a terrible blow, but still worse was to come. Alexander I died in Taganrog. Vitberg was deprived of his beloved patron and protector, the man who was the living focus of his devotion to the Russian Empire.

The new tsar, Nikolai I, was a very different character from his dreamy elder brother. A cold and disciplined military man, he had brutally put down the armed rebellion that marked his ascent to the throne. He was equally brutal when he came to sort out the mess on Sparrow Hills. He stopped work and appointed two separate investigations, one into the architectural merits of Vitberg's project, and one into its financing. The financial committee amassed large amounts of evidence of malpractice and misappropriation of funds. As chief architect, Vitberg was held responsible and he was formally interviewed by investigators. He wrote reams of rambling discourses in his defence, but these unreadable tracts only weakened his case.

The investigation established that work on the cathedral had so far cost four million one hundred and thirty-two thousand five hundred and sixty roubles, seventy-four and one quarter kopecks. Criminal proceedings were instigated at the Moscow Assizes against all the members of the building commission. The case took eight years to go through all the courts, and in the meantime Vitberg's lands and possessions were sequestered.

All the members of the commission were acquitted with the exception of Vitberg himself, who was convicted of 'abuse and unlawful actions to the detriment of the exchequer'. His assets were inventoried with a view to his paying back some part of this sum. The findings of the architectural committee were hardly less damning for Vitberg. It concluded that the foundations of the three-tier cathedral would have rested on waterlogged sand; that no building of such grandiose proportions could be made to stand on the brow of Sparrow Hills after all.

This was the death sentence for Vitberg's church. His disastrous venture was abandoned and a new competition announced. In what could be interpreted as a sly dig at the self-taught foreigner, the architectural committee proposed to invite 'the most eminent, the best and most talented artists to participate in this undertaking, for such a labour demands more than mere application, it requires the consideration of a mature mind'. No site was specified, but many of the projects submitted for the second competition still envisaged the church on Sparrow Hills in accordance with the wishes of the late Alexander I; most of the designs placed it further back from the edge, roughly where the university now stands.

In 1835, Vitberg was sent as an internal exile to the town of Vyatka. During the long legal proceedings he had lost his wife and father. Now broken and unhappy, he still believed that his grand design would one day be fulfilled.

He was allowed to come home to Petersburg in 1840, and he spent the next four years writing letters, begging favours and chasing clerks to win the right to a pension. Eventually he was granted the tiny sum of 400 roubles per annum, on which he lived until his death in 1855.

14th November, 1982

On the morning of Brezhnev's funeral the recreation room was packed. Some students had come at dawn to get comfortable seats in the front row. Vadim and Hussein came along late, and had to stand at the back. There must have been three hundred people jammed into the room.

For two days MGU had been alive with discussion of the new general secretary, Yuri Andropov. A chilling frisson had run through the hostel when his appointment was announced: a lifelong KGB man in charge, what did it mean? They said he liked Western jazz – was that good news? Mark had called Vadim at the hostel for the specific purpose of discussing the new leader. He was in a black temper. "How do you like that?" he had said to Vadim over the phone. "This should certainly put the SS back in the KPSS." Vadim was aghast at his brother's recklessness. He hung up on him for his own good. But that line about the SS was too good to waste – Mark was probably ringing up everybody he knew to deliver it.

Vadim and Hussein settled down at the back wall to watch the events. Hussein nudged Vadim. "Marvellous colours," he hissed. "Better than being there."

Vadim looked to the screen. Nothing very colourful was going on. The deceased man's body was being drawn through Moscow on a gun carriage to the accompaniment of the endless *di capo al fine* of the funeral march. His sallow face pointed skyward from the open coffin. Soldiers goosestepped by his side, and others followed the carriage carrying wreaths, his many medals and orders, and the official airbrushed portrait of Leonid Ilyich with a black ribbon on the bottom corner. In the portrait he looked a slim, alert forty-year-old.

Behind the soldiers shuffled the men of the politburo, general secretary Andropov at their head. He was wearing a dark overcoat. Marshall Ustinov, the defence minister, was the only one in uniform. They seemed to find it uncomfortable to walk at the tortoise pace of the gun carriage. Hands clasped over their groins, they waddled along like scowling castrati. Behind the politicians came Brezhnev's family: well-fed, weeping women holding dainty handkerchiefs to their noses, and broad-faced *muzhiki* who constantly tugged at their unfamiliar white collars. The dull march with its insidious melody looped to the start for the thirtieth time.

The cortege arrived on Red Square and proceeded to the necropolis behind the mausoleum. The coffin was lifted off the gun carriage and set down on a pedestal next to the neat rectangle of the pit. The mourners laid banks of wreaths at the pedestal until it looked like an Indian pyre ready for the torch. Then they withdrew and stood in a semi-circle, shoulder-to-shoulder. Identical soldiers arranged the great man's medals at his feet on a large expanse of red silk. "How many Orders of Lenin did Leonid Ilyich have in the end?" asked someone in the recreation room.

"Five," came the reply.

"*Molodets*. Good for him," said one of the girls at the front, and burst into tears. From the other end of the room Vadim saw that the tearful mourner was Lena of the *stengazeta*. For him this was the cue to turn off his brain for a while, particularly since the politburo had mounted the Lenin mausoleum and were lining up to make speeches. Vadim heard the opening line of Andropov's oration – "Comrades! In this hour of mourning, as we say farewell to Leonid Ilyich Brezhnev, our entire Party and its Central Committee declares its resolve firmly and unswervingly to carry through the strategic line in internal and external policy that was worked out under the benign guidance of Leonid Ilyich Brezhnev..." He put his mind into neutral, and did not even register what was happening on the colour TV.

He popped out of mental limbo automatically when the speeches ended. The fat ladies were queueing up to kiss the dead man's face. The scene had a ghoulish fascination about it, and it was this that brought Vadim back to earth. There was a woman whom Vadim assumed to be Brezhnev's wife – he had never seen her in public before. She wept histrionically and covered the face of the corpse in kisses. And there was the scandalous daughter Galina Brezhneva, famed on the all-Union gossip circuit for her fabulous drinking capacity and her periodic attempts to run away to the circus. She looked as old and frowsy as her mother. By Galina's side was her husband Churbanov, the police sergeant promoted by marriage to deputy minister of the interior. "They are a colourful clan, though not in Hussein's sense of the word," thought Vadim. "It's like a scene out of a Gogol short story."

Now they were screwing down the lid of the coffin. Once the box was sealed it was lifted onto two struts that lay crossways across the open grave. Two long bands, they looked like silk, were passed under the coffin and four soldiers took up position, gripping the bands tightly so as to lower the coffin into the ground. At a given signal the struts were removed. Everyone expected the lowering of the coffin to be a stately and protracted process, but instead the coffin rattled down the hole like a loose piston-head and hit the bottom with a terrific crash. It was a dramatic moment. Had a mistake been made? Did they drop Leonid Ilyich? There was a gasp in the recreation room, but nothing was said: no-one wanted to voice what everyone was thinking. Vadim had a thought of his own: "I bet he hasn't moved that fast in fifteen years." This time he was shocked at his own irreverence, but nevertheless he tucked the thought away for Mark. This was his style of joke, the kind that you don't repeat on the phone.

The coffin's thud was still echoing round the walls of the grave and across the Union when factory sirens across Moscow honked into life. This industrial cacophony blared out of the TV set and seeped in through the windows of MGU from the real world outside. It acted on the students in the recreation room like an all-clear. They stood and stretched and slowly began to file out of the room, talking as they went. Vadim let them pass ahead of him. "What a statesman," said one student as he passed Vadim. "We will not see his like again."

"We won't indeed," said his friend. "It's the end of an era."

Vadim followed them out and headed downstairs to the canteen. He had not yet had breakfast.

1829

At the time of Vitberg's disgrace, Konstantin Thon was still swanning around Italy, building conservatories for pocket money and peering down Princess Volkonskaya's cleavage for fun. The Swede's grand failure was too distant to concern Thon while he was abroad, and he was too busy to pay attention to the scandal once he arrived home.

But when in 1829 a new competition was announced for a Cathedral of Christ the Saviour, Thon had to take notice. He was the country's leading young architect; he was in the process of building the Church of Catherine the Martyr in Kolomna; he was a candidate member of the Academy of Arts. Yet his candidacy had not yet been approved by the Emperor, and so he was, despite his already distinguished career, still on probation. Unless he wanted to concede that he had reached the peak of his attainments, Thon really had to win the commission.

But he was tired. It was with a heavy heart and aching shoulders that Konstantin Thon made the first sketches. Through the long Petersburg evenings he would sit hunched over a candlelit table in his study, while the first snow flurries of autumn drew whorls and chaplets on the dark window-panes.

His old sponsor Olenin advised Thon to design his church in the Byzantine style – that is to say, to base it on old Russian rather than Ancient Greek models. In this respect, at least, Thon was only too happy to comply. He had already experimented with pre-Petrine form at Kolomna, and all of his thinking had in any case been leading him to this, to the ideas that Voronikhin had been exploring fifteen years before. Thon was now convinced that there was a peculiarly Russian genius equal or superior to the Greek, and that it too could be translated into stone. And as he worked through the winter, he realised that this was his chance to prove it.

15th November, 1982

Vadim had planned to go to the Lenin Library on the day of the funeral, but in the morning it had been announced on the radio that the entire centre of the city was closed to traffic. His business had to wait until the next day. He got up early and pulled on yesterday's clothes. It was a quiet morning in the hostel. Hussein was still asleep when Vadim left the room. He waited at the lift, and for want of anything else to do he read Lena's *stengazeta*. They had done a good job: it was nicely laid out with the same airbrushed photograph of the dead leader, under the headline LEONID ILYICH BREZHNEV (1906–82). The main body of the text was a brief summing up of his life and achievements lifted, Vadim guessed, from the official biography that had been printed earlier that year. (Mark had bought a copy less than a month ago. He had had to fight for it, he said, "like it was a French deodorant". When Vadim asked why he bothered Mark had shrugged and said it was the Soviet herd instinct: everyone else was buying them, so he did too. "And anyway, it might be a bibliographical rarity one day.")

The main text of the *stengazeta* was broken up by two sidebars: one was an account of Brezhnev's wartime activity under an informal photograph of the youthful officer in a tankman's helmet with his comrades-in-arms, and the other was an extract from his memoirs, *Malaya Zemlya*. A note at the bottom of the passage said that Brezhnev had been awarded the Lenin Literature Prize for this book. The black border – she had found some paper, then – was neatly cut and glued on. The lettering was done in thin black felt-tip – clearly no expense had been spared – though the calligraphy was not as fine as Vadim would have contributed. But yes, all in all they had managed to make a sombre but attractive product out of very unpromising material. It's not easy to straighten a crooked spindle.

The lift arrived. Vadim rode down to the ground alone. He emerged into the cold air through the high revolving doors onto the south-facing edge of MGU. It had taken him almost ten minutes to get out of the building. The bus to the metro was as empty as the lift. The metro was as empty as the bus. Vadim settled down to read a book for the twenty-minute ride to Biblioteka station. As the doors closed there came the familiar recorded announcement "...next stop Leninskiye Gory...", but then the live voice of the driver came over the intercom: "This train is not stopping at Lenin Hills, next stop Sportivnaya." Vadim was surprised. It was completely unprecedented for anything to go wrong with the metro. As they passed through the station, the train slowed but did not stop. Vadim looked in at the platform. Groups of workers were standing idle in bunches. Men in suits with pens and clipboards stalked up and down.

Sportivnaya – Frunzenskaya – Park Kultury – Kropotkinskaya – Biblioteka imeni Lenina. The exit from the metro was built into the structure of the library. Vadim emerged and crossed the broad, grey pavement to the main entrance. Once inside he queued for ten

minutes to hand his coat into the cloakroom, where the attendant
scolded him at length because the cloth tab in the nape of his old
overcoat was broken: "How do you expect me to hang it on a hook
without a tab?" the old babushka asked. She took the coat and
jammed it on a hook by its collar, then with the flat of her hand she
slammed down a square plastic token with the number 1714 on the
counter.

Vadim then went and queued for a further five minutes to hand
his briefcase into a separate cloakroom fitted out with plywood
pigeonholes. This process passed off without incident and Vadim
collected another numbered token, this one triangular. He then
passed through a booth where he showed his green library card and
picked up a control chitty stamped with a figure 10, this being the
hour of his arrival. The preliminaries were now over. He climbed the
marble staircase to the catalogues.

Here he spent two hours, wandering round the crowded maze
of the vast card index. It was a piece of detective work he was
undertaking: he wanted to find contemporary accounts of the
cathedral and of its demolition. As for the latter, he was sure the best
place to look would be in the anti-religious literature of the time. In
the catalogue he found a fortnightly magazine called *Bezbozhnik u
Stanka*, 'The Godless Worker at his Lathe'. He ordered all twenty-
four issues for 1931. Then, on a hunch, he wondered whether the
godless of Moscow had a magazine of their own. If they did, an
event like the demolition of the cathedral would certainly have been
reported. He went to the letter M to see if there was not a journal
called, say, *Moskovsky Bezbozhnik*, 'The Godless Muscovite'. But
the hunch proved false: there were plenty of magazines beginning
moskovsky, but none of them specifically atheistic. Mechanically he
flicked on through the dog-eared cards, contemplating his next line
of enquiry. He was so engrossed he nearly missed it:

Mostovsky, M.S.
A History of the Cathedral of Christ the Saviour in Moscow
M. 1891 93p. 14cm

He could not believe it. He stared at the card in astonishment. What amazed him most about it, apart from the fact that it was here in the open catalogue at all, was that the words 'Christ' and 'Saviour' were written with capital letters, like proper nouns. He had never noticed it until now, but the word 'god' was always printed with lower-case in Soviet texts. Vadim could not remember ever having seen the word 'christ' in print.

He jotted down the library reference number of the book then went and ordered it in Reading Room Four. He looked at his watch. He had a lecture at two o'clock and another at five. He had to go now, but he could be back first thing in the morning. He skipped down the marble steps, at the bottom of which, it being nearly lunchtime, he joined a hungry queue to leave the library. When his turn came he showed his card and his control chitty to a librarian in a booth. She stamped the chitty with the hour of his departure, and Vadim handed the slip of paper to a young police officer who stood hard by, leaning against the wall of the librarian's booth. Two more queues, for briefcase and coat, and Vadim hurried back onto the metro, full of the joy of discovery.

Fifteen minutes later, passing over the Metro Bridge (where again the train did not stop) he saw that the men in suits were gone and that the workers were now engaged in taking down the signs on the platform. This was not the last strange incident of the trip. On arriving back at the university he found that the old ladies whose job it was to check student passes at the entrances to the main building had been replaced by regular militiamen. "The new broom," thought Vadim as his permit was scrutinised, "I wonder if this is the shape of things to come."

When Vadim arrived at his room in V Zone to pick up some books for his lecture, Hussein immediately came out of the right-hand blok. "There you are," he said.

"Hello," said Vadim. "There are funny things going on around here."

"Here's a funnier one," said Hussein, and without another word he disappeared into his little room. He came back out a moment later with two newspapers, and made a gesture to Vadim like a magician about to do a trick.

"Look, I'm a bit late. I haven't got time for…"

"This won't take a second," interrupted Hussein, ushering Vadim in. Vadim judged that it would be quicker to humour Hussein, and he sat down impatiently on the bed.

Hussein folded the two newspapers in half, so that only the top half of the front page was showing. The visible part of both papers showed the *Pravda* masthead and a photograph in traditional respectful style of the politburo lined up on the balcony of the mausoleum for yesterday's funeral. The picture occupied the whole width of the page. Hussein slotted the papers together and with a stagy flourish he flashed one side at Vadim, then the other. Hussein clearly thought this was a great joke, but Vadim did not get it. He repeated the operation several times; Vadim could only shrug.

"Are you really so unobservant, you dolt?" said Hussein, thwacking Vadim on the head with the papers. "Look closely, and spot the difference." He put the two papers side by side on the table. Vadim looked from one to the other, but the photographs were identical, the mournful row of old faces staring ahead from the top of the mausoleum. Then he saw it: on one of the photographs the central figure was Brezhnev: Vadim looked at the date and saw that it was the paper from November 8th, the day after last week's Revolution Day parade; on the other picture the central figure was Yuri Andropov, taken at the funeral on the 15th. The only difference was that in the second shot Brezhnev was absent and everyone had shuffled up one place; the camera angle, not to mention the clothes, the poses and the expressions were precisely the same.

"Now do you get it?" giggled Hussein. "It is the Incredible Disappearing General Secretary. Now you see him, now you don't."

"Like a momentary fleeting vision," said Vadim, quoting Pushkin.

"Like the genius of pure beauty," said Hussein, finishing the quote.

Caucasus

The Caucasus, like the open palm of my hand,
Like a great rumpled bed…

– Boris Pasternak (from Second Birth)

November 1982

The next day turned out to be 'sanitary day' at the library. It was closed, and Vadim made the trip into town for nothing. He came home to the hostel and tried to do some study instead.

In the afternoon he was lying on his bed, his Advanced English Grammar open face-down on his chest. He had long since lost interest in the five varieties of conditional sentences, and now he lay, fingers laced behind his head, listening to the signs of life in the termite mound around him. The whoops and yelps of a football game drifted up from the yard below. Somewhere in a room nearby, the chubby crooner Yuri Antonov was on the radio, and his guileless melody burrowed into Vadim's brain like a weevil:

Some dreams come true, some don't come true,
Love comes to you, sometimes unseen.
And when you're glad, it stays with you,
And when you're blue, it's just a dream.

Nearer to home, Hussein was pottering around next door. He had just spent at least an hour in the bathroom, which was unlike him.

He was humming along tunelessly to Antonov's distant crooning, and in his idiosyncratic Azerbaijani interpretation the cheap song sounded like a muezzin's call to prayer. The thought struck Vadim as funny, lifting his depression for a moment.

There was a light tap on the mottled glass door of his blok. "Come in, Hussein," said Vadim.

Hussein stepped into the room, and Vadim started at the vision of spotlessness before him. He was resplendent in a black shirt and dark-brown dogtooth trousers; a broad red tie was done up scrupulously tight; his socks were white and he wore his best grey loafers; his face was pink and slightly puffy. Whether that was because he had scrubbed it raw, or because the tie was asphyxiating him, Vadim could not tell. His moustache was sleek and combed, and his face was frozen in a watch-the-birdie smile. He had a firm grip on a bunch of carnations, which he held aloft like an Olympic torch.

"How do I look?" he said through his gleaming smile.

"You look great," said Vadim, genuinely impressed. "What is it, your wedding day?"

At this Hussein abandoned his magnificent pose. "Ah, would that it were," he said, coming and sitting on the edge of Vadim's bed. "How long can a man live the life of a eunuch?"

Hussein's Russian always made Vadim smile. He had grown up in Baku, where Russian was taught in schools as a second language using classic nineteenth-century texts. So his speech was slightly bookish, but streaked through with the Moscow slang he had picked up from Russian friends. "Once a man is a eunuch, it's usually fairly long-term," said Vadim.

"You know what I mean," said Hussein. "So enough jokes. Get dressed, we are going to a party."

"We?"

"Yes. Today is the birthday of my friend Kakha Toridze from

Tbilisi. He lives on the fifth floor. Hurry or we will be late."

"Hussein, I have not been invited."

"Ah, but you are invited. You are merely unaware of the fact because I forgot to inform you. Just yesterday I was telling Kakha of my room-mate the guitarist, and he said to bring you along to his birthday, as they have no music of their own."

Vadim lay back on his cot. "Thanks, all the same, but I must do some study. I appreciate the thought, though."

"Yes, I can see how hard you are studying," said Hussein, waving at the ceiling. "The rules of English syntax are written in the cracks of the plaster. Hurry now, you will learn more at Kakha's party than you will sitting here all evening." Hussein dropped the facetious tone. "I will consider it a personal favour if you will come with me. I need your opinion on something."

"On what?"

"You'll see. Do you have a clean shirt?"

Vadim put up a little more token resistance. Then he found some decent clothes and had a quick shave. He insisted on spending five minutes tuning his guitar before they went, while Hussein hopped from one foot to the other with impatience. When at last Vadim was ready, Hussein bundled him out of the room and they took the stairs down to the fifth at a canter.

One end of the corridor on the fifth floor was a sort of exclusive Georgian enclave. Nearly all the Georgians in V Zone lived there, speaking their own language, singing their own songs, and generally creating a fairly functional illusion, in this chilly Slav wilderness, that they were back home in the sunlit, mountainous south. As soon as Vadim and Hussein emerged from the stairwell onto the corridor they smelt the warm, spicy aroma of Caucasian cuisine coming from the communal kitchen. Hussein could not resist making a detour.

"A good evening to you, Manana," he said in his most formal Russian to the woman, about thirty years old, whom they found in the kitchen. "May I congratulate you on the birthday of your husband, and present to you my friend Vadim."

Manana was chopping coriander leaf on a board. The smell was mouth-watering. She put down the knife for a second and nodded in a friendly way to Vadim. "Good evening, Vadim," she said, smiling. "A musician is always welcome at our table," she added with a nod at the guitar. "Please go and join the celebrations." Vadim thanked her. He felt an immediate liking for Manana. Like many Georgian women, she had fine, aristocratic features, but she looked careworn and her dark hair was dishevelled. She spoke perfect Russian with a slight Georgian accent, but the hard vowels and deep, throaty consonants did not grate on the ear. Perhaps it was something to do with her obvious nobility, but the accent suited her. Leaving the kitchen he felt a pang of old sorrow which he identified without undue effort: Manana reminded him of his dead mother.

Hussein led the way to the room where the party was taking place. The door was closed and all seemed quiet. Hussein knocked twice. Footsteps approached from within and a voice asked, "Who's there?"

"Kakha, it is me, Hussein." He flashed a conspiratorial smile at Vadim.

A key turned and the door opened wide. There stood a stocky, muscular man in his early thirties, his dark straight hair prematurely touched with grey. He had a strong, aquiline nose, thick glasses, and his broad smile revealed one gold tooth in his upper jaw. With his free hand he made a graceful gesture that expressed greeting and apology at once. "Pardon me, dear guests," he said in the same over-formal Russian as Hussein spoke. "We live in circumstances where, sad to say, not every visitor is a friend and a joy. Please come in, you are most welcome." Kakha had a marked Georgian accent too, and his gravelly voice betrayed that he was a heavy smoker.

Hussein introduced Vadim to his host, and the three of them

passed into the room. It was bigger than the cell-like space where
Vadim lived, but was cramped nevertheless. It had two beds and two
desks: these were MGU married quarters. The furniture had been
rearranged for the birthday party. The desks stood end to end in the
middle of the room, and the beds were drawn up as seating for the
guests. The makeshift table was crowded with Georgian delicacies:
satsivi chicken in walnuts, spiced *lobio* beans, *cheremsha* garlic
stalks, *khachapuri* cheesebread. One of the guests – Vadim's heart
flipped when he saw her – was the dark-haired American girl from
the Revolution Day party. She was sitting next to a bespectacled
young man, also foreign.

Kakha began to introduce Vadim to the other guests. Some of
them he recognised. There was a girl from his own course called
Galya. He knew her vaguely: she was a keen *komsomolka*, played a
lot of volleyball, and always wore her blond hair in two tight plaits;
then Alla – he did not know her name until Kakha mentioned it,
but he had seen her around: she was a postgraduate in the English
faculty and much lusted after for her stunning figure; she was also a
komsomol activist, but a different type from Galya: streetwise, sly,
career-minded. Vadim noted that she was smoking hard-currency
Marlboro.

"And this is my brother, Giya," continued Kakha, introducing
the man next to Alla. "Giya is *tamada* for the evening, he will lead
the toasts. The wine we will drink is from Giya's father's own vines
in the hills of Kakheti."

They were not literally brothers; Vadim understood that this was
just a poetic Georgian turn of phrase. He had heard the Georgian
word *tamada,* and knew that the art of making colourful speeches,
full of formal compliments and flights of fancy, was central to any
Georgian celebration. He greeted Giya, looking him in the eye. Giya
was wiry, sunken-faced, with thick, black stubble from his Adam's
apple to his high cheekbones. His bright eyes glowed blue in his

dark face, and his handshake was iron. Vadim was glad they were meeting as friends.

"And our guests of honour," Kakha continued, turning to the Westerners. "May I present Andrew, who has come to us from the land of William Shakespeare, Charles Dickens, Margaret Thatcher and the immortal Bobby Charlton. And Rachel, from the magical city of New York in distant America, a land of which we know very little except that it is beautiful and free."

The two foreigners laughed heartily at Kakha's introduction. Rachel clapped her hands together and rocked back on the divan seat. Vadim shook Andrew's hand and nodded politely to Rachel. But she extended her hand to him. He took it for a moment: her fingers were cool to the touch.

Vadim and Hussein were just sitting down opposite the Western guests when Manana came back into the room. She was carrying a steaming bowl of boiled potatoes swimming in butter and sprinkled with the chopped coriander. Kakha and Giya poured wine from unlabelled bottles into vodka glasses, and the two Russian women busily served food onto plates while Kakha went and locked the door. A hush settled on the company when Kakha returned and took his seat at the head of the table next to Manana. Alla stubbed out her cigarette. Giya was on his feet at the end table, his glass held elegantly between thumb and middle finger. His head was bowed as if he was composing himself to sing an aria or recite a poem, which in a sense he was.

"Dear friends," began Giya, lifting his eyes. "Today we mark the thirty-third birthday of my friend and brother Kakha Timurovich Toridze. It is a momentous day, for thirty-three is a mystical age for a man. At thirty-three a man is still young, but already mature. It is an age when one can observe the full flower of whatever gifts and talents he possesses, and Kakha possesses many. I hope it is not blasphemous to point out that at the age of thirty-three, Jesus Christ made his indelible mark on human history.

"It is an age when a man can look back proudly on his achievements, but still look forward to future triumphs, to dreams as yet unfulfilled. He hangs suspended between the naive optimism of youth and the bitter pessimism of old age; between hope and experience..."

Vadim's attention wandered from the extravagant toast and settled on Rachel. Her profile was turned to him as she listened attentively to Giya's birthday oration, and this gave Vadim the opportunity to study her close-to without risking embarrassment. He wondered why it was so obvious that she was foreign. Partly it was her clothes, of course, which were plain, comfortable-looking and well-designed, not like the garish, stripey t-shirts and the patterned skirts that the other women wore. Also she was so – what was the word? – well-groomed. Her skin was clear and her brown hair was shiny. Vadim noticed her habit of tucking the tresses behind her left ear when she was concentrating on what Giya was saying, as if she could hear better that way. She looked unspoiled and serene: Vadim doubted condescendingly that she had ever stood in a meat queue or fought her way onto a bus. She had none of the eternal weariness that Soviet women wore like a perfume, that obscured Manana's aristocratic comeliness. Rachel's attractiveness was unblighted and radiantly democratic; it belonged to no-one but her, and at the same time it belonged to everyone who looked on her. She was not on her guard, she was making no attempt to disguise any part of her personality. That was the essence of it, she was not afraid to be herself. Kakha had hit the nail on the head when he introduced her: she was beautiful and free.

The toast came to a conclusion, and they drank Kakha's health. Vadim drained his glass in one draught to demonstrate his solidarity with the sentiments expressed by Giya, though he had missed half of them in his reverie. When he placed his glass on the table he found that Rachel was now looking at him.

She smiled when his gaze met hers. "Are all you Georgians such fine speakers?" she asked.

Vadim was suddenly alarmed to be addressed by her. She looked quietly amused, as if she knew he had been gauging her. "I am a poor speaker," he said. "But then I am not a Georgian."

Rachel arched her eyebrows. "Oh. You're Russian?"

"Yes... that is, I'm a Russian Jew." He regretted this strange confession the moment he said it – but she just smiled again. "Then we have something in common. I am Jewish, too. My grandparents came from Minsk."

He had half-guessed this already – it certainly explained her fine Russian. But the confirmation of her Jewishness did not make her seem any less alien to him. Vadim could not make any connection between his blood and hers. If there were Jews on Mars, they would be first and foremost Martians. He could hardly say this to her, but he could think of no polite response.

Rachel gazed at him steadily. "If you do not like to speak, perhaps you will sing," she said, indicating the guitar which Vadim had left in the corner.

"I will be glad to, when the time comes," said Vadim. "When the company is ready."

Rachel leaned forward, as if to impart a secret. Vadim felt his stomach tense, but he inclined his head towards hers. "The first song you sing," she said gravely, "sing it for me."

Vadim said little in the course of the meal. And Rachel's request had thrown him into such confusion that he hardly dared look in her direction. He did not propose a toast himself, which, as a male guest, he really ought to have done. This was not a serious lapse of manners, however, since Kakha and Giya with occasional support from Hussein kept up a steady stream of discourse. Rachel, for her part, did not talk to him. She spent a lot of time interpreting for the Englishman, whose Russian was poor. Once, when Giya was expressing a particularly intricate and flowery thought in the course of a toast, she put her hand on Andrew's shoulder to whisper the translation in his ear. Vadim did not like that.

When everybody had eaten their fill, and even Giya's verbal inventiveness was beginning to ebb, Kakha said, "Vadim, I see that you are a quiet fellow, and this pleases me. But I ask you to sing for us now. If your song is short, we will know that you would have us understand your meaning *s poluslova*, as the Russians have it, 'with half a word spoken'. That will be a fine compliment after so brief an acquaintance. If your song is lengthy, we will know that this is an act of great generosity from one of your laconic nature. Please take your guitar and sing."

Vadim thanked Kakha and they all drank, since the formality of the request had sounded pretty much like a toast. Then Vadim took up the guitar. He plucked a couple of chords to check the tuning, and threw a glance at Rachel. She blinked at him slowly and reassuringly. It's all right, her eyes said. Between you and me, everything is going to be all right. Vadim looked away, struck an introductory chord and sang:

See here, my hand has ceased to shake.
The road leads up.
My fears have plunged down the ravine;
They won't be back.
With no more reason to delay,
I climb – and slip.
But there is not a mountain peak
I cannot take.

Of all the many unwalked paths,
Let one be mine.

Of all the borders yet uncrossed,
One is for me.
The names of those who've fallen here
Melt with the snow.
Of all the wide untravelled roads,
Give one to me.

The whole of this broad icy slope
Is bathed in blue.
The dreams of those who passed this way
Are writ in stone.
And I will strive towards my dream:
I see it now!
Two things are sacred, two things pure:
Words, and the snows.

No matter how much time may pass,
I shan't forget:
This is the place I learned to kill
My own self-doubt.
That day the waters said to me:
"Good luck always!"
But which day could that day have been?
I cannot say.

Vadim was no great performer, but he had a good, strong
voice and a fair share of natural musical feeling. He knew how to
accompany himself on the guitar, and in a small room with a kindly
disposed audience he came across very effectively. When he reached
the end of the song all clapped except Rachel, who threw Vadim the
most beatific smile and silently mouthed the words 'thank you' in
English. Vadim felt a rush of blood.

"Is that your own song?" asked Andrew with his strange Anglo-Saxon intonation.

"I'm afraid not," said Vadim, "I wish it was. It is a well-known song by Vladimir Vysotsky, the best of the Soviet bards."

"Anti-Soviet, more like," chipped in Galya, who was a little tipsy. "And he was a notorious drunk to boot."

"I don't think so," said Vadim. "There was nothing anti-Soviet about that song, was there?"

"Not that one maybe, but there are plenty of others where he mocks Soviet society and makes heroes out of bandits and misfits."

"Perhaps he thought bandits and misfits are more interesting than loggers and tractor-drivers – though he wrote about that sort of person too, of course."

"When he died," said Alla, addressing Andrew and Rachel, "they didn't even announce it on the radio, though he was a folk hero for Russians. Instead they reported that Joe Dassin had died, the French singer. He came here once or twice and gave some concerts."

"Joe Dassin was well-loved, too," said Galya.

"But Galya, think about it," said Vadim, getting annoyed. "You are in the journalism faculty, after all. On the same day two men die: one is a Russian poet who is loved or despised by the whole Union; the other is a foreign pop singer. As a professional journalist, whose death would you choose to report?"

Galya scowled. "As a professional, I would not give airtime to anti-Soviet propaganda."

"Everybody knew he had died, anyhow," continued Alla. "It was on Voice of America. They laid out his body in the Taganka Theatre. You should have seen the queue of people who came to pay their respects. It stretched three or four times round the square. It was probably the biggest queue ever in the history of Moscow – except for when Lenin died, maybe. Thousands and thousands of people, all quiet, all in mourning. There were literally mountains of flowers inside the theatre. The polleny smell from the flowers was overpowering. It was terribly hot, I remember. The Olympics were on and they had done something to the clouds so it didn't rain during the Games."

"What did they do to the clouds?" asked Andrew, puzzled.

"Oh, I don't know exactly. They blew them all away somehow. There was not a single cloud in the sky the whole time the Olympics were on. The Games were such a huge undertaking that they weren't going to take any chances on it raining for the whole month. Of course they were spoiled anyway, because of the boycott."

"That was a good summer," said Giya. "All those Pepsi Cola kiosks appeared. And you could buy real Fanta and Czech beer."

"And they sent all the children to pioneer camp," added Manana. "Why did they do that, do you think? It was so strange, there was almost no-one under the age of twelve in Moscow the whole summer long."

"Why did you boycott the Olympics, actually?" Galya asked Rachel. There was a note of aggression in her voice, as if she held Rachel personally responsible for the rude behaviour of the US government. "What did you gain by it?"

Rachel shrugged. "I think the Western countries wanted to register their protest at the invasion of Afghanistan in a way that would bring the message home. The Moscow Games were a ready-made opportunity."

"But no-one invaded Afghanistan, surely that is clear. The Soviet Union responded to a request for help from the legitimate government of the Afghan Republic."

"Friends," interjected Kakha. "Did not Jerome Jerome say that there are two topics that are never discussed in the pubs of England: politics and religion. Let us draw on the wisdom of that ancient people," – he bowed extravagantly in Andrew's direction – "and speak of other things. Vadim, perhaps you will sing for us again."

Vadim said he would be delighted. He had just the song for the occasion. He looked to Rachel. She was sitting chin in hands, eyes wide in expectation. This time he found he drew strength from her attention. He wanted her approval.

He sang:

Let us refrain from talk for a while;
Say what we must, and then be still,
The better to hear the echo within,
The meaning of all that has been said.

Let us make a break in our journey,
And take a good long look around us,
So as not to make the mistake
Of passing down the same road twice.

Let us now just sit in silence,
We all are too fond of our own voice,
Which can sometimes even drown out
The cry of the friend by our side.

In the silence we can't help but see
How far we have drifted apart;
How we thought we were galloping onward
When in fact we were running in circles;

How we imagined that big things await us;
How we believed in our own exclusivity;
How we hoped that some day, very soon,
We would see great changes to the good.

But this age is already in decline,

And, doubtless, will shortly pass away.
Yet nothing is happening in our lives,
And nothing is very likely to.

The song had the calming effect that Vadim thought it would.

"Is that Vysotsky, too?" asked Andrew.

"No, Makarevich," said Vadim. "A younger generation."

"It was very lovely, and very *à propos*," said Rachel. "Thank you, Vadim."

There was a hiatus in the conversation. No-one had a word to say.

"You know the old superstition," said Giya brightly. "When a silence falls on a celebration, somewhere a militiaman is born." They all laughed, but Galya asked: why do they say that? They laughed again. She really is a bit dim, thought Vadim.

They sat for a while longer, Vadim sang a couple more tunes, and then the guests made to leave. Kakha and Manana prevailed on them to stay for one more glass of wine, one more cup of tea, one more song, but in the end they could no longer hold their visitors hostage to their hospitality. In the doorway, Giya drew Rachel to one side. "I hope you were not offended by anything that was said this evening," he said in low tones. Then, switching into English, "Some people do not understand some things, some political things."

"Not at all," Rachel reassured him. "I had a great time, and I enjoyed the discussion." She said goodbye to Vadim in the corridor. "I'll see you again. Soon, I hope."

"I hope so, too," he said, and then his chronic lack of conversation again left him with nothing to say. He looked to his feet for inspiration and when he looked up she was gone. Andrew had gone with her. He saw the Englishman's heels disappearing round the corner and into the stairwell.

Vadim and Hussein went back to their shared room. Hussein

was whistling in his tuneless way, and Vadim was deep in thought: had he offended her at the last? When they got back to the room, Hussein followed Vadim into the left blok without invitation. He sat down on the bed and grinned broadly at his friend. Vadim thought he was going to tease him about the American. And sure enough:

"Well, what do you think of her?" he asked.

"I like her," said Vadim, guardedly. "She's nice."

"Nice! Is that the best you can say, 'nice'!"

"What do you want me to say? I only just met her."

"All the same: 'nice'?"

"She's very attractive."

"And?"

"She's interesting."

"Interesting? You have the whole treasure-house of the Russian language within your grasp, and you choose 'interesting'. Don't be such a miser. Adjectives are a renewable resource, like wheat or plutonium. Use your imagination, Vadim."

"I've said what I think, and I can't think of anything else." He was on the point of telling Hussein to mind his own business.

"But what about her womanly figure, her lively intelligence, her beautiful blond hair, the way her plaits bobbed up and down when she was angry and flushed with wine. Her sharp wit. She certainly gave you a run for your money."

"What?"

"And that heaving chest; those sporting hips. I must have those hips or die, Vadim. She will be mine."

Vadim suddenly got the picture. "You mean Galya?"

"Yes, Galya. Her name is music. Galya, *golubchik* – my little pigeon."

"But listen, Hussein," said, Vadim. "You didn't say a word to her all evening. If you want her that badly you've got to... well, you've got to chat her up."

"Chat her up? You are a common fellow, sometimes, Vadim. She is not a girl you can 'chat up'. What use are words, anyway. Words are empty noises."

"You just said they were treasure. Also wheat and plutonium."

"To you, perhaps. But Galya and I are beyond mere words. It's in the eyes, you see. When I poured her wine tonight she looked into my eyes and down into my soul, and I into hers, and I saw that she was going to love me. It is as inevitable as death."

"All the same, I would still talk to her if I were you. It can't do any harm."

"Very well, if that's what you think, I will follow your advice."

"Only go easy. Don't frighten her off."

"I know what you mean. Proceed with stealth, like a hunter."

"Yes, I suppose. A gentle approach. I think it is the best plan."

Hussein pondered for a moment. "Thank you, Vadim. I will do as you say, and I will have her."

He shook Vadim's hand in gratitude, and left the room. Vadim lay back on his bed in the same pose as when Hussein barged in on him that afternoon. He renewed his inspection of the blank ceiling.

Only now, all his thoughts were for Rachel.

Reading Room One

Not I, and not you, and not he,
Yet the same as I am, but unlike me:

– Innokenty Annensky (from The Double)

I don't know. This story is pure invention. The characters I am creating never existed beyond the bounds of my imagination. True, Mark is based loosely on my real-life brother, also called Mark. Where else would I get my ideas about elder brothers from? Originally I was going to call him Slava, but as it happens Mark is a common name among secular Russian Jews, so I thought, why change it? Funnily enough, I found it much easier to write about him once he had my own brother's name. You wouldn't have thought it would make a difference – for Slava, read Mark – but it does. It matters, the names you give things.

Yuri Prichalov's character, but not his history, is derived partly from a former acquaintance named Yuri (same principle), partly from a Jewish writer friend of mine, a *shestidesyatnik*, a man of the Sixties' Thaw, called Lev Levitsky. The story of Efim Shabad's long-short walk home from the station is true, except that the grandfather in question was my father's father and the walk was from Southfields tube station on the District Line to Longfield Street in the London borough of Wandsworth. It is roughly the same distance as from Moskovsky Station to Marat Street in Leningrad. The fishing-for-shrapnel business is almost word for word as my father told it to me. And I know a Russian lady who makes mushroom soup for her daughter in just the way I ascribe to Auntie Ira. It seemed too good a story to waste. Rachel is... well, you get the picture.

Peter Kikin was a real historical person, and he did write that letter on the 17th December, 1812. The subsequent story of the Cathedral of Christ the Saviour is all true, bar a bit of poetic licence here and there.

I've been intrigued by the Cathedral since I first heard about it years ago, but I knew barely more than Mark told Vadim. When I first decided to write about it, I planned to spend an idyllic month or two in the libraries and archives of Moscow beating a path to the primary sources, piecing together the jigsaw of history, digging up facts, uncovering telling snippets. I was looking forward to it.

Then, in the summer of 1993, I came across a book called *Khram Khrista Spasitelya v Moskve*, 'The Cathedral of Christ the Saviour in Moscow'. I could hardly believe it. Here was the first-ever complete monograph, freshly published. It was produced on high-quality paper, the print-run was 20,000, and it was filled with beautiful reproductions of old street-maps, the many different projects of the cathedral, photographs, engravings, lithographs, cine-stills, postcards, prints, eye-witness accounts and an extensive bibliography. There was an insightful and highly erudite text by Evgeniya Kirichenko, a brilliant architectural historian whose work on nineteenth-century Russian culture I had encountered before.

At first I was delighted. Here in a single volume was a mass of data on Christ the Saviour. It would have taken me years of solitary work to find this much information. But as I read the book my heart sank. Kirichenko's fine account was so exhaustive that I began to worry whether there would be anything left for me to say about the damned building. There was certainly no point in keeping that date with the archives. By the time I got to the last page I was in deep gloom. And it was not just the lack of a happy ending. I had been cheated of my big concept.

But I soon realised that I was lying to myself. Deep down it was just the idea of researching I was fond of. I knew, if I was truthful, that I would find it utterly mortifying to have to sit for weeks on end in crumbling archives in far-flung corners of Moscow, sifting through the detritus of the centuries for a paragraph's worth of fact.

I remember my last attempt at serious research. After a year's scouting-about for a thesis topic I came to Moscow under the generous auspices of the British Council to gather M.Phil material on an under-rated Russian poet named Innokenty Annensky. The very first morning I went and registered at the Lenin Library. As a Westerner I was entitled to use Reading Room One, which is reserved for members of the Soviet Academy of Sciences and high-ranking professors. I decided to start by refreshing my memory of the texts, so I opened the collected poetry at page one and began to work my way through. But I soon got bored with that. Skimming randomly through the book I happened upon this strange poem, called "Ideal".

> The vacant sound of guttering gas
> Above the death-like glaze of heads,
> And seeping boredom's black malaise
> Pervading the abandoned desks.

> And there, amid the green-stained faces,
> Cherishing the glum routine,
> To seek on faded yellow pages
> The stale unknowables of being.

I had read it before, but had never understood it. It always struck me as odd that there was not a single finite verb in all the eight lines. There cannot be many poems like that.

Then I looked up at the old men at the other tables. Some were nodding towards sleep, some were reading through magnifying glasses. One was engrossed in an alarming fit of coughing. Next to me, an old gentleman with the thickest spectacles I have ever seen was peeling an orange with his thumbnail (perfectly permissible at the Lenin State Library – in this system, where there were rules prohibiting most forms of enjoyable human activity, the Leninka was unaccountably liberal as regards the consumption of food on the premises).

With the sharp whiff of pith in my nostrils I had a moment of real insight. The little poem was about them, the dusty scholars looking for big answers in old books. The heads in the poem were their heads, made green by the coloured glass shades of reading lamps. I saw now how ludicrous they were, these distinguished bookworms, not knowing as they freewheeled to the grave that they would never find the solution to their private riddles, any more than the poem would find a main verb. But by the same token, of course, the lines were about me. Annensky, you ungrateful sod, I thought. I've come all this way to draw some attention to you, I'm doing you a favour, and all you can do is mock me.

I went for a glass of ersatz coffee in the library's grimy basement canteen. By the time I came back to my desk I knew that I would never finish my thesis. I would not be able to bear the sound of Annensky's ghostly laughter ringing in my ears.

Now I feel fine about Kirichenko's book. It saved me a lot of time. I have borrowed some facts, not stolen the ideas. It has been a road-map, but I did my own legwork. I have used the pictures as an aid to the imagination, but the only other part I have rifled is the bibliography, which led me to the original sources such as Vitberg's memoirs and the Mostovsky book. That is what bibliographies are for, after all. And I have confessed my debt to her, both here and on the page headed 'Acknowledgements' at the back of this book.

So why am I interrupting the narrative to tell you all this? Why flaunt the cogs and fly-wheels so? Glass clocks are yesterday's toy, after all. If I had to be perverse, could I not at least be original with it?

The answer is that I did not set out to be original. Not for nothing are the first three sentences of this section a quotation from *The French Lieutenant's Woman* where John Fowles pulls this very stunt. It happens in chapter thirteen, page 85, in the Picador paperback edition, the one with windswept picture of Meryl Streep on the cover. I hated it when Fowles did it to me, and I don't like doing it to you now.

But bear with me. There are reasons. It's to do with what this book is about.

It's about...

December 1982

Yes, there was a new mood in the country. Some felt it as a breath of fresh air, some as a chilly gust from Siberia. Whatever, Andropov was making a difference. Within days all the newspapers were parroting the new priority: 'Strengthen Labour Discipline'. It was not a change in policy, of course, for the party was committed to continuing on the course laid out by Brezhnev, it was just a subtle shift of emphasis, a sharpening of attention to detail, and what it meant was: we have got to stop Soviet citizens drinking themselves unconscious during working hours.

The practical measures were crude but effective. The militia began to raid vodka shops and arrest everyone who could not explain why they were not at work. Men were collared on the street and asked the same question. Vadim was stopped once at three o'clock in the afternoon. He was on his way back to the hostel from the shops, and he had a paper cone full of hot, steaming doughnuts from the stall at Universitet metro. He produced his student card by way of ID, but the militiaman said he ought to have his face in a book somewhere, not his nose in the trough, and that he would be reported to the university authorities. Vadim protested that he was stone-cold sober and that it was not a crime to be on the street in the afternoon. In the end he bought the copper off with three doughnuts.

Drunks who were past being questioned, the thousands of *alkashy* who littered the pavements of Moscow and Leningrad like plague victims, were rounded up and delivered by the wagonload to *vytrezviteli* – 'drying-out stations' – which were part police cells, part casualty ward. Here their identity was checked. Those who turned out to be respectable people (say, they had a party card in their jacket) were discreetly delivered home. After all, model citizens have birthdays too, they get promoted, their wives bear them sons, and they are entitled to celebrate once in a lifetime. As for the rest, they were given a good kicking (if the militia had the energy), hosed down, and left to shiver in the cells for the night. In the morning their heads were shaved for shame, a note was despatched to their place of work, and they were released into the light of day. Naturally, the first thing they did was go and drown their sorrows. A new and surprisingly cheap brand of vodka became available in the last days of 1982, as if intended for this very purpose. The people dubbed it *andropovka*.

At the university, the new temper took the form of komsomol meetings, compulsory for all Soviet students, where the evils of vodka, its detrimental effect on the searching mind of the young scholar, were hammered home through the use of slide shows and quotations from Lenin. The komsomol leadership, ever sensitive to subtle shifts in party policy, no longer considered it necessary to bolster their appeals for sobriety and industry with references to the speeches of Brezhnev, though he was barely cold in his grave.

These meetings spawned the inevitable crop of *stengazety*, and this time Vadim did not manage to avoid taking part. He did not mind too much, because he realised that it would be a good thing to be seen around the place engaged in some form of political activity. Now was not a good time to be regarded an outsider. This and a serious crackdown on attendance at lectures meant that he could not get to the library, and he was afraid his books would be returned to the stacks.

The busy atmosphere also kept his mind off Rachel. He had thought about her a lot in the days after their first encounter, ever hoping to bump into her in the corridor or the canteen. If he had known the number of her room he might have plucked up the courage to go and visit, but he thought it imprudent to go making enquiries just now. She was nowhere to be seen, and though she drifted into his conscious mind every day, the bright image of her in his memory began to fade. Perhaps he had just imagined her interest in him; maybe it was all just the American way of being friendly...

It was December before Vadim could sneak away to the Leninka. Andropov had come down with the first of the heavy colds that were to finish him, and immediately the reins had slackened off. A mazy flight of snow was falling, the vanguard of the white deluge to come. Settling flakes, as fine as dust, blew across the library pavement and formed shifting patterns like iron filings under a magnet. When Vadim emerged from Biblioteka metro station, he stood and watched the snow dance for a minute or two, sheltering from the painfully cold wind in the lee of a granite column. Then he scuttled across to the main doors and into the steamy, communal warmth of the Lenin State Library.

The cloakroom queue was enormous. Vadim gauged it at forty-five minutes. It was snaked up tightly like a Chinese firecracker and it filled the library hallway. The line seemed in danger of dissolving into an amorphous mass of impatient people. Arguments were breaking out like flash fires at half a dozen different points along its length.

Vadim reserved himself a place according to the accepted queue culture. First he found what looked like the extremity of the queue, and asked the person bringing up the rear, "Are you last?" Having identified the tail-ender, he took his place at their back. Then he waited for someone else to join. Once he was no longer last, he turned to the person behind him, a youth of about his own age in a natty Adidas ski-hat and said, "I'll be back in a moment". Having thus staked his claim in the presence of a witness, he went off to investigate the baggage queue. It turned out to be short, but completely immobile. All the pigeon-holes were full, so the people who wanted to hand in their bags (it was forbidden to take them into the library) had first to wait for someone to come out and remove a bag. Since it was only the start of the working day, there were far more people arriving than leaving. Vadim stood and watched the queue for five minutes, during which time five people joined the queue but only one person liberated a pigeonhole. There were fifteen people ahead of him. It was not a statistically accurate estimate, Vadim knew, but if readers kept reclaiming their briefcases at that rate it would take him two and a quarter hours to dispose of his own bag and get inside. He was ready to spit with frustration. Would he never get a look at the Mostovsky book?

"Hello, you. Too many winters, too many summers."

Vadim looked round – it was Rachel. She smiled, and the smile almost made him gasp, as if she had punched him with her red-mittened fist. She was wearing a long, American sheepskin coat and a floral Russian scarf. It ought to have looked ridiculous, but somehow it was charming. It was beautiful. She was beautiful.

"Yes, it's been a while," he said as casually as he could. Actually, the expression was 'too many summers, too many winters', but he had the good sense not to correct her Russian. "And I'm afraid we will be here all this winter too," he added, indicating the queue.

"Hm, it's certainly busy here this morning," she said, blithely casting an eye over the damp glut of people.

"I have a place in the coat queue," said Vadim. "You can jump in, if you'd like."

"Oh, I don't think that will be necessary," said Rachel. "Though thank you all the same. Give me your coat and bag, I think it's me who can do you a favour."

Vadim obediently handed over his things. "Follow me," said Rachel, and together they battled through the crowd to the furthest corner of the entrance-way. Here was a separate area of the cloakroom with a small sign: 'Reading Room One Only – Show Your Reader's Ticket.' Vadim had never noticed it before. He hung back while Rachel approached the counter. There was no queue at all. She swung the coats over the counter and stuffed Vadim's battered East German briefcase into the neck of her duffle-bag. An attendant approached from the dark depths of the cloakroom. "Two coats?" he said suspiciously to Rachel. "It's cold, cold, cold," explained Rachel in a much stronger American accent than usual. She rubbed her upper arms to make the point. The attendant laughed, took the two coats, put them on one hook, and handed Rachel the token. She came back over to Vadim. "Voilà," she said, showing him the token and her red ticket for Reading Room One.

"It seems you outrank me," smiled Vadim, flashing his green ticket for reading room four.

"It's not really a question of rank," said Rachel, grinning. "It's just another example of Russian hospitality."

They passed through the control point together and went up the stairs. "This is where our ways part," said Vadim. "I must go and sit with the mental midgets in Four while you commune with the grand dukes of academia in One."

"So be it," said Rachel. "Why don't we meet for lunch? I'll tell you about my promenade with the gods of learning, and you can scare me with stories from the slums."

"I'd like that," said Vadim lamely.

"See you on this corner at one o'clock, then," said Rachel. "Happy reading."

Vadim watched her go, then went cheerfully off to Reading Room Four. He had with him his exercise book and a pencil – nothing else was allowed. He stalked the hall looking for a suitable empty place, which ideally would be near a window, secluded, but with a view of the rest of the room, easy access to the dictionaries and with no neighbours on either side. But the room was crowded already, and he had to settle for the only spare place, in the middle of the room where to his left two girls were discussing a mutual friend's unsuitable choice of bridegroom, and to his right a man with a dripping grey handkerchief was sneezing at regular fifteen-second intervals.

Vadim's happy mood was already evaporating as he took his ticket to the issuing desk to get his books. He handed over his ticket and received two slim bound volumes from behind the counter; they were 'The Godless Worker' for 1931. "There should be another one," said Vadim, the disappointment crowding in on him. The librarian checked her sheaf of order slips: perhaps it was in use by another reader. "No, there is no slip here," she said. "Are you sure you ordered it?"

"Certain," said Vadim. "At the same time as these."

The girl shook her head. "Well, there is nothing here. What was the author and title?"

"Mostovsky," said Vadim. Then, sensing danger, "It was a book on cult architecture."

She riffled for a moment in her papers. "Well, the slip has gone astray somehow. Reorder the book, that's my advice."

Vadim instinctively felt that there was something ominous

in this. He went back to his desk and put down the two godless volumes. Then he went to check the reference number in the general catalogue – perhaps the mistake was his. He came to the 'M' section, but the 'Most-' drawer was in use. He stood for a moment, then prowled off impatiently around the catalogues – maybe Rachel was somewhere here. She wasn't. His mood grew blacker still. He came back to 'M' and now his drawer was free. He tugged it open and dived in. It took him only a moment to find the place but – the card was gone. The Mostovsky book had been removed from the catalogue. There was no way he would get his hands on the book now, and no point in protesting that the card had been there last month. For the librarians the catalogue was the only authority. It was as if the volume had never existed.

He went back to his seat in Four. Amazingly, the sick man had gone and the girls were quietly reading, but this was small comfort. He leafed listlessly through the old magazines, and gave himself over to his angry disappointment. What an absurd country he lived in, where library card indexes were subject to political purges, and where a thing ceased to be true if you could not prove it to be true.

He sat there whittling away the time till lunchtime, and in spite of himself he grew interested in 'The Godless Worker'. He had no idea the campaign against religion had been so virulent. In the April issues he read enthusiastic accounts of 'anti-Easter'. This festival of atheist enlightenment, organised by the Society of the Militant Godless, culminated in a mass icon-burning, a huge bonfire of art. There were cartoons showing crude caricatures of fat, bearded priests and hook-nosed rabbis filling their pockets with the offerings brought by their starving flocks. Another cartoon showed a church with a new sign nailed to the door: 'Museum of Atheism'. This was no less than a simple statement of fact: Voronikhin's Kazan Cathedral, Leningrad's Museum of Atheism, was a ten-minute walk from his father's flat. There were arresting photographs of *skoptsy* who, according to the text, were members of a weird Christian sect that practised emasculation of its male adherents. The pictures showed naked men, their sunburned peasant faces staring blankly from the page and a black absence where the genitalia should have been. The captions below were laconic: "Timofei Trifonov – mutilated at the age of 19." Even in the name of ideological struggle, no such pictures would ever have been printed in a Soviet journal of the prudish nineteen-eighties.

Vadim leafed on through the magazine. At the very bottom of the bundle, in the December issue, he found this:

A FUNNY STORY

There's this old woman whose outmoded behaviour
Has a fishily god-fearing flavour,
So she goes to say prayers at the church of the saviour.

But before she can say 'Our father in heaven',
Let alone get as far as 'forever, amen',
Before she can get off her creaking knees
She sees...

...A sight to make her eyes go pop,
Her old throat gasp, and her old jaw drop:
It's gone: there's not a church in sight!
God save us, that's fast work, all right!

Christ's church took fifty years to build,
Sweet jesus! Damned if I know why:
With a few large crates of dynamite
A church goes up in the blink of an eye!

Now the older folks might say it's sinful,
But I'm so glad I'm fit to bust:
That the old god-box came down to a binful
Of broken bricks, cement and dust.

It sat there like a huge fat mushroom,
And really didn't leave very much room,
For the builders of our Socialist state
To put up something truly great:

A proletarian palace, whose pinnacle
Will be seen by working folk worldwide.
A building to fill our hearts with pride!
Now, that's what I call a Soviet miracle!

– Demyan Bedny

Vadim was stunned by the poem. He did not know what to make
of it. On the one hand he was glad to have found something relating
to the church, on the other hand he was astonished by the loutish
tone of the verse and even more by the absence of any attempt to
invest it with poetic merit. It was a rhyme that a professional writer
ought to have been ashamed of, monumentally shoddy. Vadim
copied the words into his notebook. Then he looked to his watch –
it was five past one, and he was late for his rendezvous.

Rachel was already waiting. Vadim's good humour returned
as soon as he saw her. "I thought you had stood me up," she said.
They descended to the canteen in silence, down the narrow winding
corridor behind the cloakroom, down the dark stairs, past the
toilets, which also served as a smoking area: here, dismal nicotine
addicts wandered like shades in Hades, trying to kill the acrid stench
of old piss with their choking blue clouds of Bulgarian tobacco.

"You have to really want a cigarette to come down here for one," said Rachel.

"You have to really want lunch to eat in this canteen," said Vadim, as they turned left past the toilets and entered the windowless cafeteria. Vadim put the queue at fifteen minutes. "You didn't bring your red card, I suppose?" he asked Rachel.

"I did, but it doesn't work down here. It makes no sense, but for some reason the canteen is more democratic than the cloakroom."

"In Marxist-Leninist terms it makes perfect sense," said Vadim. "Social justice always starts from the lower depths and works its way up."

Rachel laughed. "But what if the attention of the lunching masses, most of whom belong to the oppressed castes of reading rooms two to four, were drawn to the bastion of privilege that is the cloakroom. They would rise up and demand an end to it. It's an explosive situation."

"Explosive is hardly the word," said Vadim. "It is ripe for revolution. The curious thing is: if the same unequal system operated down here as in the cloakroom, it would not occur to anybody to foment class struggle between reading room one and the rest. In dialectical terms, the situation would be a thesis without an antithesis, and no revolutionary synthesis would be possible. The moral is that a little democracy is a dangerous thing." At this point Vadim noticed a couple of disapproving looks in the queue, and fell silent.

When they had shuffled to the front of the lunch queue Vadim and Rachel both took a brace of fleshy-pink boiled frankfurters with an ochre blob of mustard and a doorstep of rye bread. They also had a glass of sweet chicory coffee each, and Vadim bought a slab of Red October chocolate. They took their food to an empty table in the high tiled hall of the canteen. The table was round and chest-high, like a bird-table, and was designed for eating lunch standing up. Vadim went and fetched two wet forks from a metal tray in the corner; there were no knives – "like in a lunatic asylum," said Rachel. They dried their forks with little triangles of napkin from a plastic beaker on the table, and tucked into their sausages. While they were eating, Vadim pushed the bar of chocolate across the table. "This is for you," he said. "For helping me out this morning."

"That is very sweet of you, thank you," said Rachel, and for the third time that lunchtime they lapsed into silence.

When they had finished eating, Rachel unwrapped the chocolate and broke off two chunks. She handed one piece to Vadim and bit off a square from the other. "What are you working on?" she asked, and took a sip of her tepid coffee.

"Oh, nothing important. Just an idea of my own." Vadim hesitated: was it wise to tell her? Would she think him odd? He looked at her, embarrassed again. But he could tell by her expression: she was not about to let him off that easily.

So, in low tones, he told her everything he knew, everything he had managed to find out since spring about the swimming pool and the site on Lenin Hills, about Vitberg and Thon and the plan for the Palace of Soviets. He also told her about that morning's deception, about the Mostovsky book and its disappearance from the catalogue. And finally he showed her the poem by Bedny in his notebook.

"Have you heard of Bedny?" he asked. "He was a well-known proletarian poet in the Twenties."

"Oh yes, I know Bedny," she said, flicking through Vadim's notes. "A sort of third-rate Mayakovsky, big mouth and small talent. It's my period, but not my field. I'm doing a thesis on the Symbolist and Acmeist poets."

"The Acmeists? Nobody knows much about them here."

"I know. That's because the Big Three are *persona non grata.* Nikolai Gumilyov was shot in 1921; Osip Mandelshtam died in the camps; Anna Akhmatova was called a whore and a nun, and they killed all her friends and lovers."

Mandelshtam and Gumilyov – Vadim knew their names and nothing more. "I know Akhmatova, of course," he said. "I like Akhmatova."

"I like her best, too. But as far as the university is concerned I am working on little-known Symbolists. Have you ever come across Annensky?"

Vadim shook his head.

"He was a professor of classics at the lycée in Tsarskoye Selo. He taught Gumilyov. Then he fell down dead at the train station, and his best book came out posthumously. The Acmeists all loved him."

"What did he die of?"

"I don't know exactly. A heart attack or something. Illness was his favourite thing – he was always writing about it. Illness, death, ennui and insomnia. Look at this."

She reached into her shoulder bag and pulled out a slim brown book – *Annensky, Selected Verse*. "They will confiscate that on the way out if they find it," said Vadim. "You are not supposed to bring your own books in."

"I know," said Rachel. "But I need my copy of the texts, with my notes on them." She opened the book. It was covered in little scribbles and underlinings in English. Vadim did not really approve of writing in books, but he liked her neat Latin hand with its very uncyrillic peaks and curls. She turned to a page that had a corner turned down – something else Vadim disapproved of. "A poem for a poem," she said, pointing to two short quatrains on the left-hand page. Vadim read the Russian:

IDYEAL

Tupye zvuki vspyshek gaza
Nad myortvoi yasnostyu golov,

I skuki chornaya zaraza
Ot pokidayemykh stolov.

I tam sredi zelenolitsykh,
Tosku privychki zataya,
Iskath na vytsvetshykh stranitsakh
Postyly rebus bytiya.

"Do you see the point of it?" she asked. Vadim said that he didn't. "Nor did I till this morning. It reads like a riddle, doesn't it? See if you can figure it out by this evening. I'm leaving the library at six. Come back on the metro with me – I've got a surprise for you."

She laughed at what must have been a very comical expression on Vadim's face. Then she took her book and the remains of the chocolate and left the canteen. Vadim remained at the empty bird table, inspecting the sludge in the bottom of his coffee glass.

It's about...

I have another confession to make. I lied. Soviet students did not apply to university in quite the way I have suggested Vadim went about it. The trip to Moscow, interview with the dean and all that, involved some poetic licence on my part. It would have been fairly unusual – though by no means impossible – for a native Leningrader to go to college in Moscow.

I said I might bend the facts from time to time – not often, just occasionally – and this is the first and most flagrant instance. I do not intend to signpost the others since, as I say, they are few and far between and of minor significance. I only broke the rules this time for the sake of a small dramatic/symbolic necessity. I needed the book to open in springtime in Leningrad, but the main action to take place in Moscow. I hope you will excuse me. As someone said – Hemingway I believe – the point of fiction is that it is truer than if it actually happened.

In Leningrad one used to be able to go on a Dostoyevsky tour of the city. The guide, sticking religiously to her immutable text, would show you the tavern where Raskolnikov heard the Napoleonic theory of murder; she would move on to the building where he took an axe to the old usuress and split her head like a melon; and in a courtyard crowded with climbing frames and higgledy-parked cars, she would point out the stone under which the assassin hid his loot.

It is interesting to note that Dostoyevsky himself was delighted when, just before *Crime and Punishment* was published, a poor student really did murder and rob an old lady in Petersburg. He read it in the paper and jumped for joy. It's not that he was callous; he was just a great stickler for genuine, verifiable detail. He thought a real-life homicide proved that the ideas in his book were right, that the murder made him a prophet. And I suppose even Hemingway – a much respected writer in the USSR, though mainly for being on rum-swigging terms with the world's cuddliest Communist – even he might agree that good fiction has to have had the opportunity of happening.

But this is my story. I am God here, and I will take any liberties I choose. You don't want a guided tour of the Soviet education system. It would be too dull for words, and anyway, that is not what this book is about.

It's about...

It's about raising things up and knocking them down.

Ideologies,

    idols,

        churches,

            reputations,

                truths,

untruths,

statues,

fictions,

hopes,

loves,

lives.

It's about the people who raise them up, and about those who knock them down.

Six o'clock sharp they met at the same spot at the top of the stairs. They passed through the control booth, and Vadim waited at a distance while Rachel collected the coats. He saw her share some joke with the cloakroom attendant, and she was still laughing when she came back to him.

"It's your lucky day," she said. "That nice babushka has sewn a new tab in your old coat." They dressed and went out onto the street. It was dark now, and great cottony flakes of snow were descending in languid spirals. The falling flakes were a jaundiced yellow under the halogen streetlights, but this did not lessen the soothing effect. Pale snow covered the flagstones, softened the sharp corners of the library steps, and even seemed to muffle the sound of traffic.

"How lovely," said Rachel in English. "Let's go for a walk."

"If you like," said Vadim. "Where to?"

"Let's go and have a look at your church."

They set off downhill along the last stretch of Prospekt Marksa. The high classical façade of Pashkov House, the old library building, was perched on the steep Borovitsky Hill to their right and the red-walled Kremlin lay like a curled and sleeping dragon in the wooded hollow to their left.

"Would it have been visible from here?" asked Rachel.

"Oh yes, I think so," said Vadim. "From here the dome would

have shown high above the buildings on Volkhonka. It was a huge building, as much of a landmark as the Kremlin." They crossed the busy intersection, where traffic flowed through the square and onto the Great Stone Bridge like water through a sluice. They walked slowly up the tranquil Volkhonka past the columns of the Pushkin Museum of Fine Arts.

At the top of Volkhonka, outside Kropotkinskaya metro, a lady was selling cabbage pasties from a churn. Rachel bought four and they ate two each. She remembered the chocolate in her bag and they ate that too. Then they crossed over the road and from the western side they entered the secluded park around the Moskva swimming pool.

The park was dark, but the swimming pool itself was awash in a bright white glare from high floodlights. Clouds of steam rose off the warm surface and dissolved the falling snow. The pool was full of people: older citizens ploughed up and down in straight lines, and the young ones splashed about noisily and aimlessly. All were wearing red and yellow bathing caps, which from a distance made them look strangely unhuman.

Rachel watched fascinated, and Vadim watched Rachel. The floodlights shone on the wet surface of her eyes and threw her features into sharp relief. "I think this is the weirdest thing I have ever seen," she said. "It is like walking through a forest and stumbling upon a bunch of aliens having a wild party."

"It's a witches' sabbath organised by the Soviet state committee on sports," said Vadim. He expected her to laugh, but to his delight and alarm she took his gloved hand in hers.

"Look, Vadim," she said seriously, "Are you sure you should be pursuing this Cathedral thing? Is it worth the risk?"

"What risk? I've done nothing illegal. I'm just interested in the history of the city, that's all."

"Vadim, we haven't known each other long but I think we already know each other too well for that. This is a forbidden subject, and what you are doing could be construed as anti-Soviet."

"I don't think it is anti-Soviet."

"In the end it's not your opinion that counts, is it? You are risking your university career for this. If it is no more than a hobby you should give it up now."

"I'm training to be a journalist. If a preoccupation with finding out the truth disqualifies me for that profession, then perhaps I am better off without my university career."

"All right. No need to get pompous about it." Rachel said no more, but she kept hold of Vadim's hand. At length he made an attempt to change the subject.

"You said something about a surprise?"

She sighed deeply, then turned and smiled at him. "Yes, but I thought about it this afternoon, and I think it is going to be harder to set up than I first realised. Come round to my room later on – it's 727 left-side – and I think your surprise will be ready."

He asked no more. They walked and talked for a while longer and then went back to the metro. He pointed out the walls and columns of the platform, lined with marble taken from the cathedral, and they headed back to MGU. The train did not stop at Lenin Hills – clearly the station was going to be closed for a long time. Rachel told Vadim that she had heard the closure was due to a crack in the bridge. It was found to be dangerous for two trains to be standing at the platform at one time. "And this is supposed to one of the marvels of Soviet engineering," he said. "A showpiece of the metrobuilders' art."

When they reached the privacy of V Zone's courtyard they chatted for a while and arranged that Vadim would come round to her at half-past nine. Just as a precaution, they entered the building separately.

☆

I, like my hero Vadim, am a newspaperman by profession, so let me tell you, a work of fiction is in many ways so much easier than journalism. Imaginary people are more amenable than real ones. Not once, for example, has any of the characters in this book said to me, "Don't quote me on that," or "I must see the copy before it goes to press," or "You realise everything I said here today was strictly off the record." None has slapped a libel suit on me and none of them ever will, though I have altered the words in their mouths a dozen times since I first wrote them down.

Newspapers are a frantic waste of time by comparison. When you go to interview someone for a news story, you usually know in advance exactly what you need them to say. The art of interviewing is getting them to say it, even if they don't want to. Two good lines usually constitute more than enough material for any kind of story bar the celebrity profile, but to win those two sentences you usually have to ask dozens of camouflage questions. Your interviewee talks useless dross, but you must pretend you are writing it all down, while racking your brains for new and cunning ways of eliciting the response you need, and being careful not to put him on his guard.

Even then you have to take what you get: say, for example, you are doing a story on how Lenin's tomb is to be closed to the public and the honour guard removed. Boris Yeltsin triumphantly issued such a decree on 6th October 1993, two days after he saved his skin by shelling his old friends to jelly in the parliament building. Everybody is doing the mausoleum story in the same way on the same day ("In a symbolic move that will mark a final break with Russia's communist past, President Boris Yeltsin yesterday..."), so you are looking for an angle. With luck and ingenuity, you find a young lad in the Separate Presidential Regiment, formerly the KGB uniform division, who was due to do his first turn on guard at the mausoleum the very afternoon 'Post No.1' was abolished. His boots shine like mirrors, his uniform is pressed, he has practised the goosestep till his thighs ache; his parents and grandparents and cousins have come from Siberia to see him stamp ritually across the square and stamp back again one hour later.

All this is good stuff, now all you need is for him to say: "All my life I have dreamed of standing guard over Lenin, and suddenly it has been snatched away from me. It's heartbreaking – I'll never be able to show my face in my native village of Bolotnoye again." Brilliant. Except that try-as-you-might all you can squeeze out of him is: "It's a personal disappointment, but I daresay the president knows best." Working in a foreign country gives you some extra latitude: a good many quotes can be improved by being passed through the filter of an imaginative translation, and it's not as if the boy will ever see it. You do what you can:

> …Aleksei Ivanov, 19, was dumbstruck when he heard the news while polishing his buttons in the Kremlin barracks. "It's a bitter disappointment for me," he said. "I hope the president knows what he is doing…"

Do you like the note of menace in the second half of the quote? Masterly, that. But such hard work. Fiction is a dream by comparison. Nobody thinks a good line is any the worse for being uttered by a fictional personage. Ask any writer. No-one in real life ever said "Some animals are more equal than others," and no-one said "Mediocrities always flock together, only individuals seek the truth." But if that is the line you want, you just scribble it down without anybody's say-so. Such freedom.

Now some people might say that reporters do not have the right to exploit their sources and deceive their readers in the way I have just described. But this is to miss the point. As a reporter you do not write for the public, you give no thought to the idea that your words are read by tens of thousands, even millions, of strangers. You write with one person in mind, and only one person: your immediate boss, the news editor in London. You buy him off with words, like the princes of Muscovy bought off the Mongol khans with gold. You pander to his foibles and cut your cloth to his taste. No-one else matters, least of all the readership – they can't sack you. But as long as the news editor is kept happy, your livelihood, your little fiefdom, is safe.

You learn to think of your paper as a kind of insatiable monster. All you need worry about is feeding the beast, throwing it a bone that will keep it quiet for a day, a week. When its stomach starts rumbling and it starts growling for more, you make sure that you have another juicy off-cut ready in your sack. As long as you can satisfy its hunger the beast will leave you alone. You can spend your days drinking, sleeping, ski-ing, picking your nose – any way you please, so long as there is raw chunk of something for it to wrap its great jaws around come feeding time.

But sometimes the beast gets picky, and not just any bone will do. It roars FRONT-PAGE SCOOP (they really say that) and you have to find one. You start thinking up stories that would be good scoops if they were true, which is essentially the same creative process as writing fiction, except that once you have come up with a scenario you have to go and scrabble about in the rubbish tip of the real world for enough facts and quotes to stand your inventions up. You turn desperately to your Potential Scoop File, a sort of deep-freeze for choice cuts. Is there something here you can thaw out before deadline? What about this, a local speciality: "Yeltsin has a month to live, he's on dialysis and his liver is shot." Maybe, but it is an outrageous flyer, only to be used in a real emergency (this is an emergency, dammit!).

Or this: During the cold war the KGB amassed a huge stack

of *kompromat* against the British royal family: pictures, tapes, operational reports, to be used to destabilise British society when the revolutionary moment was right. They have, among other treasures, photographs of Prince Philip sowing his pre-marital oats – all of them stolen from Stephen Ward's flat after his suicide.

Or this: In the run-up to the 1992 American presidential election, the Democratic Party bought Bill Clinton's KGB file from a black market source inside the organisation, thereby averting any embarrassing disclosures about the future president's mysterious student trip to the USSR.

These last two are pure fantasy, naturally. Even if they were true (which, of course, they are not), they would be practically impossible to pin down – no Western hack has contacts that good. How about a spectacular stunt, then? They always go down well. You could join a band of desperadoes smuggling plutonium across the old Soviet border to Pakistan – no, it would take too long to get the goods. Or here's another one: for less than the price of a set of winter tyres you could go and buy a SAM-14 ground-to-air missile at Rizhsky Rynok, Moscow's biggest flea market…

You get no further, because the beast roars again. It wants to know what's on the menu, so you tell it some fairytale to buy time, to get its digestive juices flowing. Now the pressure is really on. Once you have promised a particular dish you have to deliver, because the beast hates to be disappointed and will have your balls for cocktail nibbles. Your deadline looms and you cobble something together. You flesh it out and puff it up and stuff it with rumour and supposition. You smother your creation in a thick verbal sauce, hoping that the beast will not taste the ingredients that are lacking: solid facts, unmassaged truths, real events.

Today you are lucky. The beast swallows your peppery concoction, belches loudly and stomps off to somebody else's patch. You live to write another day. Of course you found the whole thing distasteful. You know the story was a joke, but you have a mortgage and you just booked your holiday. You know too that the beast is under pressure from bigger beasts, muscled corporate beasts who are fighting tooth and claw for a fatter chunk of a shrinking market. So you choose to watch your own back, because nobody else will. You are a mere footsoldier in an eternal circulation war, and you do not want to become its second casualty.

Vadim tapped lightly on 727. When Rachel opened the door he was surprised and somewhat disappointed to see Andrew the Englishman sitting on her bed in the left-hand blok. He glanced to the right-hand blok, and saw that the glass door was tight shut.

Rachel must have read his face. "It's all right, I don't have a room-mate," she said. "And Andrew is here to help us."

She ushered him into the blok and shut the door. "*Privyet* – hello," said Vadim, and shook Andrew's hand.

"*Privyet*," replied the Englishman. Vadim was again struck by his unpleasant accent. The strangely aspirated English p-sound, like a surreptitious fart, made him wince. Rachel had a foreign accent too, but it did not send a shiver up his spine like Andrew's.

He sat down on the bed next to the foreigner, and Rachel took a chair opposite the pair of them. There was a pause, like they were waiting for someone to formally open the meeting.

"I told Andrew about your research."

Vadim jumped up, as if he had been prodded with a needle.

"It's OK, it's OK," said Rachel, taking him by the wrist and tugging him back down. "Andrew is a friend and he is completely trustworthy, aren't you, Andrew." Andrew nodded.

"The thing is," continued Rachel, "Between us I am sure we can get you that book in the Leninka."

Vadim put his annoyance on ice. "How?"

"Easy, really. We just order it in the normal way. But not in your Reading Room Four, in Reading Room One."

"What difference does it make? If they deny its existence in four, why should they produce it in one?"

Rachel leaned forward. "It makes all the difference in the world, silly Vadim. For all your clever jokes about the Soviet class system you don't get it at all, do you. It's another world in Reading Room One. I've seen people there reading Bukharin, Zhivago, even Orwell. The rules you are used to don't apply. And so long as they have that red ticket, it makes no difference whether it is an American student or a Soviet academician who makes the application, because the first category is beyond salvation and the second is beyond sin. As for your book, no-one has burned it or torn it up. It is still in the stacks, and they will produce it if someone asks for it."

"But there is no way the duty librarian will ever let me past the door. Not unless I can convince her I am the youngest professor in the history of Moscow University."

Rachel exploded with laughter. "You're not thinking, Vadik," she said, rapping him on the forehead with her knuckles. "Obviously you can't pass for a prof, but with a change of clothing you could easily be a Westerner."

"We are about the same size and build," put in Andrew. "I'd be happy to lend you a pair of jeans and a shirt."

"This is the plan, then," said Rachel. "Andrew lends you some clothes to make you look convincingly foreign. You two go to the library and just march into Reading Room One with Andrew saying something to you in English. No-one will bat an eyelid – the worst that could happen is you get shushed by the librarian. She never actually checks readers' tickets – in theory there is no reason to, because every reader is happy with his station in life."

"Like Huxley's gammas and deltas," said Andrew.

"To be on the safe side, you keep Andrew's ticket conspicuously on the desk," Rachel continued. "The element of risk is tiny."

Vadim went through the plan for hitches. He could not think of any. "Who is actually going to order the book?" he asked.

"Me," said Rachel. "And this is the best bit: I have already ordered it for tomorrow."

Vadim's jaw dropped open, and Andrew looked a bit taken aback too.

"How did you do that?" asked Vadim. "You don't even know the full title."

Rachel clapped her hands in glee at their confusion. "I do too," she said. "I saw it in your notebook this lunchtime." Then she went serious. "Vadim, they will be on to you soon. Everything that happens in the library gets noted and reported – why do you think they record the times that people arrive and leave? The KGB has probably already been informed that you applied for prohibited literature. Once their machinery gets into motion you will be under suspicion, and under surveillance too. It won't take more than a few days. If you want to know what is in that book, you have to move fast."

Vadim saw that she was right, and suddenly he was afraid. He asked himself what would it say about him if he pursued his quest: that he was a man of unbending principle, or just an idiot? It was possible, he supposed, that the Cathedral was a foolish obsession, a habit that he had to find the sense to kick. But it was just as likely that the proper, grown-up thing to do was to pursue his research and spit on the consequences.

"I suspect that it was a mistake that that card was still in the catalogue," Rachel was saying. "It probably should have been removed years ago. You drew attention to the error, but you pointed the finger at yourself by so doing. But it's not too late. If you don't want to take it further I can just hand the book in tomorrow and there's an end to it. Any trouble you have already brought on yourself already will blow over if you keep your head down for a bit."

"No, don't do that, don't return the book" he said. That settled it, then. The prospect that the book might slip between his fingers had convinced him. It would be unscholarly and downright cowardly to turn back now that he had encountered an obstacle. If you can't pull the barge, don't act like a drayhorse.

"What time shall we meet?" he asked.

"Come to my room tomorrow at ten," said Andrew, standing up. "It's 721, just down the corridor. You can get changed there, and we will catch the train together."

"I'll see you both inside," said Rachel.

Andrew made to leave. In the doorway he turned round: "Just tell me this, Vadim. Why are you so interested in the church? What does it mean to you?"

Vadim felt he owed Andrew an answer since he was being kind enough to help him. "I just want to know what happened there," he said. "It would be nice just once to have the unadorned truth for its own sake, and that is all."

"But why the church?"

Vadim did not know what to say. He was not sure he knew how the church had cast such a spell over him. But it was something to do with the thick smog of hypocrisy that surrounded the building and made it invisible. The vilification of Thon and his work touched a deep moral nerve inside him. He hated the casual assumption that Thon was no good, and the craven way that all the commentators hid behind the authority of Herzen. He had a growing sense of mission, a knowledge that the story of the church went to the heart of something important – something important about himself as well as about the church and the system. "All I can tell you is this," he said to Andrew. "Certain people have been badly done by, and I would like to make a contribution to setting it straight."

"Do you think you might write an article on it," Andrew persisted. "The university newspaper might be interested. Part of the story involves this site, after all."

Now Vadim laughed. "No, I don't think that will ever be possible," he said. "If I ever write anything at all it will be strictly for the desk drawer, as the expression goes."

"I see," said Andrew, pensively. "Well, till tomorrow then." And he left the room.

"So then, my grail knight," said Rachel, when the door was closed, "Would you like a cup of coffee?"

Vadim was wrong.

There was nothing casual about the posthumous treatment of Thon. The architectural ideologues who wrote his name out of the official histories knew exactly what they were doing and why.

As far as they were concerned he was a guilty man, guilty by association with Nikolai, the arch-tyrant, the archetypal hard-faced tsar. As far as the Soviet critics were concerned, Thon was Nikolai's lapdog, which made him an easy target certainly, but also meant that he deserved everything he got. Anything associated with Nikolai, however remotely, was naturally bad. (Soviet guidebooks even went to the childish lengths of insisting that the statue of Nikolai outside St. Isaac's cathedral in Leningrad is a really poor piece of sculpture.)

Thon's main service for his royal master, apart from his own concrete contributions to the two capitals, was to produce an album of church designs, which Nikolai then made compulsory for all new churches throughout the Empire. No-one knows what Thon himself made of this edict – one would like to think he was embarrassed by it. Because what it meant was that no-one was allowed to express his own religious sensibility in the design of a place of worship. It meant that the state was symbolically claiming the right to control everything, even the souls of the Russian people.

Thon's designs were the only ones allowed, but naturally some churches in far-flung places slipped through the net of conformity. One such was built in the city of Vyatka. It was a charming church dedicated to the Tsar-Saint Alexander Nevsky. It was built in a kind of imposing Romantic manner (classicism had gone out of fashion with the death of the lamented Alexander). It had a large central cupola resting on a high drum consisting of a series of slim neo-Gothic spikes, like a circular Anglo-Norman picket fence. The whole structure made the shape of a Celtic cross. It was a fine piece of work – and the architect was none other than Alexander Vitberg, who here in exile finally became a temple-builder. But he did not live to see it completed, and now of course it is gone.

Nikolai would have hated Vitberg's strange spiky church, and naturally so did the Bolsheviks who knocked it down. The fact is: the two regimes, Nikolai's autocracy and the Soviet dictatorship, have an awful lot in common. Lenin and his successors managed to control souls to a degree that Nikolai could only dream of; and Nikolai, with his energy and his ruthless attention to detail, would have made a fine revolutionary if he had been born on the other side of the divide. The destruction of the physical traces of Nikolai's regime – Thon's works among other things – was a veiled admission of the kinship between them. It was a kind of psychological denial. (Vadim is beginning to prod at this sore spot in the Soviet psyche, and that is bound to provoke an angry reaction sooner or later.) But as the Ukrainian proverb has it: *Necha na zerkalo penyat koli rozha kriva*: 'Don't blame the mirror for your own ugly mug.'

Rachel plugged in a dinky little electric kettle that she had brought with her from America. It appeared to be made of plastic, and Vadim wondered that it didn't melt when the water boiled. He voiced this thought, much to Rachel's amusement. Her coffee was also Western: crunchy, dark little granules in a glass jar that, like all Rachel's possessions, was beautifully designed and just right for its function. It was the sort of useful jar Aunt Ira hoarded like gold; in fact, with its screw-top and elegant lines it would have been the prize piece in her collection.

While Rachel mixed the coffee in glass tumblers, Vadim took the time to inspect her room. The furniture was naturally the same as his, the same as everybody's in MGU. She had done her best to endow the room with some character: the walls were hung with a colourful set of prints of Bakst's costume designs for *Narcisse*. Some cushions and a knitted bedspread made her cot more like a couch. Pot plants on the windowsill disguised the insulation gap between the double windows. This foot-wide strip of windowsill served as a cold box for her milk and butter, which she kept in a bag on a string, ready to be drawn up through the ventilation window when she wanted them. Vadim was impressed that she knew such tricks of hostel life. On the table were a slim electric typewriter and a neat row of writing instruments. The tall glass-fronted escritoire was neatly divided into library and larder. On the upper shelf were her texts: the thick, blue-bound *Biblioteka Poeta* edition of Akhmatova; Mandelshtam from the same blue series, but very slender next to the Akhmatova, like a gulag inmate beside a hefty Russian babushka; there was the brown Annensky that Vadim had seen in the Leninka that morning; no Gumilyov, of course – if she had a Western edition of his verse she would surely have more sense than to keep it on an open shelf. Next to these Soviet books were a row of Western

critical works and a stack of photocopies. Then there were several
thick bundles of lined cards held together with elastic bands. Vadim
could see from where he was sitting that the top line of the top card
was inscribed with a line of poetry in Russian, below which were
scribbles in English. The line read: "I drink to my home, my ruined
home…"; he knew that was from Akhmatova, and he realised what
he was looking at: Rachel had a card index in which every poem by
her authors was separately represented – she was certainly thorough,
no doubt about that.

Rachel handed Vadim a glass of coffee, then reached for a bottle
of cognac and two teacups. She poured the drink and they clinked
cups.

"Here's to you," said Vadim.

"Here's to success," replied Rachel.

They took a sip and smacked their lips in unison.

Then, with a sudden rush of bravado, he asked the question that
had been bothering him since he first met Rachel.

"You and Andrew," he said, "are you… going out?"

Rachel feigned wide-eyed affront. "No, we're not…" – she
paused in mockery of the question – "…going out."

Vadim looked to his feet.

"Why is he helping me get the Mostovsky book?"

"Because I asked him and he's crazy about me, so you were kind
of half-right. I knew he would help once he knew what you were up
to. He thinks he knows what this obsession of yours is about." She
paused and sipped her coffee, "He thinks you are looking for God."

Vadim spluttered. "Looking for God? I don't even believe in
God."

"Yes," she said firmly. "You're looking for God. Andrew is a
Christian, you see. He spends all his spare time at the Baptist church
or in clandestine prayer meetings with his believer friends. He
thinks this fetish for a dead cathedral is your heathen way of groping

towards salvation. Your upbringing will not allow you to just go to church like a normal person – you are a Jew with an atheistic education behind you, which is a double handicap from Andrew's standpoint. So you have sublimated all your God-longing into an apparently secular task of research. But God has got his claws in you, Andrew says, and you are doomed to be saved whether you like it or not. He just wants to help you as you toddle down that Damascus road – and if he can wheedle his way into my good books at the same time, so much the better."

Vadim did not know whether to feel flattered or insulted, and his confusion set Rachel chuckling at him again. She poured some more cognac and they clinked teacups.

"To us," she said, still giggling.

"To us," and he drained his glass, Russian-style.

Her face went suddenly sombre. It was the second time that day she had effected one of these startling changes of mood, and Vadim was beginning to find it a bit disconcerting.

"Have you thought about that poem I showed you?" she asked.

"A little," he said,

"Did you manage to decipher it?"

"No, no I haven't. Is it important?"

She did not reply, but poured another round. They clinked and drank without a toast. She was breathing deeply, as if she was feeling ill, or else plucking up courage for something. "When you are in the library tomorrow I want you to remember one thing," she said. "Whatever it is you are looking for, you will not find it there. Andrew is right about that much."

Vadim did not know what she meant, but the alcohol was spreading warmly and numbingly through his limbs and he did not feel inclined to spoil the sensation by asking. "I'll remember that," was all he said.

They drank a little more, after which Vadim stood up to go.

Rachel stood up too and announced in Russian: "*Naklyukalas* – I'm plastered." It was such a slangy turn of phrase for a foreigner to use that Vadim had to laugh, and laughing they fell into each other's arms. Vadim kissed Rachel's mouth. The delicious contact sobered him in an instant, and immediately he thought that perhaps he had overstepped the mark, that he had ruined their still fragile friendship. He let go of her and blushed shamefacedly. But she did not seem about to slap his face. She smiled her smile, the one that had twice sent him into a spin, and said, "Go now. It's a bad omen to celebrate the victory before the battle." She stroked his left cheek with the knuckles of her right hand. To Vadim it seemed a beguiling gesture; he drifted out of the door and back to his monkish cell on the tenth floor.

January 1838

Konstantin Thon was a down-to-earth sort of man, so he was not overly concerned by the inauspicious start to the works. Accidents happen on building sites. It is part of the job.

From a purely professional point of view, Thon could not help but regret the unavoidable loss of the pretty little Church of the Transfiguration in the monastery grounds. It was a perfect gem. Its stubby little twin steeples were unique in Moscow, and he grew rather fond of them during the surveying works (every day the nuns and priests in their sinister black robes had eyed him from afar like he was the very devil). He had come to think of those two tapering hexagonal cones as God's salt and pepper pot.

He knew too that poor old Vitberg was upset by the deconsecration of his site. Alexander Lavrentievich, however fanatically devoted to his own design, must have understood that this was the last nail in the coffin for his cathedral. Thon would have felt more sympathy for Vitberg had his predecessor not expended so much energy on scorning his, Thon's, work. Despite the Swede's present disgrace, he still had influential friends, people that Thon would have preferred not to have ranged against him. Vitberg's bilious attitude was undignified and unbecoming.

But what falls from the cart is gone forever. Thon's work was for the greater glory of God, too; they both served the same cause, albeit under the patronage of different emperors. As for the monastery, Nikolai himself had chosen the site, which was undoubtedly the best of all the alternatives. Some 307,000 roubles – he recalled the figure even now – had been spent on buying up the land on which the monastery stood, and the holy community had been provided with a new site out to the north-east of the city at Krasnoye Selo, so no-one had been deprived of a spiritual home, still less of the roof over their head. He was certain that the Cassandras and doom-mongers would find something else to wail over.

All of which made the events of the first week of work that much more unfortunate. It had been like the material expression of a general mood of dark foreboding. Partly he blamed himself: he should never have allowed the crowd to gather and watch the dismantling of the church. But he had thought that they would very soon get bored and leave his workmen in peace, so he did not insist that the police take any measures to keep the populace at bay. So it happened that on the first day a sizeable crowd gathered to see the gold crosses removed from the two steeples. They craned their necks at the man atop the steeple, gasping and cooing as if he were a circus acrobat and not a common labourer. It might be that the presence of the gawpers distracted the climber – he could give no coherent explanation of how the accident came about – but the result was that he dropped the heavy cross. It fell to the ground and smashed like a china dinner plate. A thousand shards of gold were scattered across the churchyard.

It was a bad augury. And naturally the symbolism of the occurrence did not escape the crowd, who wept and wailed as if it were the Crucifixion itself they were witnessing. Far from quieting the salon soothsayers and the holy fools, the incident set them chattering with renewed enthusiasm. The broken cross from the Church of the Transfiguration was the prattle of all Moscow by the end of the day. Some said the evicted nuns had laid a curse on Thon's project – and the architect would hardly have been surprised if it were true. Others whispered the ancient name of the little patch of high ground where the nunnery stood – *Chertolye*, Devil's Acre. Well, if it was devils they wanted, these chattering idiots, they were welcome: the Devil take the lot of them.

After that incident, Thon gave orders that no bystanders were to be allowed inside the monastery grounds until the demolition work was completed. So at least no outsiders were present when the same man fell to his death from the same roof later in the week. Thon saw to it that his family were provided for, and everybody was put on strict instructions not to go spreading the bad news.

Konstantin Andreyevich was no longer the lanky young man he had been in Italy. Those sunny days seemed far behind him. He was still very much a don juan, but he was also a professor of the Academy of Arts, a position that brought with it financial security and a place in society, which he relished but sometimes found restricting. His respectable status seemed to have aged him, though he was only forty-four. His curly hair, still thick, was now mostly grey and he wore it short. He had grown stocky on big dinners, and though it suited his long frame to be well-covered, he had lost the hungry air that had so entranced the wives and daughters of his fellow-expatriates in Rome.

Rome, how he missed it! This project seemed such a burden when he thought of Italy. He knew he had committed himself to a lifetime's labour with Christ the Cathedral. Dear God, he would probably not even live to see it finished! In Rome he never committed himself to anything more serious than a light supper and a hand of whist. Now he had to plan decades ahead, he had to bend every thought to fulfilling the Emperor's will as regards this fatal church. All his life he had wanted to build, and now he was building himself a prison.

The first meeting with Nikolai had gone well. Thon had been summoned to Moscow soon after he was awarded the job. He had hastily packed a bag, made a roll of all the plans he could find, and set off for the old capital. The audience took place in the Emperor's apartments in the Kremlin. Thon showed His Majesty the plans, and told him who he had in mind to do the sculptures. They discussed materials: white marble from Protopopovo for the outside, the same as Vitberg had planned to use. For the interior, dark green labrador with a silver veining – it was recently discovered near Kiev and no-one had yet used it in a building; deep red porphyry from Shokshi; also jasper, and three Italian marbles – blue Bordiglio, yellow Siena, red-speckled Porto Santo – and a night-black marble from Belgium. The Emperor had looked long and hard at the plans, frowning. He complained that the drawings gave him no idea of the scale of the building. It is forty-eight and one half *sazhens* to the top of the cross, said Thon, but the Emperor just tutted in annoyance. I don't want numbers, he said, numbers don't mean anything. So as Nikolai looked over his shoulder Thon drew a human figure, like a toy soldier on the steps of the cathedral. Nikolai beamed. That's more like it, he said.

Thon had made a mental note always to include a figure in the plans henceforth, but Nikolai was ahead of him. The following week an imperial decree was published in the *St. Petersburg Chronicle* "that all who draw architectural plans or façades should henceforth depict thereon a human figure standing on the line of the horizontal, that the figure be proportionate to the scale of the plans, and that the height of the figure be fixed at two *arshin* eight *vershok*, in such wise as to render possible an informed judgement as to the height of the edifice portrayed..." Thon read the decree in amazement. How characteristic of Nikolai, he thought. He discovers the draughtsman's practice of *staffage*, and instead of just giving it his approval he turns it into a law for the whole of Russia. God preserve us from pedantic emperors!

December 1982

Vadim felt ill at ease in Andrew's clothes, but not half as uncomfortable as he felt sitting in the hushed forum of Reading Room One.

So far the plan had gone perfectly. Vadim reported to Andrew's room on the seventh floor at 10 o'clock. He was hoping to see Rachel, but Andrew said she had already gone ahead to the library. His book was waiting: she had phoned first thing to say so. Vadim's disguise was laid out on the bed: Levi's, lumberjack shirt, Birmingham University sweatshirt. Vadim felt that the sweatshirt was over-egging the pudding a little, and was moreover just the sort of item that might lead some friendly soul to strike up a conversation in the reading room. Andrew saw the wisdom of this, and they exchanged the sweatshirt for a patterned ski-jumper. Once he was dressed it became clear that his shoes gave the whole game away: the imitation leather uppers of his short brown boots were cracked and peeling; no Soviet citizen could fail to recognise them for what they were: they had 'Romanian light industry' written all over them. Andrew lent him a spare pair of shoes and with these adjustments the disguise was convincing enough. Vadim wore his own coat over the borrowed outfit so as to arouse the minimum of suspicion while they were still inside the hostel. But there was nothing he could do to disguise the jeans that poked out from beneath his overcoat, still less the smart English shoes, which were much too light for the Russian winter. They scurried as fast as they could out of the building, Vadim praying to God that they did not encounter anyone he knew, particularly Lena or Galya or one of the many village gossips of V zone. He had not even told Hussein about the scheme.

But they encountered no acquaintances, and the rest had come off easily. There was just one tricky moment when, already coatless, Vadim had to present his green ticket at the control point and collect a chitty. They had overlooked this point: the bright jumper caught the eye of the lady in the booth, who looked up and gasped in admiration of the clothing, and at the impertinence of the undergraduate who would wear such finery to the library. Vadim hurried up the stairs before she thought to ask him any questions.

Now Vadim was seated in the farthest corner of Reading Room One. His toes were still aching cold from the wait for the bus at MGU, and Andrew's shoes had turned out on longer wear to be a shade too small: his feet were killing him. Andrew was at the next desk, working away on some old newspapers, but Rachel was nowhere to be seen. Vadim drew fidgety doodles in the virgin A4 ring-bound pad that Andrew had kindly presented him with as a finishing touch to his disguise and as a sort of good-luck gift. He felt increasingly conspicuous in his idleness, and had the illusion that the attention of everybody in the room was fixed on him.

Where was Rachel? Vadim could sit still no longer. He stood up and took a walk around the room. On the shelves nearest him were the classics of Marxism-Leninism: endless tomes of Lenin's Collected Works, *Das Kapital*, the official committee-written histories of the Party, the Revolution, and the Great Patriotic War; there was the Brezhnev hagiography that Mark had bought, his memoirs and a long pamphlet section with his speeches. Vadim wandered over to the dictionary section, where three very chic Italian girls were poring over a volume of the *Great Soviet Encyclopaedia*. Vadim could not help but mark their beautiful clothes, flashier than anything Rachel would wear: all were in colourful cashmere jumpers and unseasonably short black skirts. The sight of them made Vadim feel less of a sore thumb in his outfit. In this corner of the reading room most eyes were on the Italians as they bent over the thick red book. He passed by the girls and went to the next shelf, where there was a complete set of the *Encyclopaedia Britannica*. In spite of what Rachel had told him, he was surprised to see such a heretical thing on open shelves – it was like going to the Vatican library and finding the complete works of the Marquis de Sade.

Vadim had an idea. He reached down Volume 22 – he wanted to look up Stalin. The books were packed too tight and the whole bookcase rocked unsteadily when he tugged the book out. It was the 1958 edition; Vadim opened the book and was immediately attracted to the paper, transparent as gauze and so thin that the elegant, curvilinear Latin letters seemed almost to protrude from the page, like Braille. He turned to the entry for Stalin, but could not find it. He double-checked, but no, after Stalactite came Stambulov. Hold on though: the page numbers went straight from 300 to 305, and the Stalactite article ended in mid-sentence. So there were certain ideological limits even in Reading Room One, or there had been in 1958.

Suddenly there was a mighty crash from his left. The Italians were squeaking with alarm and embarrassment: one girl clung to the bookcase and held a red tome over her head like a shield. The other two were rushing to pick up the half a dozen volumes of the *Soviet Encyclopaedia* that lay strewn on the floor. That bookcase was also shaky, it seemed: the girl had pulled down a volume and nearly brought down the whole stack with it. Vadim wondered what would be the safest thing to do – go and help them or slink off. The dilemma was solved for him by a whisper in his ear.

"Don't worry about them, good knight," said the voice. "The grail quest takes precedence over all considerations of chivalry."

"Rachel, where have you been?"

"I was in the catalogues," she said. "I kept an eye out for you, but I must have missed you somehow. But don't waste any more time, the book is on your desk."

They left the Italians to the wrath of the librarian, who was trotting over from the other side of the room, and went back to Vadim's seat. Vadim wondered whether he should say something to Rachel about their drunken embrace of the previous evening. Perhaps she was regretting it? But Andrew was still there, engrossed in his papers. Vadim did not want to broach the subject within earshot of him.

"I'll leave you to it," said Rachel when Vadim was sat down. "I'm around and about. We'll meet up at closing time so I can hand the book in. See you later." She kissed her index finger and planted it on his lips, then turned on her heel and left him alone. He took a minute to savour the warm glow of her affection – so it was no mistake, after all – then he opened the old book at the title page and began to read.

Where Sits The Pheasant

Red were the flaming
Berries of rowan.
Leaves were still falling
When I was born.

Hundreds of bickering
Church bells chimed.
It was a Sabbath day:
John the Divine.

Still I remember
The time and the place.
Hot was the rowan,
And bitter its taste.

– Marina Tsvetayeva, 1916 (from *Moscow Verses*)

December 1982

Vadim sat in reading room one for five days. It took him that long to copy the key passages into his own notebook. No-one questioned his presence, and he spoke to no-one but Rachel and Andrew.

The book contained more information about the Cathedral of Christ the Saviour than he could have hoped to amass in a lifetime. Every icon and painting was described and expounded upon, every corner of the building explored and annotated.

There was a lengthy account of the technical aspects of the construction, and these details too Vadim scrupulously copied down. The dimensions of the Cathedral were noted according to the old pre-revolutionary system of measurements and the very words, half-forgotten or never encountered by him, thrilled Vadim's sense of history. He referred to the *Great Soviet Encyclopaedia* behind him to learn that a *vershok* is 4.45 centimetres, an *arshin* 71 centimetres, and a *sazhen* two metres thirteen centimetres, that a *pood* is a little over 16 kilogrammes and a *zolotnik* 4.27 grammes; he turned to the *Encyclopaedia Britannica* for an explanation of an inch and a foot – twelve of the first in the second, why twelve exactly? – and of an ounce and a pound – sixteen! why not stick with twelve? The Western imperial terms rubbed shoulders on the page with the traditional Russian ones, and were sometimes encountered in the same sentence. He found this rattle-bag of weights and measures utterly charming, much more fun than the regular decimal rows and columns of the metric system.

The book also contained unexpected details about how the construction work was budgeted, how much the bricks cost per thousand, how much the various artists and sculptors received for their work. The total sum was noted with pedantic precision. The Cathedral of Christ the Saviour, Vadim learned, cost Russia fifteen million one hundred and twenty-three thousand one hundred and sixty-three roubles eighty-nine kopecks. He could find no mention in the accounts of voluntary donations. Perhaps the stories of how all Russia contributed to the construction of the church were no more than legend.

Each evening after work in the library Vadim went to see Rachel in her room and tell her what he had learned. She told him about her own studies, they talked about the poetry, and she gave him the slim blue Mandelshtam to read. Vadim was intrigued to find the poet writing about church buildings such as Hagia Sophia and

Notre-Dame:

Like Adam new in Eden, stretched nerves and sinews splaying,
A flexion of the muscles in its slender criss-cross vault.

Rachel told him about her life in America, and he told her about his family in Leningrad. She had never been there, so they agreed to go up together for his birthday in the spring.

On the fifth evening, after Rachel handed the Mostovsky book in, they got off the bus early and took a stroll through the university park down to the balustrade on the brow of the hill.

"All this would have been a far more beautiful sight in Vitberg's times," said Vadim as they looked down. "There was a restaurant here before the Revolution. People used to come up just for the view. Luzhniki was a big, empty, green sack until quite recently – almost until they built all that for the Olympics."

Below them the concrete oval of the Luzhniki stadium nestled in the great loop of the river. It was hemmed in by low-rise *khrushchevki*, but now it was dark and all they could see was hundreds of little rectangles of light in uncurtained windows. Amid these electric galaxies there were bright constellations of factory lights, orange streetlamps, car headlights moving like creeping comets through the moonless industrial cosmos.

"I think I prefer it this way," said Rachel. "I think big cities are beautiful at night."

They remained there until they were both chilled to the bone, and came back to the hostel arm in arm. They parted while still out of sight of the V Zone gates – a habitual precaution. "I'll go upstairs first," said Rachel. "Come by when you are out of your boots. I have some stew in the fridge." Vadim kissed her, and watched as she picked her way through the impacted snow to the gatepost. He waited five minutes, till he could stand the cold no more, and went on in after her.

There was a surprise awaiting him when he stepped out of the lift at the tenth floor. It was a new *stengazeta* consisting entirely of poems typed from the works of Marina Tsvetayeva. It hung next to the board that recorded the results of the Socialist Competition Between Floors. The *stengazeta* consisted of nine short lyrics and three smudged photographs of the poet and her family. At the top of the sheet was a biographical note clearly composed by a student – surely not Lena? – which dared to record the fact that Tsvetayeva had committed suicide on returning to the Soviet Union.

Vadim had a sudden rush of shame at his own ignorance. He had heard of Tsvetayeva of course, and he knew that some people rated her even more highly than Akhmatova, but he had never seen a single verse of hers. He found her very different from Akhmatova, whose verse was hard and flawless as a cut diamond. These poems were nervous, self-conscious, lacking Akhmatova's ladylike self-assurance.

Vadim drank in the poetry. Between each poem he involuntarily glanced left and right (what did Mark call it – the dissident twitch?). Then he ran back down the corridor to his room, fearful that some student committee might have the poster removed before he had the chance to copy it out. He grabbed an exercise book and dashed back to Tsvetayeva. By the time he reached the *stengazeta*, two other students had had the same idea: the three young men stood at the wall in silence, carefully transcribing the words into their separate notebooks.

"You took your time," said Rachel, when Vadim arrived at her room.

"I was held up," he said, and told her about the Tsvetayeva *stengazeta*. He had brought his notebook with him, along with a bottle of champagne that he had bought as a thank you for the library adventure. As Vadim opened the bottle, Rachel flicked through the poems.

"Look at this," she said to Vadim, pointing out a couple of quatrains from an untitled poem:

I miss my Russian home:
It's my eternal malady.
And now it's all the same to me
In which land I am all alone.

I crave my native tongue,
I long to hear its honeyed call.
And I do not care at all
What others speak when I am dumb.

"Poor woman," said Rachel. "It was killing her to be away, and it killed her outright to come back."

"It's a very Russian death," said Vadim. "Russians wither like cut flowers when they are away from the soil, even the sophisticated ones like Tsvetayeva. That's why exile is always seen as such a dreadful punishment for a Russian writer."

"What would happen to you if you left Russia?" asked Rachel.

Something in her voice made Vadim weigh his answer. "I think I'd be all right," he said thoughtfully. "I don't think I am attached to the country like that. But then I am not a Russian, am I? I am a Jew. You know the Stalinist codeword for Jews – 'rootless cosmopolitan' – I think I could put down roots anywhere."

"That's good," said Rachel. " That's a good way to be. Though as it happens all the Jews I know here are twice as Russian as the Slavs. Now, as my Jewish grandmother would say, let's eat."

"I'd like to meet your grandmother."

"I hope you will, Vadim. In fact I am sure you will one day. Now you stay here – it would not do for you to be seen in the Westerners' kitchen."

Rachel went to the communal kitchen at the end of the corridor, and came back with the stew, locking the door behind her. When they had finished the champagne Rachel produced an identical bottle, which she too had bought to celebrate the success of the plan. They had just popped the cork on it when the sanitary commission came knocking on her door. Rachel and Vadim kept silent, and after rattling the handle the komsomol hygiene posse went off to poke about in someone else's life.

Rachel and Vadim stayed together that night. There was no discussion beforehand and no big decision, just an insurmountable reluctance to say goodnight. He did not admit it to Rachel, but it was Vadim's first experience. At sixteen he had made up his mind not to sleep with anyone he was not in love with, and in the event had never been tempted to. The bed was narrow, and for comfort they slept curved into each other's bodies: two parallel lines like the sign of Aquarius.

In the morning they took great care that Vadim was not seen leaving Rachel's room. When he got back to his blok Hussein was in the shower. As soon as he emerged he came to the door of Vadim's room in his towel, dripping on the threshold.

"Where have you been?" he asked.

"Never you mind."

Hussein flushed. "Sorry. I didn't mean to pry. It is just that the sanitary commission was here last night, and I think you and I might be in a bit of trouble. "

"Why, what did they say?"

"Oh, the usual. They burst in like the pimpled gestapo and decreed that your desk is untidy and that it is about time we dusted the lightshades. They said they would give our blok a three out of five and carpet us at the student council unless we bucked our ideas up."

"Dear me, they are getting busy." Vadim was in too good a mood to let some stuffy committee spoil it. "They must have raided the whole zone last night."

Hussein's face fell. "No. On this floor they just did us. Do you mean to say they came to... did you see them yesterday too?"

Vadim did not reply.

"It's worse than I thought then," said Hussein, drawing his own conclusions from Vadim's silence.

"Let's not talk in here," he said at length. "It's a chilly morning, let's go and have some porridge in the canteen."

It was still early and they had no trouble finding an empty table in the V Zone cafeteria. Vadim suddenly felt in need of some sound and friendly advice. Over a bowl of oaten kasha and a cube of omelette Vadim told Hussein the whole story of his investigation into the cathedral and how it had brought him to Reading Room One. He found a delicate way of letting his friend in on the serious turn his relationship with Rachel had taken. Hussein listened without interrupting, merely shaking his head in disbelief at Vadim's folly.

"So," sighed Hussein, summing up Vadim's account, "you have been secretly amassing anti-Soviet propaganda of a religious nature; you have used illegal and deceitful means to achieve your aim; you have enlisted the aid of foreigners, citizens of imperialist states that are hostile to the Soviet way of life, and with one of these individuals you have formed an intimate personal attachment."

"Leave her out of it," said Vadim angrily. "There's no law against having foreign friends."

"Listen, you idiot," hissed Hussein, so that Vadim would lower his voice. "There doesn't need to be a law against it. The most important rules aren't written down, you know that. In the eyes of the..." He lowered his voice to a whisper. "In the eyes of the KGB every Western student in MGU is a potential spy or a provocateur. If your chum Andrew hangs out with Baptists they will be on to him for sure. You have pushed your luck, and now they may be on to you. For God's sake, Vadim, your career is at risk at the very least. They might try to blackmail you; they might pressurise your family; they could find ways to use your feelings for Rachel against you, to make you work for them; or they could just lock you up. You know all this, so why are you being so dumb?"

"We have been very cautious."

"Not cautious enough, obviously. In the first place, your Rachel is right: you were a marked man from the moment you ordered that book on your own ticket. And I would be very surprised if they failed to notice your presence in Reading Room One. If they let you get away with it, that can only mean they are biding their time. Secondly, the seventh floor is swarming with informers. It is enough for you to be seen walking down the corridor where the Westerners live for your name to find its way onto a list. And in any case you spent an evening at Kakha's in the company of foreigners. I doubt that birthday party went unreported."

Vadim raised his eyebrows. "Who?"

"Kakha is a typical Georgian," said Hussein. "He will forgive a pretty woman anything."

Vadim wanted to say something, but Hussein went on:

"Alla informs. Her special technique is taking American lovers. She pumps Americans for information, as it were. She does it for the fun of it, but she is not averse to passing on anything she learns. In return her contacts use their influence with the faculty to get them to turn a blind eye to her appalling grades. But she is playing a double game. She hopes that one of these days one of her foreign boyfriends will fall for her and whisk her away to the West."

Vadim was right about her then. He had nearly asked if the *stukach* was Galya and he was glad Hussein had offered an explanation before he had managed it. Galya was not the informer type, anyway. She was a zealot, but she was too simple-minded to be a traitor to anybody.

"Then there is Galya," said Hussein. Vadim jumped, caught red-handed in the act of an ungenerous thought. "She tells me you already have a reputation in *zhurfak* for being too clever by half. What with one thing and another your recent behaviour will have set alarm bells ringing all over the Lubyanka."

"Galya tells you the *zhurfak* gossip?" asked Vadim.

Hussein smiled coyly. "There are no secrets between us now – not any."

Vadim's raised an eyebrow. "You mean you two...?" He did not need to finish the question. The smug look on Hussein's face was his answer.

I have nothing against Galya, I think she's sweet. But Vadim's first impression of her was quite right: she was none too bright. He was wrong to look down on her though, since she had a good heart (as he is soon to find out) and her ignorance was not her own fault. A tendency to believe what she was told was her only intellectual vice. If she had been told the truth, or, better still, taught to question, she might have been able to overcome the worst effects of her limited wits; as it was, she plodded through her education by cramming her head with colossal amounts of mostly tendentious information, none of which improved her brain in the slightest.

Of course she knew she was no genius, so she worked hard. It was sheer slog that had got her into Moscow University, and sheer slog would see her through to graduation. She compensated for her mediocre gifts by throwing herself into the work of the komsomol, where she was a highly valued activist. This was where her real talents lay: she was terrifically good at organising the less enthusiastic, getting them to turn up to meetings, enlisting them to draw posters, pay their subs, turn out on frosty Saturday mornings to clear snow for the *subbotnik*. On one such morning a sleepy and cynical lad, resentful of having been bullied out of his warm bed at eight-thirty, had said to her, "You should have been born a boy, Galya, the Soviet Army needs officers like you." She knew the remark was intended as a sneer, but that only made it all the more precious to her since it could not be dismissed as flattery. She thought it was the best compliment anyone had ever paid her.

She had unfailing antennae for unsoviet heresy – her education had given her that much – and she felt them twitching at Kakha's party as soon as Vadim started singing underground songs. Giya's approving mention of Jesus Christ had also set her squirming, just a bit.

She considered it her duty as a komsomol member to say something when the first song ended, particularly since there were foreigners present. She was rather annoyed at Alla for not backing her up, since she should have known better. The subsequent exchange confirmed her fears about Vadim, whom she liked. She did not want to see him come unstuck.

Three or four years after the events described here, Galya was lucky enough to be included in an exchange group to Britain. She was put forward because of her sterling work for the komsomol and she passed a board that probed her 'political literacy', precisely the quality Vadim lacked. She joined a group of twelve similar types, plus a senior lecturer from *zhurfak* and two KGB men. They spent a week as the guests of Nottingham University.

Their host, a lecturer in the industrial economy department, had been to the USSR the previous year, where he had been shown round model factories and special schools. He had met specially selected students and no others. He had found it all most frustrating, and he determined that there would be no Potemkin villages on his leg of the exchange. He took the Soviets to Balloon Woods and Hyson Green, notorious council ghettos both. He pointed out the drunks and the prostitutes; he talked about crime figures, and the riots on the Alfreton Road and the brutal miners' strike. (Brits and Sovs got noisily drunk together in the hospitality room of Burton's Brewery at the end of a tour of the plant when the Russians, after politely quaffing a complementary couple of halfs of lager, spontaneously and prestidigitously produced bottles of vodka, hunks of black bread, and dried fish with the texture of coconut matting from the pockets of their new suits.)

The English lecturer thought, or hoped, that the Russians would appreciate the honesty of his warts-and-all approach. His method was like shooting an arrow at a target in a strong crosswind: he thought it would be dishonest to take the wind into account and he aimed for the bullseye regardless, believing that the visitors would see what he was up to and respect his intention. But Galya and most of her companions missed the point completely: they sincerely thought that what they saw was the best Britain had to offer: the best housing, the best conditions, the best beer. The experience merely confirmed all the silly propaganda they had heard about the misery of life for most ordinary people in the West. The evidence of their eyes led them deeper into error.

Yet at the same time, what Galya saw in Nottingham in 1986 was all true: the people they met in Balloon Woods and Hyson Green were genuinely desperate (they were hellish places, those estates; they have been knocked down now, thank God). All the same, truth's arrow flew wide of the mark.

But who was lying, and where was the lie?

☆

In spite of the disquieting signs, or rather because of them, Vadim and Rachel wanted to spend the day together. Vadim already felt a fatalistic calm descending on him. He knew that trouble was not far away. He had known before Hussein had articulated it for him, but he saw no gain in trying to sidestep the inevitable.

He waited for her at lunchtime outside the library. It was a bright day and the temperature had risen to a couple of degrees above zero. The snow underfoot, which had packed to a solid grey crust on the pavement over the past days, was now crumbly and soft. A treacherous sheen of water lay on top.

Rachel emerged in her funny Russian scarf and bounded down the steps to where Vadim stood. She threw her arms round his neck and kissed him. "I'm starving," she said. "Let's get some *pelmeny*."

They crossed Prospekt Marksa to the little *pelmennaya* under the Kremlin wall. The cafe was hot and steamy, like a Russian bath. They took a portion each of the little meat-filled doughballs. They drank sweet, milky coffee dished up by the ladleful from a metal urn. Rachel tried to ignore the dark brown scum that floated on top; Vadim confessed he had never noticed it.

"Where shall we go?" asked Rachel when they emerged refreshed onto the street.

"A museum?" suggested Vadim.

"No, it is too nice a day. Let's stay outdoors."

"I know then. I will take you to meet the survivors."

"The who?"

"The mute witnesses. You'll see, come on."

They crossed back over the road and caught a trolleybus. Vadim dropped eight kopecks in the perspex honesty box and tore off two tickets. "My treat," he said. The bus clicked and whirred and hummed electrically as it bowled over the Stone Bridge, then

proceeded up Dimitrov Street. Rachel pointed out the residence of
the French Ambassador. It was a little fantasy house in glazed red-
brown brick with whitestone piping. Colourful ceramic tiles were
set into the brickwork. The roof was a steep *shatyor*, like the blade
of a chisel. "What a lovely building," said Rachel. "It looks like a
gingerbread cottage."

"That is late Russian revival or early *moderne*," said Vadim.
"When we go to Leningrad you should ask my father about it. The
turn of the century is his period."

"It's my period too," said Rachel thoughtfully.

They got off two stops short of Gagarin Square.

"There is a monastery near here," said Rachel.

"The Don Monastery," said Vadim. "That is where we are
going."

They walked down Stasova Street. There was a huge humming
factory complex on their left, but straight ahead was a pinkish bell-
tower astride the gates to the walled monastery.

"It looks like a shrunken Kremlin," said Rachel.

"That's just what it is," said Vadim. All the Moscow monasteries
were fortresses. They functioned as lookout posts, and as somewhere
for the people to hide from Mongol raids."

"Early-warning stations and bomb shelters."

"Exactly."

"Is this a working monastery?"

Vadim laughed. "There are working churches, but no working
monasteries. The monk is an extinct species in Russia. This is a
museum."

"Are they all museums?"

"Most of the extant ones are. The Ivanovsky Monastery was a
KGB dungeon in the Thirties, and now it's just an empty building.
Lots were knocked down, like the Chudov and the Voznesensky
Monasteries inside the Kremlin. The Voznesensky was a gem – it

was all white and brittle, like carved ice."

"They destroyed monasteries inside the Kremlin? I thought the Kremlin was sacred."

"Not at all. They cleared away several churches and palaces within the Kremlin walls."

"How many monasteries were there in Moscow before the Revolution?"

"I don't know. Dozens. I only know some of the names. The Strastnoi Monastery, where the Rossiya cinema is now on Gorky Street, went the same year as Christ the Cathedral; the Simonov Monastery, where Thon built a bell-tower, is now a football pitch."

"Your Thon knocked down an ancient monastery, so you told me."

"Yes, but not for the sake of it. He was a builder, not a destroyer."

"How many churches were knocked down after the revolution?"

"No-one is counting, but in Moscow most of them. Moscow was known as the city of forty-times-forty churches. The cityscape was one of the wonders of the world. Golden-headed Moscow they called it, because of all the hundreds of gilt domes."

"That is a nice one." They had passed through the open gate of the Don Monastery, and were now standing before the main cathedral. It was the same faded red as the monastery walls, and it had the traditional five onion domes, graphite-grey and bulging. Away to the right, at the edge of an extensive graveyard, was the lesser cathedral. It was clearly older, and its cupola rested on a pyramid of *kokoshniki*, like a collage in aces of spades, or a tapering peacock's tail.

They made their way between the two churches, crunching through the crystallised snow and occasionally pausing to look at the headstones. Fat crows cawed and smaller birds twitted in the branches of the bare piebald birch trees. They came to the far wall, where three massive friezes and a few equally large marble figures were fixed with concrete into a row of shallow alcoves.

"This is what I wanted to show you," said Vadim.

"What are they?"

"They are all that is left of Christ the Cathedral. Three of Loganovsky's high-reliefs plus a couple of odds and ends."

"How did they get here?"

"I don't know. They say there are survivors in any massacre."

Rachel approached the first frieze. Each of the figures was about nine feet tall. A warrior-king, Dmitri Donskoi, stooped bareheaded before the bearded figure of Sergei Radonezhsky who held an icon aloft in an act of benefaction. Donskoi's captains were gathered behind him, bedecked in chainmail and armed to the teeth with spears and long-stocked axes. They were mirrored by the smaller band of hooded priests and monks who stood behind Radonezhsky. Rachel noticed that the some fingers were missing from Donskoi's hand; just the metal core of the sculpture poked through.

The second piece showed David returning triumphant with the head of Goliath. At the centre of the composition was David in a knee-length shift. To his left were grim warriors carrying the trophies of war: Goliath's breastplate and helmet. To his right a jubilant crowd waited to greet the boy hero. David himself was a winsome, almost girlish character. He seemed detached from the excitement, as if he would rather be off composing a psalm somewhere.

Next was a lonely figure of a warrior. The plaque said his name was Georgy and he was in an awkward sitting position. Then another Biblical scene: Abraham, returning with the defeated kings in irons, is met by Melchizedek. Two camels in the background seemed to smirk ironically at how the mighty were fallen. "They are very dramatic," said Rachel. "Old Georgy there looks like he is about to fall off his bar-stool."

"Yes, he does look uncomfortable," said Vadim. "He would have been mounted over one of the doorways, perched on the doorjamb.

They were all high up. They were designed to be admired from far below, which I think is why so many of the figures are looking down, why they all seem about to fall flat on their faces."

Rachel went up close to the sculptures and ran her fingers across the arm of a crouching figure by Abraham's side. The marble was rough and pitted, as if it was slowly melting away like the grubby snow underfoot. She looked up at one of the chained kings. His blank eyes gazed back at her, and there was pain and contempt in his face. "Have you come to mock us?" the face said. "Why don't you leave us in peace?"

She turned her face from his blind reproach and looked down the row of giants along the wall. Vadim was right, at least half of them were staring down at her. She shivered. "I hate the eyes on statues," she said. "They're spooky. They always look like they have cataracts or something."

"I know what you mean," said Vadim.

"Let's go," she said. "I'm getting cold."

A chill rain began to fall. The winter sun was already low in the west, but the sky was clear to the east, beyond the thick cemetery walls. Rachel saw a rainbow.

"Look at that," she said to Vadim.

"Why do they say there are seven colours in a rainbow?" he said. "I can only see six."

"Nonsense," said Rachel. She switched to English. "Red, orange, yellow, green, blue, indigo, violet; Richard of York gained battle in vain."

"In Russian we say: 'Every hunter desires to know where sits the pheasant'," said Vadim. "All the same, I maintain the last two are the same. I only see one colour after blue."

"That just shows how unobservant you are."

"Not at all. If you just looked at the rainbow as if you had never seen one or heard of one before, you would see that there are only six colours."

"Like Adam in the garden of Eden," said Rachel.

"Exactly," said Vadim.

They left the monastery and made their way back to Leninsky Prospekt. They ran for a bus and got lucky: they hopped onto the 111 to the university just as the doors were closing. Two well-dressed young men behind them were less fortunate. They raced to the bus, but the doors closed in their faces. One of them punched the bus in frustration, and when it pulled away the bus sprayed the pair of them with mud and slush. Rather unkindly, Vadim and Rachel laughed as they took their seats at the back. "They were in a terrible hurry," said Vadim.

"Anyone who gets that uptight about a bus deserves to miss it," said Rachel. "It's God's way of telling you to lighten up a bit."

The rain was turning to wet snow. It settled on the window of the bus and slid down to the bottom in great translucent gobs. The window began to steam up, and Rachel periodically rubbed a spyhole with her gloved hand.

"Do you want to hear a poem?" said Vadim.

"Is this your usual thing," she said. "To take a girl on a date to a cemetery and read her poems on the way home?" Vadim didn't know what to say – he couldn't tell whether the remark was a joke or a reproach, and he was so completely lost in love that he could not bear to do anything to displease her. His confusion must have shown in his face, because Rachel now threw her arms round him and kissed him. "Sorry, my darling," she said, tucking her head into his shoulder. "Yes, give me a poem."

He spoke the verses in an easy, conversational tone.

"The fields are shorn, and bare the woodlands,
Fog and damp rise from the rill.
There behind the blueing mountains

The sun rolls down, a silent wheel.

The rutted road is gently slumbering,
It seems to sense the truth today:
It knows the greybeard winter's coming
Is just a trice, a trice away.

And yesterday I saw it too:
Beside a fogbound, chattering hedge
That yearling colt, the redhead moon,
Was harnessed to our little sledge."

"Yesenin."

"Yes," he said.

"Meteorologically it was spot on. But a mite rustic for our present situation. By no stretch of the imagination is an Ikarus bus a little sledge."

"Oh, I don't know. Moscow is just a glorified village, after all. Nothing happens here but everyone hears about it."

Rachel squeezed his hand. They did not speak for a while. The poem had made them both feel a little melancholy.

"Are you busy tonight?" asked Rachel as the bus approached the university.

"No, of course not. Do you want to do something?"

"You introduced me to your friends; I'd like to introduce you to mine. In town."

"That would be nice."

"Be ready at seven, then. Snow boots on and earflaps down."

The bus stopped. She jumped off without a kiss or a smile or another word and left him sitting there alone.

History, they say, repeats itself. But in Russia, history does not so much repeat itself as anticipate itself. It is full of portents, precedents, shots across the bows and dry runs. For as long as there has been a Russia, the country has had this talent for predicting its own fates and misfortunes.

In the Dark Ages, reports reached the Rus-men of terrifying horsemen, sallow riders in chainmail who descended like lightning on the villages of the distant east and carried away the cattle and the women. But the raids stopped as abruptly as they had started, and distressing though the rumours were, they were soon forgotten in the heartland of the north and west, in Pskov and Kiev, Vladimir and Novgorod.

Russia had its warning when the Mongols first struck, but chose to ignore it. The horsemen of Tartary returned within a generation, and this time they were an unstoppable horde. They swept across Russia like the wind, putting entire cities to the torch and demanding tribute from the defeated peoples of Rus. They imposed a yoke that lasted for nigh on four hundred years, and left an indelible mark on the Slavs, on their language, their culture, and through generations of intermarriage on the very faces of the Russian people: the high cheekbones and broad features that signal the archetypal Russian are the physiognomical legacy of those warriors from the wastelands before Cathay.

Sometimes the pre-echoes are straightforward and literal. The uprising of 1905, Lenin wrote, was the dress rehearsal for the successful revolution of 1917. Because Lenin said it, the remark has become a cliche. But like a great many cliches it is true: 1905 was indeed the dress rehearsal. There are plenty of examples: Khrushchev's Thaw prefigured perestroika, that glorious springtime of Russian history; the little coup of August 1991 was just a curtain-raiser for the real event, the bloodbath in October 1993; and so on.

Other times the presentiments are more abstruse, more poetic, as if a kind of historical synchronicity were at work. Take Russia before the Tartar yoke, when the Russians were still basically a Viking people. The old Scandanavian word 'rus' or 'ros' means blond, and is a distant etymological cousin of the English 'russet' and, ultimately, of the word 'red'. So when Western cold warriors dubbed the Soviets 'reds', they were actually using a title that the Russian people had borne for a thousand years. (The modern Russian word for red used to mean 'beautiful'; ruddiness and pulchritude were closely linked in the Slavic mind long before the colour acquired political associations. 'Red Square' is not ideological. The name is misunderstood by Russians and mistranslated by foreigners: it means simply 'Beautiful Square'.)

And consider the murder of the Romanov family at the Ipatiev House in Ekaterinburg, 1918. It was an insignificant crime in the context of the bloody Civil War – a mere eleven people in a mass grave – but this unhappy event prefigured the exterminations of 1937. The regicide in Siberia was a deliberate transgression, a kind of original sin of Bolshevism that made all the subsequent horrors easy. Once you have blown a hole in a tsar's head and bayonetted a clutch of squealing grand duchesses, shooting peasants and workers by the truckload is no problem at all. The taboos are gone.

When the bodies of the Romanovs were discovered, I was sent to Ekaterinburg to report on it. I visited the site of the grave from which they had only recently been exhumed. I for one would be glad to be laid to rest in such a place. The open pit was in a quiet forest clearing ten miles or so north-west of the city. Tall, straight birches stood like sentries around the spot. A few paces away was a sunny, open glade where the strawgrass was knee-high. A stream ran downhill from the forest to the east, into the pit, and then out across the marshy glade. The empty grave was full of crystal-clear water. A few yards away, someone had erected a fifteen-foot-high cross made of birch logs. The cross was hurriedly nailed together; its proportions were all wrong and it was too heavy for the soft ground where it had been planted. It was leaning precariously to one side, and doubtless fell over soon after.

The Romanov grave was a serene and beautiful place; the same cannot be said of the place of their execution. The plot once occupied by the house of the merchant Ipatiev was a very sorry sight. It was a wide, uneven expanse of wasteland, like an old bombsite. Stray dogs scavenged hopelessly amid the dead trees and the rubble. There was a white-painted cross, more pleasing to the eye than the one at the grave, and a concrete slab nearby marked the site of the lower room where the shooting took place. Before the Revolution the street on which the house stood used to be called Voznesensky Prospekt, which means Ascension Avenue. The seventeenth-century Church of the Ascension is just a few hundred yards away, up a steep hill opposite the house. No doubt the family often listened to its bells (they could not see it: the windows of their prison were whitewashed). The new regime renamed it Karl Liebknecht Street in honour of the German revolutionary lynched by a Berlin mob a few months after the Romanovs met their end. The Soviet street-name bore a message for those with ears to hear: 'Don't mourn the tsar,' it said. 'We Bolsheviks have our martyrs too.'

Russian history sometimes anticipates itself in ways that are downright mystical. The Romanov dynasty was born in the Ipatiev Monastery near Kostroma, where the sixteen-year-old Mikhail Romanov was proclaimed tsar in 1613. He descended twenty-three steps from his apartments on the second floor to claim the crown. Nikolai, the last tsar, ruled for twenty-three years, and met his end in a house also called Ipatiev. On the night they died, the tsar's family was led down to the basement room on the pretext that they would be safer there as the Whites were shelling the city. The winding staircase they took on that last short walk consisted of twenty-three steps.

As for the Ipatiev House itself: the little mansion survived the Civil War, collectivisation, and the German invasion. It stood until 1977, when the local party boss, a certain Boris Yeltsin, bulldozed it on orders from Moscow. It was done swiftly in the early morning. Nobody had any chance to object. Here too, in a strange way, history was anticipating itself, for sixteen years later he merrily smashed another symbolic building, the White House in Moscow, as a matter of political expediency.

There are differences, of course. For one thing, Yeltsin repented of knocking down the tsar's house, and now the pious post-Soviet authorities have replaced it with – what else? – a magnificent expiatory church. For another, the White House was destroyed by tanks, not bulldozers. Yet the point is that Yeltsin in October 1993 did not worry his head about the rights and wrongs of demolishing buildings, because he had been there before. The taboos were gone. A house is a house is a house. And what is a tank, but a bulldozer in jackboots?

So Yeltsin's obliteration of the Romanov golgotha foreshadows his role in the October tragedy. October 1993 also marked the end of the Soviet period, two years after the country officially ended its existence. This shift is possible in Russia, for as Akhmatova once remarked in a poem, the calendar dates are often strangely out of synch with the deep tick-tock of history. The clogged heart of the Soviet Union could continue to beat for some time after its death certificate was signed.

By the same logic, the terminal illness of the Soviet autocracy began not with Gorbachev, but earlier. The Bolshevik Empire was doomed from the moment Brezhnev's coffin hit the hard bedrock of Red Square like a steam-hammer, and sent invisible cracks radiating to every corner of the Soviet world.

April 1838

By the time the last of the snows had melted, the old monastery was gone. The site on the embankment was as clean and empty as a freshly wiped blackboard.

Thon stood arms akimbo in the middle of the vast empty space, feeling like Peter the Great on the Gulf of Finland. A gaggle of surveyors and junior architects hovered respectfully behind him. In the northern corner of the plateau, gangs of navvies, stripped to the waist in the springtime sun but still in their shapeless fur hats, were carting away crumbly pyramids of earth on wooden stretchers.

"Tell me about the ground," said Thon. The chief surveyor, a small, stooping man, scurried up to his side. A hamster in a frockcoat, thought Thon, and smiled to himself.

"We have sunk three wells at varying points, as you can see," began the little man. With a sweep of the hand he indicated the three covered protuberances on the otherwise clear plane of the building site. "The depth of the wells is seventeen and one half, twelve and one half, and ten and one half arshins, their profundity diminishing in respect of their proximity to the river. An examination of the material removed from the pits allows the following analysis..." The hamster licked a finger and flicked through the pages of a large ledger he had been holding under his arm. "...the topsoil extends to a depth of two and one half arshins, where it gives way to dark sand; this stratum is six arshins deep; below this two arshins of light grit, then three arshins of yellow sand; at a depth of fourteen arshins from the surface of the deepest, northernmost well we struck hard gravel with..."

"Can I build my church on it?" interrupted Thon. He was staring at a point in the middle distance, as if he was studying the interior walls of a temple yet invisible.

The surveyor closed his ledger. "Yes, Konstantin Andreyevich. I believe the site is suitable for such a structure."

"You believe?" Thon turned on him. "This is not a question of faith, man. I need to know for sure. Will it stand or not?"

The rest of the party shrank back, afraid of being stung by the master's wrath, but enjoying the spectacle. The surveyor gripped his ledger like a shield in front of his chest. "Yes, of course," he cried. "There is no doubt of it."

"I'll not have a repeat of the Vitberg fiasco."

"You shan't have, Konstantin Andreyevich, I assure you. The ground will bear it, I can promise you that."

Thon's temper subsided as suddenly as it had flared. He returned to the meditative state he was in before. One or two of the junior architects dared to puff their cheeks or exchange a smile behind his back.

"Good," said Thon. "Let's get cracking."

Work proceeded at a fantastic rate that summer. Dozens of gangs of labourers toiled like Hebrew slaves to strip away the earth and sand and lay the bedrock bare. Once they got down to serious work the crowds of onlookers evaporated, since there was nothing to see beyond the stockade but armies of sweat-streaked men in a deepening pit.

The absence of sightseers was a blessing, since there was no telling what doomladen significance they would have put on the several discoveries made in the early stages of work. Some workmen had been digging a trench near where the refectory had stood. They had reached a depth of three arshins, so even standing at their full height they could not see out of the pit. At this level they began to turn up human bones with the sod. This was strange, for there was no record of any necropolis on the site. Some of the skeletons were in coffins, some not. Many had icons in their arms. More likely than not they were dead of the plague of 1771. The fact that some were coffinless suggested that they were buried in a hurry, before their carcasses could spread the infection. One of the foremen was foolhardy enough to voice this thought in the presence of the diggers, who immediately began to whine that they did not want to work on pestilential ground and asked to be moved to other work. But Thon would have none of it. Both for disciplinary reasons and to limit the potential for rumour-mongering, he had the same brigade keep digging till they found all the remains, and he set the blabbermouth foreman to see that they did it. At six arshins they came upon another, older cemetery. There were no bones, just the remains of coffins, but the find was all the more malevolent for that: who buries empty coffins?

The following week there was another bizarre unearthing. A navvie in a pit near the dismantled church struck brick. He thought he had come on part of the church's foundations and he went at the brick with a long iron rod. Three labourers chipped away for an hour, then in an instant they vanished, swallowed up by the ground. It transpired that the brick was the vault of a tunnel running north-east, parallel with the river towards the Kremlin, and the three labourers had fallen through the roof. They were unhurt. The site foreman had lamps lowered to them so that they could explore the tunnel further. It came to a dead end in a heap of earth and rubble fifty yards to the east, and no other trace of it was found in the course of the foundation dig. Who built the tunnel, for what purpose, and where ultimately it led, they never knew.

By the end of July 1838, 11,000 cubic arshins of earth had been removed, and the pit was in places nineteen arshins deep. The sides of the pit rose like a sheer cliff and the labourers beetled about on the bottom like ants in a soup tureen. It was time to begin work on the foundations.

Quarry-stone was shipped in from the village of Grigorievo

outside Moscow. This was the same stone Vitberg had intended
for the foundation of his church; as with the Protopopovo marble,
Thon borrowed his predecessor's research and made it work. The
stone was laid in large slabs layer by layer, starting from the deepest
corner of the pit. Each layer was levelled off, then saturated with
lime, which was allowed to set solid before the next was put down.
And so on, layer after layer throughout the rest of the year. By the end
of 1838 all the deep crags and hollows had been filled and the level
of the foundations had been raised one arshin above the shallowest
point of the pit. It was one featureless surface, like the face of the
earth at the height of Noah's flood, but solid, impenetrable.

Meanwhile, the symbols of dedication were removed from the
old site on Sparrow Hills to the Uspensky Cathedral in the Kremlin,
pending the laying of the foundation stone at the new site. This was
the bitterest of blows for Vitberg, who in his exile was following the
progress of the new cathedral with masochistic relish.

At the end of 1838 drainage to the river was installed, and the
following year the stone platform was raised another seven arshins.
On this vast immovable dish the first bricks were laid. The walls of
what would become the vaulted crypt broke the flat symmetry of the
rock-and-lime plane.

Thon promised Nikolai that the foundation ceremony would
take place before the end of the decade. He kept his word with five
months to spare. The ritual took place on 10th September, 1839, and
was no less grand than the previous occasion. Nikolai's procession
marched from the Uspensky Cathedral, past the Senate, through
the Nikolsky gates, across Red Square, which, according to one
contemporary account, "was like unto a great Church, wherein a
hallowed offering was being made, under the cupola of the very
heavens..." The procession then moved down to the embankment
at the easternmost corner of the Kremlin, turned right along
embankment, then right again at the Alexandrovsky Gardens, and

down Volkhonka to the site of the foundations.

By this time the site was taking shape. It was still a hole in the ground, but now it was a cruciform hole, its brick fringe following the line of the angles and recesses of the still-to-be church. A ramp led down into the pit on the west side and extended across the site to a covered pavilion, like a seaside pier, in the east wing. Under this pavilion the ceremony was performed. An inscribed gold cross was placed in the stone brought down from Sparrow Hills. Two slabs of Protopopovo marble bearing the names of the Emperor and the Empress were placed on top. Also buried at the site were a number of coins including thirty *poluimperials*, or golden five-rouble pieces.

The metropolitan Filaret made a speech designed to dispel the air of malediction that still hung over the project, and which had been stirred up afresh when the site on the Hills was deconsecrated. Filaret turned to Biblical precedent to make his point:

"There is in certain matters of import a special divine Providence, whereby the sublime thought is vouchsafed to one of the elect, but the honour of the deed is given unto another. Thus did David, in gratitude to God for the sanction of his reign, conceive a Temple, to be built in Jerusalem. It was a grand conception, born of one prophet and approved by another. But neither prophet foresaw the providential will before it was upon them. God appointed Solomon executor of David's plan. Likewise did the blessed Alexander, thankful to God for the salvation of his kingdom, desire to build a Cathedral to Christ the Saviour in his capital, which was consumed by fire for the redemption of Russia, but which rose again from the ashes. The thought was proclaimed abroad, and the Holy Church gave it its blessing. You alone, Nikolai, were at your brother's side in that hour; and now we see that even then the Almighty had ordained that the sacred covenant entered into by your brother be fulfilled by your own imperial hand."

☆

December 1982

Rachel called in on Vadim at quarter past seven. He was dressed and waiting. She held a bottle of wine and a cake box tied up with paper string.

"What's the cake?" asked Vadim.

"Chocolate. I forget what it's called."

"Prague?"

"That's the one."

They went and stood at the lift.

"Why do they call a chocolate cake 'Prague'?" asked Rachel.

"Why do they call processed cheese 'Friendship'? Why do they call cigarettes 'Cosmos'? Why do they call a small loaf 'Urban'? Why do they…"

"All right, I get the idea."

The lift pinged to a halt. It was empty.

"Do you remember when we got on the bus this afternoon?" asked Rachel on the way down.

"Yes," said Vadim. "What of it?"

"Those two men who just missed it. I think they were following us."

The lift stopped at the third floor and two people got in, so they could not continue the conversation. Once on the ground floor, Vadim and Rachel hurried through the central zone, swished through the great revolving doors past the smoking militiamen and out into the cold night air. The snow had not stopped since the afternoon, and the temperature was dropping. The ground was again as white and crisp as a freshly made bed. They stood on the steps, away from the revolving door – out of earshot of any passers-by.

"There's no proof," said Vadim. "It might have been no more than it seemed: two men in a hurry."

"But I am pretty sure they were in the monastery too. Did they look like the monastery type to you? And anyway there's something else. When I got back to my room there was a cigarette butt in the toilet pan – and it sure as hell wasn't me who left it there. Which means someone searched my room, and they wanted me to know it. So I started thinking if there were other signs. That's when I remembered those two."

"I wonder if they know about the library."

"Maybe not. But even if they do, I suspect that they are more interested in our relationship than in your research. The KGB loves this sort of thing: a bit of romance."

Vadim gulped. "You know I would never do anything to hurt you."

They kissed. "Nor I you, my darling, not in a million years. So long as we stick together, we can hold them off. Now let's get a car," said Rachel.

They went down to the bottom of the steps and flagged the passing vehicles. An ambulance stopped, and the driver leaned across and wound down the window.

"Where to, young people?"

"Chertanovo, Dorozhnaya Street," said Rachel.

"How much?"

"Three roubles."

"Be serious."

"Five."

The driver hesitated. He looked into the distance as if mapping out the route in his head. Rachel thought a charm attack would do the trick.

"I can see you have a kind soul," she said, tilting her head. "And we are penniless students. Take us for five and God will reward you."

"Where are you from?" asked the driver.

"Estonia," she lied.

"I could tell you weren't Russian," said the driver, proud of his perception. Hop in the back, then. But don't touch anything."

Vadim opened the sliding door of the ambulance and they climbed in. He was relieved to see the driver did not have a patient. He sat down on the empty couch and Rachel sat next to him. They were far enough from the driver to be able to speak freely.

"These friends of mine," said Rachel. "They are all refuseniks. Karina applied to leave five years ago, but they won't let her out because her father worked somewhere secret. I don't quite get it, because I asked her what he did and she said something about the postal service."

Vadim laughed. "She said *'pochtovy yashchik'* – postbox?"

"Yes, that was it. What does it mean?"

"A postbox is any closed institution, from a weapons factory to the Moscow town planning office. If you work in one you are not allowed to go abroad, even years after you change jobs."

"Nor are your children, it seems."

"Naturally," said Vadim.

"Karina is married to Misha, or was. He is just out of prison. He is not a political though, he was in for black-marketeering or some such. She divorced him when she applied to emigrate, but he is still registered at her flat, so he came back to live with her when he got out of jail. In the meantime Karina got another boyfriend, also called Misha. He is not registered in Moscow, and doesn't like to go out of doors much in case he gets asked for his documents. He is writing a book about genetics. Basically he is hiding out in Karina's flat, tapping away at his typewriter and hoping she won't go to America."

"Because then he will have to move out of the flat?"

"No, because he loves her like crazy, dumbo."

"It's a *ménage à trois*, then."

"Not really, because it's all over between Karina and Dark Misha

– that's how I think of him because he has black hair. Fair Misha, the geneticist, is the man in her life now. There is no tension between the Mishas, they get on fine. They are only a threesome because of the flat. They have this neat division of labour: Karina earns the money, Dark Misha does the shopping and a little private business on the side to replenish the larder, and Fair Misha cooks and sees to the housework."

The ambulance was now in a bleak patch of Moscow where the tower blocks jutted skyward like rows of gappy teeth. The driver turned left off the Warsaw Highway and right onto Dorozhnaya. The steely bright lights of a railway depot could be seen nearby. The locomotives hooted and screeched like night owls.

"Where now?" called the driver.

"Third turning on the right," Rachel called back "After the roundabout."

They came to a halt. Rachel got out and proferred the blue five-rouble note.

"*Tanan vaga*," said the driver.

Vadim and Rachel looked at each other blankly.

"*Tanan vaga* – 'thank you' in Estonian," said the driver, looking aggrieved. "I was there on holiday two years ago."

"Ah yes, of course." Rachel began to giggle.

"You said you were Estonian."

"And so I am," she said, giggling still. "But your pronunciation is terrible."

"Let's go," said Vadim.

"Say something in Estonian," called the driver. But they were already at the door of Karina's block, and they did not look back.

A pretty red-haired woman of about twenty-five threw open the door and threw open her arms. "Rachel, *golubchik*," she cried, and embraced the American.

"Hello, Karina. What's new?"

"What could be new?" she said, casting a glance at Vadim. "I'm still here. When they let me go to America, then there will be something new."

The Mishas hung back. Apart from their colouring they were indeed very similar: both were lean and had straggly beards, both wore the same the-world-is-a-joke expression. They might have been two forms of the same phenomenon: a yin and a yang, or a mink and a stoat. They came forward and gave Rachel a friendly kiss when she had got her coat and boots off. Ragged house slippers were issued to the guests. They went to the kitchen, which was very similar to Vadim's own in Leningrad, only smaller still. Vadim immediately noticed the blue-and-white curtains decorated with the Star of David.

A tiny table was laid for five. There was a cucumber and smetana salad, an open tin of smoked sprats, a plate of sliced salami. Potatoes were bubbling away on the stove. Dark Misha extracted an icy bottle of vodka from the freezer box of the fridge and poured a round into little bell-shaped glasses. Meanwhile Fair Misha drained the potatoes and tipped them in a big stripey bowl. On top he put a square of yellow butter the size of a fist and sprinkled it with chopped dill and spring onions. "Let's eat," he said.

"But first, let's drink," said Dark Misha.

With much shifting, shuffling and apologising they squeezed round the ridiculously inadequate table. There was barely room to raise a glass.

"You have a kitchen perfect for shrugging the shoulders in," said Vadim, making the economical gesture with elbows in, palms upturned and a sorrowful yiddishe look of resignation on his face. Rachel looked at him in astonishment, and the other three laughed.

"I'll drink to that," shouted Dark Misha. "After all, what could be more Jewish than the shrug?"

"The tut," suggested Fair Misha.

"The flinch," said Karina, and they all quietened down.

"Well anyway, let's toast before the potatoes get cold," said Fair Misha. "*Za vstrechu*, to our meeting," they all chorused. "Shalom," added Karina, and they solemnly threw back the oily liquor.

The vodka warmed their bones and eased their fellowship – which, after all, is what vodka is for. They ate the food with gusto, and drank some more toasts.

"That's good vodka," said Rachel, after the third round.

"All vodka is good, especially the second bottle," said Dark Misha.

"You sound like a Russian *muzhik*," said Karina.

"That's what I am."

"You certainly are not, you are a spivvy yid," said Karina. "And that is two big differences, as they say in Odessa."

"Actually, there is a sense in which all vodka is good vodka," put in Fair Misha. "Vodka is basically forty per cent ethanol, sixty per cent water, plus a little glycerine to make it palatable. Those have been the proportions for generations, but it turns out that forty-sixty is the ideal ratio. Less than forty and the effect is diminished; more than forty and it is inefficient, because the body can't get all the alcohol into the bloodstream."

"What do you mean, where does it go?" asked Dark Misha.

"The body dumps it."

"You piss it away, without getting the benefit?"

"In a word, yes."

"What a waste."

"Exactly. That is why Russian peasants over generations of brewing vodka in the cowshed intuitively arrived at the forty-sixty proportion. It is a kind of alcoholic natural selection. Vodka in its modern form is the perfect means of getting drunk; everything superfluous, including taste and colour, has been pared away, and all that remains is what is relevant to the task in hand."

Dark Misha looked skewily at his empty glass. "I can't believe it," he said. "Everyone is moaning about the effect of vodka on the Soviet economy, and now it transpires that vodka is the most efficient worker in the whole goddam Union."

"Now, now," said Karina. "Don't start on one of your anti-Soviet monologues. You don't want to embarrass our guest Vadim here."

Vadim smiled at Karina, though secretly he was hurt by the implication that he might not be trustworthy. But Dark Misha was not to be discouraged by Karina's gentle hint. He was moving into an aggressively philosophical stage of drunkenness. "I've been anti-Soviet and proud of it all my life," he was saying. "I don't see why after a two-year stretch in the zone I should suddenly change my world-view."

"As a geneticist I can assure you that no-one is anti-Soviet all their life," said Fair Misha. "It is an acquired characteristic, like knowing the alphabet. There's no such thing as a born *kontra*."

"Not all my life, then," conceded Dark Misha. "But ever since I got to know Pavlik Morozov, at least."

"Is he a refusenik too?" asked Rachel – and after a moment's silence all the Russians burst into unstoppable peals of raucous laughter.

"What did I say?" she asked, but they were all laughing too hard to reply. She appealed to Vadim with her eyes, but his eyes were wet with tears. She decided to let them tell her what was so funny in their own good time.

"Pavlik Morozov," said Fair Misha when the storm of laughter had subsided, "Pavlik Morozov is the number-one hero of the pioneer movement. There is not a seven-year-old from here to Vladivostok who does not know the story of heroic little Pavlik."

"He's a little shit," exclaimed Dark Misha, whose fit of laughter had left him with the hiccoughs. Karina put a stilling finger to her ex-husband's lips.

"Let me tell you about Pavlik Morozov," said Fair Misha. "Pavlik lived in the heady 1930s," he began in parody of a primary-school teacher. "The young Soviet state was surrounded by enemies; there were also hidden enemies within. Industrialisation was proceeding apace, but there was not enough food in the cities to feed the thousands of factory workers. Pavlik lived in a small village in the Urals, far from the industrial centre. He was a model pioneer, and he wore his red scarf with pride. He knew from *Pravda* of the titanic struggle going on in the cities, and he was filled with anticipation when he heard that the Party was sending its special representatives to his village to collect grain for the workers. 'Now my own family can make a contribution to the cause,' he thought. 'The grain in our barn will feed a whole brigade of workers for a month.'

"But Pavlik was pained to see that his father did not view the prospect of a visit from the Party with anything like Pavlik's own enthusiasm. And he was downright shocked when his father began hiding sacks of grain under the floorboards of their cottage. 'At least the boy won't starve this winter,' muttered old man Morozov as he went about his deceitful business. But Pavlik knew very well that he would not starve: Comrade Stalin would never allow it! Pavlik set his jaw and made a decision, which he stored away in his principled little breast.

"Not many days after there was a rat-a-tat-tat at the door. It was the Party, come to collect the grain for the city. How delighted Pavlik was to see them: three tall men in shiny boots and blue caps, rifles slung over their shoulders and their military smocks drawn in at the waist with broad leather belts. To Pavlik they were the living image of the Revolution. He would have given anything to be one of them.

"Pavlik's father sullenly led the three to the barn, and with very bad grace he helped them load the heavy sacks onto a lorry. Pavlik waited until the barn was empty, then he approached the tallest, most awesome of the three visitors and in a clear, ringing voice he made the short speech that he had been rehearsing in his head all morning. 'Comrade officer,' he said. 'You have been deceived. My father has hidden yet more grain under our house. Take it and distribute it to the workers in the factories and foundries, and pass on greetings from the pioneers of our village.'

"Pavlik looked at his father. He could tell by the dumbstruck expression on his father's face that he had no idea his son was so scrupulously honest. The two junior soldiers swiftly lowered their rifles and led Papa Morozov away, never to be seen again. The officer put his hand on the boy's shoulder. 'Show me,' he said. It was the proudest moment of Pavlik's short life.

"The three men left soon after with all the grain. The officer had said to Pavlik that his integrity would be drawn to the attention of important people in the city, that he was a credit to the pioneer movement.

"But now our tale takes a tragic turn. For as I said at the outset, there were enemies within: kulaks, sub-kulaks, bourgeois residuals from the old regime, wreckers and saboteurs. There was a band of such criminals in Pavlik's own village. When they realised that they had as formidable an enemy as Pavlik Morozov on their own doorstep they decided to act fast, before he could unmask them too. In a word, they lynched him. They beat him to death, calling him a fink and a parricide as they did it. The day of Pavlik's heroic stand was also the day of his martyrdom.

"But you know, Pavlik did not die. He lives in the heart of every pioneer. He lives in the stories that are told of him around campfires and in classrooms throughout the progressive world. His tragic life is like a shining beacon of class loyalty, an ideological template of devotion to Party and Motherland. If everyone was like Pavlik, what a very different place the world would be."

"He's a little shit," repeated Dark Misha. "I thought so from the first time I heard of him."

"But you didn't say so," teased Karina.

"Of course not," said Dark Misha. "I wasn't that stupid. And in any case, I could not have expressed the thought at that age. I just had an uneasy feeling that there was something not very nice about Pavlik. By the time I figured out what it was, naturally I knew enough to keep my mouth shut. Every school is full of little snotnoses wanting to be the new Pavlik Morozov."

"It's a powerful myth," said Rachel. "Almost Shakespearean."

"Freudian, more like," said Dark Misha.

"Freudian is right, Pavlik is a Soviet Oedipus," said Fair Misha. "It is no coincidence that Pavlik is usually held to be about thirteen years old, just entering puberty, or that Pavlik's mother never figures in the story. By denouncing his father to the secret police he consummates his incestuous marriage to his true mother, the Communist Party."

"But like Oedipus, he paid the price," said Vadim.

"On the contrary, he won the greatest possible reward, a martyr's crown," said Fair Misha. "Death is a very small price to pay for sainthood. No hero worth his salt would refuse to pay it."

History anticipates. And the really interesting presentiments are intangible, spiritual.

For the collapse of the Soviet Union was not a political implosion, but a moral one. The party was perfectly capable of feeding the entire population for years to come, and they could have kept up the arms race indefinitely. What they could not do by the beginning of the Eighties was continue to carry the burden of the immense rococo fiction they had created. The country was exhausted with the effort of it, and in the end the Soviet Union collapsed under the weight of the Big Lie.

Myths like that of Pavlik Morozov, which made treachery a virtue and put the state before the family, gnawed away at the soul of the nation. It was all part of the Big Lie. The facts as well as the moral of Pavlik's martyrdom are a lie (and the prosaic truth about him can be read in an excellent book by dissident writer Yuri Druzhnikov). Nothing about the story of Pavlik is true except that he lived, he liked spying on his neighbours, and he was murdered. Pavlik, it turns out, was a half-wit who never clapped eyes on a pioneer's scarf in his life. He was killed not by angry peasants, but by the OGPU, as the KGB was then called. Pavlik provided a pretext for unleashing a campaign of terror against the kulaks of the Urals. These stubborn farmers refused to join the collectives, and the authorities needed an excuse to herd them in or hound them out. Poor Pavlik was the excuse, a posthumous sideshow in a propaganda circus. His legend was born of a specific situation, and down the years the tale grew and was embellished in the telling. Pavlik died in 1931, an early victim of the Terror that was still to come. In his case, the events anticipate themselves in a tragic and simple way.

The Soviet edifice, it is now clear, was bound to come down sooner or later. It took a month short of eleven years to fall, from the death of Brezhnev in November 1982 to the shelling of the White House in October 1993.

I saw both events at first-hand. The passing of Brezhnev was pathetic, almost comic. But the October coup was something awesome and violent. Yet it is not the violence that sticks in my mind from those days, from that last weekend in Soviet history. It is not the luminous tracer bullets, which skipped like sprites off the flagstones at Ostankino; not the pitched battle between riot police and demonstrators on the Krymsky Bridge; not the dragon-roar of the heavy tanks as they shelled the White House at point-blank range. Most of all I remember a non-event, a semi-fictional episode.

It was on the Saturday, the day before the real bloodshed. In the afternoon anti-government demonstrators had occupied a stretch of the eight-lane Moscow ring-road, blocking traffic. They raided a nearby building-site for materials, and built impressive barricades. Many of the demonstrators armed themselves with metal spikes, long and deadly as English halberds, and there were stockpiles of Molotov cocktails at the ready. Half-bricks and chunks of paving stone were laid out on the road in neat rows, so that they could be easily picked up and thrown one after another either on the advance or on the retreat. Two battalions of OMON special-purpose police drew up opposite the barricades, and the gap between the police and the rioters formed a strip of no-man's-land the whole width of the road. Interior ministry troops poured into the area until the police lines were almost as deep as the parliamentarians'. The two hosts faced each other down. As daylight shaded into evening they stood there, combatants in an urban cold war, neither side daring to commit itself to the first act of aggression. A strong rumour passed through the ranks of Western news photographers, who were out in force, that the police had orders to go in at midnight with *cheryomukha* – 'cherry blossom', the quaint Russian name for tear gas. One of the British snappers spat in disgust: there was no way he would make the Sunday papers' deadline if they left it that late.

And then it happened: a young mother pushed a pram out into the neutral zone between the police and the barricades. She was just using it as a shortcut to the Arbat, but the photographers fell on her hungrily. She was pretty and Russian-looking: with the police in the background it made a great shot. Unfortunately, not all the photographers had got their picture by the time she reached the far side, but they asked her nicely, and she good-naturedly agreed to push the baby back along the front line. She went to and fro half a dozen times, shadowed by the clicking cameras until all the photographers were sure they had it in the bag.

I don't know, but I imagine that picture made every front page from Warsaw to Seattle.

The Mystic Art

Il est vrai qu'il n'y a pas d'art plus étroitement lié au mysticisme que l'architecture; cet art tout abstrait, tout géometrique, impossible, ne vit que de symboles, que de figures, que d'allusions; la combinaison géometrique des lignes droites est leur rhythme; les rapports qui existent entre leur nombre présentent quelque chose de mystérieux et en même temps d'incomplet.

– Alexander Herzen, quoted in *L'Histoire de l'architecture russe*, V. Kiprianoff

September 1839

After the laying of the foundation stone, the real business of building got under way. The first task was to plant the four piers that were to support the central cupola. To reduce the massive downward pressure that would be exerted through these four pillars, Thon devised a system whereby they were connected by inverted arches, thus transferring the load back and forth from one pier to the other.

That autumn the outer walls were raised to the ground elevation. The top dressing of the outer walls was begun as the walls grew taller in 1840. Protopopovo marble turned out to be ideal for the task: hard, polishable, homogenous and impervious to water. The slabs were fixed to the brickwork with cast-iron staples and anchors, and molten lead was poured into the gap. Huge chunks of the same Protopopovo stone was shipped to Italy, where the sculptor Alexander Loganovsky was making a start on the high-reliefs and the bas-reliefs. He tested the marble by carving the icon of the Mother of God of Vladimir, intended for the central attic-end on the east façade, and found it suitable in every respect.

The four great piers reached a height of forty-one feet before the cold weather came in the late autumn of 1840. In 1841 the internal walls continued to grow, and the first vaults were thrown over the inner niches, thereby connecting the outer walls with the inner pylons. This completed the socle, after which work began on installing the *zakomary*, the keel-shaped attics and the roofs. Since there were three zakomary on each wing, each roof consisted of three inverse keels, the central one larger than those to the left and right. The roofs were made of rolled sheets of red copper. The joins were folded six times and welded fast to preclude all possibility of their leaking.

It took until 1848 to clothe the exterior of the cathedral in its robe of white marble: the socle, the many pilasters, the columns and arches that made up the twelve portals, the frames of the windows, all these were cut, shaped, affixed and polished. Loganovsky's *alti relievi* were then winched up and fixed in place twenty-six metres above the ground.

The reliefs on the west side, where the main entrance was located, portrayed Christ to whom the Cathedral was dedicated, and also the patron saints of the emperors by whose decree it was erected. On the east side, facing the Kremlin, were depicted guardians of the Russian land such as Stefan of Perm and Sergei Radonezhsky; on the south side, the saints on whose feast days the battles of 1812 took place, as well as a representation of the icon of the Virgin of Smolensk: this image had been paraded through the Russian ranks on the eve of the Battle of Borodino. On the north side were the saints who brought the orthodox faith to Russia, and those on whose feast days Russian forces joined battle on foreign soil at Kulma, Leipzig and Paris.

In 1849, the four main piers grew taller still. They broadened at the top like tree trunks and merged to form a semi-spherical vault beneath the main cupola. The massive central drum was constructed in the course of 1853. All the brickwork was finished in 1854. Over the course of sixteen years, forty million bricks had been laid, each one ten and one half inches long, five inches wide, two and one half deep. The outer walls of the cathedral were three and a half yards thick, that is, twelve bricks' length.

Now the bricklayers were laid off and the metalworkers and steeplejacks took over. Their job was to build the main cupola on top of the drum, to attach the head to the body of the Cathedral of Christ. At the base of the cupola was a ring of steel a little under a hundred yards in circumference. From this ring sprung longitudinal ribs gently curving outwards then tapering in to a common point – the characteristic bulb-like shape. This vast onion dome was clad in red copper according to the same technique as had been used for the roof. The surface of the dome comprised 31,318 square feet of metal. With the other four cupolas, the total surface requiring polish and gilding amounted to nearly fifty thousand square feet. Altogether, including the crosses, four hundred and twenty-two kilos of gold went to cover the five shining heads of Christ the Cathedral.

In 1856 a new tsar, Alexander II, came to visit the site. It was now twenty-five years since his father, Nikolai I, had commissioned Konstantin Thon to build the church, and a full forty-four since his uncle Alexander I had published his Christmas manifest. And still the church was shrouded in scaffolding and tarpaulin. Muscovites had been living with the shapeless hulk for a generation, watching it expand little by little with every passing year until it resembled a Titan crouched beneath a blanket.

Konstantin Thon was now well into his sixties, and something of a titan himself. He towered over Russian architecture and was, so to speak, a pillar of the establishment. He was a first-class professor of the Academy of Arts, he held the rank of state counsellor in the Civil

Service. In 1844, Nikolai had awarded him the order of St. Anne, which automatically conferred aristocratic status on its holder. That same year he had finally married. His wife was Elena Berg, and they had a son, also Konstantin, born out of wedlock in 1842. The younger Konstantin planned to follow in his father's footsteps, but was blinded by illness in his teens. Thon officially adopted the boy in 1858.

The architect had a second, quite separate family: when he was in his fifties he made the acquaintance of Amalia Frederica Barclay, a renowned Scottish beauty, and by her he had four more children: Ottilia, Pavel, Nadezhda and Elizaveta. Amalia Barclay was the great love of his long life, the one he had been looking for since Rome. The relationship could not of course receive official blessing, ecclesiastical blessing still less, and the children were all adopted by Thon's friend Efim Guk.

Thon was more than comfortably off: he had a salary of one thousand roubles per annum, plus grants of a further one thousand five hundred. He also received money for his work on various projects: Christ the Cathedral, of course, but also the Great Kremlin Palace, and the iconostasis of Petersburg's Kazan Cathedral – masterpiece of his teacher Voronikhin.

Thon was a conservative and a monarchist who lived by government commissions. His lifetime spent in the service of Nikolai, and his album of acceptable church designs, meant that he was part of the builder police, a state official. But he was also a victim of the state system. Bryullov, his old student chum, chose to stay away from Petersburg so as to have as little as possible to do with the imperial court. But Thon, like Pushkin, thought it better to find a *modus vivendi* with the difficult emperor than not to work at all. He did not always bow his head before authority: at least once in Nikolai's militarised dictatorship Thon was 'sent to the guardhouse for a breach of subordination at the workplace'.

Nikolai had died in 1855, and Russia found itself on the eve of great changes. Like many of his generation, Thon could not wholeheartedly approve of the massive social upheaval the young Alexander was planning, but neither could he feel too nostalgic for the iron hand of absolutism Russia had left behind. And anyway, he was tired. In 1857, for the first time in his life, Professor Thon requested sick leave due to 'an affliction of the chest and worsening pains in the legs, the result of contusions received at the building site'.

He was back at his post in good time for the removal of the scaffolding, which at long last came to pass in 1860. The Cathedral of Christ the Saviour emerged from its wooden covering like a bride unveiled, and in the instant it became a spectacular focal point of the cityscape. Postcards and prints were produced in their millions from 1860 on, and within a few years the gleaming new edifice of Christ the Cathedral, no less than Tower Bridge for London or the Eiffel Tower for Paris (nineteenth-century structures both), was the city's outstanding symbol.

May 1983

Spring came late, and as the days grew long there were still patches of grey snow in some dark corners of the city. Vadim and Rachel went up to Leningrad on the Red Arrow, known popularly as the Love Train. Karina had bought Rachel's ticket so as to avoid questions about visas and permissions to leave Moscow. They splashed out on a first-class two-berth compartment and took a picnic of red-caviar sandwiches with them.

Nothing had come of their winter fears, and it seemed that the library subterfuge had passed unnoticed after all. Their love had grown more intense through the cold months, and their relationship was now an open secret in V Zone.

"This terminus was designed by Thon," said Vadim as they boarded the train.

"Let's leave Thon at home, just for the weekend," said Rachel.

"He built the one at the other end, too," said Vadim, slightly miffed.

On the stroke of midnight the train shuddered into life and began creakily to pull away. On the platform knots of people, many still wearing their winter hats, waved handkerchiefs or blew kisses to friends on the train. A platoon of young soldiers sat on their luggage, smoking miserably; a corporal stood over them, his right hand tucked in his overcoat like a portrait of Napoleon. An orchestral piece of Soviet Romanticism, Reinhold Glière's stirring *Hymn to a Great City*, was piped through the loudspeaker system to mark the Red Arrow's departure. It resounded round the station, drowning out the sound of last-minute farewells.

"I feel like I'm in Doctor Zhivago," said Rachel, as they leaned out of the window, waving at no-one in particular. "The film, not the book."

"Railway stations: the safebox of my meetings and goodbyes," quoted Vadim – from a book, not the film.

They went back to the compartment and ate their supper. Then they bought a packet of biscuits and two steaming glasses of black tea from the conductress. Since it was after midnight, Rachel felt empowered to give Vadim his birthday present. It was a copy of the slim, blue Mandelshtam.

"Where did you get it?" he exclaimed.

"It is in the hard-currency *beriozka* on Kropotkinskaya," said Rachel. "Stacks of them."

Vadim opened the book. Inside she had written the date and eight lines of Akhmatova:

Let not your heart be filled with earthly longing;
Do not be bound by home, or wife, or hearth.
And take your child's bread and give it
To the first stranger who should cross your path.

And make yourself the abject slave of him
Who once was your most hated enemy.
And to the forest beasts a brother be.
And never ask of God a single thing.

Under the poem she had inscribed a Latin 'R'.
"Thanks for the book," said Vadim. "And for the advice."
"Don't mention it," she said.

Russian history anticipates itself.

Nikolai II was not the first tsar to die a violent death at the hand of his subjects. Alexander II was hunted like a dog by a left-wing terrorist group *Narodnaya Volya*, 'The People's Will'. They seem to have been a pretty useless bunch, much prone to what the British police used to call the 'paddy factor', the tendency of our own Irish bombers to plan everything to the last detail and still find a brilliant and unexpected way of messing it up. Alexander lost count of the attempts on his life, and in the end it turned into a grim sport, a kind of deadly hide-and-seek.

The first attack took place in 1866. An aristocrat turned terrorist named Dmitry Karakozov took a pot-shot at the tsar as he walked in the Summer Garden. A peasant with the ironically prescient name of Komissarov threw himself in front of the emperor. He stopped the bullet with his body, and was given a hereditary peerage for his trouble. This gave rise to a joke both typically Russian and unmistakably Victorian:

"I say, did you hear that someone tried to shoot the tsar?"

"Indeed I did. Did you know who the scofflaw was?"

"A nobleman, I believe."

"And who was the fellow that saved His Imperial Highness?"

"A peasant."

"And how did they reward him?"

"They made him a nobleman..."

An Anton Berezovsky tried to kill Alexander in Paris the following year. And in 1879, a man named Alexander Solovyov fired five shots at the tsar, who saved himself by running away from the man in zigzags. One bullet holed the folds of the autocrat's overcoat. Later that year *Narodnaya Volya* blew up the emperor's train – he was not on it. In 1880 they managed to plant a bomb in the dining room of the Winter Palace. It exploded at six o'clock in the evening, killing and maiming forty officers of the Finland Regiment. Alexander should have been there, but he was delayed elsewhere in the palace by a guest, an unpunctual Bulgarian prince.

Narodnaya Volya could not forgive Alexander for having liberated the serfs in 1861, and thereby setting back the revolutionary cause by decades. That is, they could not forgive him for having done something right. To them, as to their Bolshevik offspring, the great emancipation was a dangerous precedent, the kind of thing that might render a revolution unnecessary altogether. All Russian revolutionaries sighed for the unquestionably despotic reign of Alexander's predecessor. Nikolai I had spent his days immersed in the minutiae of tyranny, designing buttons for cavalrymen's uniforms and blue-pencilling words in Pushkin's love lyrics. Alexander II was, within the bounds of the regime he inherited, not a bad tsar. Throughout his reign he tacked unpredictably between liberal and repressive measures, just as he had zigzagged to dodge the bullets of the *narodovolets* Solovyov. He was short-tempered, but not unremittingly cruel like his father; he was vacillating, but not hopelessly weak like his grandson. And his luck was bound to run out eventually.

At three o'clock on the afternoon of the first of March 1881, Alexander was in his carriage, heading back to the Winter Palace. It was a frosty day and there was snow on the ground. He had just attended the Changing of the Guard on Mars Field. His carriage turned at the corner of the Mikhailovsky Gardens to cross a little bridge over the Ekaterinsky Canal.

As the coach slowed almost to a halt, a waiting student named Rusakov tossed a bomb under the carriage. It exploded, killing some of the Cossack outriders and injuring several civilians. The tsar was unharmed, however, and his carriage was still roadworthy. The driver made to race from danger as fast as the horses could gallop, but Alexander ordered him to stop.

He got out of the carriage and went up to Rusakov, who was by now in the custody of the emperor's bodyguard. "Did you throw that bomb? Who are you?" he demanded, but Rusakov did not reply. Alexander looked around. On the ground lay a dead Cossack and a passer-by, a small boy. The boy was badly wounded. He lay glassily staring at the sky, opening and closing his mouth like a suffocating fish.

By the wrought-iron balustrade of the canal stood a moon-faced young man with little piggy eyes and an oily centre-parting. Alexander, his grey whiskers bristling and his baggy, bloodhound eyes flashing in anger, for some reason strode up to this person. His name was Ignaty Grinevitsky, he was nineteen years old, and Rusakov's accomplice.

Grinevitsky raised his right arm as if in salute. But in his hand was a second bomb, which he hurled to the ground at his own feet. There was a mighty explosion. When the smoke cleared the tsar and the chubby revolutionary were sitting next to each other with their backs to the railings. They leaned on their hands and eyeballed each other like two silly drunks. Grinevitsky was mortally wounded. Alexander's legs were attached to his body by no more than a few ribbons of skin and gristle. The bomb had also blown most of his clothes off, and his undervest was singed on his body. Both men were leaching rivers of warm blood that melted the fresh snow on the pavement.

The tsar was carried to a sledge. "I'm cold, I'm cold," he kept saying. One of the guards suggested taking him to the nearest house and summoning a doctor. "No," said Alexander. "Take me to the palace. I'll die there." They did as he commanded, and he expired that evening. Nikolai Alexandrovich, the future Nikolai II, was brought to see Alexander in his last hour. Nikolai was thirteen at the time, and the gruesome sight of his grandfather's suffering horrified him.

Inevitably, a church was built on the site of the assassination. It was called *Spas Na Krovi*, 'The Saviour on the Blood', and it was built in the neo-Russian style then coming into vogue. Its gold and multi-coloured candy cupolas were a deliberate echo of St. Basil's and the Kremlin ensemble in Moscow. The walls were encrusted with hundreds of ceramic tiles, and the ornament inside was made up entirely of mosaics, countless hundreds of thousands of little pieces of glass and stone, like crystals of sand on a beach, but endowed with meaning by being arranged into icons and biblical scenes. Under a canopy at the centre of the church, preserved intact, were the paving stones and the stretch of ironwork where the Tsar Liberator spilt his blood.

☆

May 1983

It was bright and sunny when Vadim and Rachel arrived in Peter's city the next morning. They walked from the station to the flat on Marat Street.

There was nobody in. "That's funny," said Vadim, "I thought Dad would be here to meet us. It is my birthday, after all." They dumped their bags, had a shower and went for a walk.

"Where do you want to go first?" asked Vadim, when they came back out onto Nevsky.

"I don't know, I've never been here before. It's your town, you decide." Vadim bit his lip and hesitated. "I know," said Rachel. "I would like to go and look for the Stray Dog."

"What stray dog?"

"The Stray Dog cafe, where the Futurists and Symbolists used to hang out."

"Do you have any idea where it was?"

"On Mikhailovsky Square. Is that far?"

"No, a short stroll. It is called Arts Square now, in front of the Russian Museum."

On the way Rachel told Vadim a story about the Stray Dog. One night, probably around 1913 or 1914, Mayakovsky was giving a poetry reading there. "You can imagine what it was like," said Rachel. "Mayakovsky, all six-foot-four of him, giving a full-blown Futurist performance. No doubt he was in his trademark yellow shirt, and maybe he had a wooden spoon in his buttonhole to add a touch of surrealism. Anyhow, there he was, punching the air and gesticulating, proclaiming his genius at the top of his voice and generally showing off."

"Words leap from my mouth like naked prostitutes from the windows of a burning brothel," quoted Vadim.

"Yes, that sort of thing. At that moment Mandelshtam came in. He happened to pass by the stage on his way to the toilet, or something. You know what he looked like: a refined little Jew with sticking-out ears and a head too big for his body. Two men could hardly be less alike. Anyway, Mandelshtam drew level just as Vladimir Vladimirovich was pausing for breath. And without breaking his stride he said in his languid voice, 'Do pipe down, Mayakovsky, you are not a Romanian orchestra.'" Rachel laughed heartily at her own story. "You are not a Romanian orchestra! What a brilliant putdown."

They turned right off Nevsky Prospekt down Brodsky Street. At the end of the road was the yellow, classical façade of the museum, formerly the Mikhailovsky Palace, and the spacious square before it. They did circuits of the square in both directions, but could find nothing – no dark, belanterned doorway, no basement breathing ancient fumes of spilt absinthe – that looked like it was once the haunt of poets and decadents.

They skirted the museum and walked the back streets until they came upon the Pavlovsky Castle, its high walls, the red-brown colour of old blood, half-obscured behind a blind of trees.

"What a forbidding building," said Rachel. "It looks like the Bates Motel, only bigger and scarier."

Vadim had no idea what the Bates Motel was, but he said, "It is meant to be forbidding. Tsar Pavel I built it to hide in. He was terrified of being stabbed, so he had the castle built with all sorts of moats and drawbridges to keep the regicides' daggers at a distance."

"And did it?"

"Sort of: he wasn't stabbed to death; they strangled him in bed with his own nightshirt. And it didn't happen there, but in the Mikhailovsky Palace, where we just were."

They turned back, taking a shortcut through the park behind the yellow palace, and they emerged at a sharp corner by a short bridge.

To the left, perched on the edge of a narrow canal, there was a church in a very sorry state of repair. Its domes were stripped skeletons, and its delapidated, tile-encrusted walls were barely visible beneath a bristling overcoat of scaffolding.

"It'll be good when it's finished," Rachel joked darkly. She peered through the forest of steel tubes. "It's a real mosaic of a church, isn't it. A proper little jigsaw puzzle. Reminds me a bit of that French mansion on Leninsky Prospekt, remember?"

Vadim said that he didn't. "Come on," he urged, taking her hand. "You haven't seen the Winter Palace yet." They crossed the little Ignaty Grinevitsky Bridge and headed up the road to the Neva.

1854

The exterior was finished, and Christ the Cathedral was now a feature of the Moscow skyline. It soared above the one- and two-storey houses of the Prechistenka quarter. It could be seen from almost any point in the city, and from most places it looked utterly majestic. Contemporary sources agree that some of the best vantage points were within the Kremlin. Looking upriver from the heights of the bell-tower of Ivan the Great, standing on the cobbled square behind the Cathedral of the Archangel, or on the narrow ramparts by the swallow-tailed merlons of the west wall, one's eye was drawn first to the new Stone Bridge in the foreground, its undulating arches connecting the north bank of the Moskva with the Zamoskvorechye suburb. At the near end of the bridge the modest eighteenth-century Church of the Adoration of the Virgin stood like an usher, ready to guide supplicants into the regal presence of Christ the Saviour.

Another marvellous view was to be had from the Bersenevskaya Embankment opposite the Cathedral where stood the Einem Chocolate Factory (later the Red October State Experimental

Confectionery Plant). The fishermen who cast their lines from the muddy bank under the factory's red walls had an uninterrupted view of the south façade of the Cathedral, a stone Narcissus admiring its reflection in the laggard water. If one approached from the west, that is, from the quiet grid of streets and alleys around Prechistenka and Ostozhenka, then the Cathedral loomed up from behind the low buildings like an alpine peak, and its long shadow on a summer's evening spread a dark mantle across half the district. From Sparrow Hills the church was clearly visible. The metropolis had spread since Karl Vitberg's day, but there was yet a long, green expanse between the Hills and the city. Close at hand, the whitewashed Tikhvinsky Church still stood in beautiful isolation in the middle of a fallow field, and it would be another fifty years before Moscow's outskirts crept up to the campanile of the Novodevichy Monastery, nestling there in the crook of the river. Away to the right, across a carpet of grass and in the distance, the envious golden domes of the Kremlin seemed to peek over the shoulder of Christ the Cathedral.

The exterior was finished, but the Cathedral as a whole was barely half-way to completion. While it was still in its cocoon of scaffolding, teams of artisans were contracted to prepare the inside walls for decoration. The plaster was not smoothed directly on the walls. Holes were drilled in the brickwork and filled with wooden plugs. Iron cramps were nailed into the wood, and lengths of hemp and tinplated wire were strung between the nails to make a framework. It was to this lath that a mixture of cement and puzzolana was applied, and when it dried it made a damp-proof gap behind which air could circulate. The plasterers were kept busy for nearly twenty years: many of the artists and icon painters who were later commissioned to adorn the walls were scarcely old enough to hold a paintbrush when the job started.

In 1854 a wooden model was made, a doll's house version of Christ the Cathedral, the interior of which was painted in oils with

the greatest possible degree of verisimilitude, so as to give Thon an
idea of how the scheme of murals, icons, and holy images chosen by
Metropolitan Filaret would look. A certain amount of tension arose
between the architects and the churchmen at this stage. The builders
wanted the lower corridor to be clad entirely in marble, but Filaret
objected that in such a case all the icons in the cathedral would be
above head height: it would be improper and unnatural if Orthodox
worshippers had to crane their necks back to make the sign of the
cross. A compromise was reached whereby some of the marble
panels had icons in the form of medallions set in the stone. At the
same time, the lower corridor was still to function as a monument
to the Patriotic War of 1812–14. The lower corridor was lined by
a progression of one hundred and seventy-seven marble tablets on
which the chronology of the war was narrated. The tablets were
mounted in groups of three on both sides of the corridor, forming
fifty-nine panels on all of which were inscribed the date and place
of every battle in the war, the names of the commanders and the
regiments that took part, the names of the officers who died or were
wounded, the number of fallen other ranks, and the names of those
who were decorated. The first panel bore the text of the imperial
rescript dated 13th June, 1812 confirming that the enemy had crossed
Russia's borders; the third reproduced the imperial manifest of 6th
July, calling for Russia to rise up and defend Moscow; the fifteenth
recorded the decisive battle of Borodino; and the thirtieth was the
Christmas Day manifest concerning the building of a Cathedral to
Christ the Saviour in Moscow, along with a representation of Thon's
Cathedral, and below it a carved sketch of Vitberg's project; the
fifty-seventh panel recorded the capture of Paris on 18th March,
1814; the fifty-eighth the peace with France; and the last was a decree
of the Holy Synod naming Christmas Day as a day of thanksgiving
for the liberation of Russia.

Other work proceeded apace while the interior rendering was in progress. The mosaic floor of the church, for example, was a work of art in its own right. It covered six hundred square sazhens and was a complex design made with marble squares and triangles of cerulean blue, raw siena, deep vermilion and Frankfort black imported from Italy and Belgium, and with the blood-coloured shokshinsky porphyry. At the middle of the abstract pattern, directly below the point of the cupola was an eight-pointed star motif enclosed in a circle. The circle was framed in a square, and on the basis of this regular central form the mosaic proliferated outwards into the four wings – its stars, diamonds, crosses, triangles and squares multiplying in harmonious symphonic repetition to the hushed corners of the Cathedral. From above, the marble floor resembled a moorish mural, laid flat and polished till it shone like a mirror.

In July 1861 Tsar Alexander II gave his seal of approval to the scheme of frescos for the walls and columns. Thon gave orders that a small section of the north-west corner should be painted first. In spite of the hundreds of drawings he had made and the hours of discussion and consultation with Filaret, he was still not sure what the overall effect would be. The first brushstrokes on the interior of Christ the Cathedral were very much an experiment. Thon decided to move cautiously on. He organised the job in such a way that the painting was done simultaneously from top and bottom: one artist perched high on wooden scaffolds, and another stood on the floor, at various points throughout the building. This arrangement was intended to save time and, once again, to aid the architect's imagination. Nobody had ever schemed an interior space of this size. There were no precedents for Thon to turn to for guidance, no church in the world to compare with this booming cavern of painted saints.

Most of the artists were drawn from the Academy where Thon had now been a professor for nearly twenty years. The Imperial Academy of Arts in Petersburg was a kind of labour exchange of talent on which Thon constantly drew, commissioning pupils that he had himself groomed for the task of contributing to his life's work. Among them are some of the great names of Russian art: Genrikh Semiradsky, Lev Dahl, Nikolai Koshelev, Vasily Vereshchagin, Vladimir Makovsky, Vasily Surikov.

As soon as the frescoes were approved, Alexei Markov, a fellow professor of Thon's at the Academy of Arts, started on the single most important work in the Cathedral, the depiction of the Lord Sabaoth that filled the semi-spherical vault below the main cupola. Markov portrayed the Ancient of Days, grey-haired and radiant, with hands spread in a gesture of blessing and creation. In his lap sat the second Person of the Godhead, portrayed as an infant and bearing a parchment with the inscription LOGOS in Greek. The Spirit of God was present in the form of a dove. At the western edge of the image in Hebrew letters was written the word 'Elohim' – Lord of Hosts. It took Markov five years to complete the painting: five working years spent lying flat on his back and in the half-dark.

A balustrade below the cupola was supported by a rich cornice that formed the top of a wide girdle or band at the base of the cylindrical drum. On this band, which in the symbolic scheme of the building connected the glorified Godhead with the world of men, were shown those who foretold the coming of Christ, witnessed His ministry, or preached His gospel. On the east side was Christ himself, bare-headed in a white tunic and seated on a jewelled throne. He bore an open book in which was written in Old Slavonic the words 'I am the Light of the World.' Gathered at the throne were the figures, seven yards tall, of the Virgin Mary and John The Baptist; of the archangels Michael and Gabriel; of Adam, Enoch, Noah, Abraham, Isaac, Jacob and Moses; of King David; of the prophets Elijah and Isaiah; the twelve apostles; Stephen, the first martyr; Emperor Constantine; Grand Duke Vladimir, and the blessed Alexander Nevsky.

These figures were painted first by Pyotr Bassin, another professor at the Academy. But Bassin's dry, two-dimensional style did not please the tsar, and the girdle was redone in the fashionable Russian idiom. The results were warmer, more flesh-and-blood, undoubtedly more in keeping with the joyful spirit of the Cathedral, but the failure was too much for old Professor Bassin, who died in shame and despair soon after his work was whitewashed into oblivion.

The frescoes in the Cathedral of Christ the Saviour were an undertaking of almost industrial proportions. But by the last years of the 1870s not an inch of bare plaster remained. The whole Cathedral was dressed in a painted coat of many colours.

During the twenty years of work on the interior, other details of the Cathedral were brought to completion. Lightning conductors were strung from the high cross, down the walls, and earthed to the river. The copper wires were not attached directly to the masonry, but passed through concealed metal sheaths, which allowed them to expand and contract with the temperature without snapping.

Fourteen bells were cast, and hung in the towers below the four lesser cupolas. The largest was decorated with six medallions in relief: the Saviour, the Virgin, John the Baptist, Alexander I, Nikolai I, Alexander II. The decorations on the bell, like everything about the Cathedral, stressed the connection between the Christian faith and the Russian land. It sang out: Russia loves God, God loves Russia.

The body of Christ the Saviour was now whole. Inside, Thon's deputy, Semyon Dmitriev, was engaged in assembling the Cathedral's soul. Ensconced in the east wing was the main iconostasis, the high partition that in every Orthodox church symbolises fallen mankind's separation from God; it is a barrier, one might even say a barricade, intended to keep the sinner from approaching the altar beyond. But at the same time the iconostasis allows the possibility of redemption: this wall has a gate.

The iconostasis of Christ the Cathedral was utterly unique. It was not the usual flat curtain – it took the form of a six-faceted tower that fitted under the eastern arch. It was a separate architectural item, in effect a church within a church. Nothing like it had been seen before in an Orthodox place of worship. Its carved marble framework was divided into four tiers, four storeys of a house in which the icons were arranged in rows. It was crowned with a sloping *shatyor* – a lacy wigwam of gold – atop which was a studded cupola like a Fabergé egg.

The iconostasis was twenty-six metres tall, almost the height of the Uspensky Cathedral in the Kremlin. It was the first thing one would see on entering through the west doors. Like an angel's folly it stood, its image reflected in the polished floor, just as the Cathedral itself was mirrored in the Moskva river outside.

The church plate and other furnishings were designed by Lev Dahl. He produced nigh on two hundred separate items of church furniture, the props and costumes in the theatre of divine worship: enamelled candlestands, silver censers for everyday use, jewel-encrusted thuribles for high holidays, plates and chalices for the Eucharist, candle-snuffers and icon-covers, rich gonfalons, lanterns and crosses on poles to be carried aloft in the Easter procession, mitres, robes and priestly vestments. Then the fixtures and fittings: balustrades and banisters, wrought bronze gates, the archiepiscopal throne, ornate offering boxes like wayside shrines for the side-chapels and the main altar, the many chandeliers and candelabra. All these too were in the warm and colourful Russian style that had grown out of the cool Russo-Byzantinism instituted by Thon fifty years before.

But by the end of the 1870s Professor Thon was out of fashion, and in some quarters his reputation was under attack. Herzen, who never ceased to see Thon as a mere lackey of Nikolai's, had delivered his verdict from afar, and he had published the opinion of his late friend Vitberg, expressed many years before ("It is a church for yokels, a simple rustic chapel."). The splenetic Stasov was yet to say his piece, but he was off sharpening his pen somewhere.

Thon's reign was over, and a new aesthetic was replacing the old. But the new wave did not see that the *russky stil* was in many ways a continuation of Thon's pre-Petrine idea, that their bright creations were in large part a change of emphasis, and that they themselves were just preparing the ground for the real flowering of the national idea in architecture.

They did not know that the best was yet to come.

Moderne

...I see it in autumn-tide clearly now; yes, clearer, clearer, oh! so bright and glorious! yet it was beautiful too in spring, when the brown earth began to grow green: beautiful in summer, when the blue sky looked so much bluer, if you could hem a piece of it in between the new white carving; beautiful in the solemn, starry nights, so solemn that it almost reached agony...

– William Morris (from *The Story of the Unknown Church*)

May 1983

They were gathered for the feast.

Yuri was in a fine and somewhat enigmatic mood. He had refused to tell Vadim where he had been that morning, and would only say that all would become clear later. Vadim suspected there was some birthday surprise in the offing.

Ira was laying wafery slices of raw onion on the herring in the kitchen, and Marina was carrying food into the main room. Rachel sat at table with Artyom; he was telling her that the Beatles came secretly to Moscow in 1966 and gave a concert for the politburo. "It was all kept very quiet, but of course the truth leaked out," he said.

"Do you think it might just be a rumour, or wishful thinking."

"No-o. I was at college with a guy whose uncle was a member of the central committee of the Communist Party at the time. He told me his uncle went to Vnukovo airport with Brezhnev to meet them. They did the one gig in the Kremlin, then left. That's what 'Back in the USSR' is all about. It's their message to the fans that they will come again, and this time they will play for us, not just for the big bosses. All the Beatles' greatest fans are here."

"That's certainly true," said Rachel. She was now considering whether it would be wise to tell this Lennon clone that her father in his youth had seen the Beatles live at the Hollywood Bowl. She did not want to freak him out totally.

"How would you translate 'big teaser'?" asked Artyom, changing tack.

"U-um."

"Or 'Sunday driver'? It's for my Complete Annotated Translation of the *Collected Works*, I've been trying to figure it out all day. What does the Albert Hall mean to you, as a symbol, I mean?"

"Not much, I'm afraid. You'd have to ask a Brit."

Vadim sat opposite, and smiled at her. She smiled back. They carried on a separate conversation without words.

"You OK?"

"Fine."

"Not bored? Not pinned down?"

"No. Loving every minute."

Efim Oskarovich fussed with the bottles of wine and vodka. He was not well today, wheezing heavily and wincing from time to time, but he was delighted to have a foreigner in the flat. He would keep apologising for the humble abode, however. "Very poky compared to what you are used to, I expect," he said.

"Not at all. It's a delightful home."

"The family's been here since before the war, you know."

"I know. Vadim told me the family history."

"The history, yes," said Efim Oskarovich, and went and flopped in an armchair.

Only Mark was subdued. He'd come up to Leningrad on the day train and had only just arrived. He had said a warm hello to Rachel, but hardly a word since.

"Are you ill or something?" asked Vadim.

"Eh? No, I'm just tired out, that's all. I've had a hard week."

At this moment Ira came in from the kitchen with the herring. Marina followed with plates of mushroom toast and open caviar sandwiches.

"All to table, please," said Ira. "Yuri, open the champagne."

"I'll see to that," said Efim Oskarovich. He took the bottle from the table and prised it off with two thumbs. The plastic cork shot off with a loud pop, ricocheted off the roof and landed in the middle of Marina's plate of sandwiches. No-one was more surprised than Efim Oskarovich. He stood stock still as wisps of vapour curled from the neck of the green bottle like smoke from the barrel of a gun.

"Hey Buffalo Bill," said Artyom, automatically. And laughing they sat down to eat.

As Artyom was discovering, Russian is a devil of a language to translate into or out of. All the renderings of poetry in this book can do no more than give a rough idea. Translation is always an exercise in approximation; there are only greater or lesser degrees of failure.

Much of the difficulty derives from the fact that every Russian root-word can produce dozens of shades of meaning. This is also the source of Russian's great richness and diversity. The base forms are not so much roots as seeds; they divide and multiply, and from the seed grows a tree that bears fruit of all shapes and sizes. Take a simple root form like *dev-* – 'girl'. In everyday use are *deva, devka, devushka, devitsa, devochka, devchonka, devstvennitsa*, and a clutch of other forms that can only be translated into English, if they can be rendered at all, with the aid of a thesaurus: little girl, girlie, lass, wench, young woman, virgin, girlfriend, maid, and so on. Even then, the English cannot convey the various notes of affection, condescension, awe or contempt that may be contained in the Russian.

Verbs are even more adaptable than nouns. With the use of prefixes and suffixes a single root can be made variously to mean 'to do something until one has had enough', 'to do something to the exclusion of all other activities', 'to do something for a while and then stop', 'to begin to do something', 'to do something in short bursts with pauses in between', 'to do something in such a manner as to exhaust the means of doing it', 'to do something that causes damage to the object of the activity', 'to do something but fail to complete it', 'to do something as an extension of an earlier action' ... the list is inexhaustible. The mix-and-match capability of the Russian language made it possible for the Soviet regime to invent sinister concepts like *nedoperevypolnyat*, a verb that consists of four prefixes nailed to the root *poln*, 'full', and means 'to fail to overfulfill one's norm to the required degree'.

At the other extreme, the identikit nature of Russian allows a great deal of scope for inventive wordplay. In 1909 the Futurist poet Velimir Khlebnikov wrote a short verse in which every word is a neologism derived from the root *smekh*, 'laugh'. It was a piece of pyrotechnical nonsense but, as sometimes happens with poets, it made Khlebnikov famous overnight. This rendering gives a flavour of *Oath by Laughter*:

O be laughsome, laugheteers!
Laugh your fill, you laugheroons!
Laugh your laughlets laughfully or be laughish laughily.
Laugh yourselves to laugheration!
In laughern laugheries belaughed
the laughkin's laughling laughie lay!
Let your laughness laugh through laughdom,

archilaughic bellylaughants!
Laughterly! laughterly!
Laughists and laughicles, belaugh the unlaughable!
Laugho, laughissimo!
O be laughsome, laugheteers!
Laugh your fill, you laugheroons!

The economy of Russian is utterly alien to English. Russian words are long, but the language makes a large investment in the simple forms in order to draw bigger dividends in the complex forms; English makes a very tiny initial outlay, but must constantly top up its account with auxiliary verbs, articles, pronouns and adverbs. Russian endings do much of the work of that vast army of English prepositions. 'Hit' and 'hammer' are three syllables each in Russian, but 'He was hitting it repeatedly with a hammer' (like the student doctor Maxwell as to the quizzical head of his girlfriend Joan) is still only two words and six syllables. To a Russian eye, the English language looks like the Soviet bureaucracy: chock-a-block with elements that perform no obvious function but claim to be vital to the smooth running of the machinery.

Single Russian words, even familiar ones, can have a completely different resonance in translation. One of the most misinterpreted words of recent times is *glasnost*. The root *glas-* means 'voice'. It is a rich vein that produces the words for agreement (*soglasie*, 'co-voice-ity'),invite (*priglasit,* 'hither-voicing'), unanimous (*edinoglasno*, 'one-voice-ly'). There is a near synonym, *edinodushno*, 'one-soul-ly', which does not even allow for the possibility of abstentions; this fine distinction was exploited by newspapers in the Soviet era for indicating how truly wholehearted unanimous Politburo votes were. In a slightly different form – *golos* – it is the usual word for a 'vote'. It is distantly related to the German *Hals*, 'throat' and maybe even to the English 'call'.

Mikhail Gorbachev did not invent the term *glasnost*. It has been part of the Russian tongue for hundreds of years, and as a matter of fact it was a favourite word of Leonid Brezhnev's speechwriters. But when Gorbachev gave the word to the wider world he was saying something very specific about Soviet society, something only dimly perceived in the usual translation 'openness'. The euphoria of glasnost was not the thrill of discovery, it was not the uncovering of something hidden. Glasnost is 'voicedness', 'giving voice'; perhaps the nearest English term is 'candour'. Glasnost was a nationwide, cathartic orgy of stating the blindingly obvious. It was news to nobody that Stalin was a monster, Brezhnev a zombie, or the nation awash in a sea of vodka; everyone knew all that already. What was so wonderful and so novel was seeing the opinions one had only dared whisper in the kitchen now trumpeted from the front page of *Pravda* and *Izvestiya*. The very word 'glasnost' contained an admission by the government that they had bound every Soviet citizen into a conspiracy of falsehood, and the word was also a promise that they would do so no longer. Glasnost knocked down one of the towers of the Big Lie, the tower called the Lie of Silence. Little by little, Soviet people began to say to each other what they had long since known to be the truth. Glasnost transformed the country into a huge confessional, and confession turned out to be very good for the Russian soul.

Perestroika is a different phenomenon, both politically and linguistically. The root here is *-stroi*, 'build'. *Pere-* corresponds to the Latin prefixes pre-, re- and trans-, and *-ka* is a feminine noun ending. Hence, rebuilding or reconstruction.

There are lots of words with the *stroi-* root, all of which mean 'building' in English. There is *stroitelstvo*, the actual process of putting brick on brick; *postroenie*, building in a metaphorical sense, as in 'building a better tomorrow'; *stroika*, a building site (or, incidentally, a demolition site); *postroika*, a building under construction; *zastroika*, a 'to-building', that is, an extension or outhouse; the word *stroi* itself means a figurative edifice, as in *sotsialistichesky stroi*, the socialist system. There was also *dolgostroi*, a 'long-build'. This was the Brezhnevian term for construction projects that, due to the indolence of the workforce or inefficiency of management, remained unfinished for years. Most of them rotted, or were stripped bare by citizens seeking free materials for their country dachas. It is a phenomenon that old Karl Magnus Vitberg would find painfully familiar.

There is also a word *perenastroika*, closely related to perestroika, which means 're-tuning' of a musical instrument. In some ways this is closer to the nub of the matter. For perestroika implies adjustment or tinkering about: it suggests that the object in question is basically sound, and merely needs some improvement here and there. Here the Big Lie raised its ugly head again: the system was in need of more than a little modification. It was rotten to the core, a whited sepulchre, and had to be swept away along with its foundations.

And that, of course, is what happened. In the mid-Eighties there was a popular quip: you start with perestroika, and you end up with perestrelka. *Strel-* means 'shoot', hence *perestrelka*: crossfire, or a two-way gunbattle. It was a prophetic sort of a joke. In Russia, they are considered the best sort.

Few remember that glasnost and perestroika were just two parts of a threesome. The other ideological keyword in the earliest days of the Gorbachev revolution was *uskorenie* – acceleration. This policy byword turned out to be true only in an ironic sense. Though we could not see it, communism's undoing, not its victory, was steaming round the bend at an ever increasing rate. Uskorenie never caught on, perhaps because everyone wanted to say something or change something, but nobody wanted to plough on down the same old track. But in the new Russia, the root *skor-*, 'fast', found alternative employment in an advertising slogan. Millions of Russians who have

forgotten all about 'uskorenie' became familiar with the rhyming TV
jingle for Western packet gravy: *Knorr – vkusen i skor* – "Knorr – it's
tasty and it's quick." Sauce for the Russian goose, no longer a source
of Soviet propaganda.

"...In Russia everything happens so slowly," Yuri was saying, his
glass of vodka poised in his hand. Mark was just pouring a shot into
his own glass because he sensed the toast was coming to an end. "So
I don't suppose I will live to see any real change for the better in this,
my native land. But my wish for you on your birthday, Vadim, is that
you will live to see a better Russia, and a better world. It will never
be the communist paradise we are promised, or any sort of paradise
actually, but maybe some day all of us will live in an ordinary earthly
place that contains less fear and more joy."

"I can drink to that," said Artyom, sincerely.

"And when that day comes," Yuri concluded, "My wish is that
you will be in the company of a loved one, someone you can share
the experience with. So here's to you, son, and to you too, Rachel.
Health!"

"Health!"

As soon as the toast was over, Ira began to dish up the roast meat
and potatoes. "Yuri, don't you think the time is right to break your
news?" she said.

"Ah. I had kind of decided not to. It's Vadim's celebration after
all, not mine."

"What's this, dad?"

Yuri grimaced. "Well I might as well tell you now, I suppose. It's
my book. I had a meeting with Stroiizdat publishers this morning,
and they have accepted it for publication."

"Dad, that's great!"

"Well done," said Mark.

"Congratulations, Yuri," said Rachel.

"We must wet the manuscript. Do we have any more *shampanskoye*?" said Efim Oskarovich.

"We do," said Ira, heading for the kitchen for the hundredth time. "But Yuri can open it himself this time. I don't want anyone to get caught in the crossfire."

"The book is a history of Russian art nouveau, I understand," said Rachel.

"Sort of. Not all of art nouveau – it's called *moderne* in Russia – just the origins of the architecture. I have a whole new theory."

"I don't think Rachel wants to hear your whole thesis right now," said Ira, returning with the bottle.

"Oh, but I do. I have been very intrigued by what Vadim has told me. If it is not too tiresome I would love to hear the outlines of it."

Mark laughed. "I don't think dad will find that too hard," he said.

"Well that's all right then," said Rachel, and turned her cool gaze to Yuri.

The bottle went pop, and Yuri handed it to Vadim to do the honours.

"I hardly know where to begin," said Yuri.

"At the end," said Rachel.

"All right. My conclusion is that art nouveau architecture in Russia arose spontaneously and organically in a specific time and place, and that it owes nothing to Western influence, and that this last also makes it practically unique in Russia."

"What time, what place?"

"Abramtsevo, just outside Moscow, eighteen eighty-two."

"Abramtsevo I have heard of – the artists' colony? Eighteen eighty-two seems about right. That was about when William Morris was founding the Arts and Crafts movement in London."

"Partly right. Abramtsevo was much more than just an artists' colony; and though Morris was contemporary, and could be said to be the inspiration for Western art nouveau, he was unknown in Russia. Russian *moderne* has different roots altogether."

"Russia had its own William Morris?"

"No. Russia had no need of a William Morris. That's the point. I'll have to go back a bit."

Rachel nodded, and Yuri took a breath.

"Right then. In Russia in the middle of the last century, architecture was a state concern. It was one expression of Nikolai's threefold slogan: 'autocracy, orthodoxy, nationality'. The chief exponent of the pompous style, which grew out of these principles was Konstantin Thon."

"Hang on a minute," protested Vadim.

"We know what you think," Yuri said. "But nobody else is in any doubt that Thon was just a court jester."

"He's not still on about that church, is he?" asked Efim Oskarovich. "In God's name, boy, haven't you got better things to do?"

"What's wrong with it?"

"Dad, not now," said Ira firmly.

"You were saying," said Rachel to Yuri.

"Yes. Well, Nikolai died and Thon began to go out of fashion. The new tsar liberated the serfs and suddenly Russia felt good about herself again. In the arts, this led to a vogue for the so-called 'Russian style'. All over Moscow these fairytale buildings kept popping up with tent-roofs and brickwork made to look like carved wood."

"Like the French embassy in Moscow?" asked Rachel.

"Yes, the old Igumnov mansion."

"And the Church of the Blood down the road. Vadim and I passed it on our walk this morning."

"Yes. That one was built at the very peak of the *russky stil*, but when a new style had already been born at Abramtsevo. Abramtsevo is the key to it all. The estate belonged to Savva Mamontov, who was a railway millionaire. Every summer he invited all the best artists in Russia to come and stay with him. One day a couple of the younger artists, Polenov and Vasnetsov, went for a walk off the estate. They were strolling through some village when Polenov noticed a piece of decorative carving on the gable of a peasant cottage. It had a long weavy pattern of stylised leaves and flowers – that remind you of anything? Polenov couldn't take his eyes off it. He marched into the cottage, offered the peasant a couple of roubles, tore it off the man's house and tramped back to Abramtsevo with it under his arm. The Abramtsevans were a terribly spoilt bunch really. They thought peasants were capable of nothing more than providing dinner. So they were all thunderstruck by this new acquisition of Polenov's – you would have thought it was a message from another world. But in a sense that plank was indeed from another world – and do you know what that world is called?"

They all shook their heads in unison like children at a puppet show.

"It is the Planet William Morris," said Yuri.

Mark giggled, and Vadim took advantage of this moment of bathos to pour some more vodka and shampanskoye. Rachel was having fun, and she was intrigued by all this. Her mind was making all sorts of connections.

"How does Morris fit in?" she asked.

"Don't you see? Think about it, where was Morris all this time?"

"Not in Moscow, surely?" said Rachel, thinking for a moment of Artyom's Beatle theory.

"No, of course not. He was in London, doing what he always did. All morning he would sit at his home-made lathe, and in the afternoon he would go inside to his desk and write tirades against the industrial revolution in England. He would burble on about how medieval craftsmen knew what they were doing, where their work would end up and how it would fit in the greater scheme of things. In short, his life was a lament for a world that had gone forever, and he lived as if he was born three hundred years too late."

"In a way he was."

"No, he wasn't. He was born three thousand miles too far west. In Russia there had been no industrial revolution. Morris's medieval world was still here, not quite as idyllic as he imagined it, but the conditions were right. The peasant that Polenov encountered that morning was a gothic artisan in the full William Morris sense of the word. So you see now how it came about: in the West. The Arts and Crafts Movement, and subsequently art nouveau, were inspired by the writings of one man; it was an intellectual phenomenon. In Russia, it all grew out of what Marxists call 'objective conditions'."

"Is that what you call them?"

"It is what I call them in the book, because I have to use the politically acceptable terminology. The label doesn't matter. The important thing is that the artists who inadvertantly founded *moderne* were inspired by what they saw in the real world, not by an article in some handbound journal with a print-run of a hundred and fifty."

Rachel nodded again. "But I don't see how you get from the peasant's plank to art nouveau."

"You are right, we are not there yet. After Polenov's discovery the whole colony embarked upon a frenzy of collectioneering. Soon they had rooms full of salt pots, distaffs, cradles, milk-paddles. They used this bric-a-brac as inspiration for their own pieces, copying and refining the patterns the peasants had made naturally, instinctively. They set up an exhibition, and displayed the pieces that they themselves made alongside the ones they collected.

"In the meantime they had conceived the idea of building something solid for the community. They had had enough of going off separately to paint and collect things. They were living together in this monastic atmosphere, after all, and some of the community were conventionally religious. For all their bourgeois lifestyle the Ambramtsevans were spiritual people. They decided to make a church."

"It's amazing," said Mark, who had been very quiet up until now. "How ideas have to take on material form in Russia. It's like that old story – Carter asks Brezhnev if he collects jokes about himself, and Brezhnev says, 'Yes, I've got two and a half campsful'. If they were so spiritual why couldn't they leave it at that? Why did they have to erect a monument to themselves?"

"I don't think they saw it that way," said Yuri. "They just wanted to leave a trace, that is all. It is a very natural desire."

"But all things pass and no-one ever leaves a trace in the end," said Marina softly. "It's pointless, like trying to write your name in the water of a lake."

"It's dangerous too," said Mark. "People who want to make a mark on Russia usually end up leaving a scar."

"About the church," said Rachel.

"Yes," said Yuri. "Well, what can I tell you? Polenov did all the research, and he settled on a strict elongated cube of a church with one elegant cupola, northern-style. But Vasnetsov got hold of his drawings and transformed them. He turned it into something more domestic, more warm and intimate. It looked like you could tug off the cupola, reach inside and pull out a biscuit. Later, people working in this vein would make buildings deliberately to look like household objects – towers like wine-bottles, roofs stacked like a pile of books and so on. It was all part of a preoccupation with a world full of real objects."

"That's interesting…" said Vadim, but Yuri was in full flow.

"Vasnetsov made the church somehow fatter and somehow jollier, like a stone santa claus. But the proportions remained perfect, all strictly according to the classical Golden Section. The iconostasis inside was simple wood, and the icons themselves were a mixture: some old ones, and some painted specially by the community – just like the wooden pots-and-pans collection in the house. I'll take you to see it one day when I am in Moscow, Rachel. It is my favourite building in all the world, and what is more, it is the first genuine piece of art nouveau in all Russia."

"It is still standing, then?"

"Oh yes," said Yuri. "It is much too significant to knock down."

"Hasn't anybody noticed its significance before?"

"Not fully. Abramtsevo is well known, of course, the church has been written about, and everybody is aware that many of the artists who worked there went on to become leading practitioners of *moderne*. But nobody has ever pointed at the church and said, look! here is the first fruit, everything else in *moderne* issues from this point; what's more, we did it on our own with no help from the West, and it is very, very beautiful."

"It's funny what you were saying about household objects," said Vadim. "Herzen said Thon's churches looked like spice-racks. He meant it as an insult."

"That struck me too," said Rachel. "Because you know who else was interested in household objects: Akhmatova and the other Acmeists. The poems are full of shoes, chairs, samovars, old maps. In the West, the cataloguing of it all is an entire industry for researchers like me. I know someone in the States who spends his life writing papers with titles like 'Silverware in the Silver Age – the Role of Spoons and Forks in Akhmatova's Lyrics'."

The Russians all laughed, but Mark took up the theme. "All writing has props and scenery," he said. "The Acmeists were surely no different in that respect."

"Oh, but they were," said Rachel. "They were using those silver knives and forks to attack the occultism of Symbolist poets like

Balmont and Bryusov."

"Bryusov? Occult?" said Mark.

"Yes, in the sense that everything, every word, for the Symbolists had a hidden meaning. The Acmeists said that they were sick of a rose always being a cipher of mystical love. They believed that a rose should be allowed to be a beautiful object in the physical world. They nearly called themselves Adamists, because a poet should look on the world with the same wonderment as Adam on the first day of creation. But to the Symbolists poetry was a kind of liturgy, and they were the priests."

"Poets always believe they are priests," said Mark. "Priests of language. Priests of feeling."

"Not the Acmeists," Rachel smiled her beautiful smile. "They believed they were architects."

"Architects?"

"Mandelshtam's first book was called *Stone*," said Vadim.

"Yes," said Rachel. "For the Acmeists, words were just as much objects in the physical world as anything else. They selected their words from the great quarry of the language, they weighed them up in their hands; they cemented them together to construct the edifice of a poem. Poetry to them was architecture with words."

"Some people might say that architecture is poetry with bricks," said Vadim.

"Thon, for example?" said Mark.

"No, Vitberg," said Vadim.

"But there is a link here," said Rachel. "I would say that the Acmeists with their domesticity, their architectural approach and their opposition to any kind of pomposity, are very close in spirit to the Abramtsevans. I would say that Acmeism is *moderne* in literature."

"Hmm," said Yuri.

"Time for a cup of tea, I think," said Ira, getting up.

"Time for a smoke-break," said Yuri, and he led the way out onto the stairwell, followed in Indian file by Mark, Marina and Artyom. Efim Oskarovich, wincing, brought up the rear, and Vadim and Rachel were left alone for a few moments.

"You have made a great impression on dad," said Vadim.

"Do you think so? I was worried I may have been behaving too... bookishly."

"No, that's the way we like it here."

"Mark doesn't seem to like it."

"He is in an odd mood. I don't know what's the matter with him today."

"Is your grandad all right. He looks ill to me."

"Yes, I think so too. He's getting on, I suppose."

"I think he is in pain."

Ira came back in with a tray of teacups and a towering home-made gateau consisting of layers of sponge bound together with toffee. This babel of a cake was crowned with a single candle.

"Goodness me, that is an impressive thing," said Rachel.

"Speciality of the house," said Ira, pleased to be complimented. "It's called a Napoleon. Which reminds me..." She put the cake down and went to the sideboard. She took a package from the drawer. It was a record in a paper bag. "Happy birthday, Vadik, with all my love. It is a small gift, but I hope you like it."

Vadim took the record out of its bag. It was a recording of Tchaikovsky's 1812 Overture.

"Play it later, when you have some time to yourself," said Ira.

"Thank you."

At this moment the smoking party returned. Ira looked alarmed. "Goodness me," she said. "The kettle isn't even on yet. Play it later, Vadim, and read the sleevenotes."

"I know already," he said.

"What do you know?" said Efim Oskarovich, easing himself

back into his chair.

"About the 1812 Overture. It was written for the consecration of the Cathedral of Christ the Saviour."

What happened next was completely unexpected. Efim Oskarovich crashed his fist down on the table, setting the teacups dancing. "For God's sake, Vadim, will you forget about that damned church!" he yelled, his face blotched with rage. "This idiot obsession of yours has gone too far. You are putting yourself in danger with your anti-Soviet behaviour."

"What anti-Soviet behaviour?"

"The church, the church! You know it is a forbidden subject, but you persist in digging away at it. Are you trying to ruin your life? Do you want to go to prison?"

"Dad, calm down," said Yuri, embarrassed by this sudden flare of temper. "You've gone purple as a beetroot."

"Don't you tell me what to do. You've been encouraging him."

"Me?"

"Yes, you, with your constant jibing and wisecracking. He thinks it's clever to go against the grain. And you are just as bad with your gifts, Ira."

"Grandad, it's only Tchaikovsky!" exclaimed Vadim.

"It's in…!"

That was as far as he got. A fit of coughing overcame Efim Oskarovich and suddenly he was struggling for air. "Dad," cried Ira, "Dad, what's happened?" He did not reply. Efim Oskarovich slipped sideways of the chair and rolled to the floor, his arms crossed on his chest like a stone crusader's. His eyes were bloodshot and watery, and his tongue stuck out blue.

"It's a heart attack," said Rachel. "Call an ambulance now."

Marina was already at the phone in the hall, dialling 03.

☆

Builders are everywhere, builders and destroyers.

Boris Yeltsin, for example, was a builder by trade. He loved the job, and he loved responsibility too. As a foreman on site in his young days he often had to use his imposing physical presence to bend surly brickies to his will. He was a hard man in a hard hat, and when he later became a high-flying party careerist he kept the knack of walking with crowds and talking with kings. It was this that made him popular when he was party leader in Sverdlovsk. And when he clashed with his boss in the perestroika years, the lawyer Gorbachev punished him by kicking him out of the politburo and sending him off to head the State Building Committee: 'You think you're so good with the proles, Boris, you go and work with them.'

Peter the Great loved building too. Like Yeltsin, he was a huge man. The first tsar ever to leave Russian soil, Peter came to the dockyards of Holland and England to learn the business of shipbuilding. This was his down-to-earth way of transforming Russia into a major European sea power: spend a few months sawing wood and shaping keels in Deptford, while away the evenings in the pub with the old salts (the road where Peter did his drinking is now called Muscovy Street, just behind the Port of London Authority), then go back home to Russia and tell the workers how it is done.

Yeltsin liked to foster the idea that he was a latterday Peter: a grand reformer, a Russian Sisyphus rolling back the rock of his country's ancient inertia. But hold on. Peter was a genuine colossus of a man. He single-handedly dragged Russia by its beard out of its medieval slumber and into the light of modern Europe, he forced his dozy country to look blinkingly on all it had slept through: the Quattrocento and the Cinquecento, the discovery of the New World and the revelations of Newtonian astronomy, the rise of sea power and the science of navigation, the splendours of Versailles and of

Wren's London. When Peter drew himself up to his full six-foot-eight inches and commanded 'Wake up, Russia! Look around you! Look west!', the whole country obeyed. He built a city that is still one of the wonders of Europe.

What did Yeltsin ever build? His proudest achievement was destroying the country he grew up in. Peter brought new foodstuffs, a whole education system, and arts and sciences both civil and martial – the very language testifies to these achievements: *kartofel, universitet, kofiy, landkarta, portret*; Yeltsin's contributions were also evidenced in the new Russian tongue: *mafiya, Viskas, markyeting, gyperinflyatsiya, milliardyer, geim-shou*. Deep down, Yeltsin knew he was no Peter the Great. But he was in no doubt that he cut a better figure than his other great historical rival and a man he detested as passionately as he loved Peter, namely Mikhail Gorbachev. Yeltsin was sure he was more courageous, more honest and more deserving of glory than his predecessor, and he wanted posterity to recognise it. Posterity looks unlikely to do him that favour.

Gorbachev's main achievement, like Yeltsin's, was a mighty act of destruction. There was probably never a political event where the symbolism of the act and its practical consequences were so in tune as in the case of the tearing-down of the Berlin Wall. After all, when they stormed the Bastille they found three loons and a cutpurse, and not a single political prisoner; the Gettysburg address was completely ignored by those who heard it; but the fall of the Wall that symbolically stood for the partition of Europe led directly to the that partition's end.

This is Gorbachev's achievement, the one Yuri hoped for in his birthday toast to Vadim: the liberation of millions of Europeans. Gorby did not order the manumission of Europe, or even approve of it; but he did not oppose it, and historically that amounts to the same thing. He remained a communist almost to the end, and this is something else with which Yeltsin constantly reproached him. Yet the fact that Gorbachev acted in the name of communism makes him all the more remarkable; Yeltsin, the first post-communist leader of Russia, used Bolshevik methods such as threats, tanks and presidential decrees whenever he became frustrated with his political opponents. This is the essential difference between the two men: Gorbachev thought he was a communist, but in his heart he was a democrat; Yeltsin thought he was a democrat, but in his heart he was always a communist.

Vadim wandered alone among the debris of the party. Yuri and Ira had gone to the hospital with Grandad, who was in a bad way. Artyom and Marina went home, and Mark had taken Rachel out for a walk. He was surprised when she agreed to the suggestion, but she was surely upset by the whole thing and needed to get out of the house. Vadim, it was felt, should stay at home to explain if anybody else turned up for the party.

He listlessly cleared away some plates and forks, but did not feel like tackling the washing-up. He wandered back and forth from room to room looking for something to occupy his mind, but nothing suggested itself. On the table was Ira's present, the Tchaikovsky overtures. It was unpleasantly quiet in the flat and, for want of anything else to do, Vadim decided to play the record.

He went into his father's room, where the record-player stood. He slipped the plastic disc out of its laminated sleeve – and a folded sheet of paper tumbled to the floor. Vadim saw as it fell that there was a poem written on the sheet in Ira's regular hand. Birthday wishes, like as not, he thought, something she was too shy to read out loud at the party. Vadim retrieved the paper and opened it.

What he read there was another staggering surprise. This scrap of samizdat was the real gift, and a very precious one at that. The

Tchaikovsky album, he now realised, was just camouflage. The poem read as follows:

'The Stone Hermit' (1933) – by Daniil Leonidovich Andreyev

Like the stone-made ark of our ancient creed,
Christ the Saviour rose above me.
Springtime by those walls and gardens,
Was filled with dreams of purity.

It was the custom of my youth
To go there at the twilight hour,
And sit down at a favourite bench
Amongst the patterned shrubs and flowers.

And in the silence I'd rehearse
The pages of my life alone,
Where birds sang in the jasmine beds
Or circled round the golden dome.

I grew to love those sacred times,
When, open to the rhyming sun,
Wise statues on high pedestals
Were ever blindly looking on.

And lost amid the marble shapes,
Barely seen in shimmering heights,
There was one bright and hallowed saint
I knew and loved above the rest.

At his high station, set in stone,
A benediction shaped his hand.

He watched the city's changing tides
Like a guardian angel or secret friend.

My white hermit! My good teacher!
Even at my own death's dawn
I'll not forget your tranquil face,
Your hands held up to a far mountain.

Vadim put down the sheet of paper. The poem expressed just
what he thought about the cathedral, or rather what he felt he
would have thought if ever he had seen it. Daniil Leonidovich – he
must be the son of the writer Leonid Andreyev. Vadim looked at the
date: a poem like this would surely have been worth a twenty-five
stretch in the Thirties – Mandelshtam had been martyred for a mere
eight lines. If this poem had circulated with Andreyev's own name,
it must have come to the attention of the secret police. Did he go to
the camps, then? If so, did he survive? What else did he write? And
biggest question of all, how on earth did Aunt Ira come by such a
thing?

Vadim went and fetched the cathedral notebook from his
cardboard suitcase. He lay the sheet next to the sneering doggerel
of Bedny's that he had copied in the Lenin Library the previous
winter. He read one then the other: hard to conceive of two more
different poems on the same subject. He put the record on. Then,
to Tchaikovsky's palpitatious snatches of 'The Marseillaise' and the
stately strains of 'God Save the Tsar' he copied Andreyev's verse into
his own notebook.

It was the evening of 26th May, 1983, the very moment of Vadim's
birth nineteen years before. If he had read the sleevenotes of the
record as Ira had advised, he would have been pleased by a striking
coincidence, a small fact that had escaped him in his own research.
The date of the premiere of the 1812 overture was given on the sleeve

as 26th May, 1883 – a century before to the very day. The occasion
of the first performance was not mentioned, but the date sufficed:
the boy and his church were astral twins, brothers in the zodiac, and
today was their shared day of birth.

In 1880 the last of the scaffolding inside was dismantled and
cleared away, and the church's interior was revealed in all its
sumptuous beauty. In September a letter came to Konstantin
Andreyevich in Petersburg, inviting him to come and inspect the
finished cathedral.

Thon was eighty-five years old now and very infirm. For ten
years he had not been to Moscow, and he had delegated the final
stages of the work to his deputy Dmitriev. He knew he was not really
up to the long journey. These days he hardly even left the house,
as his legs could not support him for more than a few steps. But
he had lived with Christ the Cathedral for the greater part of his
life. God had granted that he should live to see the project through
to completion; the least he could do was make the trip to the old
capital and give thanks in the temple that he himself had raised. He
decided he would go to Moscow if it was the last thing he did.

On the morning of the inspection Dmitriev came to meet
Konstantin Andreyevich at his Moscow lodgings. They exchanged
warm greetings. "It is grand to see you looking so well," said
Dmitriev, but in fact he was shocked to see how the master had aged
since last they had met. Thon wheezed asthmatically as he heaved
himself into the carriage. He spoke very little along the way. He was
breathless and almost sick with nerves. "I have waited a long time
for this day," was all he managed to say. And he clung to Dmitriev's
arm like a frightened child.

The carriage approached Christ the Saviour along the Kremlin

Embankment. Thon strained to see out of the window, but he caught only a fleeting glimpse of his handiwork before the curve of the road took it out of his range of vision. But a few moments later the south-eastern corner of the cathedral hove into view like a great ship emerging from a sea-fog. From the corner recess Loganovsky's high-reliefs – 'David returning from his victory over Goliath' and 'Abram and his confederates greeted by Melchizedek' – looked down on him like the sailors on the ship.

They came to a stop. A young man, one of the junior architects, opened the carriage door on Thon's side and bowed low. At that moment the fourteen great bells in the towers rang out in greeting. A hurrah went up from three hundred workers and builders who stood amassed on the southern steps and on the gallery below the main cupola. They waved their hats and clapped and cried, "Bravo, Konstantin Andreyevich! Hail the architect."

The joyful welcome was more than Thon's frail nerves could stand. His held tight to the carriage door, his legs buckling beneath him, and he began to weep.

Four workers hurried up to Thon with a sedan chair. Dmitriev and the young man who had opened the carriage door eased Thon into the seat and covered his knees with a plaid rug. The four workers lifted the chair on its poles and carried Thon up the broad steps. At the door a line of engineers, architects and artists was waiting to greet him. But such was Thon's agitation that he was barely able to acknowledge their presence. He merely raised a hand like a Roman judge as he was borne past the welcoming committee, and hoarsely he whispered thank you, thank you, thank you.

Now he was inside the church. He was dizzy with emotion as he cast a clouded eye round the interior. It seemed to him that the church swept him into its embrace, that the vaults and arches inclined towards him and gathered him in like a prodigal son. From the columns and the walls, the niches and the arcades, the painted faces of the saints and the apostles seemed to smile down on him in confirmation of this. Through the film of his own tears he thought he saw the figures move. He knew this was foolishness, but their silent welcome was no less real to him than the raucous cheering of the labourers that he could still hear outside. As soon as he set eyes on the hushed cavern, Konstantin Andreyevich knew his life was complete. He had come home, and it was a stone paradise of his own making.

He asked to be set down by the main altar, in front of the iconostasis. Most of the church was awash in a gold-green glow, but here a cold light streamed in, diffusing in the deep recess and throwing a steely clear luminescence on the frescoes. The octagonal iconostasis was before him, set in the eastern wing of the cathedral like a precious stone. The standing icons on its four tiers stared past him unseeing, immovably serene sentries before the throne of God. He looked up at the shallow little steeple atop the iconostasis with its fragile tracery woven from gold.

Now he turned his attention to Vereshchagin's canvases. From here he could best see the 'Deposition'. Two grim disciples were lifting the naked, lifeless body of the god-man to the ground. One of them perched on a rough ladder that rested against the right arm of the cross; the other stood on the ground, holding the Redeemer's legs in an awkward grip. A third disciple, young and beardless, crouched on the ground, a white winding-sheet draped over his knees. Behind him stood the mother of Jesus in the garb of a nun. Her face was stony with grief. With her left hand she clutched her dead son's wrist; rivulets of blood had congealed between his fingers and similar red dribbles streaked his punctured feet. Pale sunlight illuminated the dead man's skin and made it glow. Even from here, Thon could see the smoothness of the man's body against the hard, knotty texture of the cross. It was a masterful piece of art. Looking at it he was reminded of his own helplessness – that he, like the dead

Christ, relied on the strong arms of friends to hold him.

Weeping still, he asked to be moved the centre of the mosaic floor so he could inspect the cupola. He threw back his head and looked into the eyes of the Lord Sabaoth, high above him. He gazed up at the image of God, whose arms were spread in blessing, from whose head issued fans of light.

Thon toured each of the four arms of the Cathedral, returning at last to the eastern niche. Suddenly the shape of the iconostasis reminded him of the tent-roof of the church in the old Alekseevsky monastery, dismantled on his orders more than forty years ago. It was then that a magical thing happened. For the remaining moments of the tour of the Cathedral, Konstantin Andreyevich found that he looked on everything with new eyes. It was as if he had never seen anything here before this day, as if he had never commissioned the paintings and icons, never drawn a curve or measured an angle or touched a stone or paced out a square. He did not have a thought for the years of work he had put in, and could not perceive the Cathedral as the material result of his years of effort. To him it was a new creation. His feelings for Christ the Saviour were now composed entirely of a sense of awe and wonder before something majestic and sublime. The Cathedral had broken free of him, and he willingly let it go. All he could see in it now was a pale reflection of the glory of God, and that was as much as his frame could stand.

In a state of utter exhaustion Konstant Andreyevich was carried out of the church and back to the waiting carriage. He tried to make a speech, but had not the strength. He just thanked the labourers for their effort, and promised to return to Moscow within the year to take personal charge of the preparations for the dedication of the Cathedral of Christ the Saviour.

But it was not to be. Konstantin Andreyevich Thon died the following winter in Petersburg, having seen his masterpiece in its finished state once and once only. Thon's funeral was a grandiose

affair, as befitted a man with a lifetime of public service behind him.
The oration contained the following words: The name of Konstantin
Andreyevich Thon will live long in the memory of our people; so
long as the joyous chimes sound from the heights of Christ the
Saviour, Orthodox folk will make the sign of the cross and recall the
name of the man who in the name of the Blessed Redeemer created
a temple and a monument to the glory of our nation and to the woes
of its people, a man who by so doing raised a immovable monument
to his own self, under the vaults of which young artists will, for
many years to come, study the builder's art.

At the time this necrologue was spoken, young artists had one
month short of fifty years in which to study the builder's art under
the cathedral's vaults. The bells, we know, ceased to chime within a
generation; some Orthodox folk continued to make the sign of the
cross, but by the time the finale came they were very careful when
and in whose presence they performed that small ritual.

Even if Thon had lived another year, he would not have seen the
consecration of his church. The ceremony was delayed for two years
by the assassination of Alexander II.

On the day he was murdered by Ignaty Grinevitsky, the Tsar
Liberator had been due to sign a decree granting Russia a limited
parliament. Had he done so it may be – just may be – that Russia
would have been set on the road to constitutional monarchy. Many
of the horrors of twentieth-century Russian history might (only
might) have been avoided. It could be that the assassination of
Alexander II displaced Russia's historical orbit and set it on a new
course, a collision course with revolutionary bolshevism. That is
not to say that but for pudgy little Grinevitsky and his home-made
bomb, Christ the Cathedral would be here today. The Cathedral,
and the rest of Moscow too, might in any case have been shelled to
dust in 1941. The Germans might have won, and historic Moscow

might now be as extinct a city as historic Dresden. Christ the Cathedral might by now have become an Audi showroom or a smoky bierkeller.

Or, conversely, the Cathedral might have made it through the twentieth century in one piece. It might have been here yet. Perhaps in some other universe Thon's cathedral still stands, and its marble walls are at this moment ringing to the heavenly strains of Rachmaninov's *Night Vigil*, not reverberating to the clatter of the last metro out of Yugo-Zapadnaya.

An High Place For Chemosh

Then did Solomon build an high place for Chemosh, the abomination of Moab, in the hill that is before Jerusalem.

– First Book of Kings

May 1983

The room was dark and the curtains drawn. Ira closed the door gently behind Vadim. He stood still, allowing his eyes to grow used to the gloom. He could hear his grandfather wheezing, and assumed that he was asleep. But then the old man spoke up. "Come over here. I want to talk to you," he said. Vadim approached the bed and sat down in the chair by its side. "Turn the lamp on," commanded Efim Oskarovich. "Let's have a look at you."

Vadim did as he was told. Efim Oskarovich was lying propped on a pillow. His hands were by his sides on top of the counterpane. His face was ashen. He seemed to have lost five kilos in weight since the previous evening. Vadim wondered if that were possible.

"How are you, Grandad?" he asked.

"I'm dying, as you well know."

"Don't say that, Grandad."

"I do say that. Let's not lie to each other. Not today."

Vadim said nothing.

"I'm sorry if I embarrassed you and your American friend," said Efim Oskarovich. "I spoiled your birthday, and that is unforgivable."

"There'll be other birthdays."

"Not for me there won't."

There was another awkward pause. Vadim voiced the question that had kept him awake all night.

"Did I give you the heart attack?"

"No, son. I've known it was coming for a while now. I brought it on myself."

"You knew you were ill? Grandad, why didn't you go the polyclinic? They might have been able to avert it."

"I've been on borrowed time for more than forty years, Vadik. I never should have known you or even your father. Now I want to go out with dignity, not beg some doctor for a few more weeks or months."

Pause again.

"How is your Rachel?"

"Concerned for you. Upset too. But she'll get over it," he said.

"I'm sure. She's a strong girl, that one. Much stronger than you. You will need to lean on her when they really start leaning on you."

"I don't think it will come to that."

"It has already come to that," said Efim Oskarovich sharply. "For God's sake, boy, I'm not blind."

Ira came into the room. "I think it''s time you rested, dad," she said, looking daggers at Vadim. "You must not get excited."

Vadim made to leave.

"Stay there," said Efim Oskarovich.

"But..." started Ira.

"I said he is to stay," he interrupted. "I haven't finished talking to him. Now leave us alone for ten minutes or you really will finish me off with all your fussing."

Ira quickly retreated to the other room.

"That wasn't very nice," said Vadim.

"Don't you worry about Ira. I'll make my peace with her later. It's you I need now."

He swallowed.

"I've got something I want you to know, something about me. I'm telling you now because I don't want you to find out after I've gone and think the worse of me for it. The truth costs nothing when you are on your last legs. Maybe that's why death-bed confessions are so popular."

Vadim smiled. Efim Oskarovich smiled too, or maybe it was a grimace of pain.

"I know what Ira gave you for your birthday. The whole thing. I suppose you have been wondering where she got that poem from?" Efim looked at Vadim, eyebrows raised. Vadim just nodded. "She got it from me. You might say she stole it from me."

"Stole it?"

"There are ways of telling when someone has been through your belongings. She took it from my papers without telling me and wrote it out for you. That's stealing, isn't it?"

Vadim didn't know.

"I first came across that poem some time in the Fifties. Lots of stuff like that circulated in those days, after Khrushchev's speech. They were exciting times. Stories about the camps, by people who had been in the camps. I was given that poem to read by a friend of your father's. Someone he knew from the army. He was like you, too interested in everything, and naive with it. But I had been through the mill by that time. I knew what I was doing. I copied out that poem and kept it." He went silent for a moment. "You didn't know I was fond of poetry, did you?"

"I didn't."

"Well, you were right, I'm not."

"So..."

"So why did I keep that poem."

"Yes."

Efim Oskarovich was breathing heavily now, like a man plucking up courage for a big leap. "This is not a confession, Vadim. It is not absolution I am after, and I make no apologies. I have tried always to be honest in my life. I never grassed when I was in the camps, and I never flinched at the front." Vadim was perplexed. His grandfather had never so much as mentioned his imprisonment before. The boy felt a strange prickling in his neck. He had not yet guessed what Efim Oskarovich was about to tell him, and in the present instant he was not sure he wanted to hear it. He wished the interview was over with, or that Ira had tried harder to kick him out earlier. "Are you listening to me, Vadim?"

"Yes, I'm listening," he said. "Grandad, we know you did right in the war, and you were rehabilitated after the camps, weren't you? You don't have to justify yourself to anyone, least of all your own family."

"I know. It's not the family I am addressing now, it's you alone. And I told you this is not penitence. I just want you to know the truth. It is something I did years ago, when I was too young to know any better. For God's sake, lad, have you not puzzled it out for yourself? I was one of the people who tore down your precious church. I helped demolish the Cathedral of Christ the Saviour."

The idea for a Palace of Soviets was originally mooted by Sergei Kirov at the first Congress of Soviets in 1922. From the tribune he said that the Palace "should be an emblem of the coming might, the triumph of communism, not only here, but in the West too. It is said of us that at lightning speed we are wiping from the face of the earth the palaces of the bankers, the landowners and the tsars. And it is true. In their place we shall raise a new palace, a palace of the workers and the labouring peasants. We will put all our worker-peasant creativity into this monument."

Like so many of the peripheral figures in this story, Kirov was right without knowing he was right: from the very start, he linked the idea of a Palace of Soviets to the destructive power of the new regime. And this was some years before the real pogroms of buildings and people began: in 1922 most of the city's ancient architecture was still intact, and most of the citizenry was still there to see it.

The Congress passed a resolution, promptly forgot all about it, and that ought to have been the end of the whole idea. But less than two years later, in the bitter winter of 1924, Lenin died. His posthumous cult took off, and there began the slow metamorphosis of Marxism from an untried economic theory into a compulsory state religion.

The new faith needed its holy places. Lenin's body was at first installed in a makeshift wooden mausoleum on Red Square. The winter cold kept his corpse in natural deep-freeze inside this temporary temple. While he lay there, an ambitious young architect named Balikhin wrote a proposal that the Palace of Soviets earlier described by Kirov should be combined with a memorial to Lenin. Balikhin had thought the whole thing through: "The best place for it," he wrote, "is the square where the cathedral of Ch. Saviour stands [by 1924, people were already a little squeamish about writing the word 'Christ']. As a monument of history and art the cathedral is worthless. There is no sound reason for preserving it, at least none which cannot be overcome on the path to materialising this magnificient idea." Balikhin sent his immodest proposal to *Pravda*, hoping they would publish his scheme. "There is no more worthy way to immortalise the memory of LENIN!" he wrote in a covering letter.

But he was in for a disappointment. The editor of *Pravda*, who seems to have been a good judge of copy but a bad judge of history, returned the typescript with a dismissive note: "We will make ourselves a laughing-stock, and deservedly too, if we start publishing plans for tearing down whole blocks and vast buildings." And that, again, should have been that. But Balikhin tucked his plans and manifestos away in a drawer and waited. He knew his idea was ahead of its time, but not by much. He knew the deep symbolism of his scheme would prove irresistible in the end.

The idea lay dormant for six years, the second of its three long hibernations, and emerged again in 1931. The timing is significant. The Revolution was slowly fading from the national memory. Boredom and disillusion were setting in. The previous year Mayakovsky, drummerboy of the Revolution, had taken a revolver and blown a large hole in his chest, the surest sign yet that the enthusiastic romanticism of the early days had gone. (Just the week before the unspeakable Bedny had said to him, in the course of an argument about art, "You shut your mouth, Mayakovsky, you are a dead man already." This, as we know, was the second time in Mayakovsky's career that a fellow professional had asked him to be quiet; it is the sort of thing that can get a poet down.)

The revolution had lost its momentum. The people, especially the young people who were the nation's future, needed a way to restore their confidence in the new order, to fire their imagination and recapture the revolutionary optimism of the early days. They needed bread and circuses. The bread was being expropriated from the peasants: Pavlik Morozov met his sticky end in the summer of 1931 and was immediately beatified – the boy-god of perfidy. The circus was provided by the Palace itself: it was to be a project on such a scale that the whole Soviet people would be able, would be obliged, to contribute. The Palace of Soviets was not just a big building. It was a focus for the energy of an entire nation, something real and tangible to build when the goal of building socialism seemed too abstract and too distant.

On 17th April a letter was sent out to all the leading architects of the Soviet Union inviting them to submit a design by the end of June.

The brief was broad and simple: the palace was to reflect the spirit of the age, it had to be big enough to house party congresses, and it had to be an architectural monument for the capital. The suggested site for the palace was on Okhotny Ryad, where the Gosplan building now stands.

Among those called to take part was Balikhin, now an established avant-gardist and leader of the Association of new Architects, ASNOVA for short. He freshened up the drawings he had prepared seven years before and sent them in. Despite the brief, Balikhin's plan placed the Palace on the square where Christ the Saviour stood. His design took the form of a 100-metre cube: "The sides of the cube will be a diary of the world union of socialist republics, on which each new republic joining the USSR will be inscribed, until eventually, written in red on the top line, will appear the date of the world revolution, the day of the formation of the Global Union of Soviet Socialist Republics." Yes, Balikhin was a man ahead of his time: what he was proposing was the ultimate *stengazeta*.

Representatives of all those involved in judging the competition met throughout that summer. In the voting council there was much discussion of the site. The one mentioned in the original brief was meant only as a suggestion, but still the overwhelming majority felt that Okhotny Ryad would be the best place for it. Six meetings were held between 25th April and 2nd June. The Cathedral of Christ was not even mentioned until the third meeting, when it was suggested as a site by a member of Balikhin's ASNOVA group. The proposal was ignored, but at the next meeting Kryukov, chairman of the Construction Administration, announced that the government members on the committee were unhappy with the direction the talks were taking. They felt that Okhotny Ryad was too neutral a spot. (They were right, of course: though Gosplan is one of the biggest and squarest buildings in the centre of Moscow, it is easy to walk past without even noticing it's there. At ground level it is just a faceless stretch of wall.) The architects came up with a new site: Kitai-Gorod, the oldest part of the city apart from the Kremlin itself, just to the east of Red Square. It was put to a ballot and passed. Only Balikhin, present in person on this occasion, demurred. He doggedly cast his vote for Christ the Cathedral.

The architects on the council were being very dim. They completely failed to take the crashing hints that were being dropped, and they never twigged who Balikhin's backers were. Voroshilov himself sent a message to the fifth meeting asking the architects to reconsider. To add extra pressure, the meeting was held in Molotov's office in the Kremlin. But again the council failed to do what the political authorities were demanding of them. Perhaps they really did not understand what the party wanted, perhaps they believed that the government was genuinely interested in their professional opinion, that they were more than just a rubber stamp. Certainly, they did not know how ridiculous they looked, baying for Barabbas's blood and asking that Christ the Saviour be spared. Whatever their thinking, they again recommended Kitai-Gorod, adding as an afterthought that Bolotnaya Square, on the clown's frown of an island in the Moscow River, might be a good second choice. Now Molotov, or rather Molotov's boss, lost patience with the talking-shop he had set up. At the sixth and final meeting the architects were simply told that it was to be the Cathedral of Christ, and there was an end to it.

In fact, Stalin had paid a quiet visit to the site the previous day, the latest in a long line of Russian rulers to cast an eye over the little hillock of Chertolye. It was then, if not a long while before, that the final decision was taken: 1st June 1931 is the day that sentence of death was passed on the Cathedral.

Efim Oskarovich seemed to have got a second wind.

"We began by building a wooden fence round the site. The fence was made of tall four-metre planks roughly nailed together. We didn't bother to trim them to length – what was the point? We didn't think the job would take all that long and the stockade was only to stop people seeing what was going on. It took a couple of days, but soon the whole cathedral was penned in like a milch-cow.

"While I was still fence-building, other brigades got down to the real work. One crew was detailed to strip the main cupola, while others got on with the four smaller ones. They started from the bottom of the dome and spiralled their way up to the point. The gold sheets came away in neat squares. They were lowered to the ground with ropes and pulleys and stacked in a pile inside the church. Piled up like that they looked like one of Ira's Napoleon cakes, and a soldier stood on guard to make sure nobody took a bite.

"Once the fence was finished I was sent to help with the cupola. From an engineering point of view it was fascinating. As the gold came away you could see the whole intricate construction – a real cat's cradle of girders and wires. Credit where credit is due, I thought it was a grand piece of work. If you ask me, it was a shame that such a fine construction had been covered with gold for all those years.

"We had all sorts of problems getting the cross down. It must have been a good three metres tall, and it was immensely heavy. We undid all the bolts we could find joining it to the pinnacle of the cupola frame, but some were rusted solid, so even when we had done all we could to loosen it, the cross was still standing fast. Also it was hard to work up there because we were exposed to bitterly cold crosswinds: you couldn't work on a stubborn bolt for more than a few minutes at a time. In the end we just attached long ropes to the cross, fed them down to the ground, and tugged it off its perch with brute force. The top of the cross broke off, and the rest of it tumbled down the side of the cupola and got stuck in the metal spars. It looked like a gold fly in an iron spider's web.

"We used the same method for the cupolas themselves. We pulled them off in chunks. Long ropes were attached to the building at one end and to heavy tractors at the other. When everything was ready, one of the foremen would blow a whistle and we would all have to get out of the way. Then the tractors would slowly take up the tension and draw away from the cathedral in low gear. You would hear a creaking and a snap of metal and section by section the dome came crashing to the ground."

Efim Oskarovich twisted his body to open the drawer of his bedside table. He pulled out an old photograph and handed it to Vadim. The picture showed a group of workers in high boots, long trenchcoats and cloth caps, posing in one of the corner towers of the cathedral. Some had their hands thrust in their pockets, others squatted on their haunches, all had adopted the self-conscious, formal posture of people unused to being in the lens of a camera. In the foreground was the naked framework of the cathedral roof and a stretch of supporting wall, already partly dismantled. One bare-headed young labourer sat in what looked like a very precarious position on this rickety brick wall, his arms folded and his feet resting on a bent girder. He stared haughtily down into the camera.

"That's my brigade," said Efim Oskarovich. And pointing to the young man, "And, that's me, showing off as usual." He flopped back on his pillow and continued his story with his eyes closed. Vadim kept hold of the photo as he listened, trying to make the connection between the venturesome youth who peered out at him across the decades and the old man who now lay wheezing before him.

"The cathedral looked very odd without the domes," Efim Oskarovich went on. "Disproportionate, also undignified and kind of tragi-comic. I only ever saw one other sight like it and that was later, in the camps, when new inmates arrived. With their new-shaved heads, their look of self-pity and bewilderment, and the prison jackets that came down over their fingers, they made just the same impression – part-sad, part-funny, but mostly just clumsy.

"Just after that picture was taken, we took the bell out of the tower. That was easy: we just lifted it off its hinges and tipped it out. It fell point-downwards and buried itself in the ground like a bomb dropped from an aeroplane. Other brigades had a harder job if they were dismantling parts that were earmarked for some other use. The fellows who stripped the marble from the inside walls were under strict instructions not to damage it in the process. Each slab was carefully numbered before it was prised off the brickwork. As soon as they took it down it was loaded onto horse-drawn carts and taken across the road to Palace of Soviets metro station, which was being built at the same time. There must have been a fantastic quantity of marble in that building. Every day for three months they shipped out six or seven wagonloads. Such riches, Vadim, you can't imagine."

On 13th July, 1931, as the preparations for the quartering of the Cathedral began, a second open competition for the Palace of Soviets was announced. One hundred and sixty designs were submitted. Twenty-four entries came from abroad, and an astonishing one hundred and twelve were the work of amateurs. All the projects were put on public display in August 1931, even as the job of clearing the site was in progress.

It would be churlish to suggest that the Palace designs were anything less than stunning. The idea of a beacon for the socialist world caught the imagination of some of the greatest architects of the era. All of the inventiveness and innovation that had characterised the art of the Twenties was here on show, but at the same time many of the designs were forward-looking, even futuristic.

Alexander Vesnin contributed a bulbous design that looked like Yuri Gagarin's space helmet; Moisei Ginzburg and Gustav Hassenpflug dreamed up an Art Deco teasmaid; Nikolai Ladovsky's building had a dome that slid open so that, as he explained in an accompanying note, "delegates could receive greetings direct from the skies". Viktor Olenev's palace was shaped like a huge number six, for did not the Soviet Union constitute a sixth part of the world?; Alexander Vlasov made a model that looked like a great spider; Yakov Doditsa and Alexei Dushkin took the beacon idea literally, and drew a glowing glass building that was in effect a six-hundred-foot lightbulb, casting its electric glare over the whole city at night.

Looking at the designs, one sometimes has to pinch oneself so as not to forget the scale of the objects in the drawings, that they were intended to cover three blocks and tower to the heavens. For example, Nikolai Vasiliev's amusing project was called The Ship of State, but his bright orange snub-nosed ship resembles nothing so much as a fairground dodgem; it is the Bumper-Car of Bolshevism. Joseph Urban imagined a large slice of pie, and this, like Olenev's, is presumably a reference to the USSR's share of the global cake. Naum Gabo envisaged a big frilly thing: from above it is a stone doily, and in perspective a dung beetle with wings spread. Auguste and Gustave Perret submitted a doodle on the back of an envelope, and it looks like, well, a doodle on the back of an envelope. Le Corbusier's blueprint is, predictably enough, a piece of machinery, and it even seems to have some moving parts: his rough drawings show the main corpus of the building revolving like a cam head. Berthold Lubetkin presented a spaceship, pure and simple: his pictures show a classic flying saucer on the launchpad. Walter Gropius's design is as mechanical as Le Corbusier's; his brilliant palace is a circular sliderule, or a colossal cog for all the little cogs to convene in.

But the designs that came closest to the spirit of the age (and to the taste of the Client) were those that looked like buildings, not buildings trying to look like something else. Vladimir Shchuko and Vladimir Gelfreikh planned a monumental Babylonian box, a pumped-up Ark of the Covenant. Alexei Shchusev, the man who built the final Lenin Mausoleum, offered a classical Greek temple writ large, its colonnades and arcades shrinking into the distance like tightly packed telegraph poles in an urban prairie. This design featured a tower with a giant human figure aloft, an idea that appealed to the Palace Committee. But none of these won. The prize went to Boris Iofan, an architect who, like Thon, learned his trade in Rome and who, like Vitberg, had friends in high places to help him win the commission.

These are not the only points of contact between Iofan and his two unfashionable predecessors. Like them, he was setting out to build a monument to a national victory, a victory ascribed to the greatness of the Russian idea. All three set out consciously to build the biggest edifice in the world, to outshine the West, and to make it a place of gathering and – for this is not stretching the point – a centre of worship. Like Thon, Iofan was at once a willing servant of the state and a prisoner of the state's demands on him. Like Vitberg, he was destined never to see his building complete. But, as Evgeniya Kirichenko points out, he continued to believe in it long after it had become clear it would never be built.

Iofan's design was recognisably in the manner we now know as Stalinesque Gothic or Totalitarian Wedding-Cake. He can claim to be the author of modern Moscow's most distinctive architectural style. In Iofan's original drawings the wedding-cakiness of the structure is particularly marked. The bottom two levels of the building are square and the top two are round. On the flat roof, perched on the edge, stands the lone figure of a liberated proletarian, like a plastic bridegroom gesticulating wildly at the skies or at the absent bride. Though this proposal triumphed over those of the greatest architects of the age, Iofan's – it was made clear to him – was in need of a good deal of revision. Its main fault, in the opinion of Molotov, who now officially headed the Palace Commission, was *prezemistost*, 'groundliness', in other words it was too short. At 200 metres it was only twice the size of the Cathedral it was replacing, barely any bigger than the present university building.

The plans for 1933, the year the Palace was originally due to have been completed, show a fifth tier plonked on the top. The liberated proletarian had at Stalin's personal suggestion been replaced by a Lenin. A separate competition was organised for this statue. Twenty-five sculptors took part, and the commission was awarded to Sergei Merkurov. His Lenin was seventy-five metres tall, almost twice the height of the Statue of Liberty. Lenin's arm was raised like he was hailing a taxi, or waving cheerily at his own mummified body away on the other side of the Kremlin. He was wearing a flowing overcoat and he was bareheaded. In short, he was the archetypal piece of leninoplasty, one might say the platonic ideal of the genre. All the three-rouble desk-busts of the Great Leader, every mass-produced town-square Ulyanov, all the plaster heads like moulded boulders in the vestibules of institutes, police stations, in the 'red corner' of every factory and school, all the countless thousands of seated lenin statues, thoughtful lenin statues, jut-jawed exhortational lenin statues, all the slant-eyed Central Asian lenins and the swarthy Caucasian lenins, the striding-into-the-future lenins, the suffer-the-little-children grandpa-lenins, the lenins-and-stalins, the lenins-on-armoured-cars, the apocryphal waving-goodbye lenin who had one cap in his hand and another on his head (they say the sculptor was made to chip it off in the night), the subversive lenin on Lenin Square, Erevan, whose left hand was posed such that, from the right angle, it looked like his dick was hanging out (I saw it, it really did – there was even a KGB man stationed at the offending spot to move along snickering tourists), the granite lenin-in-Razliv-writing-stateandrevolution-on-a-treestump, the leaping lenin in Leningrad known as the ballet-dancer, they all owe a debt to the lenin-that-never-was, the invisible mother of all lenins, the largest figure in the history of statuary, the never-to-be-built Lenin of the Palace of Soviets.

While the statue competition was in progress, major changes were made to its huge pedestal. It was deemed that the five-tier version was still far too stumpy. Shchuko and Gelfreikh were drafted in to help Iofan get it right, to make it bigger and more impressive. The corners of the building were populated with busy muscle-bound caryatids, proletarian gargoyles all frozen in the act of building communism; the capitals were decorated with bas-reliefs of marching masses. The three discs of the upper levels were teased out, extended like a telescope. The fourth tier was stretched to make a deep drum; the fifth tier popped up like a top-hat; a sixth tier was added as a footrest for Lenin's huge boots; Lenin himself continued to grow like Pinnochio's nose until he reached a fully tumescent one hundred metres. His index finger alone was as long as a lamp-post, and standing on the ground he would have been able – on tippytoes – to touch the point of the cross on the Cathedral of Christ.

The building he balanced on was now over four hundred metres high, taller than the Empire State, which of course was the point of its upward pandiculation. The gigantomanic tendency that Vitberg and Thon had just about kept in check now superseded all architectural and artistic considerations. In the real world, Lenin would have been invisible above the navel on all but the clearest of days; his upper body would have been permanently lost in the clouds. This is not apparent on the jaw-dropping artists' impressions of the Palace drawn in the mid-Thirties. In these pictures he towers above an all-new Moscow in which the only recognisable feature is the Kremlin, reduced to a dinky little toy castle at the feet of the enormous Palace. All the rest is a fantasy to make Albert Speer gasp – the old Moscow has been wiped clean like a blackboard; a grand processional thoroughfare, Palace of Soviets Avenue, half a mile wide, runs south-west along the precise axis of Vitberg's mystic thread; the Avenue is lined with symmetrical towers and colonnades; there are gardens, fountains, neat squares and, like tiny mites in this Jack-and-the-Beanstalk world, there are Soviet people going about their business. Images like this were widely published in the 1930s. Everyone knew that this was the world of tomorrow, the society they were here to construct.

The sketches by Shchuko and Gelfreikh are so obviously cinematic, bi-planes flying in chevrons over the building and great phalanxes of the faithful demonstrating with red flags in the foreground, that one cannot help feeling the authors missed their true calling: they should really have been set designers for Cecil B. deMille. And there is an important key here: when you look at the drawings you suddenly get the feeling that it was not New York the Soviets were trying to outdo, but Hollywood. For who is this paper Ozymandias, teetering on the pinnacle of the skyscraper? What is that monstrous giant doing up there? The bi-planes are the clue; in fact, they are a giveaway. Why, it's King Kong in a three-piece suit.

Efim Oskarovich stopped to cough. He took a sip of water, then asked Vadim to find him a smoke. Vadim went to the kitchen, where he found a blue packet of Kosmos on the breadbin. He lit a cigarette from the gas stove and brought it glowing to his grandfather. "Who decided what was to be done with all the art?" he asked.

"There was a whole army of art historians and museum curators going round saying what had to be saved and what could be smashed up," said Efim Oskarovich. "They worked hardest in the early stages. All the furniture in the church, also the priests' vestments, the candlesticks, plates, goblets, bibles, not to mention the dozens of icons, were taken to one corner of the cathedral where the valuables commission noted them down in a big book and sent them off in sledges – it was snowy by then. Hundreds of thousands of roubles' worth of stuff – I don't know what became of it all, but all the priests' clothes were thrown on a bonfire. The commission was only interested in antiques. I dare say some of it found its way into private hands, because a lot of the objects they turned their noses up at were actually very pretty. But I did not see any pilfering going on myself."

"Was it hard work, taking the church down?"

"Hard, but enjoyable. Everybody went at it with such determination and enthusiasm. That was the tone for the nineteen-thirties. We all believed we were building a new society. We weren't stupid; we realised it was a symbolic task, clearing the way for the Palace of Soviets. It was a slow job, moving that mountain stone by massive stone. At the start we used logs as rollers, like they did in ancient Egypt, but that was very inefficient. One day I went to one of the foremen and said, look, why don't we lay a track into the church and move the stuff out on flat bogeys. It'll be so much quicker. The foreman put it to the higher-ups, who said they thought it was a grand idea. I was put in charge. We laid a circular track – in one entrance and out another – with two long cars. One team loaded up on the inside, and another unloaded on the outside by the embankment, while I co-ordinated the whole thing. My mates teased me about my promotion: Efim's gone up in the world, they said. Next thing you know he'll be building a dacha next to his railway.

"The tracks worked well for flat slabs, like the marble and labrador, but it did not cope so well with big, irregular shapes. I remember we tried to put one of the angel statues onto my invention. This cherub was about three metres tall. We put a noose round its neck, lifted it off the ground with a crane. Then six of us manoeuvred the statue onto the wagon. It did not have a single flat edge, this little angel, and it kept blowing about in the wind. If it swung your way the only thing to do was duck, because it weighed a tonne. It must have been a laughable sight, half a dozen grown men trying to put a giant, disobedient baby to bed."

Efim Oskarovich laughed silently at the memory, but his giggle turned into another fit of coughing. As soon as the attack subsided he took another drag from his cigarette. Vadim guessed that his grandfather's cherub was part of Loganovsky's 'David and Goliath' one of the pieces in the Don Monastery. He took advantage of the pause to put another question to him. "Did you see the explosion?"

"Yes, I was there. We had been working for a couple of months when it became clear that there was no way we were going to finish the job by New Year. The architects were very keen that the cathedral should be gone before the start of nineteen thirty-two. They wanted to get down to work in time for the fifteenth Revolution Day."

"Nineteen thirty-two would also have been the centenary of Thon's project. He started work in eighteen thirty-two."

"If you say so. I don't know if that concerned the bosses or not. In any case, when it became clear that the walls of the cathedral were just too solid to be chipped away with pickaxes they sent in a group of explosives engineers. A day was set and we had to finish removing all the innards before then."

"It was the fifth of December, nineteen thirty-one."

"You know best. I remember it was very cold and clear. The main explosion was scheduled for lunchtime. We were not allowed to hang around on the day, but I was interested to see the finale, so I went and climbed the fire escape of the first house on Gogolevsky Boulevard. I got onto the roof and found that practically everybody who lived in the building was there.

"The first explosion was really shocking. It nearly knocked me off my feet. The ground jumped and all the women on the roof screamed. I saw only one of the four towers come down. It just deflated, and a huge ball of brickdust rolled out from the church like a slow, red wave. The cloud looked so solid, like a living thing. I thought we would be suffocated, but the dust somehow dissipated and turned into this eerie pink mist. It hung over the wreckage for the rest of the day, for days after too. I don't remember how many separate explosions there were altogether – four or five maybe. It was an impressive sight, I can tell you."

"I suppose that was the end of your job."

"God, no. There was still a lot of work to be done clearing the rubble. I came early the next morning, when it was still dark. The ruins were very dramatic by moonlight – all jagged and Gothic. I was one of the first on the site. Bits of the walls were still standing. There was half a doorway at one corner with a statue of a bishop or a saint on top. He looked like a fanatical old stylite.

"The job was more straightforward now, because there was nothing slated for salvage. It was just a question of getting rid of the huge slag-heap. We climbed all over it like dung-beetles. The pile of debris must have been twenty metres high and a hundred metres long. We lay long wooden chutes up the hill and started clearing from the top. Whole bricks down one chute, broken bricks down another, granite down another, to fleets and fleets of waiting trucks who ferried it away to various building sites."

"They used the bricks for new buildings?"

"Of course. Waste not, want not. There was a lot of building going on in those years, as well as lot of demolition – don't you forget that. It took at least a month to move the rubble, maybe it was two. Everything was done at top speed because the Palace of Soviets was supposed to have been finished within two years."

"Two years – it's unreal."

"Maybe. But in those days everything seemed possible. We

believed in the future, and that meant turning our back on the past."

"But the Palace didn't get built, did it. The old was wiped away and nothing replaced it."

"In this case, yes. But you know the Cathedral was doomed from the start. I remember one of the brigade saying that when they knocked down the Alekseyevsky monastery, one of the evicted nuns put a curse on the site. She said no other building would ever stand in its place. We just fulfilled the prophecy."

"Yes, I have heard stories like that."

"And you know the ancient name of that part of town: *Chertolye*, Devil's Acre. The *oprichniki* tortured people to death there. It has been an evil spot ever since."

"It is not proven that the *oprichnina* had a base there. And the word *chertolye* is probably from *cherta* – boundary, not *chert* – devil."

"Never mind what's proven. The people remember it that way, and the people are never wrong about such things. They never forget a place of execution or a word of malediction."

1935

The vestments of Christ the Saviour were divided up and alloted. The main beneficiary was the nearby metro station, which was lined with Protopopovo marble and opened to passengers in 1935. The dark labradorite went for the plinth of the Moskva Hotel, then under construction. The brick, that huge mountain of it, was shared between the Mossnabbyt building trust and the Lenin Institute.

The gold and other precious metals all went to the state coffers, and the octagonal iconostasis was sold abroad for hard currency. It was purchased by Eleanor Roosevelt, who donated it to the Vatican. The marble tablets bearing the names of the heroes of the Patriotic

War later surfaced in Moscow University, along with the jasper columns from the portals. One of the fourteen bells went to the river port in the north of Moscow; two others were given to the Moscow Arts Theatre.

Three of Loganovsky's friezes were spared, as we know. For more than twenty years they lay around in pieces on the grounds of the Don Monastery. They were finally assembled at a far wall in the late Fifties. A few other pieces of artwork were also reprieved: Semiradsky's *Last Supper* went to the vaults of the Tretyakov Gallery, Vereshchagin's *Adoration of the Magi* and *The Anointing of King David* to the State Historical Museum, along with two other pieces by Semiradsky and one by Surikov.

There is one other place where one can to this day see the strange remains of Thon's Cathedral: it is another metro station, Novokuznetskaya on the orange line. It inherited twenty-one ornate marble benches, which now line the platforms and the central vestibule of this busy changeover stop. These great long thrones have solid scrolls for arms and are carved with vine leaves as thick and juicy as steaks; other have a winding oak-leaf design or a pattern like fish scales. They seem too grand for the narrow concrete platform, but the benches have set the theme for the whole station. It is designed as a monument to Soviet arms, just as the Cathedral commemorated the military victories of Tsarist Russia. Above the benches in the central corridor of the station is a long frieze depicting acts of heroism from the Second World War, and down the middle runs a row of lamp-posts, perhaps a faint echo of the celebrated Yablochkov electric lamps that were installed outside the Cathedral on the death of Alexander III. On the platforms above the benches are little medallions of Suvorov, Kutuzov and Alexander Nevsky, another small nod to the past.

If Kropotkinskaya station glories in its stolen raiment, then Novokuznetskaya feels like an apology for the lost splendour of the church, or at least for the obliteration of the feat of soldiery it honoured. The tribute is a tacit one, however. There is nothing in the station to say what the benches are or where they came from. Yet seated on the cool seats one can still feel, in spite of the noise and the rush-hour bustle, a solemn, churchy kind of stillness.

And here's a funny thing: among metro-workers, Novokuznetskaya is considered the best station on the line to be assigned to. Underground men are no more or less superstitious than anyone else in Russia, but they say that you don't get ill when you work at Novokuznetskaya, and all the aches and pains you do have just seem to fade away like mist.

But all this was in the past or in the future. By 1937 the gaping pit of the Palace had been carved out. The solid raft of Thon's foundations had gone along with the rest of his work, and behind a high fence, guarded day and night by armed soldiers, the mechanical diggers gnawed deeper and deeper into the bedrock.

Iofan and his team now knew the size of the job ahead. The completion date had been put back to 1942, the end of the third five-year-plan, much more realistic than the two-year deadline stipulated when the competition had been announced. Soviet architects made regular trips to the USA to study the techniques of skyscraper-building, a skill that – for all its bombast – the Soviet Union did not possess. Special workshops were set up to solve the acoustic and optical problems posed by the Palace of Soviets. New kinds of steel and brick were developed specially.

For the task was truly Herculean. The Palace was to have room for 25,000 visitors at a time, the main conference hall alone was intended to house 15,000. There was to be a library big enough to hold half a million books; there were to be countless reception rooms, kitchens, buffets, guardhouses, lavatories, reading rooms, auditoria, press centres, workshops, switchboards and smoking rooms. The only thing about it that seems rather small is the carpark:

there was to be space for a mere 400 vehicles. But in the traffic-free 1930s, and in a country where public transport was not just an urban convenience but an ideological statement too, such a carpark would have seemed vast.

In 1938 Stalin appointed himself to the Construction Committee, thereby underlining the importance he personally attached to the project. The early stages of building proceeded apace, and it was decreed that there would be no winter break for the builders. In the last days of the 1930s, the first shoots of its metal framework appeared above the fence. The Stone Bridge, built along with the Cathedral a hundred years before, was dismantled. A new and bigger one was constructed a little further downstream in anticipation of the cohorts of demonstrators who would soon come marching from the Zamoskvoreche suburb to the Palace. Plans were also laid to narrow the Moscow River so as not to cramp the new building, and to give the embankment a more even curve. The building materials were stacked high on the site, vast concrete fins set in the ground marked the line of the exterior walls, and great cranes stood like nodding brontosauri above it all. There was little doubt that the palace would be completed on schedule.

Then Nazi Germany attacked the Soviet Union. The Soviet state was suddenly in danger of being toppled. In October 1941 the metal carcass of the Palace, built and awaiting assembly on site, was turned into hedgehog tanktraps. Work on the Palace was officially suspended in December: Stalin issued a decree to that effect on the 19th, when the Germans were on the point of occupying the capital as Napoleon had done 129 years before. But Moscow did not fall that winter. In 1942 girders earmarked for the palace were shipped to the Urals for railway bridges.

The Palace was not cancelled, merely postponed. All the administrative machinery under Iofan remained in place, and it was given various odd jobs to do during the war, such as carrying out repairs on Lenin's mausoleum. After the defeat of Germany, the palace apparatus was entrusted with building the seven spiky skyscrapers, or *vysotki*, which are now the most distinctive feature of the city's skyline. These seven sisters are like offshoots from the roots of the Palace of Soviets. They are all gigantic, particularly the Moscow University building, but they would have appeared positively runtish next to Iofan's finished creation. And as the German architectural theorist Karl Schloegel has pointed out, each of the *vysotki* is turned to face the empty space where the Palace of Soviets should have been. If those stones could speak they would all be crying out: where's Mummy?

Stalin died in 1953. Millions wept in the streets, millions more – in many cases the same people – inwardly sighed with relief. In 1957, as Khrushchev's Thaw gained momentum, the question of the Palace of Soviets cropped up again. The palace administration had already been broken up amid whispers of corruption in the organisation. Now it was said that the water-table by the river would not have borne the weight of the tallest building on the planet. So it happened that the same two charges of embezzlement and bad surveying that scuppered Vitberg's temple now put paid to Iofan's.

Schloegel thinks that the rumours of professional incompetence must have been fabricated. He thinks it was just a face-saving way of ditching Iofan's by now inappropriately Stalinist project, for surely no serious architect would fail to test the bedrock? Schloegel might be right, but perhaps he does not see how easily the refusal to perform miracles for Stalin could be taken as indifference, or worse, treachery. Promising the utterly impossible was a way of proving one's devotion. This is the most perverse thing of all: the bigger the lie you told the Great Leader, the more eloquently it spoke of your love for him.

At any rate, the site by the river was abandoned, the name of the metro station was changed from Palace of Soviets to Kropotkinskaya, and a new competition for a much more modest palace was announced. The location for the new building? None other than Lenin Hills, hard by the university. However, not one of the twenty-one designs was deemed suitable. Eventually the government settled for an unobtrusive glass shoebox of a building that was built inside the Kremlin close to the Trinity Gate. They called it the Palace of Congresses. It was finished in just two years and was opened in 1961, the same year in which the Moskva outdoor swimming pool received its first eager bathers.

And so the story of the cathedral of Christ the Saviour comes full circle: the temple that Vitberg originally planned for the Kremlin went to Sparrow Hills; from there it moved to Chertolye and was built by Thon; his monument to a unique redeemer and a special victory metamorphosed into Iofan's great spike, which celebrated another victory and a different redeemer. This second saviour never became concrete, but the idea lived on. Like an unquiet spirit it flitted back to the Hills and tarried there a while; then it returned to its starting-place, finding tangible form in the grounds of the old fortress. It stands there now, blank and anonymous as a paving stone. Like an enlightened Buddhist soul, it has been purified of all the selfness and vainglory that marked its earlier incarnations.

Kremlin – Sparrow Hills – Chertolye – Lenin Hills – Kremlin. Turn and turn again. You could plot the protracted fate of Christ the Cathedral on a diagram, like the hours on a clock face. You could fill in the key dates from 1812 to 1961 and mark the key sites: Kremlin at twelve o'clock, Chertolye at six, the Hills at three and nine. It would make a kind of mandala in time and topography. It would be a very picture of the wheel of life.

Moral Geography

Like salt, a star melts in the brimming barrel,
And blacker grows the gelling water's skin.
Death is more pure, my woes more savoury,
The earth more righteous – and more frightening.

– Osip Mandelshtam

June 1983

Vadim went to Leningrad for his birthday and stayed for his grandfather's funeral.

The wake was a traditional affair. Ira used up all her depleted reserves of caviar and tinned ham for the feast. The family sat down to eat at three in the afternoon and did not get up till after midnight. On the table throughout the meal stood a glass of vodka with a slice of black bread across the top, the symbol of Efim Oskarovich's absence. The men got solemnly and single-mindedly drunk, and they wore their hangovers like black armbands for two days.

Rachel went back to Moscow the day after the ruined birthday party. Yuri assured her that she was welcome to stay, and Vadim begged her not to go, but she did not want to intrude on a family affair. Mark also returned to his studies as soon as the funeral was over, but Vadim lingered in Leningrad. In spite of their long talk, he had the feeling that something had been left unsaid between him and his grandfather, that if he just hung around for a while the message might bleed though to him by some kind of ghostly osmosis.

Vadim asked Ira if he could have the photograph of grandfather on the cathedral roof, and she gave it to him gladly. There was another item: a green-tinted picture postcard of the church from the turn of the century. It was in mint condition and it showed the monument to Alexander III (Vadim had never seen a picture of it before), the ball-shaped electric lights, and the dizzy butte of the church's white walls behind. The words '*Moscou, Vue du Temple du Sauveur*' were printed in gilt letters in one corner. The postcard was a genuine antique – no telling now where Efim Oskarovich had found it – and Vadim inherited this along with the other snapshot.

Vadim talked to Rachel by phone most days. She rang from the inter-city call-box in V Zone. She constantly asked him when he was coming back, but Vadim could not give a definite answer. "I miss you like hell," she said. "Life goes on, you know."

"I know. I'm not grieving, I'm just thinking."

"Well, come and think here. You need to talk to someone – and I need to talk to you."

"What about?"

"It's not a telephone conversation. Get down here, there's lots of news."

Vadim had barely put the receiver in its cradle when the phone rang again. It was Hussein.

"That's amazing," said Vadim. "I have just this second been speaking to Rachel."

"I know, I was behind her in the queue."

"You were listening?" said Vadim.

"Yes, but don't worry, it's not a profession with me, or even a hobby. In any case I got no answers to the main question."

"Which is?"

"Which is, where are you? It's been nearly two weeks. You should know that questions are being asked about you. The word absenteeism is being bandied about."

"Your usual source?"

"Naturally. But there's more."

"What?"

"It's not for the phone."

"God, not you too?"

"Yes, me too. Hurry back, I mean it. You are in..." The phone clicked to an electric warble as Hussein's supply of coins ran out.

Big trouble... hot water... deep shit. One of these certainly. Vadim was not worried about the lectures he had missed. He knew he would be able to catch up with the work. It was the business of making up reasons for his absence he found so tiresome. He could just tell the truth, that a close relative had died and he was at home for the funeral, but that would not cover him for two weeks' absence. At best it would win him some sympathy, and he did not want to sell his grandfather's memory that cheap. So he pulled on his shoes and went round the corner to the Moscow Station for a ticket.

It was so familiar a journey that Vadim could make it with his eyes shut. And since it was the overnight train, that is what he did. Eager as he was to see Rachel, he did not go straight to the university on arriving in Moscow, but went out onto Komsomol Square – Three Stations Square, as it is known – to find some breakfast.

It was one of the first really summery days of the year. The light was clean and bright as a freshly laundered shirt, and at this early hour there was little traffic and no acrid petroleum smog. There were a few people around: some ragged railway porters slept on their feet, their arms drooped over the arms of their barrows. Knots of sunburned Armenians and colourful Uzbek women picked at their gold teeth with sharpened matchsticks where they sat. At their feet were bundles of dried apricots and shelled walnuts destined for the market. A militiaman was gingerly poking a lifeless drunk with his toe.

In the centre of the square, three orange water-trucks turned in ever-widening circles. They moved in unison like a corps de ballet, spraying wet doodles on the dusty surface as they went. Vadim watched until the trucks had spiralled out to the point where, on the next circuit, they would soak his shoes unless he moved on. The Uzbeks for some reason stayed put, as if daring the trucks to douse them, and as he entered the steamy *stolovaya* beside the station he heard their outraged shouts and the terrifying Asian curses they heaped on the Russian drivers' heads.

He had some kasha and fried eggs. He took his time about it, wanting to plan his moment of arrival at MGU so as not to wake Rachel at too indecent an hour. After a second cup of chicory sludge he descended into the metro and boarded a train on the red line. At Sportivnaya the recorded announcement said, "Next stop Universitet." Lenin Hills had been cut out of the recorded loop. The station itself, when they passed through, was stripped bare. A framework of girders had been fixed to the glass walls of the platform like the bars on the windows of a mental ward. The view of the river had gone.

When Vadim got back to MGU he went straight to 727 and knocked for Rachel. There was no reply. He called her name – she might be sleeping, or maybe she took him for the sanitary commission – but still no answer. Just his luck, thought Vadim, today of all days, when he had been killing time at the station, she chose to make an early start. Pinned to her doorjamb was an empty cigarette packet containing some slips of paper for messages – all the Americans had them. Vadim considered writing something but then thought better of it. Best call back later.

Vadim went off towards the stairs. Passing down the corridor he saw that the door of Andrew's room was ajar. He knocked and pushed the door open, and was embarrassed to see the Englishman on his knees and head bowed by the narrow bed. Andrew did not seem annoyed by the intrusion, however.

Hello," he said, getting up. "When did you get back?"

"Just now," said Vadim. "How are you?"

"Fine. Seen Rachel yet?"

"Not yet."

"Ah no, of course. Anyway I'm glad you dropped by because I have something for you." Andrew first went and shut the door of the blok. Then he reached into the back of his wardrobe and brought out a book. "I was sorry to hear about your grandfather," he said. "I understand it was quite a blow for you. I would like you to have this." He held out the book to Vadim, who took it.

It was a Bible. Vadim had never seen one before. The cover was made of soft blue plastic, a fact that immediately advertised the fact that it was printed abroad. By force of habit Vadim turned to the back page: there was none of the information that by law was given in all Soviet printed matter: no order number, no tirage, no price and no printworks specified. This omission alone made the Bible seem like a very exotic thing indeed. The paper, Vadim noted, was unbelievably smooth and thin. The print did not show through the page, it had left no impress on the surface of the pages, and in spite of its tiny size it was clean and black as a government Zil. Vadim opened the book in the middle. "...I am like a pelican of the wilderness: I am like an owl of the desert. I watch, and am as a sparrow alone on the house top..." The language was archaic, but not completely opaque like the Slavonic liturgy. Even on the evidence of one or two sentences he could see that it was translated into rather beautiful Russian.

"Thank you," said Vadim. "This is extremely generous of you."

"Not at all," said Andrew. "I didn't buy it, I just carried it out here. God's postman, ha ha. I want you to have it, because you will appreciate what it has to say."

Vadim looked up from the page. "I am not a Christian, Andrew," he said.

"I know. That's exactly the point."

Vadim slipped the book into his cardboard suitcase. "Do you know where Rachel is," he asked. "I was expecting to catch her home."

"Yes, she went early to see the man," Andrew replied. "To nip this thing in the bud before it goes too far."

"What thing?"

"Why, this business with the KG..." Andrew stopped and reddened. "You don't know?"

"No, I don't know. What the hell is going on?"

"But your own... but surely Rachel told you about it?"

"Andrew, I have not been here for two weeks. She said on the phone that she had some news, nothing more. What's this about the..." He lowered his voice "...the KGB?"

Andrew wrestled with his conscience.

"You might as well tell me now. The secret is out anyway, and you will just make it worse if you keep me in suspense."

"All right," said Andrew. "But not in here."

They went down to the V Zone canteen.

"Rachel will kill me," said Andrew. "I just assumed you were in on all this."

"I wasn't. Tell me from the beginning."

"Well, she was approached through... a third party. They said they wanted to talk to her, and implied they would make problems for her friends if she refused. They mentioned your name and the name of a *refusenik* acquaintance of hers."

"Karina?"

"I don't know what she is called."

"And Rachel agreed?"

"Well, she thought that there was nothing they could really do to harm her," – Vadim snorted – "...and she did not want to spoil her friend's chance of emigrating just because she was too cowardly to stand up to a KGB man. So she agreed to meet the fellow once, just to put their minds at rest about her. That was the definite arrangement they made: a one-off meeting. It happened about a week ago."

"So how come she is seeing the man again today?"

"He rang her up yesterday afternoon and asked when is the next meeting. She said there would be no more meetings and he acted as if this was a complete surprise to him, as if she was breaking off a beautiful friendship. Rachel reluctantly agreed to go and see him again first thing this morning, just to tell him that there would be no more cosy chats."

"Dear God! And she thinks they will just shake hands and say cheerio?"

"Well, what else can they do, Vadim? She is an American citizen, after all."

"What can they do? Andrew, they can do any damn thing they please."

Vadim left the Englishman to his breakfast and went to his room. There was a note tucked in the door and his heart leaped when he saw it. He opened the slip of paper:

Comrade Prichalov, Vadim Yurevich.

You are invited to be present at a plenary meeting of the komsomol, faculty of journalism, at 10.00 on Thursday, at which your disciplinary record will be discussed. Attendance is compulsory.

Central Committee of the VLKSM, MGU

"A trial date," thought Vadim. "The day after tomorrow. Hussein was right, I am in deep."

Inside, tucked in the door of his room was another note, and another disappointment. "*If you are reading this,*" it said, "*then you must be back. About time. My advice to you is go to a few lectures, be seen, put a few stitches in the tattered overcoat of your reputation.*

I shall see you later. Hussein." It was sound advice and he took it.
He knew, in any case, that it was better than hanging around in the
hostel like a lost dog, waiting for Rachel to come back.

He spent the day in conspicuous study, and returned to V Zone
at around six; this time, finally, the note he was waiting for was
there. No signature.

"*I am home. Everything's fine. Come and see me.*"

Vadim threw himself down the three flights of stairs and sprinted
down the seventh-floor corridor. He burst into her room. She stood
facing him in the hallway, feet planted like a soldier at ease, and arms
akimbo. He swept her off the ground and they tottered through the
door of the blok and toppled onto the bed.

It was a while before they felt like talking. Vadim was the first to
speak.

"Why didn't you tell me about the KGB?" She did not seem
surprised to be asked. Vadim guessed rightly that Andrew had
already confessed to giving the game away.

Rachel stroked his head. "How could I have told you? I couldn't
say it on the phone, could I? I kept asking you to come back, but you
wouldn't."

"How did it go today?"

"All right. It is just the one man, Nikolai Palych. He is very
charming – and actually rather good-looking. We met outside the
Moskva Hotel and he took me to an empty room there, the same
place we met the first time. On the first occasion he asked me
about American universities and how I like it here. He said he was
interested in US politics and would be interested to hear my views. I
didn't tell him anything. I said I was interested in poetry, not politics,
and mostly just nodded and smiled and acted friendly. This time was
much the same, only more tense. I told him I could not possibly see

him any more, and he looked so upset I nearly changed my mind on the spot."

Vadim shuddered. "You told him that, then?"

"Of course. I only agreed to one meeting to clear the air."

"And to help Karina."

"Ye-es. And for one other reason."

"Oh?"

"Because I have applied for another year here – to do some more archive research and to be with you."

"Another year? Oh, that's great, Rachel. Really wonderful."

"Yes. But Nikolai Palych could block it if he wanted. He made that very clear in a hinting sort of way. I just wanted to let them know I have nothing to hide."

"Hm, I can see the sense of that. But I don't think they will just let it lie."

"Don't worry. He practically promised they would let me back after the summer. Then we can just be together while we decide what to do."

Vadim kissed her. In eight months she had acquired more street wisdom than he had amassed in twenty years of Soviet life. They sat quietly for a few minutes and then Vadim asked a question that had been at the back of his mind all day.

"How did they contact you in the first place? Andrew said something about a third party."

"Yes. I was wondering when you were going to ask me that, and I am afraid you are not going to like the answer."

"What is it?"

"They made Mark do it."

"They what! Mark did what?"

"They forced him. They called him in on the day he came up to Leningrad for your birthday. They made him pass on the message that they wanted to meet me."

"The bastard."

"Now don't be stupid. He just passed on the message. He could hardly have refused. He told me about it in Leningrad and set up the first meeting when we got back to Moscow. He was just a messenger. He did nothing wrong, and nothing I did not agree to."

"Why the hell didn't he tell me?"

"I told him I wanted to tell you myself. But then Efim Oskarovich died, and I thought you had enough worries. I meant to talk to you about it beforehand, but you weren't here, were you. I didn't know you would stay two weeks up there."

"I'll kill him."

"You'll talk to him. He wants to explain. I said you would go to see him once I had told you. I suggest you arrange to meet up for a brotherly chat tomorrow afternoon. I am going to see Karina."

"Does she know about all this?"

"Yes, I told her. She has had lots of dealings with these people and knows the score."

"Perhaps I should come to see her too."

"No, she wants to see me alone. I think she has fallen out with Fair Misha."

"Oh?"

"Yes. She wrote a letter to Gromyko asking to be allowed to emigrate. He hates it when she does quixotic things like that. He thinks it is just asking for trouble."

There was a light knock on the door. Vadim and Rachel looked at each other; suddenly they realised they had not locked it.

"Rachel, it's me, Hussein. Is Vadim there?"

"Yes," she called. "Come in, Hussein."

He stepped in and bowed from the waist to Rachel, and shook Vadim's hand. "Hello my friend, glad to see you back."

"Good to see you, too."

"Forgive my interrupting, but Vadim, there is an important

phonecall for you on the tenth floor.

"A phonecall?"

"An important one."

They both sensed the urgency in Hussein's voice. "I'll be back in a minute," said Vadim, and left with his room-mate.

"What's the panic," asked Vadim as they bounded back up the stairs.

"It's them, Vadim, the *Komitet*."

"How do you know, did they say so?"

"No, but it's them, all right. You'll see."

They trotted down the corridor to the phone booth by the lift. The floor-commandant was there, holding the receiver respectfully at arm's length. Vadim took the phone.

"Hello?" he said.

"My name is Nikolai Palych. Do you know who I am?"

"Yes."

"I would like to meet you."

"Yes."

"I will see you by the ski-jump on Lenin Hills at seven o'clock tomorrow. Is that all right?"

"Sounds fine."

"Till tomorrow evening then."

Click.

"What did he say?" asked Hussein.

"Is it anything serious?" asked the floor-lady, husky with excitement.

Vadim was annoyed she knew. Now his business would be telegraphed round the hostel. "Later," he said to Hussein, and went straight back downstairs to Rachel.

The next day at noon Vadim was sitting on the edge of the fountain in the courtyard of MArkhi, the Moscow Architectural Institute. The yard was full of students, many of them carrying unwieldy metre-square canvas stretchers in sheaths made from old sheets. All of them looked terribly bohemian, and quite certain of their own brilliance. None had that mousy air of the students at MGU. Not for nothing did MArkhi have a reputation as the most anti-Soviet college in Moscow, and not for nothing was it situated two minutes' walk from the Lubyanka.

"Hello, brother," said Mark. Vadim had not seen him approach. "Got a ciggy by any chance?"

"No. No, I haven't."

"Ah. Be back in a minute."

Mark wandered off to a group by the door and cadged a cigarette from a rather attractive hippy girl in a yellow sarafan. He stayed to talk to them and Vadim watched from his seat by the fountain. He was struck by how perfectly Mark fitted into this. This was his natural milieu, the MArkhi crowd. He looked like a different person here on his home patch, and Vadim found himself wondering whether he knew his elder brother at all.

Mark finished his cigarette, bummed another, and came back to Vadim. "Are you hungry?"

"No."

"Me neither."

"Let's go for a walk, then."

They left the institute, turned right and right again onto the steep incline of Kuznetsky Most.

"Are you angry with me? If you are I will apologise. Just say the word."

"I was yesterday. I am not now. Yesterday I couldn't understand why you put Rachel at risk. Now I'm just a bit jealous about you and her having secrets that I was not privy to."

"She was at risk, anyway. Being with you puts her at risk, and vice versa."

"Yes, I know."

"The thing I don't understand is why they have not come to you. You know her best, after all."

"They have come to me now. I have been summoned to meet them this evening."

"Who? Nikolai Palych?"

"Yes. What's he like?"

"Smooth bastard. You'll like him. He's Rachel's case manager. Her guardian angel. Where are you seeing him, in the Lubyanka?"

"No. Up by the university."

"Neutral territory, that's good. It means they don't want to put the frighteners on you. Not yet, anyway. It means they haven't made up their mind how to handle you. The main thing is to disappoint their expectations. Not to let them think you have any potential. Be wishy-washy, give the lukewarm answer to anything they ask. Don't defy them, because they relish a struggle. Bore them. In the end they have to put a tick or a cross by your name. If they put a cross, that means you are not *perspektivny*, not worth the effort to cultivate, and with a bit of luck they will leave you in peace."

"Is that what you did?"

"Yes. But it takes discipline. They try to provoke you, make you lash out at them. But the moment you poke your head out, they grab you by the hair and drag you into the open. The only sensible tactic is to roll up like a hedgehog and sit it out."

They were now on the corner of Stoleshnikov Alley, by the basement beer-bar known as The Three Steps. The queue to get in was surprisingly short, barely past the steps that gave the bar its name.

"Do you fancy a drink?" asked Mark.

"No, better keep my wits about me."

"But beer isn't alcoholic. Not in this bar, anyway."

"All the same. Maybe later."

They walked on up the hill in silence towards the statue of Yuri Dolgoruky. Vadim broke the pause.

"Mark, let's get out of here. Let's go to America."

"Whoa, hold on a minute," laughed Mark. "Who do you think is going to let you go?"

"We are Jews, we can apply. They would let us out eventually."

"I'm not talking about Soviet power, blockhead. I am talking about dad. Not to mention Ira – it would break her heart, you know that."

Vadim grimaced. "Well, she may have to get used to the idea. Rachel is not going to want to stay here forever."

Mark stopped and turned to his brother. "I didn't know things were that advanced with you two."

"They're not. Not yet. But she is coming back after the summer break for another year. I'm just mapping out the possibilities, the likelihoods. Say we get married and go to the States. Once we were there I could call you over. Not just you, dad and Ira too."

"Dad and Ira might not want to go. I might not want to go."

"You'll want to go, you hate it here."

"Vadim, I like it here. I don't want to live anywhere else. You must follow your own path, of course, but I am staying here whatever."

They sat down at Dolgoruky's feet on Sovetskaya Square. At the Aragvi Restaurant a few paces away, the elderly uniformed doorman had barricaded himself in behind the door with a broomstick. He was refusing even to see the hungry little queue on the street.

"You hate it here," repeated Vadim. "You always have. It's a dustpan, you said it."

Mark sighed. "It's not so bad, really."

"It's the bumhole of the world."

"Yes, that's nearer the truth, I think," said Mark. Vadim looked at him sideways. "Yes, you've hit the nail on the head there."

"Is there a joke coming?"

"No, not a joke. In fact, probably the most serious thing I have ever said to you. Let's move on." They got up and headed up Gorky Street towards the Garden Ring.

"You remember geometry at school?"

"Barely. Why?"

"Do you remember the answer to the question 'Do parallel lines ever cross?'" said Mark.

"Yes, they cross at infinity."

"Well, half-right. That is just the same as saying they never cross. Let me put it another way: we are walking parallel to each other now. Will we ever bump into each other?"

"Yes, at infinity."

"No! We've just been through that."

"No, then. We will never bump into each other."

"Wrong again. You are thinking in two dimensions, think in three."

"Are you sure this is not a joke?"

"No joke. Think, Vadim, three-dimensional geometry. We are walking north on a spherical planet. Parallel lines on a flat surface never meet, but on a sphere they converge at the top. If we keep walking next to each other, due north and exactly parallel like this, we will bump into each other when we reach the North Pole. Moreover, we will know we have reached the North Pole precisely because we have bumped into each other."

"So?"

"So imagine that the moral universe behaves in the same way as the physical universe."

"The moral universe?"

"In that universe I am an Eskimo."

Vadim laughed. "What are you talking about?"

Mark stopped walking. "I mean that I need to inhabit a world where the lines of moral force conflict. It is the only way I have of knowing where I stand. I can be sure I am doing the right thing precisely because I find myself in disagreement with the system, with 'socialist morality' and all the rest of it. If the Soviet Union was not here to tell me I was doing wrong, I wouldn't know I was doing right. The USSR is the north pole of the moral planet. I need this freezing environment, Vadim; in warmer climes I would lose myself completely."

"You can't tell me that the party tells you what's wrong and what's right. You don't need them."

"But I do. I really need it to be that straightforward. They speak, therefore they lie. Anything more complicated than that and I get confused. But you are different. You can happily move around between the tropics, where the lines do not meet. You, Vadim, can make daily decisions on how to act on the moral planet with nothing but your own judgement for a compass. You could easily survive in the temperate moral climate of the free world, but I couldn't. I would find all that decision-making exhausting. It would sap me. I haven't got the energy or the confidence. Here in the moral Arctic we dress to protect ourselves against the blizzard outside. We wear the same clothes every day, rarely poke our noses outside the igloo, and we stay reasonably warm."

"Don't you want to live in a normal country?"

"No."

"Read whatever you like, say what you like?"

"I can do that already – by torchlight and in whispers. That's the way I like it. You take your Rachel and emigrate to the West if you want to, little brother, but I am staying put. I like my chains, they make me feel important; if they took them off me now I would be so lightweight I'd just float away."

I once went to the provincial town of Ryazan, on assignment for a newspaper. I had been sent to interview a charming English lady who had just walked to the North Pole. She had arrived back on the plane only that morning and she was aching for a hot cup of tea.

Ryazan was a desperate place. It was Saturday morning, and there was not a drop of tea to be had in the entire city. I offered her a hard-currency Digestive biscuit from my briefcase, hoping that in some Pavlovian way it would make her feel like she had had the cuppa she yearned for. It didn't, but it was the start of the conversation.

She told me about her journey. She described a surreal place where there was no sound save the anguished groaning of the frozen earth beneath her feet. A place where the landscape would change overnight: once she went to sleep in a boundless snowy desert and woke to find herself crusoed on a platform of ice no bigger than a tennis court. In the evenings she cooked great pans full of spaghetti in melted snow and went to sleep in her hat. She came to look on her Russian fur hat as home.

She described pressure ridges to me, "like Everests reduced to rubble". She had to climb these mountains of ice-cubes in her skis. And she told me about the pole itself: the world's roof smells salty, like the seaside, but silent, silent, silent. You know you have arrived because the horizon suddenly becomes curved and you can't turn your back on your shadow. It goes with you whichever way you look. You can circumnavigate the world with no more effort than it takes to walk round a lamp-post: five paces, and you are Sir Francis Drake.

I gave her another Digestive. I felt she had earned it. She took the dry biscuit and looked wistfully over my shoulder, as if she expected that cup of tea to materialise out of thin air somewhere behind my left ear. Then she smiled and said this:

"At the Pole everyone is stripped of their social baggage, no-one can be any better than they are. You know, I think that we have elevated the way we live to total artifice. We have lost our way. The fact is, in order to be happy all you need is just a bowl, a spoon and a flat place to sleep."

"Who's there?"

"It's me – Rachel."

Karina opened the door on the latch. She closed it, took off the chain, and opened it again.

"What's the matter?" asked Rachel.

"Are you alone?" She hustled Rachel into the hallway.

"Yes..."

"No tails?"

"Not that I saw. Where are the Mishas."

"I sent them away for a few days. I'm sick of the pair of them."

"Is that why you are frightened? Because you are here alone."

"I'm not frightened, Rachel dear, but you should be. Come on through, there is someone here I want you to meet."

Karina went ahead into the main room while Rachel took off her shoes and slipped on a pair of *tapochki*. Something filled her with foreboding, something more than Karina's melodramatic words. She padded through to the other room, where a smartly dressed lady of about thirty was sitting with a cup of tea in Karina's armchair.

"This is Carol," said Karina as the woman stood up and extended her hand. "She is a friend of mine and a compatriot of yours – from the embassy."

"Pleased to meet you," said Rachel suspiciously.

"You too," said Carol in a preppy accent. "I've heard so much about you."

"Have you now?" Rachel looked with raised eyebrows at Karina.

"I've known Carol since she was a student here. She was my link with America then, like you are now."

"Irex exchange," said Carol. "I did my masters on the Soviet legal system."

"Sounds interesting," said Rachel, trying to sound bored. "And good preparation for the state department, no doubt."

"Yes." She cleared her throat. "Let's sit down, shall we?"

The Americans both took seats. Karina hovered like an over-eager waitress. "Tea, Rachel."

"No, thanks," said Rachel sharply. "Why don't you sit down and tell me what's going on here?"

Karina's face fell. "Don't be angry with Karina," said Carol. "She wants to help you."

"So why the ambush?"

"It is not an ambush, Rachel. Karina asked me along as a... well as a consultant, you might say."

"Why didn't you consult me first, Karina?"

"How could I? You know what the phones are like."

"I'm not here in any official way, Rachel. I really am just a friend. Karina was worried that you might be in trouble, and she told me a little about it."

"She had no right. There are no problems I can't handle."

"Well, that's good. But Karina did the right thing. No-one knows anything but me, and I'm not about to tell anyone without your say-so."

"I should hope not!"

"But it can't do any harm to put me in the picture. It will put everyone's mind at rest and will be like extra insurance for you if need it."

Rachel raced through the permutations in her mind. She had no idea what hysterical colours Karina had put on her story, and thought that it might be better to give her own sober version. Perhaps it was a mistake to be angry. Perhaps she should just play it cool, say she had a brush with the KGB but now it was all over. If she said nothing and walked out, this Carol would naturally assume the worst and file some kind of report. These diplomats were sneaks, they never did anything 'unofficially'. The very fact that she had said she would tell no-one contained a hint that she could if she had a mind to. And Carol was right about the insurance, not so much for her as for Vadim. If someone at the embassy knew about him, if she could sell the situation to this Carol woman as a human rights issue, it might make it harder for the KGB to lean on him in her absence. Karina had told them God knows what already, she might as well have the state department for her as against her.

"What do you want to hear?"

"Just tell me the whole story, from the beginning."

Rachel gave her account of the harassment by the KGB. She stressed that yesterday's meeting was the second and last, and she did not dwell on her relationship with Vadim except to say that he and his brother were more at risk than she herself.

"They are not our problem," said Carol. "How close are you to this boy Vadim?"

Rachel flushed. "You mean do I sleep with him?"

"No. Why should I mean that?"

"Because that's how you guys operate. You think communism is a venereal disease. A person has sex with a Russian and the next thing you know he is passing secrets to Castro."

"And do you?"

"Pass secrets to Castro? No."

"You know what I mean."

"I know what you mean and you can shove it. I've had enough

of this, I'm going home." Rachel went out to the hall to put on her shoes.

Karina came after. She had not followed the whole conversation in English, but she realised she had made a mistake. "I will ring you tomorrow," she said. "Perhaps we can meet."

"I don't think so," said Rachel. "Not till I have cooled down."

Carol came to the doorway. "Don't go yet, Rachel. I think you should come with me to the embassy. I think you should tell my superiors what you have told me."

"I'm going home and I am not talking to you or anybody. I wish I'd never opened my big mouth."

"I really do think you should come with me. I am going to have to report this and I think our people will want to hear your account first-hand."

Rachel blanched. "You said this was between us."

"I know, but that was before I knew the full extent of it. You are in serious trouble, honey. They are trying to recruit you. Whether you like it or not, I have to think of your safety as an American citizen in a hostile country."

"So you lied to me from the start."

"I did not. I genuinely didn't know how big a deal this was. But come with me back to the embassy now. I'm sure we can straighten this out very quickly."

"And if I don't come."

"Well then, for your own safety, the embassy might have to get in touch with your exchange program back home and request that they decline your request for another year's study out here."

Rachel laughed bitterly. "Just the same bag of tricks as the other guys. There's nothing to choose between you."

"There is a whole world of difference, Rachel. They are trying to hurt you, and we just want to keep you out of harm's way. Come on, make it easy on yourself."

Rachel pulled on her jacket. She hesitated for a moment longer. "I'll give you an hour, but only because you are blackmailing me. I've got to be somewhere else at six."

"An hour will be more than enough," said Carol. "My car's round the corner. Let's go."

Vadim knocked on Rachel's door at six sharp. His heart sank when she was not there.

She had promised last night to brief him on Nikolai Palych. He wanted to know more about what the man was like, how he might handle him. He wanted her to tell him it was all going to be all right.

He could hear American voices in one of the open rooms further down the corridor. Perhaps Rachel was there? Should he go and knock? No. If she was there she would come out herself as soon as she saw the time. He could see if Andrew was in? Again no. He would want to talk about religion, and Vadim was in too nervous a state for that right now. Best not loiter here. He decided to go and wait in his own room, and come back here at quarter-past.

Hussein was not in either. Vadim paced up and down, sat down, stood up. For something to do, he took his new Bible from the place where he had hidden it in the void behind his wardrobe. He skimmed through the pages of the book, and again he was struck by the magnificence of the Russian:

"Thy lips are like a thread of scarlet, and thy speech is comely: thy temples are like a piece of a pomegranate within thy locks. Thy neck is like the tower of David, builded for an armoury, whereon there hang a thousand bucklers, all shields of mighty men..."

Love poetry in the Bible. He had no idea.

There came a light knock – too light to be the sanitary commission. Vadim hurriedly put the Bible away. He glanced at his watch: twenty-past. The ancient verse had distracted him, and now she had come looking for him.

No. It was Andrew. Uncharacteristically he pushed past Vadim and into the room. "Shut the door," he said urgently.

"What is it?"

"Shut the door quickly and come in here."

Vadim did as he was told. Later, when he thought it over, everything that was said from this point on seemed to be in slow motion, every word and every movement seemed to involve a huge expenditure of energy, as if they were conversing under water.

Vadim now stood face to face with the Englishmen. They both stood unnaturally to attention, like rival sergeant-majors.

"When did you last see Rachel?" demanded Andrew.

"I'm just going to see her now. I was with her... first thing this morning. Why?"

The trace of a wince crossed Andrew's face. "Do you know what her plans were for today?" he continued.

"Yes, I do. Nothing special." Alarm was rising from the pit of his stomach. "Don't you think you better tell me what's up?"

"I don't know. I thought you might."

"Well clearly you know something. Is she hurt?"

"No, nothing like that. Let's sit down." They moved like reflections of each other. It almost made Vadim laugh. Now they sat in identical poses side by side on the bed.

"Well?"

"I've just been with some of the Americans. They are in uproar. There's been some kind of scandal. Rachel was at their embassy this afternoon – was that part of her schedule?"

"No, not as far as I know. What scandal? Is she still there?"

"Yes. Well, no." His voice was trembling now.

"Yes or no, Andrew? For God's sake, tell me what is happening."

"One of the other Americans saw her there earlier on. She was just leaving. She seemed to be under arrest or something. He said she looked upset, kind of punch-drunk. The thing is, Vadim, they were sending her away. Something happened, and the embassy decided to put her on a plane out of here. Vadim, I'm really sorry, but she has already left the country. She's gone."

A Final Toast

I drink to my home, to my ruined home;
To the evil I've lived through;
To our being together, but being alone;
And I drink to you.

I drink to the lies on lips that betrayed me;
To the deathly cold in men's eyes;
I drink to a world which is cruel and coarse;
And to God, who would not save me.

– Anna Akhmatova

June 1983

Friendship Street tried hard to be a genteel corner of Moscow. It was in the prestigious south-west of the town, rising like a river in the Lenin Hills. It was lined with trees and had a grass verge, but the greenery was sparse and sickly, half-choked by fumes from the heavy traffic. An unending torrent of cars and lorries flowed down the broad highway, into the funnel of Mosfilmovskaya and down the Bersenevskaya Embankment to Kiev Station and the Kalininsky Bridge. The road was dotted with foreign embassies, but generally not of the most prestigious kind, that is, not the kind that bring above-average grocery shops and hard-currency *beriozkas* in their wake. Most of Eastern Europe was here: the German Democratic Republic was at No.56; Hungary, Romania, Bulgaria shared fences on the Moscow streetplan as they do borders on the map of Europe; there were some iffy socialists in the neighbourhood too – the Federative Republic of Yugoslavia at 46, and the Democratic People's Republic of North Korea at 72. Malaysia added an exotic touch at number 50, and Sweden sat politely but uneasily in this company at 60. All did their best to ignore the leper of the bunch, the Socialist People's Arab Libyan Jamahiriya at number 38.

Presiding serenely over them all, like a breezeblock Buddha, was the squat, minimalist mass of the Chinese Embassy, Friendship Street 6. The building stood in the centre of a great, empty compound surrounded with a high fence. And just outside the fence was a ramshackle edifice, little more than a prefabricated shed. This shed was a beer-bar, and it did as much as anything to lower the tone of the district. It was nameless, like most of the bars in Moscow, but the students who came here called it The Taiwan – it being situated just off the coast of China.

This is where Vadim came when he heard the news from Andrew. At the moment when he should have been meeting Nikolai Palych he was just starting on his first mug of sour beer; now he was finishing his fourth or fifth. Try as he might to drown his sorrows, they kept bobbing up to the surface like an unweighted corpse.

He cast an eye round the room. It was full of miserable men, most of them twice his age or more. There were no women. Smoking was not allowed in the bar, but every man in the place had a cigarette on the go. They all held their smokes under the table, which made them crouch uncomfortably with their chins hanging over their ale-pots. In their free hands some of the men grasped vodka bottles from which they surreptitiously topped up their beers. This wicked cocktail, known as a 'bottle brush', had been given a new name by Vadim's generation: they call it 'the neutron bomb', because it wipes out the people but leaves the building standing.

The air inside the bar was blue with smoke and profanity. Vadim could hardly breathe. He felt sick, but he drained his glass before leaving. He planned to walk back to the university but found that he was too unsteady. He rolled to the bus-stop and vomited in the gutter.

Vadim arrived back at his room still in a daze of misery and intoxication. When he entered the block he saw that Hussein and Galya were sitting staidly on the bed in the room on the right, bent forward, hands clasped, like Baptists at prayer. "Everywhere I go these days there is someone talking to God," thought Vadim. He said hello and retreated quickly to his own room. He did not want to embark on a postmortem right now.

He threw himself on his bed and stared at the ceiling. The cracks turned circles over his head like distant vultures. He had been there less than a minute when there was a timid knock at the door. Vadim's heart sunk. "Can we come in," said Hussein, putting his head gingerly round the door.

"I suppose," said Vadim ungraciously.

Hussein and Galya entered almost on tiptoes. They sat down at the two chairs, and took up the same prayerful pose. Vadim did not take his eyes from the ceiling. Galya threw a glance at Hussein, a glance that said: get on with it.

"I'm really sorry, old friend," Hussein began. "You must be feeling terrible."

"It doesn't matter," Vadim said.

"If there is anything..."

"I know. Thanks."

There was a break. Galya cast the same look at Hussein and Vadim spotted it this time.

"What now?" he asked.

"Vadik, I know it is not a good time. But we want to talk to you about the komsomol meeting tomorrow. You know you are on the agenda?" said Hussein.

"Yes, I got a note."

"Have you thought about how you are going to handle it?"

"I have the perfect plan. I am going to forget it."

"Not turn up?" exclaimed Galya. "Vadim, you can't do that!"

"Why not? There aren't many problems that won't go away if you ignore them long enough."

"But you will make it worse for yourself if you do that."

Vadim got up on his elbows. "Galya, I really don't give a shit."

"Now hold on, Vadim," said Hussein angrily. "Don't you dare swear at Galya. She is only here now because she wants to help you. So why don't you sit up, shut up and listen to what we have to say. Of course, if you prefer to wallow in booze and self-pity, just say the word and we'll leave you to it."

Vadim considered for a moment whether to make his misery complete by offending his friend – and decided against it.

"I beg your pardon, Galya," he said, swinging his legs off the bed. "Excuse me for a moment while I go and wash my face." He went outside to the toilet. There was a cigarette butt unfurling soggy-brown in the bowl. He crossed to the bathroom, cleaned his teeth, and put his head under the shower for a minute. He came back sodden, but feeling much better.

"Have you been smoking in here?" he asked Hussein.

"No. You know no-one smokes in here. What makes you ask that?"

He checked the panel in the wardrobe. The Bible was gone from its hiding-place.

"What are you looking for? What's going on?" asked Hussein.

"Never mind now," said Vadim. "What did you want to say, Galya?"

She took a deep breath. "Well, first of all, you should know that tomorrow's meeting is not a komsomol initiative." Her voice sunk to a whisper as she said this. They all moved closer together so that their heads where almost touching.

"Who then?"

"Lena got called to the personnel department – two days ago. You know she is komsomol organiser. There were two men there from the... well, you know. They asked all about you, how hard you study, what the other students think of you. Well, Lena was frightened: she said what she thought they wanted to hear. She figured they would not be asking if they did not already have something against you."

"Good logic," said Vadim.

"Impeccable," said Hussein.

"Lena apparently came out with some vague stuff about how you do not take your studies as seriously as you might, how you sometimes avoid taking active part in the work of the komsomol. They asked her about religion. She didn't know what they were driving at, but she said..." Galya hesitated.

"What did she say, exactly?" pressed Vadim.

"She said she knew that you are a Jew."

Vadim clapped a hand to his forehead and drew it down across his face. "Brilliant."

"I don't think she meant it to sound like that. They were pressurising her, she had to say something. Anyway, they suggested that someone like you should not be in the organisation, that the komsomol should consider withdrawing your membership. She said she would make sure it was on the agenda for the next meeting."

"Did she tell you all this?"

"Yes, in strict confidence. She doesn't know that... she doesn't know about Hussein and me."

"Why do you think she told you?"

"She was shaken by it, and a bit ashamed. She has never come in contact with them before, and now she is worried that if you get thrown out of the komsomol you will be kicked out of the university too."

"Well naturally I will. If I am not fit to be a young Leninist, they won't let me continue to stay on at the university. Do you know the KGB men's names?"

"No. Lena said one of them was rather good-looking."

Vadim smiled, and Hussein said, "Why do you ask that?"

"They have been leaning on Rachel for a while," explained Vadim. "Her man is called Nikolai Palych. I was meant to see him earlier today."

"You were meant to?"

"I didn't go."

Hussein and Galya recoiled into their chairs. Hussein whistled through his teeth.

"That was very dumb. You are in way over your head now. I don't think anyone can drag you out."

"I know," said Vadim. "The game is up."

"No, that's not true," said Galya firmly. "It doesn't change anything. Our plan is still the only hope."

"Our plan?"

"Galya thought it up," said Hussein. "I think it is your best shot."

"Thank you, Galya," said Vadim. "Tell me."

They closed in a huddle again. "When the chairman proposes excluding you from the komsomol, I will table a motion suggesting that we downgrade the punishment to a severe reprimand. You will have to eat humble pie beforehand, say that you accept the criticisms of your behaviour and promise to change. There must be no jokes and no hint of irony, otherwise I will have no justification in proposing the motion. Someone will have to second the motion. It can't be Hussein, because that's too obvious. I can't line anyone up, because that would be too risky. It must not look like it has been staged. I will act as if the idea occurred to me in the course of the meeting – after all, it is just the sort of soppy thing I would say, isn't it – and we will have to hope that someone takes it upon themselves to second it."

"Why should anyone do that? It will be obvious the leadership wants me out."

"Yes but I think the rank and file will jump at the chance to go easy on you. Everybody knows you, and nobody will want to vote for spoiling your life. They will resent being asked. My proposal will let everyone off the hook, because they can do their komsomol duty without doing too much damage to your future."

Vadim turned it over in his mind. "If the KGB wants me kicked out, then they will find a way even if this works."

"That is possible," said Galya. "But you know, a thing like this looks much better if it comes from the grass roots. They know that, that's why they approached Lena. They want your peers to do the dirty work, because if the authorities penalise you it looks like persecution. And once you have been formally reprimanded by us, they cannot very well punish you again for the same lapse. That is the way it works, like inoculation."

Vadim scratched the back of his head. "I don't like the idea of a public confession. It will be a bit dishonest of me."

"I knew you would say something like that, you haughty bastard," exploded Hussein. "Well I'm sorry, but you can't afford that kind of luxury at the moment. Why can't you go through the motions like everyone else? It is not as if anybody is asking you to believe a word of it. Don't be honest, be humble for once. It's not a bad virtue and it's one you have been short on recently."

"All right, all right. I'll do it."

"Well, isn't that big of you."

"No, I mean, thank you. Thanks for dreaming it up. I mean it."

Hussein and Galya got up. "Well then," said Galya brightly. "We'll see you there in the morning, then. Be early, that looks good."

"I will. Good night."

When they had gone Vadim undressed and got into bed. But he could not sleep. He adopted the familiar pose: hands laced behind his head, gaze fixed on the ceiling, and so he remained all night. His head was full of thoughts, but none of them was for the ordeal of the next day, all were for the past. His face was stone and betrayed no emotion. But occasionally he would whisper a word under his breath: "Rachel."

I can't tell you how disappointed I am in her. This is not what I had in mind at all when I invented her. She was supposed to be the best thing that ever happened to Vadim. She was going to bring him out of himself a bit, give him the confidence he lacked, teach him a thing or two. I wanted her to be the agent of his redemption. She was meant to save him.

I had planned that they would unite against the forces trying to drive a wedge between them, that they would draw strength from their shared tribulation, and that in the end they would go and live happily ever after in the West. The last thing I wanted was a tragic turn of events this near the end of the story. It's not good news for the film rights. But it's too late now. What's done is done.

I shan't bore you with what they put her through at the embassy. Some of what was said was true, and some of it wasn't. She had a lengthy and emotional discussion with a minister counsellor from Washington DC and a first secretary from Boston who, apart from their diplomatic duties, or rather as part of them, ran errands for a three-letter organisation the name of which did not appear on their business cards. These two gentlemen told her in a most forceful way that the KGB had their claws in her and that she was in serious danger, which was kind of true. They told her that the very fact she had met with a KGB man was enough to be used against her for blackmail purposes, that the KGB would certainly have tapes and pictures and videos that they could doctor and fake and make into anything they wanted; that at any moment she might find herself waking up in a KGB hospital with a brainful of drugs and not know who the hell or where the hell she was. All this was unlikely, but none of it was entirely beyond the bounds of possibility. She knew that. They nearly blew it when they suggested that Vadim might well be working for the KGB too – she was sure that wasn't true. But they were deadly serious about everything they said, and that shocked her. Also they bullied her and frightened her and told her she was naive and silly, that she was putting herself and other people at risk for the sake of a holiday romance. They made her feel like a traitor to her country, which hurt: all those years of pledging allegiance to the flag take their toll on even the most independent psyche.

It was all very humiliating and unpleasant for her. It was without doubt the most harrowing experience of her life. But it had the desired effect: it wore her down. When they flicked the nice-and-nasty switch the other way and started telling her that she had nothing to be ashamed of, that through no fault of hers that she had been sucked in over her head, that there was a plane to New York that evening and she could be beyond the reach of the Soviet secret police and in the safety of the United States before the day was out, well, she agreed through her tears to go. In that moment she was doing it as much to get away from her own people as from the Soviets.

She did not go back to the university to pack her things, that was all taken care of later. She wrote no letters and made no phonecalls – they were very strict about that. While she was waiting in the embassy's cultural section, she bumped into one of the Irex students who had come in to collect the mail, and she told him she was going. But there was no opportunity to write a note or even pass a message. She was driven to Sheremetyevo Airport in a diplomatic Chevrolet

with leather seats – which was a treat – and she went home in the
clothes she stood up in.

But couldn't she have toughed it out? She was a free citizen of
a free country, wasn't she? No-one, not even the President of the
United States himself, could order her to go home if she didn't want
to. She could have told them all to go to hell and marched out of
the secure lead-lined room where the interview took place, out of
the building, out of the compound, onto the metro and all the way
back to Vadim's room on the tenth floor of V Zone of the MGU
main building. He would have comforted her and marvelled at her
strength of will and held her so tight that it squeezed the breath
out of her. It would have been a wonderful night for both of them.
The next day they could have gone to Palace of Weddings No.1 and
applied for a marriage license. That way, whatever happened, sooner
or later they would have been together. She had that option, no
matter how much psychological pressure she was subjected to. She
had every right to tell them to go to hell and mind their own goddam
business and she could have flounced out of there and nobody could
have done a damn thing to stop her. All the minister general and
the first secretary could have done was tut-tut and shake their close-
cropped blond heads and file a report.

It would have been great. That was what I planned for her from
the beginning. So why didn't she do it, when it would have been so
good to put one over on those guys? Why didn't she?

I'll tell you why, if you want to know.

Because she didn't love him enough, that's why.

The meeting was unusually well-attended. The komsorgs, like
party whips, had been rallying the idle and indifferent. All the
first year of *zhurfak* were there, as were all who lived on the tenth

floor with Vadim. Galya, when she arrived, was glad to see Vadim already there, sitting contritely at the front, wearing a tie and and his komsomol badge. With him were two other disciplinary cases, room-mates who had been caught blind-drunk in their blok on the day their exams finished.

Hussein walked in a minute or two later, and since Lena was nowhere to be seen Galya risked exchanging a few words with him.

"How was he this morning?" she asked.

"Resigned, depressed."

"Why aren't you wearing your badge?"

"I lent it to Vadim. He couldn't find his and I felt his need was greater."

"All right. Go and sit down. See you after."

Hussein went and took a seat near Vadim. Shortly afterwards the komsomol committee arrived, headed by Lena, and took their seats behind a table at the front. Galya was disturbed to see that Lena was accompanied by an older student, Sergei Tolchkov, whom she recognised as a full-time official of the central committee of the Moscow University komsomol organisation. Vadim also recognised him: he was the postgraduate who had made the speech at the Friendship Evening on the day he first saw Rachel.

The official business was dealt with swiftly. Tolchkov was introduced and he gave a short talk on a recent exchange trip to Bulgaria and brought fraternal greetings from the students of Sofia University. The talk came to its dull conclusion. Lena stood up.

"I would like to thank comrade Tolchkov for conveying the good wishes of the Bulgarian comrades to us. It is obvious that he brought many interesting thoughts and impressions back with him."

"And a suitcase full of training shoes, no doubt," muttered one of the accused drunkards next to Vadim. No-one else heard it.

"Now we come to the last item on the agenda," Lena was saying, "Two disciplinary matters. First there is the matter of comrades

Kradkin, Oleg Mikhailovich, and Raikov, Alexander Stepanovich. Both admit to violating the conditions of residence in the hostel of the main corpus of MGU and to being in a state of intoxication when routinely visited in their room in V Zone by the sanitary commission. Comrades Kradkin and Raikov, do you have anything to say?"

The two of them stood up. The one who had muttered to Vadim, Kradkin, did all the talking. Raikov hung his head, a study in repentance. "We would like to say, Sasha and I, that we did not mean any harm and we regret breaking the rules," said Kradkin. "We promise in future to act in a manner more becoming to young Leninists, and we apologise to our comrades and fellow-students for falling below the standards expected of us."

"Right," said Lena. "Despite your apology, such a lapse cannot be entirely overlooked, especially at a time when the Party and the whole country is striving for more discipline in the work-place. It is proposed that you both be handed down a severe reprimand. This is a more stringent punishment than a simple reprimand, and reflects the seriousness of your behaviour; at the same time it is less than a very severe reprimand, and this is in recognition of your undertaking not to offend in this way again. It is, in other words, a final warning. Is that understood?"

"Understood," said Kradkin and Raikov in unison, and sat down.

Lena put the punishment to the vote. It was passed unanimously.

"Good result," said Vadim to Kradkin.

"Yes," he whispered back. "We thought we were going to get a boot up the arse and out of here. We'd have been in army uniform before we knew it."

Vadim turned his attention back to Lena. He saw that she was troubled. She shuffled papers and glanced his way, but would not meet his eye. "It is a good sign that she is not enjoying this," he thought. "She will be as glad as anyone of Galya's let-out." Galya had also spotted Lena's confusion and was thinking along different lines: they must have suspected she wouldn't have the stomach for it, that's why they sent Tolchkov.

"...And the other disciplinary matter concerns comrade Prichalov, Vadim Yurevich," said Lena. "In the light of serious ideological errors and repeated lapses in discipline, it is proposed to revoke comrade Prichalov's membership of the All-Union Leninist Communist Union of Youth." A frisson of scandal passed round the room. For most of the students present this was the first they knew that Vadim was in trouble this bad. The quicker-witted had already realised that they would each be called upon to cast a stone. "What do you have to say for yourself, comrade Prichalov?" asked Lena, still not looking his way.

Vadim stood up. "I apologise if my conduct has been in any way unbecoming of a member of this organisation. I have no quarrel with the komsomol," – Galya groaned – "and I promise to try harder to act like a true Leninist in future." He sat down.

"Has anyone else anything to say on this matter?"

"I do," piped up a voice from the back. It was a lad from the tenth floor with whom Vadim was on nodding terms: his name was Fedya and he was a *stukach* assigned to the French contingent on Rachel's corridor. Rachel had once told Vadim that the French girls nicknamed him *le cochon en pantalon marron* because he always wore a brown suit when he called on them, and because he shamelessly ate every scrap of food in their larder. "It's a good phrase, the pig in brown trousers," she had said. "It could be the title of a collection by some minor Futurist poet."

Vadim smiled to himself at this reminiscence. He came back to earth only when he heard Fedya speaking his name. "...Prichalov often hums the tunes of anti-Soviet songs in the kitchen. He has been heard to make jokes about the Socialist Competition Between

Floors, and he did not take part in last week's subbotnik, when our floor undertook to disinfect the corridor and rid V Zone of cockroaches."

"Anyone else?" said Lena.

"He hasn't been to class much recently," ventured one timid girl from Vadim's own group. Then, immediately regretting her remark, "But I expect there was a good reason."

"There was," called out Hussein. "He was burying his grandfather. He missed the cockroach purge for the same reason, Fedya. And incidentally, how do you know the tunes he hums were from anti-Soviet songs unless you listen to those songs yourself?"

Fedya blushed, and there was a ripple of laughter and clapping.

"Now then, comrades," put in Tolchkov. "This is a serious matter, we are not here to joke."

"Who's joking?" said Hussein.

"That's enough from you, I think. You are clearly biased in the comrade's favour. I say we move to a vote on this now."

"Can I say something first?" It was Galya.

"Yes," said Lena. "Go ahead, Galya."

"In view of comrade Prichalov's sincere apology, I propose that we show leniency and change his punishment to a very severe reprimand. This would show Leninist wisdom, and is no less than we did for Kradkin and Raikov just now."

"That is a fine idea, Galya," said Lena, gushing with relief. "Is there a seconder?"

"If I may interrupt you for a second, comrade chairman," Tolchkov was on his feet again. "Before you vote on this I should like to make a few remarks in my capacity as a member of the central committee of the MGU komsomol."

"Please do," said Lena, deflated. "Please do."

"A comrade just mentioned Leninist wisdom. And she was quite right, we should certainly act wisely in this situation. I hardly need remind you that the very heart of Leninism is Vladimir Ilyich's brilliant insight that the revolution is made and sustained by a hard core of dedicated revolutionaries, professional frontliners striving to build a new society. General Secretary Andropov has laid special stress on this, and we, as young Leninists, should take careful note of the Party's lead. We are the Party cadres of the near future; our generation may well be the one to lead the Soviet people out of the era of developed socialism into the reality of communism. We want no timeservers, no careerists in our ranks as we undertake this historic task. You should be aware that the eyes of the Party, of all our senior comrades, are on us at this moment. We must be sure to act with a high degree of ideological vigilance. I say our vote should send a resounding and unanimous – yes, unanimous – message of reassurance to all those comrades who are watching us closely, listening to our deliberations."

Tolchkov sat down. His meaning had been lost on no-one in the room. None had the courage or inclination to speak. Vadim too remained silent: he knew it was all over now.

Lena cleared her throat. "In the light of comrade Tolchkov's remarks," she said hoarsely, "I think the proper thing to do is proceed straight to a vote as per the agenda." She coughed. "All those in favour of excluding Prichalov, Vadim Yurevich, from the ranks of the komsomol, please raise your hands."

The hands went up. Some without a qualm, some hesitantly. A few students raised their arms half-way by way of a disguised protest. Oleg Kradkin, when he lifted his arm, whispered out of the corner of his mouth, "Sorry, Vadim, nothing personal." Lena's hand was up, as it had to be, and so was Galya's. The last person to add his voice to the mob was Hussein.

She didn't love him. I was horrified when I realised this was so.

Rachel was escorted to the plane in a daze. Her emotions had taken a terrible battering and she was numb to the outside world. She barely noticed the customs check, which was very brief since she had no luggage. Passport control passed her by. She did not get a fit of giggles when the boy-soldier behind the screen stared at her glassily for thirty seconds. She did not give him a cheery *do svidaniya* when he finally handed back her documents.

Up to this point her reactions were what you would expect, what I was expecting. To all appearances she was a bereaved person. Even the embassy official, the one from Boston, who came with her to the departure gate felt sorry for her, and these CIA men are not easily moved to pity. He left her only when the flight started boarding. She shook his hand and politely said thank you. Thank you for what? – she did not know.

Once on the plane, it was her misfortune to find herself seated next to a chatty Californian businessman who was going home after ZUB-83, an international exhibition of dental equipment. He had spent a drunken week in the Hammer Centre with some friendly bureaucrats from the Soviet Ministry of Health. He was sure he had a major deal in the bag, and he wanted to tell Rachel all about it.

Rachel did not want to listen. As soon as the seatbelt lights went out she escaped to the toilet where she sat and sobbed for half an hour. Then she washed her face and went back to her seat and instantly fell asleep. When she woke up they were already out of Soviet air space.

Rachel summoned a passing stewardess who, she noticed by her name tag, was also called Rachel. This insignificant coincidence cheered her a little. Rachel asked for a gin-and-tonic. The stewardess Rachel brought the drink with a charming smile that suggested she lived for such moments. Our Rachel found everything about the drink-serving process extraordinarily pleasing. The plastic tray was a nice, deep blue colour; the Gordon's miniature was so dinky; the little ring-pull tonic opened with a delicious crack and fizz; the ice cubes had funny holes in them, like they always do on planes; unfortunately there was no lemon, but Rachel was not about to quibble.

She mixed herself the drink, keeping back a drop of gin and a splash of tonic for a top-up. She took a first sip, and that was when the emotional dam gave way and wave after happy wave of relief broke over her. She was overwhelmed by the most blissful feeling of release. She felt like she could fly – then she remembered that she was flying, and she laughed. The burden of her love affair with Vadim fell away from her like a sack of stone. She put it behind her. And once she had taken affectionate leave of him, the rest was easy. Before the ice was melted in her plastic glass she had said goodbye to the whole rotten ballgame: the queues, the empty shelves, the *stukachi*, the habitual misery of her Russian friends, the grime, the emotional intensity, the ubiquitous smell of cabbage and dark tobacco, the daily slog, the transparent propaganda, the weather, the hostel, the roaches, the buses, the entire cantankerous, pointless, unpleasant, bottomless wretchedness of the USSR.

Good riddance to it. She was going home, and she would not be back in a hurry.

It is fifteen minutes on the red line of the underground from the university to Kropotkinskaya.

Vadim stood all the way. When he got out, he spent a few minutes on the platform. He went up to one of the columns. It was flecked with pink and grey. The marble was very beautiful, but today the effect struck him as dull and kitschy. The platform looked like a millionaire's bathroom, he thought, opulent but tasteless. He flattened his palm on the column, and its coolness reminded him of Rachel's cool fingers the first time she had touched him.

He walked to the eastern end of the platform. The hanging signs were swaying in the dank draught, like stale breath, that always preceded the arrival of a train. He noticed that the name of Lenin Hills had been scrubbed off the sign: so it was closed forever then.

Vadim left the platform and went up to the surface, emerging by the exit on Gogolevsky Boulevard. There was a plaque on the pink doorway: "Metro Station Kropotkinskaya, built 1931–35, architectural monument, protected by the state." He crossed the road and sat down on a bench by the statue of Engels, at the point where Kropotkinskaya Street meets Metrobuilders' Street.

He saw how the ground seemed to swell up from this point towards the militia box on the corner by the Ostozhenka cafe, and how it fell sharply away, like the lip of a volcano. Treetops peeked out of the deep hollow where the Moskva swimming pool was located, but there was no sign of it from here. It was sheltered from the bustle of the street by the park and the lie of the land.

He pulled a notebook and pen out of his jacket. "It must have looked good from this angle," he wrote, "and in this light. In the low evening sun, the golden domes would have burned like furnaces. They would have been dazzling. From here I would see two façades at once, two of Loganovsky's high-reliefs, and at least nine of the bas-reliefs. I would have the full effect of the sheer size of it. Also, I would see the neat beds of flowers and Andreyev's old hermit who, if I am right, was mounted on the kokoshnik of the central vault on the west side."

He crossed over Metrobuilders' to the cafe, then turned left across the top of Soimonovsky Alley, so that he was on Volkhonka Street. He walked down the road. To his left was an ordinary street scene, with shops and buildings; to his right a man-made precipice, the edge of the yawning hole dug for the Palace of Soviets. Vadim now stood on Volkhonka with his back to the Pushkin Museum. He was on a high platform that, it struck him, was like a miniature copy of the one on Lenin Hills. "From there you look down on Moskva the city," he noted, "And from here you look down on Moskva the swimming pool." Why did they call the pool 'Moscow' Was that really the best they could think of?

Ten metres below he could see dozens of heads bobbing about in the water like apples in a barrel. He could hear the excited cries of children as they splashed about in the water. The diving board, a dramatic parabola in pre-formed concrete, rose up like a disembodied Norman arch opposite his vantage point.

He watched for a few minutes then walked further up Volkhonka. He turned right again and descended into the park around the pool. There were maples and pear trees. He was on a path of blue asphalt that sloped away to the blue and yellow tiled outer walls of the loathsome great soup bowl. Some of the tiles were of thick frosted glass, and he could see ghostly pink bodies moving around in the changing rooms behind. He left the path and went onto the grass. He was near a set of steps leading out onto the unnamed little street at the eastern edge of the park. He figured he was now standing on the place where the iconostasis had been, or rather he was standing beneath it, for the floor of the cathedral would have been several metres above his head.

He felt nothing, however, no historical vibration, no echo down the decades. So he headed round the pool to where the greenery was thickest. Absurdly, he found himself scanning the ground for some small shard of marble or even an old piece of brick, any sign of the past life of the location. There was nothing, of course. All he encountered was some kind of public toilet hidden in the undergrowth roughly on the site of the statue of Alexander III enthroned – a vulgar, though doubtless unintentional gag. He laughed anyway. "I feel like an Egyptologist," he thought. "Or like someone looking for dinosaur bones. How extraordinary to think that there are thousands of people in this city who, like Grandad, remember the Cathedral, who saw it and walked around inside it, or even prayed in it, and now it has disappeared utterly. I don't see it, and they don't talk about it. It might as well never have existed."

He emerged onto the Kropotkinskaya Embankment and crossed the road to the riverside. Sitting on the embankment wall he took a minute to survey the magnificent sight to his right: the crowded ensemble of the Kremlin was spread before him like a table laid for a giants' feast. In the foreground were the towers of the ancient fortress: the butiloid Water-Pump Tower on the southern corner nearest to him; the climactic ziggurat of the Borovitskaya; then, at intervals along the river wall, the Annunciation Tower, the Magazin Tower, the Second Nameless and the First Nameless Towers. Vadim smiled to himself as he counted off the last two: for five hundred years these little brothers had stood guard over the city, and nobody had ever thought to honour them with a name. These red spires were set against the flat white and yellow façade of Thon's Great Kremlin Palace; to the right of the palace, the shining cupolas of the Archangelsky and the Blagoveshchensky Cathedrals and the two uneven peaks of the bell-tower of Ivan the Great made an untidy scuffle of golden heads.

Vadim looked beyond the Kremlin, and through the pollution haze he could make out the top-knot of the Cathedral of St. Basil's the Blessed at the eastern extremity of Red Square. He knew now that St. Basil's had also been slated for destruction as it impeded the progress of Stalin's cohorts across the square on high holidays. Now the very idea of Moscow without St. Basil's was unthinkable, but then who a hundred years ago could have envisaged a Moscow without Christ the Saviour?

Beyond St. Basil's loomed the grey massif of the Rossiya Hotel, mercifully obscure from here. A whole medieval suburb, the narrow streets and twisted alleyways of Zaryadye, had been razed to make space for that square monster. Was one church anything to grieve for in comparison?

Vadim got up and walked away from the Kremlin. He stopped at the intersection with Soimonovsky Alley and looked back. There was nothing to see: no buildings, no evidence of town-planning, just a row of trees and a fast stretch of road connecting the Kremlin with the Garden Ring at the Krymsky Bridge. His eye scanned the empty patch of sky to his left, looking for somewhere to settle, and alighted for want of anything else on the iron pylons overlooking the pool. He realised that it was this blank space, this architectural vacuum, which was the most telling evidence of the Cathedral's once having lived. Christ the Saviour was conspicuous mostly by its massive absence. Vadim was standing a few hundred yards from the political heart of the Empire, and there was nothing here to see but a glorified puddle. It was a dead zone, a numb spot on the face of the town.

Vadim crossed the road again and started up a gentle slope through the park. The trees formed a canopy; it was chilly here and he felt like he was in a tunnel. He was suddenly overcome with a rush of claustrophobia, and he made to cut through the bushes and out onto the street to his left. Then he became aware of a rich and familiar fragrance. He stopped and breathed deeply. It was coming from the bushes. It was jasmine. The smell was so strong it blocked out the chlorine fumes and the usual urban stench of car exhausts. His heart flipped: this was the scrap of history he was looking for. He knew from Andreyev's poem that there were jasmine bushes in the Cathedral gardens, and here they still were. They were a genuine link to the past, better than a relic, better than the salvaged alti-relievi at the Don Monastery, because they were alive and whole. He plucked a sprig from the nearest bush and tucked it in his jacket pocket. Then he carried on uphill towards the metro.

He had now come almost full circle. He glanced to his left at the little baroque church of Elijah the Commonplace, tucked away on Third Commonplace Alley. "Built in a day," said the plaque on the wall. Could that be true? Vadim didn't know, but he wanted to believe it. Old Elijah must have felt a very poor relation next to Christ the Saviour. Now he was the only church left for several blocks in any direction. Probably his very insignificance saved him. Built in a day? Maybe, maybe not. The point is he was still here two hundred years on.

At the top of the small hill Vadim stopped again. The pool was now on his right, and there was another low wall from which it was visible. Vadim leaned on this wall with his head in his hands and thought of Rachel, spending her first morning back in New York. He tried to despise her for her betrayal, but could not. He just wanted her back, if just for half an hour so they could at least say a proper goodbye. For a moment he was overcome with regret and self-pity. He gave himself over to it, whispered her name under his breath again.

"Vadim." A voice spoke his name behind him. It was the voice of a man. He span round. The speaker was a fair-haired man, late-twenties. He was in a brown jacket and dark tie. He wore a home-knitted jumper and scuffed training shoes. He smiled as if apologising for barging in on Vadim's misery.

Beside him stood a second man, rather older, slightly shorter, bald. There was a car by the kerb opposite the Ostozhenka cafe, ten metres from where they stood. The engine was running, the back door was open, and a third man sat behind the wheel, looking straight ahead.

"Come with us, Vadim," said the first man. "There are some things we need to talk over." His voice was all sympathy, without a hint of menace, but Vadim's stomach turned.

"Nikolai Palych?" he asked. The man nodded and smiled again. His colleague glanced at his watch and squinted up the road. Vadim too looked to see who else was in the vicinity. There were no pedestrians on Soimonovsky. The nearest people were outside the bakery on the corner of Kropotkinskaya, sixty metres away across a busy road. There were a few diners in the Ostozhenka cafe. But what difference could witnesses make to this?

"What is there to say? What do you want to talk to me about?" asked Vadim.

"It's not street talk. Get in the car and we'll discuss it at the office. It won't take long, I promise you."

Vadim's courage was slowly returning after the initial shock. "Are you arresting me?"

Nikolai Palych chuckled, and the other man scowled. "Of course not," said Nikolai Palych. "We just want to have a chat with you, check you are all right."

"I'm fine, thanks. And I'm busy just now. I don't think I have anything interesting to tell you, anyhow."

"We'll be the judge of that, son," said the second man. "Now stop wasting our time and get in the car, or it will be the worse for you."

Vadim looked at Nikolai Palych, whose eyes were pleading.

"No," said Vadim.

"Do it," said the second man.

"No," he repeated. Then a strange thought popped into his head, something from his reading about the Cathedral. "I claim sanctuary," he said.

"You what?"

"I claim sanctuary. This is hallowed ground, and you have no right to touch me here."

Nikolai Palych looked at him with such sympathy and sorrow that for a moment Vadim thought he was going to burst into tears.

The other man snarled and spat a bubbly gob of phlegm on the pavement.

Vadim had had enough. He turned on his heel and set off back down the hill. What exactly happened next he was never sure because it all came about terribly fast, but two hands grabbed his arms and two other hands grabbed a handful of hair and the seat of his pants, and he was somehow propelled headfirst into the back of the car. To his credit he kept calm, and he didn't scream or struggle. But having his hair pulled made his eyes water, which was unfortunate because he didn't want them to think he was crying.

The five-minute ride to the Lubyanka was uncomfortable, but not unbearably so. He lay on his stomach with his nose in the hot plastic upholstery of the back seat. The second man was in the front passenger seat. Clearly he had found it distasteful to abduct Vadim because he kept saying things like: "Why did you go and do that, you stupid little shit?" and "Nutty son of a bitch, what did you think you were playing at?" Nikolai Palych meanwhile was in the back with Vadim, in fact he was sitting on him. Every time his colleague produced an angry remark, Nikolai Palych patted Vadim comfortingly on the head and said "There there, now. There there."

Nikolai Palych sat behind a scarred desk in the windowless room. The desk was bare but for a cardboard Aeroflot calendar and a green phone. Behind him hung a dusty portrait of Dzerzhinsky. Vadim sat opposite Nikolai Palych, sideways on. There was a narrow table in front of him, forming a T-shape with the writing desk. On Vadim's table was a pen and a few sheets of blank paper. The other man, who still had not introduced himself, paced impatiently up and down behind Vadim's back. Vadim tried not to pay attention to him, but his footfalls and his sibilant breath made the hairs on Vadim's neck bristle.

Nikolai Palych lit a cigarette. "Why didn't you turn up yesterday?" he asked. He did not sound angry, just disappointed. "We were expecting you at seven."

"I was busy yesterday," said Vadim, "Preparing the case for the defence."

"Ah yes, the comrades' court. We heard about that. How did it go?"

"They kicked me out."

Nikolai Palych tutted and shook his head. "That's bad news. I'm very sorry to hear that. If only you had come to me yesterday. I have some friends in *zhurfak*, I could have had a word and saved you all that distress. It will be much harder to help you now."

"Thanks all the same," said Vadim.

"Oh, don't thank me. It's no hardship to help a good fellow."

"No, you misunderstand me. I mean: thank you, I don't want your help."

Nikolai Palych was not offended. He leaned across and took a sheet of the paper from in front of Vadim. Deftly he rolled it into a cone and tapped the drooping ash of his cigarette into it.

"Well you are going to need someone's help, Vadim."

"Yes," chimed in the other man. "Especially now that it turns out your little girlfriend is a spy."

Vadim twisted round in his seat. "She is not a spy!"

"No? Then why did she up-sticks and run away in such a hurry, tell me that? What did she have to be so afraid of, eh?"

"She's not a spy," repeated Vadim lamely. He looked to Nikolai Palych, who smiled and made a little loop in the air with his cigarette. It was a comforting sort of gesture, as if he was saying to Vadim: don't mind my friend, he's got a suspicious nature.

"You know best, Vadim," said Nikolai Palych. "After all, you knew her much better than any of us." Nikolai Palych paused, and carefully stubbed out his cigarette on the paper cone. "I only met her twice," he continued, but I really liked her, I liked her a lot." He flicked the cone to shake the ash down to the bottom. He peered into his ashtray, then looked up suddenly: "You did know I had met her?" Vadim nodded. "She loved being in the USSR, and I know she was very fond of you. She told me so herself. That's what I can't understand, Vadim. If she was happy here, why did she leave so suddenly? It is baffling to me. And I was really hoping you could shed some light on it. So what do you think, Vadim? What made her do it?"

Vadim shrugged, trying hard not to let any emotion into his voice. "I don't know," he said. "I don't understand it either."

"It's a mystery," said the second man. "A riddle wrapped in a mystery inside an enigma."

"Ha!" laughed Nikolai Palych, grinning at Vadim. Was he inviting Vadim to join him in mocking his colleague?

Perhaps the second man realised he was being teased, because suddenly he became aggressive. He came round to the front of Vadim and gripping the edge of the table leaned close to his face. Vadim could smell garlic and stale tobacco on his breath.

"How long have you been a believer?"

Vadim was taken aback. "I am not a believer."

The man snorted. "Don't lie, believers aren't supposed to lie. We know you loiter in monasteries. You have spent the best part of a year gathering anti-Soviet religious propaganda, and you have made contact with illegal Baptist groups."

"I haven't done that!"

"You have, dammit. They passed you a Bible only the other day. Who was that intended for?"

"For me. It was a present to me, from a friend."

"Strange present for a komsomol member, isn't it? And there is no need to be so coy about your English pal. We know all about him and his activities."

"I don't know anything about any activities. I don't know him all that well at all."

The man snorted again. "So why the lavish gifts, then?"

"Lavish gifts? One book?"

"A Bible! Have you any idea how much a Bible is worth on the black market?"

"Now then, Boris Borisovich," said Nikolai Palych, "Let's not be unfair to Vadim. He's an amateur historian, that's all. He's just interested in books. The Bible is a book like any other, and a very important one in the history of European culture. Isn't that right, Vadim?"

"Yes, that's right." He was grateful for the note of reason.

"Books are wonderful things," Nikolai Palych went on. "Your father has written a book, hasn't he?"

"Yes." Vadim was reeling now. "Yes. It is coming out at the end of the year."

"Unless the publishers get cold feet," said Boris Borisovich.

"What?"

"Publishers are nervous people. They hate scandal. They can't risk investing money in a print-run and then having to pull it because the author is anti-Soviet."

"My father isn't anti-Soviet! And his book is about nineteenth-century architecture, how can that possibly be anti-Soviet?"

"Well, if he is not anti-Soviet, where did you get your objectionable opinions?" said Boris Borisovich. "How come your brother slanders the Soviet way of life every time he opens his mouth?"

Again Nikolai Palych stepped in. "Boris Borisovich, please. Yuri Efimovich is a long-standing party member. And anyway, it is Vadim we are interested in just now, not his father or his brother." Boris Borisovich scowled his familiar scowl and returned to his impatient beat behind Vadim's back. Vadim stared at the table, his head in his hands. Nikolai Palych lit another cigarette and picked up his paper ashtray.

"No-one is accusing you of anything, Vadim. Sure, you have bent the rules, but who in Russia doesn't do that? That business in the Lenin Library, that showed initiative. I'm not condoning it, mind, but it was clever and daring, and I like that. Sometimes I feel we could use more of those kind of qualities in the Service." There was a splutter from behind; Nikolai Palych ignored it. He lowered his voice, taking Vadim into his confidence. "We know you are not a villain, Vadim, we are not stupid. But there are some things we have to check out. If an exchange visitor from a capitalist country suddenly makes a dash for the exit, we have to ask ourselves why. That's our job."

"But you asked me in before that happened."

Nikolai Palych glanced at his colleague. "I know. There were some things we needed to ask you about anyway, about your contacts with foreign citizens."

"Is it illegal to know people from other countries?"

"Of course not. Your friends are your own affair. But acquaintance with foreigners brings with it certain responsibilities, certain duties. You know that. You are a komsomol member, after all, and a bright lad to boot. Everyone at the university says so."

"Who?"

"Everyone. Now listen. All we want from you is an hour of your time. We would just like you to jot down what you know about Rachel. She's gone now. Think of it as a kind of tribute, a memoir. You keep a journal, don't you? It shouldn't be hard for you. We would just like to know from you what she was like. We would like to know the same things you would tell a friend who had never met her."

"Why?"

"It's for our records, so we can close the matter. Probably no-one will ever even read it. Just write down for us the kind of thing you used to talk about; what her opinions were about various things – art, poetry, religion, politics. What did she like to do in the evenings, where did you go together, what are her friends like? I expect she introduced you to friends? It's a kind of pen portrait we are interested in. We want to put her in context."

"I don't think I want to do that."

"Now don't be hasty, Vadim. It is half an hour of your time and then you can go home. It will cost you nothing and will earn you a great deal of good will. You've been going through a rough patch. Everybody has rough patches – in their education, their marriage, their career – it would be a shame if one little blot on your copybook spoiled your whole future. On the other hand, if you do me this favour it will make it much easier for me to go to the dean of the faculty and say, look, give Vadim a break because he's a decent sort really and he's on our side. I'm sure I can make the dean see the sense of that."

"I told you, I don't want your help. I'll fight my own battles with the faculty."

"That's the spirit, well said! But a little reinforcement can't do any harm, can it? Just jot down a few thoughts. Whatever you write will be between you and me, I promise."

Vadim said nothing. He picked up the pen.

Nikolai Palych stood up. "Boris Borisovich and I will just go and get a bite to eat now. We'll be back in an hour. If you haven't finished by then, don't worry, you will go home anyway. You can come back in and finish it off another time."

The two men left the room, locking the door behind them.

Vadim paced the room. For an hour and a half he walked to and fro and wrote not a word. He spent the time in terror, chewing the pen, preparing himself for the ordeal of arrest. He was convinced he would be beaten, and that was what frightened him most of all, more than the thought of imprisonment. He did not know if he could withstand even the threat of physical violence.

Vadim stuck a hand in his pocket and found the sprig of jasmine he had torn off the bush a lifetime ago. Nervously he began to strip off the leaves and tear them into tiny pieces. The pungent smell filled his lungs as it had done in the park. The green juice stained his fingertips. He was on the last leaf when the key turned in the door. Vadim nearly jumped out of his skin. Instinctively he backed to the wall.

It was Nikolai Palych, alone this time.

He came over to the table, saw the clean sheets of paper, and sighed. "You are making a mistake, Vadim," he said without malice.

"I'm sorry," Vadim mumbled.

Nikolai Palych took a sheet of the paper and the pen and wrote a 925-number on it in big figures. "This is my work telephone," he said, folding the paper and handing it to Vadim. "Give me a call if you change your mind. But do it fast. In a day or two it will be out of my hands."

Vadim hesitated, then took the paper. "You are letting me go?" He hardly dared ask the question.

"Yes, you can go." Nikolai Palych opened the door and called down the corridor. A uniformed soldier wearing blue shoulder tabs – he was no older than Vadim – came and stood in the empty oblong room, ready to escort Vadim back to the world.

Vadim made to leave. On impulse he turned in the doorway and looked at Nikolai Palych: he was sitting on the edge of the table, sniffing the jasmine twig.

"I shan't be ringing you," said Vadim.

"I know," said Nikolai Palych. "To hell with you." And he gave Vadim a big, friendly wink.

☆

The V Zone lift was out of order. Vadim had to climb the ten storeys back to his room. There was a note tucked in the door. It said: *Please come by and see me this evening. Kakha.* Vadim did not want to sit alone. Glad of the invitation, he went straight back down to the fifth floor.

Kakha opened the door and seized Vadim in a fierce, Georgian embrace. His jumper smelled richly of tobacco. "Come in," he said. "We have been waiting for you. Where have you been?"

"For a long walk," said Vadim.

They passed into the room where he had first met Rachel. Manana was there. She came up to Vadim, took his face in her hands, and kissed his forehead in blessing. Hussein was there too: he sat on the bed in that same hunched pose, wringing his hands like Cain. The table was laid, and suddenly Vadim realised that he was ravenously hungry. Manana felt this instinctively; she steered him into a chair, planted a spoon in his fist and brought a plate of *chakhokhbili* stew and a hunk of *lavash* flat bread from the kitchen. Vadim fell wordlessly on the food. Kakha disappeared for a moment, then returned with a bottle of cognac and three tumblers. While he poured two generous fingers into each glass, Hussein spoke.

"Vadim," he said, "I betrayed you. I am asking you to forgive me, but I understand perfectly if you can't. You won't want to share a room with me now, so I am moving in with Kakha."

Vadim put down his spoon for a moment. "Hussein, don't give me all that Caucasian honour nonsense, please. The cause was lost. If you had made a spectacle of yourself and gone down with me, then I would be the one eaten up with guilt now, not you. You took the only realistic option, which was to keep your head down. Even Galya understood that."

"No, Galya was braver. She did not want me to tell you this, but she was supposed to play the part of that snake, Fedya. Before the meeting she was approached and asked to make a speech accusing you of un-Soviet behaviour. She refused."

"That was very brave of her, and kind. I will thank her when I see her."

"But what about me, do you forgive me?"

"I will forgive you if you stop whingeing." Vadim extended his hand to his friend, who took it with a smile.

Kakha picked up the glass. "Let's drink on it."

"Oh, I can't drink," said Vadim, still feeling yesterday's beer. "Not today."

"You must," said Kakha. "This is a solemn moment."

"Yes, you must," said Hussein. "And I wasn't whingeing."

Vadim picked up his glass and the three of them chinked. "To what shall we drink?" he said.

"To the better part of valour," said Vadim.

"An obscure toast, overly succinct, but I like the ring of it," said Kakha.

"What does it mean?" asked Hussein.

"It is an English proverb. It means don't cross swords until you know you can be victorious."

"Ah, the English," said Kakha. "Such a wise people. If I were not a Georgian I think I should like to be an Englishman. Not for nothing did the poet Lennon (the earth is his pillow) write that Georgia was always on his mind. We have a deep affinity, the English and us."

They drank, Kakha poured another round, and they drank that too.

"I am going to be kicked out of university," said Vadim gloomily.

"And I am going to be married," said Hussein, gloomier still.

Kakha roared with laughter as Vadim's jaw dropped. "When did this happen?" Vadim exclaimed.

"A day or two ago," said Hussein. "Galya and I want to stay in the capital when we graduate. With her komsomol record, she ought to be able to get a placing here. Once we are man and wife, I will apply for permanent residence in Moscow. It is another reason why I could not risk standing up for you today, and why Galya's refusal to accuse you was all the more noble. It cost her precious goodwill."

"I see," said Vadim.

"We must drink to this," said Kakha. He called to Manana, who all this time had been doing washing in the bathroom. "Join us for a toast," he said, "and we will share our own news."

Manana came in from the bathroom and took a fourth glass from the cupboard. She also brought a fresh bottle of cognac, since the men had just polished off the first. Kakha prised off the cap with a knife, and poured out four shots. They raised their glasses and when Manana had sat down at the table Kakha made his announcement. It naturally took the form of a toast.

"We live in a strange land, my friends," he began. "We live in a land beyond the looking-glass: all is upside-down and inside-out. In all the world, for example, when people celebrate they throw open their doors and sing at the top of their voices; here, in our looking-glass world, we pull down the shutters and speak in whispers. We are confused, like the English girl Alice, but we are frightened too, because when the Cheshire cat smiles, we see that his teeth are daggers.

"We live in sad times, my good friends, when it is a badge of honour to be reviled by one's peers. Yes, it is a strange, topsy-turvy land we live in. It is the Soviet Socialist Republic of Absurdistan. Manana and I, we cannot leave this place altogether, but we see no reason to remain in its citadel. My studies shall soon be over; we shall leave Moscow and return to Tbilisi. We want to live among our countrymen and our kinfolk. We want to speak the language we were born to. In short, we want to build a raft of peace and sanity on which to sail this mad ocean.

"We will gain much when we leave here, but we will lose much too. This give-and-take is in the nature of things, it is almost a universal law. Hussein here has announced his intention to trade his freedom for a lifetime of love, and this is a very common example of the universal law at work. Vadim has suffered great losses these past days, and it may seem to him that he has gained nothing for his pain. But let me say this, I see a new Vadim today. I do not know what exactly has happened to bring it about, but he has acquired a flinty edge that was not present in the dreamy musicmaker I met in this room last year. Vadim has the air of a warrior about him now; I feel sure this new strength will stand him in good stead. It is his compensation."

"So let us drink to the universal law, and (though it is bad form to mix toasts) to our own selves. And if we never meet in this company or this location again, the memory of this moment will gradually gain value in the repositories of our mind. To us, then, our gains and losses."

"To us," echoed Hussein and Manana.

"To us," said Vadim.

We are near the end.

Vadim was indeed expelled from Moscow University, and within the month he was drafted into the Soviet Army. After basic training he was shipped at night to Tadjikistan, thence to Afghanistan, where he served two tours. Nothing terrible happened to him in the war. He got typhoid, and twice came down with hepatitis, but he was never wounded. He could be said to have got off lightly.

But he saw too many horrors and atrocities on both sides. There was one occasion when his unit took an Afghan village. The Soviet soldiers rounded up the men of the village and made them strip to the waist. Some of the men had bruises or grazes on their right shoulders, clear proof that they had been firing rifles. They were roughed up and questioned, but none would say anything. Then Vadim's platoon commander, a senior sergeant from Krasnodar, took the family of one of the Afghan partisans and herded them into one of the huts near the village square. There was a mother and about eight children. The father was tied to a tree in sight of the hut. Then the sergeant ordered one of the tanks to drive over the hut. The tank reversed over it two or three times. Its caterpillar tracks were soon clogged with a sticky red porridge of blood and daub. The Afghan villager was in a frenzy. He screamed and screamed, but suddenly went limp and stopped screaming. Vadim was sent over to the man. He approached cautiously with his gun at the ready – it could have been some kind of trick. He prodded the man with his AK. But the Afghan was dead: his heart had burst at the sight of his family's massacre.

Vadim kept a diary in Afghanistan, as he had always done in civilian life, and when he came out of the army he wrote some naturalistic short stories about the war. Some of these anguished tales were published in literary journals during the glasnost years, and Vadim made a small name for himself as a writer. But he could never write up the incident that left the deepest mark on him. He never put down on paper how he had killed a man.

It happened in May 1985, the last month before his demobilisation. Vadim had gone through nineteen months of active service without shooting anyone dead, a shameful state of affairs for a *dyed*, a 'grandad' with most of his service behind him. He was careful not to advertise the fact around the barracks.

Then one night there was a huge scandal in camp. The regiment was stationed on the edge of Kabul, so there was a large and willing market for anything the soldiers could steal from stores: flour, spoons, underpants, petrol. The barracks, like all such installations, were encircled by two rings of barbed wire in between which ran a six-metre strip sown with anti-infantry mines. But there were blank spots in the minefield, invisible crossings to the outer wire. Everyone in the regiment knew where they were and used them for conducting business with the locals.

On that night, a corporal from another platoon had gone to the edge of the compound to trade. What exactly happened nobody knew, though it was easy enough to guess once his body was found in the morning. The soldier had got into some sort of argument with his clients and they had cut his throat.

The regimental commander called a full parade and raised hell. In the afternoon he gave a separate haranguing to the duty officer responsible for the guard the previous night, and to the one taking over that evening. The new officer was still smarting when he came to brief the guard detail, which included Vadim. He threatened them with a dozen refined forms of torture if the guard was anything less than exemplary. Vadim had heard it all countless times before and was in any case too demob-happy to care that much about a little black-marketeering, but all the same he understood that the officer was serious. The orders were clear: if anything moves out there, if you see a shadow or hear a rustle or a whisper, you shoot at it. There was to be no perimeter buy-and-sell that night.

Vadim got the three-to-five watch, the worst of the night because it was the hardest to stay awake through. For the same reason it was the most popular among the camp merchants. At three o'clock sharp Vadim took his post in a low tower on the eastern corner of the compound, and settled down for his shift. By about half-past four it was beginning to get light. Vadim was pinching himself to fight the drowsiness and thinking how soon it was to demob, and how strange it would be to go home. He closed his eyes to dwell on the thought.

Then he heard a noise like a footfall on gravel. He was an

experienced soldier by now, murder virgin or no, and he took no chances: he pointed his Kalashnikov into the darkness and fired off all thirty rounds. Then he crouched down to reload. It seemed to take a feverishly long time to unclip the curved magazine and snap a new one into the underbelly of his AK, and during those four or five seconds the Afghans shot back. One bullet punctured the tin roof of his lookout post. Vadim's belly froze. His back was cold with sweat and he was almost blind with fear and fury. They were out there, they were armed, and they might be coming his way. His weapon was reloaded now, and the shots aimed at him had given him a rough fix on his enemy. He peered out of his post, and there they were, the dushmani, three pale figures in the first glimmer of dawn. With a bang and a whoosh a flare went up from the adjacent post. It burst brightly in the sky, and now Vadim could see them clear as daylight about a hundred metres away. He could see their hunched pose and the panic on their bearded faces; he saw them look at each other as if to say: what the hell do we do now? Maybe they were already in retreat, it was hard to tell, but the main thing was that they were still a threat. Vadim took aim and fired, and this time he got one. His AK was loaded entirely with tracers – *dyed's* privilege – so he saw the long trajectory of the bullet that killed the Afghan, how it dipped before it struck him in the chest. The dushman twitched like a stringed puppet, then crumpled to the ground.

And that was the end of it. The other two ran away into the darkness as the flare faded. An APC was sent out of the compound soon after, and its crew gingerly retrieved the body.

Whether the Afghans were coming to attack the camp or to buy some rice, there was no way of telling. But the camp commander gave Vadim the benefit of the doubt, and recommended that he be awarded a medal 'For Valour', his only decoration of the war. He received the medal back home, a civilian again by that time.

Later, as a result of his small success as a writer, he was offered an editing job on a respected literary journal in Moscow, and he moved to the city he now considered home. Vadim supported the democracy movement of the late 1980s. In August 1991 he kept vigil for three nights at the White House with many fellow Muscovites and Afghan veterans. He was in the cheering crowd that watched the demontage of the statue of Dzerzhinsky; he actually wept as the steel cable tightened round the monument's neck and dragged it off its pedestal. In October 1993, when Yeltsin's tanks rolled into Moscow down the same two roads that Napoleon's armies had taken, when the big White House on the embankment was shelled and burned, Vadim stayed indoors and watched the whole thing on CNN.

He rarely visited Leningrad these days, and could not get into the habit of calling the town of his birth Petersburg. He rarely saw his father, who was still trying in vain to publish his book on *moderne*. When in Leningrad, Vadim usually stayed with Ira or with Mark. (Mark was married now and had a flat of his own. He had set up a small advertising agency in 1987, one of the first in the Soviet Union, and was doing very nicely.)

And Vadim had no peace. Two ghosts haunted him. One was Rachel – there was a small corner of his heart where his love for her still glowed bright. The other was the man he killed outside Kabul. Every day, if only for a moment, Vadim's mind would turn to that mujahideen. The memory would not be laid to rest, and he began to have a recurring dream about death. He wrote it down in his diary after it came to him in the very last days of his soldiery, but the same dream often recurred, even when the war was long past. Here is the dream as he first recorded it in a forty-four-kopeck exercise book in June 1985. It is the last word in Vadim's story.

I was walking purposefully across a dry and rocky stretch

of ground. I was near my destination when a shot rang out from behind. I fell to my knees and noted calmly that I had been wounded in the leg. I stayed on my knees for a second, my head bowed like a man at prayer. Then another bullet struck me in the back and I was hurled forward by the force of it. Suddenly I was in excruciating pain. I lay face down in the dust as waves of agony broke over me. It was more than I could bear. I did not care what happened, so long as the pain stopped. I closed my eyes and willed it to end, the sooner the better.

I felt Death approaching from my right. He seemed to be walking towards me out of a thick night-fog. He was not a person: I perceived him just as a patient presence in the blackness. He was immense and imposing, but not in the least threatening. A line of poetry popped into my head. I cannot remember it now, all I know is that it was very beautiful. I could not say whether I was remembering the line, or whether I had made it up. I said to myself, "Did I read that somewhere, or did I just write it?" And the question was probably my last conscious thought.

I became aware of someone to my left. I turned to him and saw that he was my Life. He was like a twin brother. I knew it was time to take leave of my Life: we shook hands warmly, and though I did not see his face, I was sure that he smiled at me. I did not feel the need to review my past; I had no thoughts for friends or loved ones. All I had to do was bid farewell to my Twin, my Life.

Meanwhile Death had come much closer. He now rose up on my right like a cliff. I raised my eyes to him, but all I could see was the towering, shimmering rock-wall. I was alone with him. He leaned over me and enveloped me in his darkness. I felt I was being wrapped in the folds of his garment. Then his hand drew near, and in that instant I felt the heavy load of my humanity fall away. It just dropped off like a discarded skin or a suit of armour. I sighed with the marvellous sense of liberation: until that moment I'd had no idea *that nature weighed so heavily upon me.*

Then the hand of Death closed over me. With two fingers and thumb he extinguished my being like a candle.

Chertolye

In one of Anna Akhmatova's essays on Pushkin she makes the point that it is impossible to imagine the court intriguer Dantès lying mortally wounded in the snow at Chernaya Rechka while the poet rides home in his carriage to a breakfast of eggs and porridge. Alexander Pushkin was bound to die in that duel – otherwise he would not be Alexander Pushkin. By the same token the Cathedral of Christ the Saviour, like Christ himself, had to die young. It is the tragedy that makes the church and the man what they are, or were. The Soviet bard Vladimir Vysotsky knew this. He sang:

> At the age of three-and-thirty Christ the Poet met his end,
> (He had said: thou shalt not kill, for killing's murder.)
> So they nailed his hands to stop him ever working with a pen,
> And to make the job of thinking that much harder.

Christ the Man rose again, it is said. And after the collapse of communism, various organisations in the new Russia set about trying to bring Christ the Cathedral back to life. In metro stations and underpasses, on street corners and in the recesses of the cavernous toy shop Detsky Mir, legions of old ladies stood collecting roubles for the restoration of the cathedral. They usually had a little trestle table on which stood a collecting tin flanked by a couple of candles. Alongside there was often a photocopied picture of the church under a protective sheet of cellophane. Perhaps those pious babushkas didn't realise, or if they knew they didn't care, that hyperinflation was eating up their pennies faster than they could gather them. Perhaps they believed that, like the loaves and the fishes, their ten-rouble coins would somehow be transformed into the millions of dollars needed for the task. Perhaps they subscribed to the old myth that the lost Church had been built on a mountain of widows' mites, and thought it could be done again.

But money was the least of the practical obstacles. As the public rehabilitation of the church gained momentum, a question arose as to whether the Stalinist engineers who dug the foundations for the Palace of Soviets had destroyed the geological footing of Thon's cathedral, along with the unique construction that he invented specially for the purpose of supporting the massive weight of the church. Those enthusiastic demolition men, it was said, had torn out the very bedrock, like an offending eye. Meanwhile, some pessimistic quantity surveyor calculated that if all the brick factories in Russia did nothing but work for Christ the Saviour, it would still take them months to produce as many bricks as were in the old cathedral. And where now would they source the jasper, the copper, the gold – and the marble? They couldn't take it back from Kropotkinskaya metro station. Where could the new post-Soviet state find the stonemasons, the silversmiths, even the bricklayers, the carpenters and the plasterers – not to mention the great artists, the Vasnetsovs, the Vereshchagins, the Loganovskys? Where in the new Russia was an architect to measure against Konstantin Thon?

But people wanted to acknowledge the loss of Thon's church, and were looking for ways to do it. There was, for example, a serious proposal to project a giant hologram of the cathedral into the empty space above the swimming pool. An architect named Yuri Seliverstov suggested that a full-size three-dimensional outline of the church be made in scaffolding. That metal skeleton that would give an impression of the scale of the building, and its ribby minimalism would have evoked the denuded cupola in its last days. It was a clever and eloquent notion, but it was not to be. Because Yuri Luzhkov, the mayor of Moscow, had plans of his own. Like the believers with their rattling tins, he wanted to see Christ the Saviour incarnate, to clone the church and re-install it on the very spot from which it had been uprooted 60 years previously. And he had the central funds and the political clout to make it happen.

The pool was dismantled late in 1994, as winter set in. An immense quantity of cement was poured into the empty hollow, making a huge, slowly congealing, grey lake. This flat expanse, once it hardened, became the foundation not of the church itself, but of a huge box-like pediment intended to raise the ground level to the same elevation as in tsarist times. For the natural hillock of Chertolye had been turned into a scooped-out bowl; the high ground that Thon had once built on no longer existed. The new artifical dais would function as a kind of shelf, on which the church would be displayed like a souvenir of itself. It was also to serve as office space for all manner of ecclesiastical bureaucrats, as well as containing a suite of rooms for the patriarch, and an underground carpark. There was to be a new subterranean church dedicated to the Transfiguration – a thoughtful reminder, but not an actual re-creation, of the little nunnery church that stood here before Thon.

The foundation stone of the new Cathedral of Christ the Saviour was laid on 7th January 1995 (Christmas Day according to the Orthodox calendar). Construction work began immediately afterwards and proceeded at an astonishing pace, as both the ecclesiastical and the municipal authorities wanted their cathedral finished in time for the millennium. A church that took most of a lifetime to build the first time round was to be erected and dressed within the timeframe of an old-fashioned Stalinist five-year-plan.

Modern materials and methods speeded things along, of course. The outer walls were raised inside two years (it took Thon a decade to reach that point); they were made up of many prefabricated slabs of concrete, lifted into place by a forest of tall cranes. In 1996, as the reborn cathedral took shape, two plaques were unveiled to commemorate all the generous donors – not the subway babushkas with their tins, but the new super-rich of Russia and wealthy foreign well-wishers. Once the outer carcass of the church was complete, some of the art that had been spared in 1931 found its way back to Chertolye, among it some fine works by Vereshchagin. But most of the icons and the furnishings had to be created anew.

A strange controversy arose around the restoration of the high-reliefs above the doorways. The fashionable artist Zurab Tsereteli was commissioned to re-create exact copies of Loganovsky's originals (mercifully, the remnants of those exquisite marbles were not removed from the Don Monastery). Tsereteli's figures were cast in *dekorativit*, a synthetic material named and patented by his own studio. The finished high-reliefs were naturally designed to be white, like the walls of the church. But when they were put in situ, they somehow looked cheap and slightly plastic. So they were taken down and replaced with versions in bronze – a medium that Tsereteli was more familiar with. His metal substitutes are an obvious point of difference with Thon's church, and also one of its most unsuccessful elements. Rendered in dark-brown metal, those biblical heroes look like a bunch of chocolate Santas and Easter bunnies. Another incongruous innovation – one that would certainly catch Thon's eye – is the panoramic viewing platform installed beneath the main dome. From ground level it spoils the roofline, and makes the main cupola look oddly detached. It is there, presumably, to make the building pay its way as a tourist attraction, not merely be a house of God.

The new Cathedral of Christ the Saviour was completed on schedule in 1999. It was consecrated in the summer of 2000 and – like its predecessor – immediately became a focal point of the city. But I wish that the new powers in Moscow had left well alone, and not tried to atone for the sins of their fathers. The real Cathedral of

Christ was gone. The men of the new Soviet order ripped it apart and blew it to bits, and it was dishonest and foolish of their successors to make it look as if nothing of the sort had ever happened. The church that you can see today, the one that Rachel visited when she returned to Moscow thirty years on, is no more than a passable simulacrum of Thon's masterpiece. She didn't like the repro version when she saw it – even before she happened upon Pussy Riot's upsetting piece of political hooliganism. And I don't like it either. It's not right. It's a imperfect copy, a palpable fake.

Russia has wasted too much time on façades and phantoms. Mayor Luzhkov and those who supported his plan would have been honouring the past, and telling a better truth about their nation's history, if they had preserved the hole in the ground and a gap in the skyline. As Vadim always knew, the real Cathedral was present by being absent. Its columns had rested, it may well be, on the torture chambers of the *oprichnina*; it swept a more ancient place of worship out of its path; it was born of the disgrace of Karl Magnus Vitberg, an honest and ill-used man. It was damned from the moment the displaced nuns of the Alekseyevsky monastery whispered, "The devil take what men plant here". And even as Luzhkov's pale counterfeit was going up, there were those who said that the vast plinth on which it stood was not solid enough to support it forever...

In May 1994, at the time when I was thinking about writing this book, a group of Moscow artists organised a one-day art-fest, a *khepening*, in the abandoned Moskva swimming pool. Individuals and groups were asked to come to the site on a certain day, bringing something with which to 'fill' the dry pool. The tiled floor was divided into plots where all the contributions were displayed. Exhibitors brought paintings and sculptures representing every shade and current of the new Russian avant-garde. Some came and performed sketches or dances, or played music in their allotted space. A friend of mine stood on his head and arranged his legs in an inverted V, so as to be a human pyramid. To my great delight I was invited to take part too. I contributed a short text for the exhibition catalogue, thereby staking my own small claim in Chertolye's history.

Now, many years on, I like to remember the place as it looked then. On the grass near the pool a modest chapel had been built. It was about the size of a bus-shelter (one dared hope that the green earth would bear that small burden). The open-sided wooden structure stood near the site of the Cathedral's altar, on the east side of the park. It held a single icon, and on its tarred roof was a toy cupola no bigger than a football. Most days people could be seen in this little shrine, taking shelter from the pealing rain, or praying God's mercy on their long-suffering land.

Acknowledgments

I owe a great debt of gratitude to the Russian architectural historian Evgeniya Kirichenko. I have never met her, but her brilliant monograph on the Cathedral, *Khram Khrista Spasitelya v Moskve*, made this book possible.

I would like to thank some Russian friends: Slava Ponomaryov and Tanya Meshchanova, Andrei Malyshev, Oleg Blotsky, the entire Zharkov family. Many thanks are due to the following people who read the manuscript, gave me advice and encouragement, or helped in practical ways: my brother Mark Bastable and my cousin David Harsent; my partner Kim Davies; Paul McGregor; Reg Wright; Sarah Spankie; Claire Wrathall; EJ Knapp; Alison Moore; Ian Denning.

The cover of the book shows the Cathedral of Christ roughly to scale with the proposed Palace of Soviets. The background is taken from the decorative endpapers of *Generalny Plan Rekonstruktsii Goroda Moskvy* ('General Plan for the Reconstruction of the City of Moscow'), designed by S.B. Telingater, 1936.

4629457R00187

Printed in Great Britain
by Amazon.co.uk, Ltd.,
Marston Gate.